37
Downing Street
A Farnham Family Saga

Sarah Lysaght

First published in the United Kingdom in 2012
by Elusive Spirit Publishing

ISBN 978-0-9571850-0-5

Produced by
The Choir Press, Gloucester

Contents

Acknowledgements

In loving memory of my dear nana Doris.

For my dad, who brought me up to be honest, kind and trustworthy and with whom I share many traits, a little scepticism being among them.

My deepest thanks go to my darling husband for all his encouragement and support throughout. I couldn't have done it without him.

Thank you must also go to Phil for her tireless proof reading; to The Choir Press for their help and assistance in getting my manuscript to print; to the Farnham Museum for the many hours they allowed me to spend in their research room and for their kind permission allowing me to publish my front cover; and to all my family and friends who showed an interest and enquired regularly.

Prologue

As a young child, I had never considered the childhood my parents had experienced or the length of time that my grandparents had lived. When you are a child, you think that the world revolves around you and you alone. Your parents and grandparents appear to have always been there, always looked the same and never age. Trying to imagine them as children is an impossible task for such an inexperienced and immature young mind.

My parents had both been born in Surrey and moved away from the area before my birth. I have fond memories of visiting my grandparents in Farnham during the school holidays. A wealth of love and an abundance of laughter were always present during those visits. I don't doubt my sister and I were spoilt rotten by our grandparents.

Not until I became a parent myself did I begin to question my foundations. No matter how hard we try not to be like them, we do tend to share some characteristics with our parents. I often hear myself saying things to my children which my parents said to me and I expect the same behaviour from my children as my parents expected from me. You hand these things down, often unaware you are doing it.

What and who has made me the way I am? Whom do I resemble the most? Where do I get my traits and interests? Many of these questions I have been able to answer after becoming interested in researching my family tree. I have spent many years searching my family records, using the internet and visiting relevant history centres, libraries and museums.

The following is an account of what family life was like for some of my ancestors. I hope you enjoy reading it as much as I have enjoyed writing it.

Chapter 1

1889

Neither Edwin nor Mary could have known what events lay ahead of them when they met by chance on that late summer's day in 1889. It had not been particularly hot that summer, and July had been unusually wet resulting in building projects slipping behind schedule. The team of bricklayers who had been engaged were working on five fairly large cottages in Kingston upon Thames. At last, by the September, the weather had turned glorious and work had begun again in earnest.

Edwin was nineteen years old. He had been hard at work in the baking sun, bricklaying alongside his father and brother. Together they had travelled the seven miles every morning and night to and from their home in Sutton. Edwin had begun his working life when he was a young boy, following in the footsteps of his grand-father, father and brothers as a bricklayer and labourer.

The men had been working on the site solidly for the past twelve weeks in all weathers and now they were about to start work on the last property. Roofers, painters and glaziers had also now been employed to complete the cottages already worked on.

When Mary had arrived on site she had immediately caught Edwin's eye. Mary was slightly older than Edwin by about eighteen months although, just by looking at her, you would not have known. Her skin was smooth, pale and unblemished and her hair, curly and black and immaculately groomed, sat tall upon her head. She was truly a vision of beauty to Edwin. He had never seen such a pretty girl.

Edwin was one of five children and was named after his father. He had two older brothers and two sisters. When he was a child, his father had moved the family periodically, searching the county of Sussex for work as a bricklayer, and his wife, Harriet, was often forced to take on dressmaking work in an attempt to make ends meet.

In the 1870s times had been hard for the family. Money had been short and Harriet had often not known how she was going to feed her family. At times, she had battled fiercely to hold her family together. Her husband was very partial to his ale and thought nothing about spending his weekly earnings, as soon as he had received them, down at the local ale house. So in her mid fifties, Harriet was finding it a struggle to feed and clothe her family. She and her youngest daughter had resorted to taking in other people's washing to gain an extra income, while her husband merrily drank the rest away.

As a child, Edwin had never had new clothes. Upon his back he wore his brother's hand-me-downs, shirts and britches which had been darned by his mother. His shoes displayed many holes, patched as best she could by his mother. He had never known that contented feeling when leaving the table with a full stomach nor the comfort of a soft bed with plenty of warm covers. He had been used to sleeping on an old threadbare mattress which lay upon the cold stone floor. Throughout his young life he had always been left with a feeling of wanting more. The one thing, however, that Edwin and his siblings were never short of was their mother's love. Throughout her life, Harriet always managed to stay cheerful and this had rubbed off on her children. For all of his faults and no matter what her husband would fling at her, she had never stopped loving him as well.

Edwin considered he was nothing like his own father. As a young man he soon recognised that there could be more to life and as soon as it was possible, he was determined to go and find it. Then, one day, Edwin and his father were labouring as bricklayers on a building site just outside Kingston upon Thames. That was the day he met Mary.

Mary was one of six children. She had been named after both of her grandmothers. She had one much older brother named Charles whom she loved dearly. She had seen less of him while growing up, as he had married when she was only eleven, but this hadn't stopped them from remaining close. Mary also had a younger brother who was an annoyance to her most of the time as he teased her continually. Her two older sisters, Jane and Alice, had very successfully set up and run a dressmaking business from the family home until they had left to get married in 1881 when they handed all responsibility over to Mary. She also had a younger sister called Emily who was her favourite.

Mary's father was Thomas. He was a proud man. He had worked hard throughout his life to achieve a status where he was able to run his own small business. He was a house decorator and on occasions employed small numbers of men to work for him. Thomas's two sons had followed their father into the same profession. Mary's mother, Jane, had always felt privileged never to have worked. This was mainly due to the fact that her husband was always so careful with money. He in turn had passed this common sense on to his children. They had all realised from an early age the importance of spending money wisely, not taking it for granted and the value in saving for a rainy day. Mary's family had inhabited the same street for more than two decades and enjoyed a fairly comfortable life.

Mary's grandfather had been a baker and although her father had not wanted to follow into that work, he had wanted to emulate his father's success. His decorating business had prospered, and he thus achieved this ambition. He had over the years employed men to work for him on larger scale projects, and now he had his sons working with him. He thoroughly enjoyed his work.

Her father and two brothers had just begun a new job near Kingston upon Thames, decorating and glazing the newly built houses there. It just happened to be the same building site upon which Edwin and his family were working. On this particular morning, Mary had travelled with her father and brothers by horse and cart and was to continue on into the town on business. She was a dressmaker and had a couple of new customers in Kingston for whom she had completed some work. Her father and her brothers, James and Charles, had been employed to paint the cottages inside and out and glaze their windows. They had not been on site as long as the bricklayers and roofers and had kept themselves to themselves.

Thomas, James and Charles climbed down from the cart dressed in their painting overalls and carrying their lunch of tongue sandwiches which Jane had lovingly prepared earlier that morning. Mary shuffled across to where her father had been sitting and took the reins from him. As she did so, there was a whistle from one of the men working on the site, followed by a cheer and mischievous laughter. Mary looked up to see about fifteen men all staring back at her. It was a daunting sight for even the boldest of women. "Get on with your work, lads," responded Thomas, trying to spare his daughter's blushes. "Have you never seen a woman before?"

"Not one so pretty," remarked one labourer, working up on the roof.

"Aar, leave the poor girl alone," piped up Edwin who was mixing his mortar only feet away from the cart. Turning to Mary he said, "You get on with your business, Miss. Never mind this rough lot."

"Thank you. I will," Mary spoke quietly but confidently, yet at the same time registering how handsome the bricklayer was. She noted in those few seconds that the bricklayer was fairly tall and slim, had thick, dark, wavy hair and smoked a pipe, and that even though he was a labourer he appeared pretty clean. It seemed to Mary that he could easily have been more suited to a number of other occupations, rather than a bricklayer. He somehow stood out from all the rest. As Mary flicked the reins across the horse's back to encourage it to move forward, Edwin shouted after her. "Make sure you have a good day now, Miss."

"I will, thank you," replied Mary, and she was gone.

*

Mary spent the rest of the day in and around Kingston upon Thames. She had some errands to do for her mother and four clients to visit. She had spent the last eight years running the dress-making business from her parents' home in Edgell Road, Staines. Her sisters, Jane and Alice, had both married bricklayers the same year, leaving her to run their business. They had previously purchased a second-hand sewing machine and paper patterns and gradually everything else they had needed for their business, slowly building it up over the last decade. It was a job which had paid well, considering they were women, and a job for which the family had gained a very good reputation. Through their diligence they had managed to earn a decent living, helping their parents considerably, and now it was Mary's turn to prove her worth. This was a role which she appeared to be fulfilling with ease.

Mary was returning to Kingston with various items she had altered for her customers. She was to deliver a jacket and dress, both of which she had sewn from scratch, and she had some new orders to collect. She also had to call into the milliner's shop, just outside Kingston, for a new pattern book and some more material. Mary also needed to purchase some groceries for her mother which she did after she had stopped briefly to eat her lunch in the park. It had taken her most of the day before she had completed all her errands. Throughout the day, the memory of her morning's encounter with the labourer would slip back into her consciousness. As she returned to collect her father and brothers, she couldn't help feeling nervous and excited at the prospect of seeing this man again. As she pulled up and stopped the horse outside the new cottages, her brother Charles leant out of an upstairs window where he had been painting the frame and shouted, "We've nearly finished for the day, Sis. We'll be out in a moment."

Mary acknowledged his words with a wave. As she waited patiently for her father and brothers to arrive, she couldn't prevent her eyes from scanning the site for the handsome bricklayer she had met that morning. It took a few moments before she noticed him. Edwin was crouching down at the side of the fourth incomplete cottage, where he was apparently cleaning off his tools with a rag and some water, as it was nearing the end of his working day. Two men, one older and one younger, approached him as he gathered up his tools and Mary correctly assumed they were his father and brother because of the strong resemblance they had to each other. As the three men left the building site they walked past where Mary was sitting in the cart. Edwin's father and brother acknowledged Mary with a friendly nod and kept walking but Edwin stopped. "Hello again," he said.

"Hello," replied Mary.

"Did you have a successful day?" enquired Edwin.

"Yes thank you, I did. I have some new dressmaking orders to keep me busy."

Edwin noticed his father and brothers had stopped and were waiting for him. They had all planned to go for a drink at the local inn after work. "I'll catch you up in a minute, Dad," Edwin shouted down the street. He turned back to Mary. "So, you're a dressmaker?" he enquired.

"Yes, I work from my home in Staines."

"My mother was a dressmaker some years ago now," said Edwin. "She still sews a little." Mary was secretly delighted for they already had something in common. "So what else have you been doing in Kingston town?" asked Edwin.

"I had some finished garments to deliver and some errands to do for my mother. I also enjoyed my lunch under a shady tree in the park."

"That sounds better than eating your lunch on a building site."

"I will no doubt need to return again next week to do more of the same," replied Mary, a little forwardly. At that moment her father and brothers turned up.

"Well, I'll look forward to seeing you again next week then," smiled Edwin. Mary smiled back and shuffled across the seat to allow her father to take back the reins.

"Goodbye then. Oh dear, I'm sorry, I never asked your name," Edwin said a little embarrassed.

"It's Mary," was her reply, releasing Edwin from his embarrassment.

"And I'm Edwin. I'll look forward to seeing you again next week then."

"Yes. Bye, Edwin," and the pair parted company.

"Looks like Sis has an admirer," teased her younger brother.

As the cart pulled away Thomas warned his daughter. "Mary, I don't want you talking to the lads from the site. They're not the type of men you should be mixing with. You can do so much better."

"Yes father, but Edwin seems harmless enough."

"Mary, I am not prepared to discuss it any more." No one dared say any more on the matter for the rest of the journey home.

Thomas was a proud, confident man and his children were expected to respect his wishes. That evening after dinner he warned Mary again, in front of her mother, not to talk to the labourers at the site, as most of them were common young men and only after one thing. Mary thought she understood what her father was implying, but felt sure that Edwin was not one of those kinds of men.

The following week after Mary's needlework and dressmaking jobs were complete, she returned with her father and brothers to Kingston upon Thames. This time Mary and Edwin spent a little longer in each other's company, unbeknown to Thomas. They waited until he had disappeared inside one of the cottages to start his painting and arranged a secret meeting place for lunch, far away from the building site. It was to be at the local park and somewhere where they would not be spotted by their families. This was how they began to get to know each other over the next few weeks, grabbing their chances whenever and wherever time and people would allow. Even during those early days Mary instinctively knew she and Edwin would spend the rest of their lives together. Somehow it just felt so right.

Thomas had his suspicions the two were secretly meeting. He managed to find and make contact with Edwin senior on the building site one morning and they agreed to meet for lunch at the local Inn to discuss their children. Once together, the two men were surprised to find they had plenty in common. They actually enjoyed each other's company and swapped stories about work and family life. They discovered they had both had to struggle to get to where they were today and both had experienced the loss of a young child along the way. They returned to the site later than they had intended as they had become carried away in their conversation.

A month passed and Edwin's work was almost finished on the site. Bricklaying was all but complete and roofing work had begun on the last cottage. Thomas and his sons had plenty more work to complete before they were finished and Mary was still making frequent visits, usually weekly, to Kingston upon Thames with them. One Thursday as they sat together in the park during one of the many lunches they shared, Edwin informed Mary that tomorrow would be his last day on the site. "Well, we knew this day would come eventually," commented Mary, very matter of fact.

"Yes, but it seems to have passed very quickly," said Edwin. He looked down at his shoes and muttered, "Too quickly." As Mary was far from shy she took Edwin's hand in hers and squeezed it. "I hope you don't mind Edwin, but I have taken the liberty of asking around in search of work for you."

Edwin was surprised. "No, I don't mind," he said.

"My sister and her husband need some work doing on the house they have just moved into in Staines. I said you might be able to help."

"I am. I could. What is the work?"

"I think some of the outside walls need repairing, but you'll have to ask them."

"It sounds promising."

Mary continued, "I realise it would be some distance from your home and family, so if you need a place to stay, Emily, my sister, has a spare room. She is looking to rent it out."

"It seems as though you have it all worked out for me," Edwin said, smiling.

"It's only a small job, compared with what you've been used to. It shouldn't take you too long but if you do take it, it would enable you enough time to look for another job."

"Or you," laughed Edwin. "But it sounds like a plan and I do rather like the idea of spending more time with you." He paused. "I was wondering how we were going to continue seeing each other. I have rather enjoyed our secret liaisons."

"Well, that's another thing," said Mary, looking rather concerned. "I don't want to lie to my father any more."

"You haven't been lying," said Edwin.

"No, not exactly, I know. But I have been deceiving him and seeing you behind his back and against his advice." Edwin felt unable to disagree with her this time. "If you decide to work for my sister and brother-in-law and live at their house, I want to be able to tell my father the truth and let him know that we are seeing each other."

Edwin needed a mere second to consider her comment before he agreed. "No more creeping around and seeing each other in secret. So when do you want to tell your family?" he asked.

Mary was a little taken aback by his prompt and positive reaction and thought for a moment. "Well, how about you call for me on Saturday afternoon? I should have told my father by then and we can go and visit Arthur and Emily and make the necessary arrangements."

"Great. I can be with you about two o'clock?"

"I'll look forward to it," smiled Mary. As they looked deep into each other's eyes, they both felt it was right to make this commitment to each other. Not just the commitment to meet up on the Saturday, but a commitment possibly for the rest of their lives. In unison they both leant forward and their lips touched. A thousand little shock waves made both their bodies tingle with pleasure. They felt both sick with desire and excited to the core. Their first kiss was as special as it should have been and would be the start of their journey through life together.

Edwin met Mary as arranged on that Saturday afternoon. Mary had broken the news of her and Edwin's friendship to her father the previous evening. He had taken the news incredibly well which worried Mary slightly, but she didn't know why. On the Saturday morning when her father and brother had left for work, Mary began to explain to her mother about the feelings she had for Edwin. "He's kind and thoughtful and honest. I'm sure he feels the same way about me as I do about him." Her mother could keep it a secret no longer. "Your father had suspected something was going on between the two of you. He went to speak with Edwin's father one day on the site, to gauge what type of family they were."

"He did? And what did he discover?" asked Mary, worriedly.

"Well, you mustn't let your father know that I've told you this, but he and Edwin's father met up one lunchtime for a drink and appear to have hit it off straightaway. They have visited the inn a couple more times since that first meeting. They had both guessed, correctly as it happens, that their children were secretly meeting with each other." Mary was a bit surprised by her father's devious behaviour and a little angry with him.

"So, just because father gets on with Edwin's father, he has given me his blessing to walk out with Edwin?"

"I'm not sure you have his blessing, but he's not going to stop you from seeing Edwin," replied her mother. Jane managed to calm her daughter down through this response. "We would like to get to know him a bit better ourselves though," continued her mother.

"You can," grinned Mary. "He's coming round later."

"Oh, Mary, I wish you could have warned me. Look at the state of the house." Jane was a proud woman and madly set about cleaning and tidying her house in time for Edwin's visit.

Edwin was reliable and prompt, knocking on the back door as the parlour room clock chimed two. Mary introduced Edwin briefly to her mother before leaving for her sister's house and Jane in turn invited Edwin for his tea. Edwin accepted the invitation graciously and the pair left with a spring in their step. He took the job and the room at Arthur and Emily's house and the two couples enjoyed the afternoon together, discussing Arthur's plans for the job and making arrangements for when Edwin could move in his belongings.

Edwin had made a start at getting to know Mary's family and the pair continued to get to know each other well. Mary told him all about her many nephews and nieces. She knew she shouldn't have favourites and explained to Edwin that if she did, it would have to be her brother's fifth child, Alice Clara. Alice Clara was six years old and had been named after her aunt. She was very sweet and caring, always seeing the good in everyone. She carried a wise head on her very young shoulders and Mary believed she would go far.

The evening was spent at Mary's house with her parents and her younger brother, Charles. Edwin and Charles hit it off straightaway. Throughout the evening they shared their building experiences and swapped stories. Thomas listened to the pair, joining in with the conversation by adding his twopenn'or every now and then. The house became relatively lively as the evening continued. Mary and her mother enjoyed the male companionship. Beer flowed at a steady but sensible pace, good food was enjoyed by all and friendships were forged.

The building work which Edwin began at Arthur and Emily's house was finished in no time at all. It was completed with competence and reliability. The couple were very pleased with Edwin's hard work and had no hesitation in verbally recommending him to a local builder who was overrun with work and looking for reliable bricklayers. Through their recommendation, Edwin gained more work which enabled him to stay in the village of Staines and continue living at Arthur and Emily's house. More importantly of course, he could continue to see Mary. Soon, the two of them were regularly meeting at Arthur and Emily's house.

Before long it was Christmas and the first time that Edwin and Mary had spent any length of time apart. Edwin left to stay with his family in Sutton over the Christmas period and Mary spent her Christmas at her parents' home. Emily and Arthur missed the pair terribly; their house had never seemed so quiet. Mary and Edwin longed for the New Year when they could see each other again regularly. When the New Year arrived, they spent the next six months getting to know each other better and spent more and more time in each other's company. Arthur and Emily felt as though they had two new lodgers, not just one, as Mary was spending much of her time at their house. The four of them got on very well, sharing meals, conversation, walks, attending the church service on a Sunday morning and enjoying evenings in by the fire. Arthur and Emily had not been blessed with a family as yet, which had made socialising a lot easier.

During the summer of 1890, Edwin and Mary were enjoying lunch together in Arthur and Emily's garden in Gresham Road. Edwin usually met Mary for lunch if he was working close by. The weather was hot and Mary had made a picnic for them to enjoy. The cool lemonade was going down a treat as they sat and talked in the sun. Arthur was at work and Emily had gone shopping with a friend. It was one of those few occasions when they had the house to themselves. They enjoyed these rare moments together.

Edwin thought it was time he let Mary know just how restless he was becoming. The subject they found themselves discussing that day over lunch didn't surprise Mary as she had already recognised there was something troubling Edwin.

From that very first instant that Mary had spotted Edwin on the building site, she had always thought the job of bricklayer's labourer hadn't suited him. Not because he wasn't skilled in his work, but because the job just didn't appear to suit his stature. So it came as no great surprise to Mary when Edwin started to explain that he desired something better for himself, and for his future wife and any family he may have. He explained that his ultimate goal was to run his own business and for it not to have anything to do with the building trade. The only problem was that Edwin had no real idea what it was he wanted to do.

Mary admired his honesty and determination. She was one hundred per cent behind him in whatever he chose to do and desperate to help him make a decision. They spent the rest of their lunch time, before Edwin had to get back to work, discussing his various options, but these appeared limited. They concluded he must pursue the dream to run his own business. The couple knew this wasn't going to happen overnight. It was going to take some planning; plenty of hard work, many long hours and certainly more money than the couple had managed to save to date.

It was Christmas Eve when Edwin and Mary's lives were set upon a new path and their lives were changed for ever. Edwin had been in the pub at lunchtime with Thomas and Charles. They had all overheard a conversation with a group of fellow bricklayers who were planning to leave for Portsmouth in search of work. They were going to cross the water at Portsmouth for the Isle of Wight, where bricklayers and labourers were needed for a grand building scheme of improvements that were taking place on the island. Edwin listened intently to the details and the excitement in the men's voices. It appeared that the wages being promised were much more than the bricklayers could earn on the mainland. Edwin was a little sceptical, but this could prove to be the lucky break he desperately needed and he knew he had to take that risk. That afternoon he took some time to make all the necessary arrangements and spoke with Thomas.

Mary had taken the cart into town, as she had an errand to run. She had arranged for a portrait of herself to be painted especially for Edwin as a Christmas gift to him and had secretly sat for the artist a few times so as to get the picture accurate. Mary was very pleased with the end result and knew Edwin would love it. She was eager to see his reaction when she presented him with her gift the following day.

When Mary arrived home that evening Edwin was waiting for her and couldn't hold back in giving her his news. He had thought about what her reaction would be, all day, and planned in his head how he would tell her. He hoped she would support his decision. Edwin had reached another important conclusion that afternoon, one that could affect the rest of their lives. Edwin had decided to ask Mary to marry him.

Mary opened the door to her home, clutching her framed portrait wrapped in brown paper and tied up with string. Her father was sitting beside the fire cleaning his shoes and her mother was preparing the tea. At first she didn't notice Edwin as he was obscured behind the door. As she walked into the kitchen, Edwin thought she looked even more beautiful than she had the day before, and boldly told her so. Before she turned to face him she carefully placed her gift out of his sight. Call it a woman's intuition, but Mary knew he was bursting to share some news. "What's the matter with you?" she asked, tilting her head to one side. "Have you had one too many down the pub?"

"No, I'm as sober as a judge," Edwin grinned, "but I do have something I want to discuss with you." He was bubbling over with excitement. Thomas and Jane who were sitting by the fire were pretending to be disinterested in the conversation.

Turning to her parents, Mary asked, "Can we use the parlour please, Mother?" Her mother responded with a smile and a nod. Mary showed Edwin through to the parlour which was usually only used on special occasions. The parlour contained her family's best furnishings. In the centre was a table and chairs. A display cabinet held a tea service and some other breakable items and on the walls hung a couple of fairly expensive looking paintings. As soon as they were inside the room, Mary couldn't hold back any longer. "Well, what is it?" she asked, excitedly.

Edwin looked straight into Mary's eyes and replied, "I'm going away." There was a moment of silence between the couple and Mary's heart sank into the pit of her stomach. Edwin could see the disappointment in Mary's eyes so he continued quickly. "There's some work going on the Isle of Wight and they're promising to pay good wages, so I thought I'd take the chance and join the other men who are going too." Mary was shocked. This was not what she had expected. She hadn't been prepared for such an announcement. She had been hoping for a different kind of proclamation altogether. For a moment she was unable to mutter a single word. She felt sick with sadness and then a feeling of anger came over her. She believed that Edwin had not even considered her feelings when he had made this decision. When she finally found the courage to speak up, Edwin stepped in before she could begin. "I know what you're thinking, Mary."

"Do you?"

"I'm not running away from you."

"You're not?" she questioned.

"No. I want you to come with me."

Stunned and still hurting, she replied, "Well how can I do that? My parents would never allow it." She paused and then continued with renewed confidence, "Not unless we were married that is."

"I've already thought of that," replied Edwin.

"Have you?"

"Yes. Now it's my turn to have a plan and for you to listen," he smiled. "Will you sit down so that I can explain?" The couple both pulled out a chair each from under the table and sat down facing one another. Edwin leant forward and pulled Mary's hands towards him and held onto them tightly. "I'm leaving in two days' time, because if I don't, I run the risk of there being no work left by the time I get there."

"Two days?"

"Yes. It could take me anything from three days to a week to get there." Mary looked so sad. She was thinking about how different this Christmas was going to be now, knowing they only had a couple of days left together. How much she had been looking forward to it, and now she wasn't sure when she would see Edwin again, if indeed she ever would. "Please don't look so sad, Mary. Listen to my plan."

"I'm sorry, Edwin. It has just come as a bit of a shock."

"Once I get on to the island, I'll secure a job and find a place to stay. I believe there are plenty of boarding houses. It shouldn't take long before you can come and join me."

"You know I'd love to, Edwin, but how will we get my parents to agree?"

"Yes, that could prove difficult," smiled Edwin. "I guess I'll just have to make an honest woman of you."

"Oh, very romantic" sighed Mary, who had always dreamed of this moment, and in those dreams it had been so very different.

Although sensing her disappointment Edwin teased her further. "I can do romantic." He broke free from holding Mary's hands and started to crawl across the floor towards her. When he was kneeling right next to Mary, she started to giggle.

"Get up you silly fool," she mocked.

Edwin ignored this comment and rummaged inside his jacket pocket. He looked up at Mary with his big blue eyes, grinned, and proudly held up an engagement ring. He'd purchased it only that afternoon in a pawnbroker's in town and managed to barter with the shop owner and get it for a good price. He felt it was well worth spending some of their savings on the ring, as he hoped he would be able to make it up quite quickly with his new job on the Isle of Wight. "Will you marry me, my darling Mary?"

Without even having to contemplate the answer, Mary almost shouted her answer. "Yes, of course I will." She blushed pink with embarrassment at sounding so forceful. Edwin gently placed the ring upon her finger. It fitted perfectly.

The pair stood up together. Edwin pulled Mary towards him and they kissed. They both wanted that kiss to last for ever. When they had both got their breath back it was Mary who spoke first. "Well that was the easy bit."

For a split second Edwin wondered what she meant. "What do you mean?"

"Now all we have to do is go out there and tell my parents."

"Oh, yes I see." Edwin pretended to sound concerned. "Do you think they will be unhappy about our news?" he enquired.

"My father will be, as you haven't asked his permission first."

Edwin paused for a moment and tried to look worried but he couldn't keep the pretence up for very long. Laughing he said, "Well it's a good job I did that this afternoon then isn't it?"

"Oh, Edwin." Mary frowned at him for teasing her and it was closely followed with a smile of relief and a playful smack on his arm. "Just before we tell them our news, I have something I want to give you," she said excitedly. Mary left the room in a hurry saying, "I'll be right back." Within seconds she had returned, clutching the brown paper package. "I had meant to give you this tomorrow on Christmas morning," she said, "but I think you should have it now." She handed Edwin the package and he untied the string and removed the paper. Stunned, he stared at the portrait of his beautiful Mary and was lost for words. "I don't know what to say," he said eventually.

"Don't you like it?"

"Yes, it's beautiful. You're beautiful," he said, looking straight into Mary's eyes. "Can I take it with me?" he continued. "Then, when I'm missing you, I can look at it and it will feel as though you are there with me."

"Yes, I'd like that." Mary was truly touched by Edwin's words. Edwin and Mary embraced and kissed again. They were both happy and terribly sad all at the same time. Mixed emotions were uncontrollably rushing around inside their hearts. Mary spoke first. "We had best go and tell my parents," she said.

The couple left the parlour and returned to the kitchen where Thomas and Jane had thought they would never reappear and share their news. At one point they had wondered if Mary had turned down Edwin's proposal, the couple had seemed to be taking so long. When Mary had rushed from the room to fetch the portrait, Thomas and Jane had thought the worst. They soon realised it was to retrieve the gift Mary had purchased for Edwin. Thomas's and Jane's daughter was positively glowing when she gave her parents the good news. There were plenty of hugs, hand-shakes and congratulations filling the house that night. Edwin was invited to stay for his tea and the couple's health was toasted. The serious conversations were left for after the meal.

Edwin and Mary's plans for the future were discussed in great detail that night, leaving nothing to chance. Edwin was to spend Christmas with Mary's family, so that the couple could be together as much as possible before Edwin had to leave. Thomas had agreed to give Edwin a head start, by taking him in the cart to Woking. It would take about twelve miles off his journey and Edwin thanked Thomas for his kind offer. Thomas surprised his daughter when he gave them a small sum of money. "Call it an early wedding present," he said. They both looked astonished. "It's not much mind you," Thomas added, embarrassed. "I would have liked to have given you more."

"I don't know what to say, sir." Edwin had replied. "Thank you very much. We will put it to good use, won't we Mary?"

"Yes we will. Thank you, Dad. We really weren't expecting anything like this." Mary embraced her father.

"I know," smiled Thomas, who recognised his daughter as an autonomous woman. He was delighted to see his daughter so happy. He knew he was doing the right thing in letting her go and was certain he was giving her to a trustworthy man who would always love and care for her.

Edwin and Mary had no gift for each other on Christmas morning but the day remained very special. They did their utmost to enjoy their last couple of days together but both were apprehensive about Edwin's departure. When the day finally arrived, they found saying goodbye to one another incredibly difficult, even though they planned to be together again soon. Both of them had tears in their eyes as Edwin left. In trying to spare his daughter's feelings, Thomas had decided that Mary should say goodbye to Edwin outside her home and that her father would travel alone with him to Woking. Mary watched her father's and Edwin's figures decrease in size as the cart disappeared further and further down the road, until they were no longer in sight. Mary knew she would only have to wait about six weeks until they could be together again but it already felt like a lifetime. That day couldn't arrive quickly enough for Mary.

Edwin's journey was not particularly long but it was a fairly arduous one. Hitching rides with journeymen and travellers had proved more difficult than expected and it was because he was travelling over the Christmas and New Year period. He finally arrived on the island on New Year's Day, six days after he had set out.

The Isle of Wight is a small diamond-shaped island, situated south of the county of Hampshire. It is separated from the south of mainland England by as little as three miles of water called the Solent. Edwin considered himself lucky when he spotted a boatman just about to set off across the Solent for the island. It was just after lunchtime and the man was on his way home after making a trip to the mainland. His boat was laden with all sorts of produce and Edwin could clearly see the man had had a few beers during his shopping trip. "Excuse me, sir, could I ride with you across to the island?" enquired Edwin. "I'll pay you for your time."

The short stout man spoke with a gruff voice and slightly slurred speech. "If you dare to risk it son, then climb aboard. Joe's the name." And then he laughed heartily, as he could see Edwin's face contained a look of concern as he tried to decide if he should risk a boat ride with a stranger. "Only joking with you lad. Mind you, I could do with some help with the rowing, if you would be so kind."

"I'll have a go," smiled Edwin. "I've never been in a boat before, never mind rowed one. There's not much call for them where I come from." He climbed in and immediately lost his balance causing the boat to rock back and forth violently. Joe began laughing again.

"You'd better develop some sea legs if you're going to stay on the island for any length of time," he teased. The pair chatted continuously during their short crossing. It had been a little unsteady in parts and their vision of the island obscured by mist, but it wasn't raining and the temperatures were pretty mild for the time of year. As he disembarked Edwin realised he had thoroughly enjoyed his first trip on a boat.

Stepping from the boat onto dry land, he and some other men who had just arrived on the island were directed by a messenger boy towards Ryde, the island's largest town. Located in the north-east of the island, it was a modern town with a half-mile long pier and four-mile long beaches. Here, Edwin was told where he could sign up with the building firm that had been hired to make the improvements to the island. Edwin followed a group of men who were making their way up from the water's edge to the streets of Ryde.

Edwin was concentrating on not losing them and trying to get his bearings so he almost missed a sign in the window of a local shop. Fortunately it caught his eye and he stopped to read it. In doing so he caused two men who were behind him and not paying such good attention, to bump into him. "Sorry mate," one of them muttered briefly and then they were gone. Edwin didn't even acknowledge them; he was too engrossed in the sign. It read:

Assistant required.
To help with day-to-day running of Fishmonger's shop.
No previous experience necessary.
Must be prepared to work hard.
Apply within.

Edwin instantly recognised this as the opportunity he had been waiting for. It could be the chance he needed to get out of the building trade and might allow him to save for his and Mary's future. It might even enable him to set up on his own one day. He confidently hammered on the shop's closed door and seconds later a medium-sized man greeted him politely. The fishmonger and poultry merchant's name was Edward Hooper. Edwin introduced himself and explained why he was in Ryde and, more importantly, why he was bothering Mr Hooper on New Year's Day.

There had been a Hooper's Fishmongers on the island for over fifty years. The trade had been passed on through the family, starting with Edward Hooper's great grandfather. Edward had gained many years' experience from growing up with a father and grandfather who were fishmongers. They had handed down all their knowledge and expertise which had enabled Edward to become so successful. The family's reputation preceded them and they had all worked and lived at the same premises in Ryde for many years. Edward Hooper had grown up in Ryde, alongside his wife, Jane, who had lived only a few doors away with her father who ran a grocer's shop. Edward and Jane had married in the spring of 1867, and set up home over the fishmonger's shop with Edward's father. It was on these premises they had brought up their own family. Edward was now forty-seven and he and his son ran the shop together. Recently Edward had recognised his son's disinterest in the family business and knew he had to do something about it. Employing a new member of staff would be a start.

After a brief chat with Edwin to discuss the work involved and his wages, Mr Hooper agreed to give him a week's trial. After this time he said he would review the situation. Edwin didn't find out until much later that week that plenty of his fellow bricklayers had been turned away from the building site empty handed, as there just wasn't enough work for the numbers of men that had descended upon the island. Edwin was pleased he had made the hasty decision to enter and enquire about work in Mr Hooper's shop.

Edwin was soon to discover that Mr Hooper ran his shop on Pier Street with precision. Edwin admired this and aspired to do the same. During his first week in Ryde, Edwin and Mr Hooper had got to know each other well and Edwin had told him all about Mary. Mr Hooper had also been a great asset in finding Edwin a place to live. He had told him about a house on Monkton Street that very first day when he had arrived and allowed Edwin some wages in advance to secure rooms there. Edwin had written to Mary during his first night on the island and told her about the turn of events. He couldn't wait for the return post to read her reply. He wasn't disappointed. He received her letter the following week and she was every bit as thrilled for Edwin as he was. He had only another four weeks to wait and Mary would be joining him.

Hooper's Fishmongers was where Edwin learnt his new trade, a trade that would become important to him and Mary for the rest of their lives. To begin, Edwin was taught how to bone, skin, de-scale and trim the various types of fish. He soon learnt how to remove the heads and insides, as many of Hooper's customers requested this. Edwin soon came to realise that fishmongering is a skilled job that demands a detailed knowledge of fish. He was lucky to have such a good teacher as Edward Hooper. Edwin was eager to learn and as the days went by he became quite skilled at what he did. This encouraged Mr Hooper to have Edwin accompany him on the trips he made to Ramsgate by train to purchase his fish, which in turn pleased Edward's son greatly, as he had always found the trips a trifle boring. Edward bought fish wholesale and prepared it for retail sales. He had premises for storing and collecting stock at Ramsgate. Edwin accompanied him on one occasion shortly before Mary arrived on the island. The two men were away for three days.

Mary finally joined Edwin during the first week in February. They were thrilled to see each other and Mary literally fell into Edwin's arms as she lost her footing when she stepped out of the little rowing boat that had brought her to her new home. It made Edwin laugh as he fondly remembered his first experience on a boat only weeks earlier. Once on the island she experienced a feeling of being a million miles away from the hustle and bustle of mainland England. Her first week was very busy. Edwin was working of course, but took every opportunity to introduce his future wife to the people he now knew. Working in a shop all day had certainly enabled him to get to know the local people quite well and he enjoyed sharing this knowledge with Mary.

When Mary was introduced to the Hoopers she was an immediate success. Jane Hooper discovered Mary was a dress-maker and engaged her services to alter a few of her garments that would no longer fit and this was how Mary acquired her first bit of business. Edwin showed Mary around the sights of the town. They looked around the church and decided they would like to be married there. They enjoyed many walks along the beautiful beaches, beside the sea and along the cliffs, taking in the magnificent views. While Edwin was at work, Mary planned for their wedding and began to secretly redesign herself a wedding gown from one of her favourite dresses. She spent many hours sewing while Edwin was at work and sometimes into the evenings.

*

Mary had only been on the island for two weeks when Edwin left for Ramsgate again with Mr Hooper. Edwin and Mary missed each other terribly. On his return he was pleased to find Mary waiting for him at the dock. He was exhausted from the trip but couldn't wait to get home to listen to what Mary had been doing and hear the news about the town. Mary regaled Edwin with the sights she had witnessed in the village that week. How they laughed about Mr West's new Arab bicycle which he had purchased from John Harrington and Co. "First, he clambered onto the seat, not very gracefully mind, but seemed quite confident and upright to begin. Within seconds he had began to wobble and was swaying across the road as though he had been drinking in The Eagle all night." Edwin began to laugh. He knew this gentleman well, but couldn't quite picture him on a bicycle. Mary continued, much to Edwin's delight. "After a few more seconds he hit the ground hard, stopping everyone in their tracks from going about their business."

"Oh dear," Edwin sniggered.

"Everyone looked concerned, but was relieved as he picked himself up."

"Did you race to his rescue, darling?" Edwin tried to keep a serious face.

"I couldn't. Just like everyone else I was slightly dumb-founded."

"So what happened next?" enquired Edwin.

"Well, the poor man tried to cling on to some dignity, brushed himself down and climbed back on to the contraption." Edwin knew what was coming next and couldn't stop himself from chuckling. Mary continued. "As he wobbled off down the road, the crowd that had gathered started to turn away and resume whatever it was they had been doing before, but I kept a watchful eye on matters and blow me down he came off again." Edwin exploded into fits of laughter. "He repeated this several times," shouted Mary so as to be heard over Edwin's guffaws. "The poor man must be covered in bruises," laughed Mary. The pair couldn't stop themselves and laughed together until their bellies ached. It was a pleasant feeling to be together again and to not have a care in the world.

With three weeks to go until their wedding, Edwin and Mary attended church every Sunday to hear their banns being read. They were married on 1 March at All Saints Church in Ryde. Edwin was twenty-two and Mary twenty-three. All Saints was a large and imposing church in a highly prominent location, positioned at the junction of Queens Road and West Street, a stone's throw from where Edwin worked on Pier Street and where Edwin and Mary lived on Monkton Street. It was designed by the architect, Sir George Gilbert Scott and had been built less than twenty years earlier.

All Saints was considered to be one of the finest parish churches in England. Its elaborate alabaster and marble sculptured work and rich murals by Clayton and Bell, who also produced most of the stained glass windows, just went to prove why many of the local people referred to it as the "Cathedral of the island". The church dominated the skyline, particularly when looking from the Portsmouth area of the mainland, and would have been the first thing that Edwin saw of the island when he had approached two months prior to his wedding, if it hadn't been such a misty day. Set on top of the highest hill in Ryde its steeple could be seen from a great distance.

Although the church was rather grand, Mary had wanted a simple ceremony. They arrived at church on their wedding day feeling both nervous and excited. The congregation was small as Edwin and Mary had no family members at their ceremony. The church was all but empty, except for the few acquaintances from the village who had come out in support. Even the Hooper family were unable to attend because of work commitments.

Edwin and Mary were married by Alexander Poole, Vicar of the parish. As they had no family members present, their witnesses were George Beazley, the parish clerk, and Mary Beales, who worked as a parlourmaid for the vicar. Mary wore her restyled dress for the ceremony which she had worked on for the last three weeks. It was a cream coloured full-length gown which she had lovingly altered especially for her big day. Edwin had guessed she'd been working on a dress as she had hurriedly hidden it away on occasions when she had heard him coming in from work. He had been given strict instructions not to enter the room on numerous occasions until instructed to do so by Mary, thus giving her time to hide anything which might give him a clue to what she would be wearing.

At times he had felt quite left out of the preparations but had never tried to sneak a look at the dress before the big day. He had spent the time wisely and written to his family to inform them of his good news and fortune. When he eventually saw Mary in her wedding dress, it had been well worth the wait. If he hadn't known her better, he would have thought she'd spent a fortune on it. All those hours of sewing while he sat alone in the evenings had been worth it. Mary looked stunning. The dress featured a high neckline and large front yoke made from lace. This lace yoke was very wide, almost extending from shoulder to shoulder, rounded at the front and forming a deep "V" on her back. The dress had wonderfully large puffed sleeves, which were very full to the elbow, then continued in a long cuff to her wrists. The bodice of the gown was fitted to the waistline. The skirt was gathered at the waist and fell naturally over her hips. A button on each side of the centre gather held her lace train in place. The gown also had a button closure on the back. She wore a simple but elegant veil. She was a remarkable seamstress.

Edwin was wearing a three-piece suit which he had borrowed from Mr Hooper's son who had worn it recently to a big family wedding. It consisted of a grey, knee-length topcoat with matching waistcoat, contrasting dark trousers, cream coloured shirt with a short turnover collar and floppy bow tie. Edwin's hair had been trimmed especially for the day.

It was the happiest day of the couple's life, a day the pair would remember for the rest of their lives. That evening was spent together and alone. They enjoyed a wedding supper which Mary had been preparing for the last week. For their main course they had fish, a delicious whole salmon and prawns, given to them as a wedding present by the Hoopers. That night was the first time that Edwin and Mary had given themselves to each other. They had abstained up until now. It had been Mary's decision and Edwin had respected her wishes although at times they had both found the decision almost impossible to stick to. Waiting to consummate their marriage vows had made their wedding day even more special for them. They went to sleep that night, content and happy, ready for whatever the rest of their lives could throw at them. Little did they suspect that a new life had already begun to grow inside Mary.

It was December 1891 and Mary and Edwin were having breakfast together as they did most days. "I think the baby will be born today." Mary said as she poured her husband a cup of tea. This comment took Edwin a little by surprise. He almost choked on his breakfast and was a little unsure as how to answer his wife. "Oh, do you? How do you know?" and as soon as he had asked the question, he wished he hadn't.

"It's just a feeling I have," said Mary, noticing Edwin's embarrassed look.

"Oh, all right then love." He stood up to leave. "I'll see you later then," he said, bending to give her a kiss on her cheek, not really knowing how she wanted him to respond.

"Have a good day," replied Mary, slightly perturbed by her husband's lackadaisical behaviour on what she knew would turn out to be a far from normal day. Edwin left his wife that morning for work, both excited and terrified. He was about to become a father for the first time and had no idea what was expected of him or how to behave. His role had been, up until now, to earn the money to put the food on the table and a little bit to put by to save for the future. He had no idea how this was all about to change.

Later that day their first child was born. It had been a particularly long labour which Mary had been informed was normal with a first child. She had been experiencing terrible backache for most of the day which had nothing to do with all the cleaning, washing and sorting she had been doing. She had damp-dusted the woodwork and surfaces in the house, hand-washed and hung out to dry the dirty clothes and tidied the cupboards; anything to try to take her mind off her labour pains. When her contractions had become more insistent she went to fetch her neighbour, Dorothy Parsons, landlady of the local inn who was well versed in these matters. She had helped many a newborn into this world and over the last few months had become good friends to Mary and Edwin. Dorothy had promised she would look after Mary and help her during the birth.

As soon as she heard the knock on the back door, Dorothy knew who it would be. She had seen Mary the day before and could tell just by looking at her belly that she would be due any time soon. She had many years' experience at this game and given birth to eleven of her own. "Won't be long now, dearie," she had called across the street. Mary had waved, nodded and smiled back.

Dorothy opened the door.

"I think the baby's coming, can you come?"

"Of course dearie, I'll be right with you." She turned and picked up a bag that she had already packed the previous evening and had waiting by the door. "Jack!" she bellowed. "I'm off round to Mary's. Open up for me if I'm not back in time." Jack was Dorothy's youngest son, still at home and unmarried as yet. Dorothy's husband had died a few years back and Dorothy was glad of Jack's company and his help with the Inn. He had been the only thing that had kept her going.

"All right, Mum, I will," was his reply.

Dorothy shut the door behind her and the two women walked

the short distance back to Mary's house. Mary stopped twice on the way, both times because of a contraction. Dorothy reassured her that it was all quite normal. Once in the house and upstairs, Dorothy helped Mary to prepare the bed. As they placed a final thick layer of newspaper under some sheets that they had already stuffed with paper, Mary's contractions became very strong. Dorothy wrapped a towel around the iron bed head for Mary to hang on to. The contractions were now spaced about two or three minutes apart and lasting for over a minute. Mary just wanted to push. "Try to wait a little longer, dearie," Dorothy told her.

Mary was in labour for just over two hours. The most embarrassing part for her was when she lost all control of her bladder and bowel movements, and soiled the bed. Mary was horrified when she realised what had happened. Dorothy on the other hand had seen it all before, many times, and wasn't fazed in the slightest. She cleaned up the mess and was able to steer Mary's mind back to the matter in hand pretty quickly. Mary's throat was dry and she felt nauseous. It seemed that just as one contraction ended, another began. "All right, dearie, get ready to push," Dorothy instructed. Feeling exhausted already, Mary prepared to push. Lifting her arms above her head she grabbed hold of the towel tightly. "Hold your breath and count to ten while you push," suggested Dorothy. Mary did as she was instructed. "Push!" shouted Dorothy.

After what felt like hours of pushing but in reality was only minutes, Dorothy exclaimed, "That's great, dearie, I can see the baby's head. You're doing just great. The worst bit's over." Once the baby's head had eased its way out, there was a short moment of relief for Mary and then more pushing began. Dorothy helped to guide the shoulders and torso out. "It's a boy!" she exclaimed. "Well done, dearie." Dorothy wrapped the baby in a clean towel and rubbed him rather briskly. He began to cry loudly. "Not much wrong with those lungs" she observed. Dorothy almost threw the child at his mother because she was so used to handling young babies. As Mary cradled her baby for the first time, an incredible feeling swept over her. She was completely exhausted but at the same time elated. While Mary admired her baby, Dorothy cut the umbilical cord without mother or baby even noticing. Mary was so engrossed in her new son that she also hadn't noticed she was still having small contractions. Both the woman admired their handiwork, touching and caressing the baby's tiny hands and feet. Then, after a few minutes Dorothy enquired, "Shall we see if he wants some of his mummy's milk, dearie?"

Dorothy lifted the baby into position, while Mary moved aside her upper garments. The baby latched on straightaway and it couldn't have been a more natural situation for Mary. Her hard work was done, or so she thought. Another few minutes passed, then Mary shouted out in alarm, "Ow! Why do I feel like I want to push again?"

"Oh that's normal, dearie," said Dorothy reassuringly. "There's nothing to worry about. It's just your body doing what's natural. Just one more push and you're done," she continued. Mary did as she was told and delivered the placenta. She had no idea what had just happened but she trusted Dorothy implicitly and knew she was in capable hands. Dorothy went to work again and cleaned up around the new mother and her baby. She was thorough and worked quickly as time was getting on and she must be getting back to her business. If she didn't leave soon she would return to irate customers and a bad-tempered son.

When mother and baby were clean and comfortable and she had fetched a pot of hot, sweet tea for Mary, Dorothy left for the inn. She hadn't gone far when she bumped into Edwin returning from his work. "Congratulations, dearie, you have a son," she grinned, proud to be his informant.

"Do I?" replied Edwin, a little embarrassed. "Thank you."

"No problem at all, dearie. It's all in a day's work," and then she was off on her way again.

Edwin entered the house feeling tired after his long day and apprehensive about what was about to greet him. The house was quiet. It seemed as though the place was empty, not how he had imagined it to be with a new baby on the premises. He made his way upstairs and slowly opened the bedroom door to find Mary asleep in their bed and their son lying perfectly still in her arms. Edwin just stood there, mouth open wide, eyes filling with tears, taking in the beautiful scene that met him. He was so proud of his clever young wife. She stirred and noticed her husband standing there in the doorway.

"Hello, Edwin, have you had a good day?" she whispered.

"Not bad," he replied stumbling over his words. "What about you?"

"Interesting," she smiled.

Edwin moved towards his wife with a look of caring concern. "Are you all right though?" he enquired.

"Yes, I'm fine," replied Mary.

"And what about the baby?" he enquired.

"Well, he certainly made an entrance into the world but he's strong and he's healthy," Mary said with a smile and right on cue, their son opened his mouth and started to cry. "I think he's ready for another feed," said Mary.

"Can I hold him quickly?" asked Edwin. Mary handed the baby to his father. Edwin cradled his son in his arms for the first time and felt elated and terrified all at the same time. Mary looked on, full of pride for their achievement. Life was certainly going to be very different for the couple from now on. They had previously discussed a name for their first-born child and Edwin had asked if it were a boy, could they traditionally name him after his father? Mary had agreed and now Edwin recalled their conversation. "Are we going to call him—?" but before Edwin could finish, Mary had answered.

"Yes, if that is what you wish."

"Edwin it is then, after your dad," Edwin said, looking down at his new son.

"Or Teddy?" said Mary.

"Or Teddy," laughed Edwin.

A few days later they sent their good news to their families by letter. Mary was thrilled to receive, by return post, a small package for the baby from her parents containing a long-sleeved nightgown, a square-necked cotton dress which had been embroidered and a shawl. Mary's mother had made these clothes herself by hand. Mary sorely wished her family could be there to experience her and Edwin's happiness. She missed them all, greatly.

Chapter 2

1892

It was the spring of 1892 when Edwin began to experience a feeling of restlessness and crave a change. He felt quite established at what he did for a living, but couldn't help wanting more. At the same time Edward Hooper was having a similar problem with his son. Mr Hooper's son didn't want to continue with the work his family had been doing for generations. He no longer had the desire to walk in his father's shoes. He wanted to break that cycle and Edward Hooper had recognised his son's restiveness for some time now. The boy had talked to his father about selling the long-standing family business and using the money to purchase a hotel that he'd heard was coming up for sale.

Edward Hooper was seriously considering his son's proposal. His health was beginning to fail him and he was always feeling tired. He knew he wasn't getting any younger and he had been thinking about calling it a day and selling up. He knew his son would make a go of the hotel and didn't doubt he would make an excellent hotel proprietor. All he needed was to make sure he raised enough money from the sale of his fishmonger business to make it viable.

Edward considered his options, and then approached Edwin with the proposal to purchase his family business. He knew he would continue his good work and wanted to give him first refusal. Edwin was both incredibly grateful and overwhelmed by Edward Hooper's generosity; Mr Hooper was giving him an excellent opportunity. Unfortunately, however hard the two men tried, sadly they could not reach common ground upon a settlement. The business was simply worth more than Edwin and Mary could afford or had been able to save. Mr Hooper was not in a position where he could offer to delay payments for Edwin as his son needed every last penny to purchase the hotel. So the two men were bitterly disappointed when they were unable to reach a compromise and do business together. They were also very aware that this meant that soon they would have to part company.

Mary had known about their meeting and had hoped for a positive outcome. She had some news of her own to give Edwin when he returned home and hoped he would be in a pleasant mood. She had been watching for his return from the shop, through the front window of their small property. Teddy had just been fed and was sleeping in the back room. When she saw her husband approaching she opened the front door for him. He smiled at her as he walked in and without a word began to unbutton his coat.

"How did it go darling?" she enquired with some hesitance.

"Not a good outcome, I'm afraid dear," Edwin replied. He hung up his coat on the hook by the door and slumped down into his chair, looking exhausted. "We simply can't afford to buy it." He sighed, frustrated.

"So what do we do now?"

"I suppose it depends on how quickly Mr Hooper sells the shop. He says I'll be able to stay on until it's sold, but after that it will depend upon the new owner."

There was a short silence between the couple, until Mary could contain herself no longer. "Edwin?"

"Yes dear?"

"I know it's not a good time to tell you this or for it to have happened, but we're going to have another baby." Edwin leapt out of the chair.

"Oh Mary. Are you sure?" He looked pleased.

"As sure as I can be," she said. He pulled her close and held her in his arms.

"What are we going to do if you have no job?" she asked him.

"Where are we going to find the money to clothe and feed us all?" She was starting to worry.

"It won't come to that," he whispered gently, trying to reassure her. "I will find something, I'm sure."

Without thinking she replied, "I suppose you always have the building trade to go back to if there's nothing else," but the words escaped from her mouth without thought and as they did she immediately regretted them.

"That would really be the last thing I would want to do Mary. I don't want to ever have to do that if I can help it. I enjoy what I do now and I want to keep doing it. I'll find something. I'm sure of it."

"I know you will, darling, I know you will."

A short time later, once they had digested each other's news, Mary wrote to her parents and explained the situation with Edwin's job, and about how she was going to have another baby. Mary tried to sound positive but it was difficult. She desperately hoped her family would be able to help them. Her father, Thomas, wrote back almost immediately, greatly concerned for his daughter and son-in-law. He promised to help as much as he could, and to keep his eyes and ears open for any opportunities that might present themselves back in the Staines area.

Over the next few months Edwin and Mary asked everyone they could think of, if they were aware of any property becoming available to rent. They bought newspapers, scanning them for possible premises but there was nothing that they could afford. Time was running out and Edwin was becoming very anxious. Mary had noticed he had not been sleeping well at night and that his appetite had declined. In turn this was having a negative effect on Mary. She was doing her best to stay optimistic but under the circumstances it was near impossible.

When Edwin's job came to an end at the Hoopers' shop and the business and premises had been sold, the new owner had no need for Edwin's services. He had a large family who were all used to working in their father's shop and there was no room for Edwin. He found himself unemployed and the family was in a desperate situation. They had some money put by which they could live on for a short while but it wouldn't last them very long.

Just as they were about to give up all hope, a letter arrived from Mary's father. A feeling of utter relief swept over them both as Mary read it out aloud to Edwin.

Dear Edwin and Mary,

I have good news. A property has become available on Laleham Road in Staines, which your mother and I think would be ideal as a Fishmongers. There are facilities out the back for storage, and rooms above for you to live in. The lease is for one year. Mother and I were very excited when Emily told us about it last Thursday.

We are sure you will not mind, that we have taken the liberty of securing it with a deposit of eight pounds and six shillings. It is not a small sum, we know, but we have faith in you both and know you will repay us as soon as is possible.

We hope you are able to leave soon, and arrive safely. We both cannot wait to see you again and to meet our grandson.

God speed, my darlings,

From your loving Father and Mother.

There seemed little point to hanging around, so the following day Edwin and Mary packed their belongings, excited once again about their future. Mary longed to see her family and for them to meet Teddy. The couple said their goodbyes to the friends they had made in Ryde and enjoyed a last meal with the Hoopers in their new home at the hotel. The two men discussed the new lives they were embarking upon and wished each other success in their new ventures. They vowed to stay in touch. It was an emotional time for all. Edwin and Mary felt torn about leaving Ryde. Plenty had happened on this little island. They had made a great many friends in such a short space of time and they were going to miss them all.

Edwin was pleased they had spent time with the Hoopers. He

had wanted to see how Mr Hooper's new hotel business would suit him and his son. He felt he owed a great deal to the man. After all, it was he who Edwin had learnt a new trade from. He had become quite skilled at it during his stay on the island. Mary had given birth to their first child there, an experience they both would never forget. They promised themselves they would return one day, as they finished packing up their belongings ready to leave the following morning for Middlesex. Their journey home to Staines took four days and was not easy with a young baby. When they arrived Mary was exhausted but her family were extremely happy to see them and made a big fuss over Teddy, who enjoyed all the attention.

After a meal of stew and potatoes, Thomas and Edwin discussed going to visit the premises in Laleham Road the following morning. It was also to become the family's new home. The shop was situated on a road which ran along the bottom of Edgell Road, where Mary's parents lived, and Gresham Road, where Arthur and Emily lived. It was an ideal situation from a business point of view but also because Mary could be close to her family again. Edwin couldn't express his thanks enough to Thomas, and they sat up till late discussing Edwin's plans, while Mary, Teddy and Jane went off to bed. Both Edwin and Mary slept better that night than they had in a long time.

The next day was Saturday. Edwin, Thomas and Mary left early to inspect the building, while Jane stayed at home and looked after Teddy. It wasn't difficult for Thomas to organise this time off work, as he had a number of men working for him at this time and after all, he was the 'boss'. Upon first inspection, the premises were ideal, but they were filthy, and would need a substantial clean and plenty of scrubbing before Edwin would be satisfied enough to open up his new shop in there. He also had to think about buying stock for his premises and using the contacts he'd made while he was in Ryde to arrange this. Mary began work on the upstairs which had been just as neglected.

The pair worked incredibly hard over the next four days, while Mary's mother and sister shared the care of Teddy. Teddy was having a great time, meeting lots of new people and visiting new places. His grandmother and aunt enjoyed spoiling him. Thomas was also kept busy for, after his normal day's work, he had promised to paint a sign to go above Edwin's shop window. When it was finished it read 'Quality Fishmonger' in dark green letters.

The family were able to move into their new home on the Thursday. By then, Mary was more than happy with the condition of the upstairs, Edwin's fish and poultry had arrived and Thomas had fixed the sign above the shop. The following day was Friday, and Edwin was able to open the door of his new shop to his waiting customers for the very first time. He and Mary had hardly slept the night before as they were so excited.

Edwin was overwhelmed by a feeling of absolute pleasure as his first customers entered the shop. He was captain of his ship for the very first time in his life and it was a proud yet terrifying moment for them both. Edwin was desperate for the business to be a success, and Mary was desperate for him to succeed. She knew he had worked hard for this moment and didn't want to see him fall at the first hurdle. It did concern them that they owed her father so much money. They didn't want to be in anyone's debt, not even her father's. They were both proud and determined to pay back Thomas as soon as was possible.

The fish shop's first day was very busy. There had been a steady stream of customers coming and going throughout the day. Edwin hoped it would be this busy every day but realised as the day had gone on that some of their customers who had visited were there just to be nosy. He had greeted those customers in the same way as his others, with courtesy and diplomacy, but he was able to tell them apart from the genuine ones due to his past experience and because they bought very little or nothing at all.

That evening Edwin and Mary were completely exhausted as they walked the short distance to Edgell Road. Mary's mother had promised to cook them dinner that night in celebration of their first day in business. As they walked, they laughed together, discussing some of the odd requests they had received during their first day in business.

"Did you notice that scruffy looking man who came into the shop early on?" Mary asked. "He was very thin. I suspect he was a tramp."

"Not until the smell reached me," recalled Edwin. "It was that, which made me look up."

"He asked me if he could have any of the leftover fish heads, tails and guts."

"Did he say what he wanted them for?" asked Edwin.

"He said he wanted them for his pigs."

"What did you say?"

"I explained we had a bin out back that he could help himself to any time." Mary looked deep in thought. "The trouble is, I can't help wondering if they were really for him."

"Mary! You didn't ask him that did you?" Edwin looked concerned.

A little annoyed by her husband's reaction, Mary replied. "No. But can you imagine if I had? I might have lost us one of our best customers," she said sarcastically.

"I hope we aren't soon to consider him one of my best customers," replied Edwin seriously.

"But he would be doing us a favour if he was to empty our bin regularly."

"You must think he'll be back again then?"

"Yes I do." And then she paused, deep in thought. "Edwin, do you think we could help him out every now and then and leave a little extra out in the bin for him?"

"Not if he's really giving it to his pigs. I'm not having good fish going to waste." Mary looked at Edwin and Edwin looked at Mary and they both laughed. "Let's just see if he comes back first shall we?" replied Edwin rather sensibly.

As the couple arrived in Edgell Road, Edwin commented, "Most of the townsfolk around here seem very pleasant."

"They are," said Mary. "I think many of them came out today in support of what we have done. There were plenty of faces that I know quite well from when I was growing up in the village. I'm sure many of them will become our regulars."

"I hope so," smiled Edwin. "I really hope so."

Until that moment Mary hadn't realised just how much she had missed her family and all that used to be familiar to her in Staines. In particular, the company and support of the other women in her family, her mother and sister Emily were of great importance to her. Emily and Arthur were very taken with Teddy as were her parents, and Emily and Mary had plenty of catching up to do. Mary was especially pleased her family would be around to help her when her second child was born.

By December Mary was heavily pregnant and expected her baby in less than eight weeks. She had been feeling very tired recently. It had been an exciting and busy last six months, but the hard work and long hours she had put in helping her husband in the fish shop were beginning to take their toll. The one good thing to come out of all their hard work was having the ability to pay back Mary's father, the money he had given them to set them up in their successful business. This was a real achievement for Edwin and it was with great pride that he handed over the final, outstanding sum of money to Thomas.

"So, what will you do with the spare income you'll have next month?" enquired Thomas.

"Well, if you take a look at Mary, it just might give you a clue," Edwin laughed.

Both men turned to look at Mary who had collapsed into the chair next to the fire, her belly bulging out in front of her. She was positively glowing and looked truly beautiful with the firelight bouncing off her face. Pregnancy really suited her. Both men laughed out loud.

"Hey!" shouted Mary. "It's your fault I'm in this condition. I could always arrange for you to have a separate bedroom," she jested.

"Whoops, I think we've upset her," her father teased. He turned back to Edwin. "Careful lad or you'll be sleeping with your fish." Edwin stood up and walked over to Mary putting his arm around her shoulders. "You wouldn't do that to me love, would you?"

"I might," she replied, "unless I can come up with an even better solution."

That atmosphere and banter continued throughout both households over the Christmas period. It was one of great celebration and light-heartedness. Both Thomas's and Edwin's businesses were thriving and the families were united at Christmas once more. It felt right to thank the Lord for their good fortune, so they all attended church regularly every Sunday and even more so at Christmas. Mary had always known the church while growing up and attended regularly with her family, whereas Edwin's upbringing had included the church a little less often. He was aware he had been christened and attended church with his mother as a young child, but had only started going again regularly since he had known Mary. He didn't find it a chore, but did recognise that without Mary's influence, it might not happen so often.

Mary's brothers and sisters had all visited the family home at different times during the Christmas period. There was a consistent explosion of laughter and chattering throughout the house in Edgell Road and their front room had experienced plenty of use. Edwin had renewed his friendship with Charles and they had visited the public house on many occasions, sometimes returning home rather worse for wear and having to redeem themselves the following day. Mary and Emily had caught up with each other's news over the past six months. Emily had confided in Mary about concerns she had about not having had any children yet. Mary had tried to reassure her, saying if it was God's will, then it would happen, and to try not to worry, but she knew that her words had done little to help her sister's plight.

Edwin and Mary had also enjoyed a visit from her brother James and his large family. His wife, Charlotte, had given him five sons and two daughters so far. Charlotte had given birth every other year. James had joked that Mary was following in Charlotte's shoes and Edwin's face had been a picture. Mary had enjoyed little Alice's company again. She was now seven years old and even more of a delight to spend time with. She showed a big interest in Teddy and wanted to help with his every need. She showed a very mature interest in Mary's pregnancy and made Mary promise that she could come and help when the baby was born. It was a happy time for them all and one filled with great expectations for the New Year ahead.

Christmas had also been a busy time in the shop and this had enabled Edwin to save some extra money. He had decided he would try to do this, wherever possible, every month. It would be easier now that he had no debts to pay back. At the moment his shop premises did not belong to him but one day soon he hoped he would be able to afford to purchase them for his own.

Edwin and Mary's second child was born on 14 February: a daughter, born at home in Laleham Road. She was a beautiful looking baby with thick black hair and dark eyes, just like her mother. Jane had been in attendance during her granddaughter's birth, while Mary's sister Emily helped Edwin downstairs in the shop and kept Teddy occupied. Edwin had been sent to fetch Jane and Emily first thing that morning and they had arrived in the nick of time. Mary had barely made it into the bedroom before her daughter put in an appearance. She had only had a few contractions, when suddenly the baby was there. There had been hardly any time for even the need to push. The birth had been a piece of cake compared with Teddy's entrance into the world. Mary's second child was much smaller when compared to her brother when he had been born and that had made Mary's job a lot easier.

"You're in a bit of a hurry. You don't want to go rushing through life at such a speed. Slow down little lady," remarked her grandmother. "Take time and enjoy it," she said, as she kissed the child on her nose and then handed her to her mother. "Well done Mary. You have a daughter. Does she have a name?"

"I like Mabel," replied Mary, cradling her new baby. "Yes, Mabel Winifred I think. Do you like it?"

"That's beautiful," replied her mother, "just like she is."

Jane helped Mary to get cleaned up and then went downstairs to fetch Edwin. "You can go up now Edwin, they're ready for you." Surprised to see Jane back so quickly, Edwin asked if everything was all right. "Perfect," replied Jane. "Go and see for yourself."

Edwin rushed upstairs clutching something behind his back which he had had hidden under the shop counter. As he reached the top of the stairs he stopped outside the bedroom door for a second, to listen. There was not a sound coming from the room. He entered the room slowly and quietly, a little unsure as to what he would find. He walked over to where his wife lay with her eyes shut and sat down on the edge of the bed.

Mary's face was a little flushed and she had a few beads of perspiration on her forehead. She opened her eyes as Edwin sat down. "We have a daughter," she said, delighted.

Edwin leaned towards them and glanced at his new daughter for the first time. He could only see her little face sticking out from the blanket and a strand or two of her dark hair. "She looks just like you," he smiled. Mary thought so too.

"Do you realise what day it is today?" he asked.

"Yes dear, but I thought you had forgotten with all this going on."

"Never," he replied. In the four and a half years they had known each other, Edwin had always given Mary flowers on Valentine's

Day. "You have given me the most special love token today and I thank you for that," said Edwin. "Just look at her, she's as beautiful as her mother, if that is possible."

Mary beamed, full of pride for her achievement. Edwin bent down to kiss his clever wife on her forehead and said, "These are for you my darling." He produced a small bunch of snowdrops from behind his back and handed them to Mary. He had asked Jane if he could pick them for Mary earlier that morning, as they had left the house in Edgell Road in such a rush. He had managed to grab a handful on his way past.

"They're beautiful," said Mary. "Thank you."

"Not as beautiful as you and our daughter." Edwin's every word was sincere and Mary loved him for that.

"Well, we have one of each now," remarked Mary. "Shall we stop there?" she joked. Edwin just grinned. Could life get any better?

Teddy greeted his new sister with a little less enthusiasm. He was walking now and he was into everything. When Edwin introduced his new daughter to her brother Teddy was almost too engrossed to even look up. He was more interested in playing with the wooden blocks his grandfather had given to him earlier. Thomas had brought home some offcuts of wood from a site he'd been working at the previous week, sanded down the blocks and painted letters and numbers on their sides. The boy was delighted with his grandfather's gift.

Teddy was playing quietly with his blocks on the floor around Edwin's feet, while Edwin warmed himself by the fire, cradling his daughter. Thomas and Jane were fussing over Mary and arguing over who was next to hold the baby. Emily and Arthur had called in earlier with a small gift for the baby, and now Mary was feeling quite exhausted. Her mother had offered to look after Teddy for a few days but Mary had thanked her and said "I will have to get used to having two children one day, so it might as well be sooner, rather than later."

"As you wish dear, but you know where I am if you need me."

*

The family over the fish shop in Staines had grown from three to four and for the next three months life for Edwin and his family was good. They attended their parish church regularly, where Mabel was baptised about two weeks after her birth, as Teddy had been when the family lived in Ryde. Mary had two healthy children, and although she felt completely exhausted most of the time, she somehow managed to find time to help her husband in the shop. Edwin's business went from strength to strength and he successfully managed to save a little money each month. They counted their blessings, for they had many.

As promised, Mary's niece Alice was allowed to come and stay for a few days and help with the new baby. Her father had dropped her off and stayed for his supper. Mary was thrilled to see her brother again. They had plenty of catching up to do. James filled Mary in about where he was working and how Charlotte his wife was coping with their ever-growing family. When he returned a few days later to collect his daughter, she was reluctant to return home with him.

Mary had been concerned at first about how she would cope with Alice. After all, the child was still only eight years old. But Mary need not have worried as Alice had been a godsend. She was able to recognise when Mary needed help and immediately leap into action to undertake her task, whether it be to look after her cousins or carry out household chores. It made Mary feel quite tired just watching her. She skipped from one task to the next, humming a merry tune. Jobs were completed in no time at all and then she moved on to the next. Mary had no need to follow her around to correct or finish anything. Alice was quite exact, detailed and thorough in her work. At the end of her stay, Mary was sorry to see her leave. The two had become very close.

If Mary had any spare time these days, it was in the evenings when the children had gone to bed and she would spend it making clothes for them, or repairing her own and Edwin's. On one occasion, Edwin had returned home after a trip to the docks and had asked her if she could repair his trousers for him. Edwin had managed to split the seam in both pockets, because of the heavy filleting knives he carried around with him. He also had a small tear on the left leg, where he had caught it on the corner of a wooden crate.

"What on earth do you do with your trousers?" she toyed with him, holding them towards the candle to get a better look. "You must stand around all day with your hands in your pockets, gossiping to anyone that will listen." Mary enjoyed pulling his leg, especially after he had been away from her for a while, and Edwin enjoyed their banter. He missed Mary and his family terribly when he was away.

"You cheeky mare," he teased in return. "If you knew how hard I really worked."

"Work!" she continued. "You don't know the meaning of work. You try running a shop while your husband is away, keeping house and looking after two children and mending clothes all day. It's not easy, especially when you have a husband who keeps disappearing whenever he feels like it, off to the coast for a week at a time."

Suddenly, Edwin looked hurt. "You don't mean that do you Mary?" Mary looked up from her sewing and saw Edwin's hurt and concerned face.

"You silly sod, of course I don't mean it. I know you work as hard as any man."

Edwin smiled, walked over to his wife and knelt down next to her. "I knew you were only pulling my leg really," he said.

"You did?" Mary believed her husband wasn't so sure.

"Well, I hoped you were only teasing." He paused. "Do you miss me when I'm away Mary?"

"Of course I do," she said, looking deep into Edwin's eyes. "Every time you go away it seems to get harder, not easier." Edwin felt the same, but they both knew it was a necessary chore. They both wanted only the best for their family and if that meant working hard to get it and making sacrifices, then so be it.

"I hate having no one to talk to in the evenings about my day," Mary continued. "I can't bear having to go to bed by myself, and do you know the worst thing?"

Edwin was kneeling on the floor, holding onto Mary's hands. "What is it my darling?" he asked caringly. "What is it?"

"When I get into bed at night, I don't have anyone to warm my feet on." Mary laughed out loud. Edwin had had enough of her teasing and grabbed her around the waist and started to tickle her. "Get off me, get off," she squealed, in between her laughter.

Dropping her sewing onto the floor they embraced, and then kissed. They embraced again, and held tightly onto each other for quite some time, enjoying the warmth of each other's bodies, both of them feeling as though they never wanted to let go of the other. Edwin pulled away first and said, "Shall we go to bed then?"

"What a good idea," agreed Mary. She looked deep into her husband's eyes, smiled and continued, "and then I can warm up my feet." Edwin chased her upstairs, into the bedroom and onto the bed, where they fell into each other's arms

It was the following week when a letter arrived for Edwin, informing him that the lease on the shop and their home in Laleham Road was due to expire. It was hard to believe a whole year had passed. Everyone in the family knew Edwin and Mary would renew the lease or maybe try to purchase the property as soon as they had managed to save enough money, so they all were surprised and confused when Edwin informed them of the contents of the letter. No one was more upset than Mary.

"They're not going to renew the lease," Edwin told her.

"I don't understand. Why ever not?"

"It doesn't say. It just says we have a month to get out."

"One month? Well, can we afford to buy the property Edwin?"

"No. We just don't have enough saved yet." He paused. "Even

if we did, it's not up for sale. The letter states that the premises are neither up for renewal nor for sale. It goes on to say we have a month to vacate."

"Oh Edwin, what are we going to do?" Mary began to cry.

"We'll think of something dear." He tried to reassure her while all he could think about was the great effort they had put into the place and how they were about to lose it all.

Edwin, Mary and their two children were forced to leave Staines a month later and went to live in Dorset. The news had come as a big shock to the whole family and had taken some getting used to. Thomas and Edwin had looked everywhere for suitable premises. The fact was there was just nothing available. The last month had flown by and Mary had tried to spend as much time as was possible with her family. Time was precious and Mary had no idea when she would see them all again.

Then Edwin had been lucky enough to see a notice, in a local paper, that a fishmonger's shop was available for rent, in Dorset. It included accommodation for a small family and the rent was manageable, so after some quick consideration Edwin and Mary decided to take the property and move to the All Saints district of Dorset. It was a long journey, over one hundred miles away from Mary's family home. The thought of having to move home again, after such a short space of time and now with two young children in tow, was giving Mary sleepless nights. And then there was the thought of being so far away from her parents and sister Emily, who over the last year she had come to rely upon so much for her extra help and support.

Poor Teddy was going to miss his grandparents, aunts and uncles terribly and Mary knew her parents had become very attached to both of their newest grandchildren. It was a wrench for everyone concerned, but the couple knew they had little choice. They tried to stay strong and were determined to make the best of it.

There had been a fishmongers shop on High East Street, Dorset, for some years. For the last few years James Hibbs had run the business and lived on the premises with his wife and children. Edwin and Mr Hibbs corresponded by letter, to finalise the details. Hibbs had informed Edwin how he had lived on the premises for the last ten years, at first as a lodger, and later when he had taken over the running of the fishmongers shop from the previous occupant, who had decided to sell up, move away and live abroad.

Hibbs explained that he now had the opportunity to try his hand at something else and was looking to rent out his shop to someone who would continue to run a fishmonger's on his premises. He gave Edwin information about his business income and explained it was 'a good little earner'. It turned out not to be making as much money as Edwin was making in Staines, but it was more than enough for the family to get by on and still be able to save for the future.

When the day finally arrived for Edwin to move his family, Mary thought her heart would break. As the train pulled away and began the hundred-mile trip to their new life, Teddy wiped away the tears that poured from his mothers eyes. He waved frantically to his grandparents and they waved back. He recognised that his mother was distressed and sensed that a change was taking place, but he was too young to understand what was really happening. He was more excited about going on a train journey and after a few miles his enthusiasm had rubbed off on the rest of his family.

So Edwin took over the rent and running of the fishmonger's shop on High East Street in Dorchester. There were other shops on High East Street and Edwin and Mary got to know their owners quite quickly. There was a butcher occupying number fourteen, a baker at fifteen, a widow who owned the greengrocers at number ten, Mr Baker, a pastry cook and confectioner occupied number nine, and at number sixteen, Fred Barnett was the licensed vict-ualler of The Phoenix public house. The family settled quickly in Dorchester. Mary made plenty of new friends, some who became regular customers in the shop and others she met through the church or in the park while out with the children.

Edwin became good friends with Fred Barnett of the Phoenix, who was single at the time and conveniently ate nothing but fish. The man never touched meat and that made good business sense to Edwin and the pair often laughed about it. Edwin would often carry a parcel of fish, wrapped up in newspaper, along the road with him to the Phoenix for Fred's dinner. The two men would spend the occasional evening together, sitting at the bar chatting and sometimes on Sundays when Mary was at church with the children, Edwin would use Fred as an excuse to get out of going with her, saying Fred needed the company.

Another Christmas came and went and this year in some ways it was very different from the last. Edwin and Mary spent Christmas in their new home in Dorset with their two young children. It was a very quiet Christmas that year, when they saw very little of anyone else. They both missed the company of Mary's family and the comings and goings of various relatives. However, there was one little thing that this Christmas had in common with last year's and that was that Mary was expecting another child.

Chapter 3

1894

Mary kept in regular contact with her parents and sister via letters. She had of course informed them she was expecting another child and they had written back expressing their delight. Mary found that regular letter writing made the fact that she was unable to visit her parents a little more easy to bear. She enjoyed letting them know about Teddy and Mabel and wrote to them about many funny tales to do with the fish shop. The letters she wrote helped her to miss them less. She knew her parents shared her letters with Emily and they often wrote back with news of Emily and Arthur. Mary looked forward to receiving their letters. One simple letter could brighten her day and keep her going for weeks. She would read it over and over again until she almost knew it by heart.

One such letter she received contained some news she had been waiting to hear for many years. Arthur and Emily were at last going to have a child. Mary couldn't contain her excitement and rushed into the shop to tell Edwin. He was as thrilled for them as Mary. "Our babies will be born within months of each other," smiled Mary. "What a shame we don't live a little closer to one another. It would be so lovely for them to be able to grow up together."

"Mary, sometimes you have a very simple outlook on life," replied Edwin. "Life is rarely that straightforward." Edwin didn't mean to belittle Mary in any way and she admired him, as sometimes he could just be far too practical and realistic.

It was the middle of May when Edwin and Mary's third child, Lillian, was born. As was the norm for Edwin, he stayed well out of the way during the birth and tried to keep himself occupied with work.

The butcher's widow, Susan Haywood, had been appointed the job of looking after Teddy and Mabel. Now almost two and a half years old, Teddy was proving a bit of a handful. He couldn't understand why he wasn't being allowed to see his mother and was becoming very agitated about this. He had been suffering from a cold for the past two days and his parents had put his recent awkwardness down to him feeling a little under the weather.

Teddy's carer, normally a patient woman, was trying everything she could to occupy the boy and keep his mind off being away from his mother. While she finished her chores, Teddy and Mabel played with her two children on the kitchen floor. Then she took them out for a walk down into the town to replenish her food stocks, as it was Friday. As they passed the fishmongers on their way back, Teddy spotted his father, and pulling away from the woman ran inside the shop.

"Dad, Dad, where's Mam?" he shouted at the top of his voice.

"Calm down Teddy," his father told him as he picked him up and held him close.

Edwin had never known his son to seem so troubled and tried to reassure him.

"It won't be long now Ted, and we will all be able to go and see your mother. I think she might even have a surprise for us all." Teddy looked up at his father, with his big round eyes and managed to force a smile. "Now off you go, back with your sister and I'll come and get you when your mother is ready." Teddy did as he was told with the thought of what his surprise could be racing around inside his tiny head.

The baby was born reasonably healthy but she was smaller than Mabel had been when she was born. During her labour Mary had been helped by her friend and neighbour Mrs Paul. The labour hadn't been too bad. She was becoming quite a professional at it now. Once she and the baby had been washed and made comfortable, Mrs Paul left and Edwin was allowed into the bedroom. He entered carrying Mabel, Teddy at his side. As the door opened Teddy flew past his father like a whirlwind so that he could get to see his mother first. He stopped dead in his tracks when he noticed she was cradling a baby in her arms. His mother beamed a warm smile at Teddy which reassured him slightly.

Teddy slowly and quietly stepped up to the bed where Mary was cradling Lillian. He leant over the baby to get a better look. "A baby," said Teddy with raised eyebrows. He never asked, but he did wonder how it had got there and where it had come from.

"Yes, Teddy. It's a baby, another baby sister for you. Her name is Lillian," replied his mother. Teddy leant in even closer.

"Where's my surprise?" asked Teddy.

"Surprise?" Mary seemed confused and looked over to Edwin at which point Edwin stepped in to explain. "I told him earlier, that you might have a surprise for him later."

"Oh I see," said Mary. "Baby Lillian is your surprise, Teddy." Teddy didn't look too impressed with that news, and the disappointed look on his face made Edwin and Mary smile.

"So she's called Lillian is she?" enquired Edwin, who was standing at the end of the bed holding onto Mabel.

"Yes dear, I'd like to call her Lillian May. A pretty name, don't you agree?"

"Yes, a very pretty name, for another very pretty daughter," replied Edwin.

Teddy leaned forward to see what everyone was fussing about and as he did released the loudest and wettest sneeze straight at his mother and new baby sister. Both Mary and Edwin burst out laughing and poor Lillian began to cry loudly because of all the commotion.

"It's time for bed I think Teddy," said his mother, looking over at Edwin for back up. "Yes," Edwin agreed, "I think we've all had enough excitement for one day."

Edwin's and Mary's household had an established routine.

Mary was determined this should continue over the next two days, and that it should remain just like any other weekend. Edwin worked all day in the shop on the Saturday, whilst Mary continued with the job of motherhood, the only difference now being that she had three children not two. On Sunday, Mary took all of her children with her to church, which again was a normal occurrence while Edwin chose to visit Fred at the Phoenix. The two men usually spent an hour or so there on a Sunday afternoon, reading their newspapers and catching up with local hearsay, and today he had the excuse that he was going to wet the baby's head.

When Monday morning arrived Edwin started work in the shop and Mary made a start on her ever-growing pile of washing. Later on that morning Mary noticed Lillian had started with a runny nose. A few hours later her runny nose had turned into a full-blown cold equipped with sneezes and a cough. Lillian in herself seemed unperturbed. Although Mary noticed she was a little unsettled when she put her down for a sleep, she was feeding well and seemed quite bright and alert when she was awake so Mary had no reason to particularly worry. The following Sunday was Lillian's christening and although she was worse the family were reluctant to cancel the proceedings.

It wasn't until Lilly and Teddy still had their colds a week later that Mary started to feel more concerned. Lilly had started to cough more and more frequently. She was also becoming quite distressed because of it. Lilly was sometimes impossible to feed and often Mary struggled to keep her milk down. Quite often Lilly would have a fit of coughing after a feed, usually followed by vomiting. Teddy had been suffering as well but Mary was less concerned about him as he was stronger than his baby sister and seemed little affected by his affliction.

After a brief discussion with Edwin, Mary decided to consult a doctor about Lillian. During her visit the doctor seemed a little callous in his diagnosis. Mary decided to ignore his curt behaviour, believing he must be overtired due to his heavy workload. She was blatantly aware that there were other babies and children in the village suffering with a similar illness because of the numbers of mothers and children in the waiting area. However, the doctor had managed to reassure her that she was doing the right thing by keeping the baby warm when taking her out for walks and to continue trying her with her feeds. He suggested Mary might want to add some liquorice, elderberry or garlic to the child's feeds. "It may help her to keep the liquid down. And some mullein would help ease her breathing and soothe her sore throat and cough," the doctor had added as they had parted company. Mary acknowledged his comment, said thank you and goodbye.

Mary was aware that mullein was a plant which had a long history of use as a medicine. She could remember her mother saying that she had used it and that it had helped her many a time when her children had been sick. Her mother had once described a time when James had been very poorly. He had had difficulty breathing properly and complained of earache after contracting a particularly nasty cold when he was about two years old. Mary's mother had used mullein on that occasion. It had proved to be an effective treatment for James and Mary was sure the same would be true for little Lilly.

Over the next week Mary tried the mullein and the other medicines the doctor had suggested. She added them to Lilly's feeds, but none of them seemed to be having the desired effect. If anything, Lillian's cough had increased and changed in sound. She now seemed to be making a "barking" sound and at times Lillian even seemed to be having trouble catching her breath.

Teddy's cold, on the other hand, appeared to be recovering and his cough had improved since taking the medicine. It was tiny Lilly that Mary and Edwin were fraught with worry about. "I just don't understand it," sighed Mary. "How can they both have colds in June?"

"I don't know, my darling, but you're doing all the right things. You've been going for walks in the fresh air and making sure they take their mullein. Look at Teddy, he's improved already. I'm sure Lilly will do the same in a few more days," reassured Edwin.

"Yes, I'm sure you're right. It's just so hard not to worry. She's so little."

That night Mary was up most of the night with the baby. Lilly had a terrible fever and was continuously coughing. She was now unable to keep down any of her feeds. She made a terrible sound when she coughed. It sounded as though she had a great amount of fluid in her throat which she just couldn't dislodge. It appeared she was gasping for air. Her face had reddened and at one stage she actually stopped breathing for a few seconds. Mary was beside herself and refused to leave her baby's side. Lilly's coughing had exhausted her frail little form and she finally fell asleep around 2am. Once her baby was asleep Mary covered her with another blanket and fell asleep herself in a chair next to Lilly's crib.

The following morning Mary awoke to discover her beautiful baby daughter had died during the night. Lillian May had lived for just eighteen days. She had died from whooping cough and there was nothing Mary, nor anyone, could have done to save her. It took Mary and Edwin many months to get over the death of their daughter. If the truth be known, they would never truly forget the experience or the daughter they were never really allowed to get to know.

A small funeral was held for Lillian May at All Saints church in Dorchester. Mary's parents arrived the day before. Edwin had written the difficult letter informing them of his daughter's death and begging them to arrive as soon as possible. When they did he was relieved, as no matter how he tried he had been unable to comfort his wife. Mary was inconsolable.

At the funeral Mary put on a brave face. She realised how glad she was they had gone ahead and had Lilly baptised. Just one week earlier they had almost postponed the baptism as Lilly's health was deteriorating. Now Mary was relieved they hadn't. For decades Christians had believed that baptism was essential for a soul to enter heaven and therefore a baptism should take place as near to the birth as possible. Infants who died before baptism were deemed ineligible for salvation and were not buried on consecrated or holy ground. This would have made Mary's torment much worse and she was grateful for this one small mercy.

Mary's parents were a huge support. Now in their sixties, the journey had proved long and tiring but this hadn't deterred them. They knew something of what their daughter was going through as they too had once lost a young child. Mary had been four years old when her two-year-old brother George had died. Mary didn't remember him but the memory of him had stayed with Thomas and Jane all these years, as Lillian's would stay with Edwin and Mary.

Emily had been too upset and too pregnant to accompany her parents on their journey to Dorchester. Now into her third trimester she had broken down when they had told her the distressing news. She had been looking forward to having her baby at the same time as her sister and now that dream had been snatched from them both. It was too far for Emily to travel and she knew she would be of no use to Mary anyway. She sent all her love with her parents and made her mother promise to explain to Mary how much she loved and missed her sister, and the distress she felt for her. After the funeral Mary sobbed in her mother's arms, "I wish Emily was here."

"She would be no use to you, my darling," her mother said gently. "She would be a constant reminder of what you have lost." Then she paused. "Emily has recently been through a similar loss of her own."

"What?" Mary suddenly looked up at her mother, bewildered. "She's lost her baby too? Why did she not write and tell me."

"No, sorry, you misunderstand me. Her baby is fine," reassured her mother. "What I mean is she has previously been pregnant and lost a child." Mary was shocked. "And I suspect it has happened to her more than once," her mother continued. "She's never spoken of it, but I suspect she has lost other babies."

"Poor, poor Emily, I knew they had been trying for a baby for a long time but I never thought … Why has she never told me?" Mary asked her mother.

"I don't think she would have told me if I hadn't have popped round one day and found her in bed. She was very matter of fact about it as though it wasn't the first time it had happened."

"Oh poor Emily. Why didn't she say anything?"

"Well, I suppose it's not something one wants to talk about, is it?"

For a short moment Mary's mind had been taken off her own predicament and she was more upset about her sister's loss but it wasn't long before she remembered her own misfortune. With her mother still holding her close she asked, "Why did Lilly have to die, Mam?" Mary began to cry again. Huge tears plopped from her sore, swollen eyes and her mother could do little to stop her own eyes from weeping. "I'm afraid I don't have all the answers dear," her mother replied, wiping away a tear from her own face. "But I do know that God never gives us trials we cannot endure. You will get through this Mary. I promise. Our faith is nothing if it is never tested." Mary listened to her mother's wise words and felt a little comforted.

The following days and weeks were difficult for Edwin and Mary. They knew they would get through this tragedy because they had each other and they still loved each other more than either of them could describe. Nothing could change that love. Edwin made it clear to Mary just how he felt about her but he made no demands upon her in the bedroom and waited until she was truly ready before they made love together again.

A month later when Edwin and Mary received news of the birth of Arthur and Emily's daughter, all they wanted to feel was happiness for the pair but the news just seemed to open up their slow-healing wounds and expose all their feelings of loss all over again. It took Mary some weeks before she felt able to write to her sister and pass on her best wishes. Emily had nothing but understanding for her sister and when they finally got together a few months later, no one would have known that either woman had ever lost a child.

The days and weeks turned into months and then before they knew it a whole year and a half had gone by since the death of Edwin's and Mary's daughter. Edwin's business was thriving and he and Mary had a tidy sum of money saved away by the Christmas of 1895. Edwin had been discussing what they might do with the money when Mary interrupted him. "I think we might have to put any plans we have on hold for a while," remarked Mary nervously.

"Oh yes, and why is that?" asked Edwin hoping his suspicions over the last few days were going to prove correct.

"Because," and Mary waited a few seconds so that she could get the words out without bursting into tears, "we're going to have another baby," she whispered.

"That's wonderful, Mary. Well done love." Edwin spoke gently to his wife as he knew she was still feeling vulnerable. Mary looked worried. She really didn't want to lose another baby. The thought of history repeating itself drove little daggers of pain and panic in and out and through her heart.

"What's the matter?" Edwin asked. "It is good news isn't it?"

"Yes, dear, it's wonderful news but it's impossible not to think about Lillian."

"How about we try to concentrate on this baby and you," said Edwin, his sensible streak showing itself again and Mary knew her husband was right.

With Christmas and New Year both over, Mary was trying hard to look positively to the future and to the birth of her next child when she received a letter from Emily who had some news of her own.

She and Arthur were also expecting another child and it was due about a month before Mary's.

When Edwin finished his work in the shop he went upstairs to find some solace and his family. On his way upstairs Edwin observed that the children were already tucked up in their beds and there appeared to be no smell of dinner wafting in from the kitchen and the table hadn't been laid. He found Mary sitting in the armchair almost in darkness, staring into the flames flickering in the fireplace and holding a letter in her hand. Noticing Mary was obviously distressed over the letter's contents, Edwin enquired, "Are you all right, my dear? Is it bad news?"

At first Mary didn't acknowledge or even hear her husband. She was so deep inside her own thoughts. "Mary, are you all right?" Edwin repeated his question louder this time. Mary finally looked up and registered her husband's presence. Without speaking she handed Edwin the letter. He read its contents quickly and then understood why Mary was sitting quietly all by herself. He handed her back the letter. "I understand your concern Mary."

"I can't help worrying Edwin. History seems to be repeating itself."

"What do you mean? In what way is history repeating?"

"You know what happened the last time Emily and I were expecting a baby at the same time." Mary paused and looked back into the orange flames which seemed to be dancing about in the fireplace. Edwin was unsure as how to respond. "I don't think I could manage if I lost another baby," Mary continued.

"You won't have to, my darling." He tried to reassure her but didn't feel as though he was doing a very good job.

"There are no guarantees Edwin. If the Lord wishes it, there is not a lot we can do."

"No, I suppose you may be right, so there is no point in worrying about it then is there? You'll just make yourself poorly and that won't help anyone. Try to think more positively, darling." He hoped he had said enough to convince her but couldn't refrain from giving a little more advice. "Just don't overdo it Mary. You know what you're like."

Ignoring his last comment Mary was distracted by her thoughts again. I must write back to Emily she thought. I bet she's feeling the same way. Emily was and it was only to be expected. Before she had received her sister's letter the same thoughts had gone through Emily's mind and she and Arthur had had a similar conversation. The two women wrote to each other more in those next seven months than they had ever done previously. They wrote weekly, sharing their hopes and worries. Letter writing proved comforting, knowing they both were experiencing similar feelings.

In June Mary received news that Emily and Arthur had had a baby girl. They had chosen to name her Margaret and Emily had tried to reassure Mary by explaining in her letter that the baby was happy and healthy, had a good appetite and slept well. Emily went on to say that Margaret was the spitting image of her father. Emily had done her best to reassure her sister in her letter but Mary's time couldn't come quickly enough. Mary just wanted it over and done with. She needed to know her baby was going to be all right like her sister's, but the next few weeks seemed to drag on for ever.

That time dragged for Emily also. She seemed to have to wait for an age to receive news of Mary's baby. As the days went by she feared more and more for her sister but when at last she finally received the news she'd been waiting for she squealed with relief and delight and danced around the room with her eldest daughter in her arms. Two-year-old Dorothy thought it was great fun and chuckled joyfully. Arthur thought she had gone completely mad and baby Margaret wasn't impressed at all, crying loudly as her father tried unsuccessfully to soothe her.

When Emily eventually came back down to earth she set about writing a six-page letter to her sister telling her all about Dorothy's and Margaret's progress, where Arthur was working at the moment and asked so many questions about Mary's new baby she almost ran out of space on the page. At the end of the letter she had just enough room to ask when the two families could all get together again.

Mary's baby was finally born on 16 July. It was a boy and Edwin and Mary decided to call him Lionel Gordon. Mary hadn't enjoyed this pregnancy because she had the constant fear at the back of her mind that something would go wrong. It hadn't and Mary was hugely relieved as Lionel was a big boy, healthy and strong. He had weighed much more than Mary's other babies. He had a fine set of lungs and a huge appetite. There was not much wrong with him. In fact, he was perfect. Edwin was extremely pleased that he had another son and believed, correctly, that this would help enable Mary not to compare this baby to the one they had previously lost.

It wasn't many months before the two sisters were able to organise for their families to meet up in Staines. Edwin had agreed to close his shop for a week, which had been unheard of before, but Mary had managed to convince him they all needed a holiday. He recognised how much his wife needed to visit her home town and family and how the last two years had taken their toll on her. Circumstances had affected him also and he now felt the timing appropriate to take a break from his normal daily routine and spend some quality time with his growing family.

It proved to be a wonderfully happy time for the two families. Teddy, Mabel and Dorothy got on so well and played beautifully together without bickering or falling out once. The men took time to enjoy themselves with visits to the local pub while the two new mothers compared notes on their new babies, synchronised their feeding times and changed their babies' napkins together always laughing and joking about something, usually their husbands.

Time had been made for a trip to the local park where the fathers had taken turns in pushing their babies' perambulators and the mothers had played hide and seek behind the Park's tall trees with their older children. The two families enjoyed vibrant mealtimes all squashed together around Emily's and Arthur's dining table and it had been pleasing to be able to laugh together again. During this time life could not have been sweeter, but unfortunately both couples were realistic and well aware that in life things never stay perfect for very long. This was why they all made the very most of their reunion and their time spent together.

As if right on cue, a couple of months later Edwin found himself looking for new premises for his business and a new home for his family. The family were once again thrown into turmoil. Edwin had received a letter one morning about the lease on his business premises. After the feelings of anger and frustration had subsided he showed it to Mary.

"I can't believe this is happening to us again," Mary said despondently.

"Neither can I, dear, and just as everything was running so smoothly."

"Are we ever going to be able to settle ourselves in one place for good? I hate to think where we could end up next."

Edwin responded optimistically. "I don't know yet but let's not panic. We have a couple of months to decide and enough money saved this time so things could go in our favour," smiled Edwin. Suddenly the realisation of what Edwin was implying dawned on Mary and her face lit up.

"Are you going to look to buy a property then?" she enquired.

"Absolutely," Edwin answered with determination in his voice.

"Oh, Edwin, wouldn't it be wonderful if we could find somewhere to settle and not have to move again?"

"Most definitely," he sighed. "I cannot deny it has been terribly frustrating to have to keep moving every couple of years just as the business is beginning to thrive." He continued a little more cheerfully. "Every time we move we seem to have accumulated more junk and more children." He paused. "I just can't do it any more."

"I know what you mean dear. Teddy should start school soon. I don't want to have to keep moving him every time he has just settled in somewhere."

"I think it would do us all good to have a permanent family home," continued Edwin. "I think we deserve it. Don't you?"

"Oh yes. I do. I do."

"I was hoping you'd say that."

Edwin and Mary had made their decision. They knew it wasn't going to be easy and could appreciate just how much hard work and commitment was needed to fulfil their ambitions. Neither of them was afraid of hard work and both had proved this over the last seven years. So it was fortunate that neither of them knew just what really lay ahead for them.

Chapter 4

1897

Edwin's challenge was to find another suitable building to accommodate a fish shop where the premises could also be turned into a home. With an ever-increasing family which showed no signs of slowing, suitable and affordable premises were proving harder to find than Edwin had anticipated. Just as he was beginning to feel he had exhausted all possibilities, a chance meeting brought to his attention a property which was for sale in Surrey.

Edwin was in Ramsgate at the time meeting with the dock manager to inform him of his change in circumstances. The lease on his shop in Dorset had only two more weeks before it expired and Edwin had agreed to let the dock manager know his new address as soon as possible. As he was leaving the dockside office, he literally bumped into his brother-in-law James who was trying to come in. James was of course married to Mary's sister, Alice. The two men had become firm friends when a few years earlier James had left his job as a bricklayer and followed Edwin into the fish trade. At the time he and Edwin had corresponded by letter and Edwin was able to give James some useful tips and important contacts which had enabled him to set up his own business. Now it was James's turn to help Edwin.

James and Alice had moved to Windlesham in Surrey and rented a shop where James sold fresh fish and meat. James had always said it had been the best move he had ever made and that he would be eternally grateful to Edwin for all his help and advice. Edwin had not seen James for some months and so was surprised, yet pleased to bump into him at the docks. James was just as pleased to see Edwin. "Hello, mate, don't get to see you here very often now. I'm usually over in Billingsgate but have a bit of business here today."

"Well, it's good to see you," replied Edwin as he shook James's hand.

"How's business and the family?" asked James.

Edwin explained his situation and James looked genuinely concerned for his brother-in-law. "I bet Mary's worried, isn't she?"

Edwin nodded. "You could say that." James then told him about a property he had recently visited. "Listen, I looked at a property only last week with the intention of buying it myself. It was perfect but unfortunately a little out of my price range. We've not managed to save quite that much yet."

"Where was it?" asked Edwin, his interest captured immediately.

"It's in a place called Farnham, not far from Woking."

"Oh yes, I've heard of it," replied Edwin.

"I know you and Mary have been saving for longer than Alice and I, so I'm sure you will be able to afford it. Anyway, it's standing empty at the moment. You could move in right away. It's in quite good condition and there's plenty of room upstairs for the family." James was able to describe the property in enough detail for Edwin to become excited. Edwin and James continued their discussion in a local coffee house and enjoyed the hour they spent in each other's company, their heads locked tightly together in both business and personal issues.

Edwin could hardly wait to get home and tell Mary about his chance meeting with James. "Visiting Ramsgate today may prove to be more valuable than I anticipated," he explained to Mary after he arrived home late that evening. Mary had been working on yet another pair of Teddy's trousers which he had put his knees through. "I bumped into James and he told me all about a property that is up for sale, in Farnham. I think I'll go to see it tomorrow and if I think it's suitable I will have no hesitation in making arrangements to buy it."

"Oh Edwin, that sounds wonderful. I've heard Farnham is a lovely town. The children would love it there." She paused for a second then asked. "Did James speak of how Alice and the children are?"

"Briefly, he said Alice was busy with the baby and that she hadn't been sleeping too well. It's been keeping them up most nights and they're both worn out."

"Oh dear, poor Alice, maybe I'll drop her a line."

Edwin continued. "We spent most of the time discussing the property in Farnham. I don't mind telling you, I'm quite excited about it. Are you?"

"Of course but I just don't want to get my hopes up too much. I couldn't stand the disappointment if it wasn't suitable for some reason. So let's just wait and see what happens after you've visited the place."

"That's very sensible of you my darling, but it is hard not to be a little eager, isn't it?"

"Yes dear, it certainly is."

Edwin left very early the following morning for the town of Farnham. He travelled by train, having to change twice, arriving in Farnham some three hours later. He had warned Mary he might have to stay overnight in Farnham if the property was right and he was unable to finalise the details in one day. He left Mary in charge of the shop along with Fred Barnett's wife, Ellen. Mary had gone round to the Phoenix the night before and asked Fred if she could borrow his wife the next day. Fred had been very obliging and said he was sure he could spare her for a day or two if need be, and Ellen had joked she'd be glad of a change of scenery. Mary and Ellen got on very well. They were the same age and had always found each other's company refreshing. Mary was able to enjoy a giggle with Ellen but knew she would work hard as well. Spending a whole day in each other's company was a pleasure for both women.

Edwin arrived in Farnham around eleven that morning. Armed with directions from James he made his way from the town's busy station platform, along Station Hill and on to South Street where he made a left turn into Union Road. It was then only a short distance around the bend to the top of Downing Street where James had explained he would find the property. In total his walk had taken him around five minutes, no time at all from the station, just as James had described.

After turning the corner Edwin tentatively made his way along and up Downing Street trying to take in everything and gain a real feel for the place. He hoped he would not be disappointed with the property. Traffic passed him continuously and there were plenty of people about. Delivery boys aged between twelve and sixteen on three-wheeler bikes with boxes or baskets fixed on the back, whizzed past him at speed in their urgency to deliver the goods on time. They were dressed smartly in suits and caps in order to give the right impression to their customers. As soon as they had completed their delivery they would return to where they were employed in order to load up for their next job. Worried they might be disciplined by their employers for late deliveries they worked extra hard, pedalling quickly, loading and unloading, backwards and forwards all day.

There were other boys pushing small carts laden with produce for delivery to local homes and other shops. Horses and their traps belonging to the people of Farnham and surrounding areas were left parked outside shops along both sides of Downing Street while their occupants made their daily purchases. Horses pulling carts or vans were laden with all sorts of goods travelling to and fro, up and down the length of the street. The noise and smell gave Edwin a real sense of the busy town and its people, going about their daily business. For some reason it felt right for Edwin to be there and part of this hectic, exciting town.

Edwin made his way up the right-hand side of the street passing a tea dealers, tailors, a greengrocer, and then a pub called The Bird in Hand. Edwin knew he was nearly there as James had mentioned the Bird in Hand. He had said it was one of the less expensive places to stay if Edwin needed to do so overnight. James had said he could definitely recommend the ale there. Edwin passed another general store and next door to that was the building he had come to see.

The building was split into two properties, appearing ostentatious with its painted façade and three pineapple-like pommels which decorated the parapet. On the right-hand side it housed the Coffee Tavern while the left side stood vacant. The four-bay building was marked by five fluted giant Ionic pilasters, and its two centre bays incorporated large windows with a blind arcade above.

The property consisted of three floors covered with a slate roof which was in a good state of repair. On the first floor above the doorway was a deeply recessed and architraved square window. The building dated from about 1855. Edwin peered through a split in the wood which was boarding up the bay window. From what he could make out, it seemed the building had been previously used as a butcher's shop. The butchers hooks used to hang the meat up and some large wooden chopping boards had been left behind.

Edwin was early for his two o'clock meeting with the agent dealing with the property so he worked this to his advantage and went to take a good look around the outside. He liked what he saw. The property appeared to be in a reasonable state of repair. The brickwork was sound, the wooden window frames had been well maintained and there was enough space in the back yard for extra storage if he should need it. He had decided upon the amount he would be willing to offer for the property and was sure his offer would be accepted.

As he still had some time before his meeting with the agent he decided to use his time wisely and explore the town, allowing him the opportunity to check out any competition. He was pleased to discover that there were only two other fishmongers operating in Farnham and they were right over the other side of the town. They should cause me little concern, he thought.

During his walk around Farnham town he discovered the Bush Hotel which was over 300 years old. He was impressed as it boasted extensive gardens and grounds, tennis courts, bowling green and a hall, capable of dining 140 people, together with stabling. The hotel was run by Charles Hart whom Edwin met when he called into the bar for a swift drink to quench his thirst. There were other hotels in Farnham such as The Lion and Lamb, The Railway, The Queens Head and The Ship, but Edwin thought none compared to the impressive Bush Hotel.

Edwin passed Farnham's Police Station situated on Union Street and the Volunteer Fire Brigade inside Engine House on East Street, both of which Edwin hoped he would never have to call upon for their services. Shortly after one o'clock Edwin headed back to Downing Street where he enjoyed a late lunch in the Coffee Tavern, situated next door to the vacant property. He chose a table next to the window, so as he could keep watch for the agent whom he had arranged to meet. The coffee house's owner was a very hospitable man who had gained a wealth of knowledge about the local people and was only too willing to share this knowledge. He was eager to explain that among Farnham's many inhabitants there were also some affluent businessmen, such as John Henry Knight, George Sturt and Harold Falkner.

John Henry Knight came from a wealthy family and according to the coffee shop owner had invented the first ever British petrol-driven car. The man told Edwin of how very recently Mr Knight had been summonsed for driving his car in Castle Street without a licence and for speeding.

He went on to tell Edwin about George Sturt who had lived in Farnham all his life and upon the death of his father taken over the family's wheelwright's business in East Street. Unbeknown to Edwin at this time, he and George Sturt would meet a few times during their lives, when George would make and repair wheels for Edwin's cart. Later in his life George Sturt would realise his true ambition, which was to become a writer and Edwin and Mary would enjoy reading George's books about rural life in and around Farnham.

Lastly, the coffee shop owner told Edwin of Harold Falkner, a man in his early twenties who had just set up his own architect's practice in Farnham. With his friend Charles Borelli, a wealthy businessman and property owner, he would later campaign actively for the preservation of local buildings on which he would then do restoration work. Himself once a builder, Edwin would come to admire this man greatly over the years for his work and improvements he would achieve around the town. Edwin didn't know it yet but he would grow to share Harold Falkner's love and concern for Farnham's historic buildings. Inside the coffee shop, the two men's conversation came to an abrupt end as Edwin noticed the agent waiting outside the next-door property. He apologised to the coffee shop owner and made a hasty exit.

After a thorough inspection of the property Edwin left feeling both relieved and apprehensive. He had managed to strike a deal and the two men walked the short distance together to where the agent's office was situated on West Street to sign the necessary papers. Edwin believed the property was ideal. He couldn't have wished for better. James had been right and Edwin was sure Mary would love it. By the time the paperwork was complete it was getting late and Edwin knew he would be unable to make it home that night. He made his way back to the Bird in Hand on Downing Street to enquire about a room for the night.

That evening he was able to go over the paperwork while enjoying a rather basic but tasty meal. He later sketched some ideas down on paper that he had thought of while he had been inspecting the premises. The following morning Edwin had time to take another quick look around the town before he had to catch his train home. He discovered the town's famous castle. He had no idea how he could have missed it the day before except that his mind was obviously on other matters. Seated north of the town, Farnham Castle was founded in 1129 by Henry de Bois, brother of King Stephen and Bishop of Winchester. The castle was reputed to be a powerful fortress with parkland adjoining and covering over 300 acres. Teddy's going to love this, thought Edwin.

Situated at the junction of Castle Street and The Borough was the Corn Exchange. The building had been erected in 1865 in place of the old market house. Edwin took a look inside this building where there were offices, shops, assembly rooms and a market hall where Farnham held its corn market every Thursday. At the corner of this building Edwin admired a tower 88 feet high which contained a four-dial clock.

Edwin was pleased his trip had turned out to be worthwhile and successful. When he returned to Dorset, he was feeling very positive about the future. He had made some useful discoveries and contacts during his visit to Farnham, and he had been able to set out some plans on paper for a few alterations he would need to do to the inside of his new property. He couldn't wait to let Mary know how he had got on.

Ellen Barnett was just leaving the fish shop after helping Mary solidly for the last two days. "I'm completely shattered," she said as she was leaving for home. "I don't know how you manage to run this shop, look after the house and take care of those children."

"It's a case of having to," Mary replied. Ellen didn't have children and had up until then no idea how exhausting they could be. This experience had opened her eyes and made her realise how easy she had it at home. But she had no intention in sharing her new-found knowledge with her husband.

Mary eagerly awaited her husband's arrival and was still serving in the shop when Edwin walked through the door. She had Lionel strapped to her belly, asleep in a sling. Teddy and Mabel were playing out in the street and when they spotted their father, followed him into the shop. Mary breathed a sigh of relief to see her husband home safely. "Oh Edwin, it's good to see you. How did you get on?"

"It couldn't have gone better," he smiled. "You are now looking at the proud owner of a property in Farnham."

"Really!"

"Yes, really," he replied as he picked up Teddy under one arm and Mabel in the other. Swinging them gently and looking at them in turn he asked, "How do you two little ragamuffins fancy moving house and going to live near to a real castle?"

"Yeah! Whoopee!" shouted Teddy and Mabel together. Teddy was very excited at this prospect. Mabel was really only copying her big brother as she was too little to understand what was happening.

"I'm ready when you are," smiled Mary.

"That's my girl," beamed Edwin.

The family moved themselves and their few precious belongings into their new home a couple of weeks later. The few pieces of furniture they owned travelled by train with a removal company and then by horse and cart to Downing Street. As soon as Mary stepped off the train she felt a connection with the town. When she saw their new shop premises and home she turned to Edwin and asked him how on earth they could afford such a place.

"It seems a very smart and affluent area. Are you sure you've brought me to the right place?"

Edwin laughed at her making fun of him. "What do you think of it then? Do you like it? Do you think we can be happy here?"

"Oh yes Edwin, I'm sure we can."

Teddy and Mabel had already run off and were exploring the upstairs of the property, making a right din. When Mary inspected the area downstairs she recognised that it would need quite a bit of work doing on it before Edwin would be satisfied to open it to the public. They discussed this and Edwin explained to Mary exactly what he wanted to do and the changes he wanted to make to the ground floor, sharing with her the sketches he had made in the Bird in Hand during his first visit.

"I reckon it should take about a week, two at the most before we can open properly. That should also give me enough time to sort out a new supplier," Edwin informed his wife.

"Are you going to change suppliers then?" asked Mary.

"I think I should after talking to James. He now purchases his supplies from the Billingsgate Market in London. We also discussed the port of Grimsby."

"Grimsby? But that's miles away from here. Why Grimsby?" enquired Mary.

"That's where most of the fish comes into at the moment and apparently they are extending the railway to Grimsby Docks. Rumour has it that when it is finished it will be quicker and cheaper than getting supplies back here from London."

"That sounds unlikely," commented Mary sceptically.

"It does, but I wouldn't be surprised if it happens. It won't be finished though for another couple of years so for the time being I will have to use Billingsgate."

Behind the room which was to be their shop, was another room which Mary intended to use as her kitchen. It housed a large black, cast-iron cooking range, comprised of coal grate, oven and smaller top oven and back boiler for hot water. It's in need of a good clean thought Mary. A stone sink sat on the opposite wall with a cast-iron pump from where they could get fresh water. Mary had decided this room was where the family meals would be cooked and eaten. It was big enough to include a table, chairs and dresser. From this room were stairs leading to the first floor. There was also a door leading down to a cellar. Beyond the room was the back entrance which led out into the back yard which housed a brick-built privy.

When Mary took her first look around upstairs, she was pleasantly surprised. The living area was in need of some tender loving care but would be comfortable for the time being. It was extremely spacious compared with where they had come from and Mary couldn't help feeling their furniture would become lost in this grandiose room. It was bright and airy compared with their last property which could feel quite gloomy even in the summer months. Mary liked the fact there were plenty of windows to this property which would allow light into the room and aid Mary with her needlework. It was a good place to house her trusty old sewing machine.

The front living room area had a small fireplace depicting swags of flowers held by ribbons on the frieze and repeated on the jambs. The hood featured a chalice overflowing with fruit. The fireplace was tiled both sides with a set of green tiles with floral slips. There was a large window to the side which looked down onto Ivy Lane, a small square window above the shop doorway and a large arched feature above the window to the front of the shop. Mary instantly loved the position of the property as it had a beautiful view of the town's parish church opposite. Edwin had made a good decision when he had purchased this property, she thought. There would be many notable buildings in Farnham which would become very familiar to Edwin and his family over the following years, Farnham's Parish Church of St Andrew's probably taking precedence. From his shop, Edwin would soon be able to look out straight across the street into Upper Church Lane, where he would clearly be able to see the church and all that was going on.

St Andrew's dated back to the twelfth century and consisted of a chancel, nave of six bays, aisles, transepts and an embattled western tower with four pinnacles, containing eight bells and a clock with chimes. The church had been restored in 1862, the tower restored in 1865 and great improvements and additions were also made in 1886. A monument to William Cobbet, an MP who had died in 1835, was positioned opposite its north door. The church had several stained-glass windows. Mary had already fallen in love with it from the first minute she had set eyes upon it.

The family would attend their first Sunday service at the church the next weekend and most Sunday services thereafter. Mary looked forward to having any future children christened there and hoped one day she may even witness her children being married in St Andrew's.

It wasn't long before their furniture arrived on the cart and with help from the removal men, Edwin unloaded it and carried it up the stairs or into the kitchen area. The bedrooms were larger than they had been used to which was a good thing as Mary had no idea just how large her family was going to get. Teddy and Mabel were very excitable at bedtime and baby Lionel had taken quite some time to settle. For the time being Lionel was to stay in his crib in his parents' bedroom. That night Mary and Edwin had the best night's sleep they had had in months. They woke the following morning feeling refreshed and ready for whatever life was to present to them.

It didn't take the family long to settle into their new life in Farnham. Edwin and Mary soon realised that the town was as popular with visitors as it was with its townsfolk because of its wealth of history and in particular that surrounding its castle. Teddy of course was really taken with the castle when his father took him to see it and the grounds during their first week there. He enjoyed listening to his father's tales and hearing about the castle's bloody history.

The town itself when Edwin and his family arrived in Farnham had many modern conveniences. It was lighted with gas by a company in Wales, run from premises in East Street, and its water supply came from two reservoirs containing 183,000 gallons. Farnham's council had recently spent over £14,000 on a new and extensive sewage system and Edwin planned to soon have the latest design in flushing toilets installed into the back yard privy.

Edwin's property was situated in a prominent part of this popular historical town, near to the top of Downing Street. Farnham at the time had a wealth of other shops. On Downing

Street alone there were two pubs, the Hop Bag run by Fred Dollery and the Bird in Hand run by Ed Eagleton. Next door to Edwin's shop and moving south along Downing Street there was the Coffee Tavern, a general dealer, upholsterer, dairyman and greengrocers, tailor, tea dealer, shoe maker and a seed man and florist. Walking north back up along the opposite side there was a grocers, plumber and metalworker, draper, sausage-maker, shoemaker, baker and confectioner, umbrella repairer and a hairdresser. It appeared that the needs of the Farnham people were clearly being met, and now there was to be another fishmonger.

As true as his word Edwin's shop opened for business in less than two weeks. He and Mary had worked long and hard to get the premises just as they wanted them. The frontage to the shop was finished also. To the left was the entrance into the shop and on the right an open window onto the street displayed many varieties of fresh fish which sat upon a huge marble slab. The open display window allowed Edwin's customers to view his selection of fresh fish before they bought. The slab of marble gently sloped upwards into the shop from the street and onto it Edwin poured buckets of ice to help preserve his fresh fish for longer. He had arranged the display with great care to attract the eyes of the passing public. Above this opening was a roller shutter which he was able to pull down at the end of the day, after he had removed any leftover merchandise and wiped down the marble slab. High above his shop was a sign displaying his name and his trade.

To enter the shop, customers could use the door to the left. Once inside a purchase could be made at a cashier's desk positioned towards the back of the shop. Directly opposite the shop's entrance was another door which led down into a cellar where Edwin kept his supply of ice in a refrigerated area. In a separate storage area on the ground floor he used a copper vat for boiling crabs, lobsters and shrimps. The vat was heated by burning wood and coal below it. The children always knew when their father was boiling lobsters as they could hear them screaming. Edwin explained to his children that this was simply the air coming out of their shells as they were being cooked. It was a sound that none of them, including Mary, particularly enjoyed listening to.

Edwin now bought his supplies from the market at Billingsgate. It was always an early start for Edwin on the days he went to Billingsgate, arriving by 7am to get the fish back to Farnham in time for his customers. It was essential he was physically fit as there was plenty of bending and lifting when transporting crates and boxes of produce and the work also involved standing for long periods. Working conditions were often cold and very wet. It was a job for a younger man like Edwin, but even he was beginning to feel the strain.

Fishmongers could sell fish whole or as fillets, cutlets or steaks, and might prepare fish to individual requirements by boning, skinning, de-scaling and trimming for their customers. Edwin was skilled in all areas of this trade. His customers often asked him to remove the head, insides and other inedible parts of a fish. He could also prepare shellfish and other seafood, dressing crabs and preparing lobsters, prawns, scallops, oysters, clams and mussels.

Edwin's customers were able to choose a herring by its roe or ask to have a sole filleted on the spot. His work involved a significant amount of skill and practice as well as a genuine passion for all types of fish. Edwin was good with his hands and able to work confidently and quickly with food. He had recently made a decision to expand his trade within Farnham and decided to sell poultry in his shop as well as fish. Edwin had his poultry hung up outside above the window for all his customers to inspect. He often gave advice on how best to cook the fish and poultry he sold and picked up many handy tips from customers and fishmongers alike whom Edwin had became acquainted with over the years. Most evenings it was 9pm before he had finished cleaning up in his shop. Edwin worked hard, long hours for himself and his family to ensure they all received a decent quality of life.

*

The family had been in residence in Farnham for a couple of months when Jubilee Day celebrations were held on 22 June to commemorate Queen Victoria's sixty years on the throne. The local council had met back in March to discuss their plans, around the same time the family had moved into the town. They had voted upon a sum not exceeding £50 which could be spent upon the celebrations. All the businesses and houses on Downing Street and other main roads in the town had been instructed to decorate the front of their properties appropriately, so red, white and blue Union Jack banners were draped from the buildings along both sides of the street and across the road. Larger flags attached to poles were secured through upstairs windows. Edwin set about this chore the day before the celebrations and the rest of the family came out to watch him perform the task.

"Can I hold the ladder for you?" shouted an excited Teddy who had just arrived home from elementary school. His mother had been greatly relieved that Teddy had settled in so quickly at school. She had wondered if he might have been difficult with this new situation.

"Thank you lad, but give your mother your school bag first, so as you have both hands free to catch me when I fall."

"Don't tease the poor boy," interjected Mary. Teddy didn't comprehend his father's humour and handed his bag quickly to his mother.

Edwin expertly climbed the ladder which he had borrowed from a neighbour. Unlike the other properties, his had only one opening window upstairs facing onto the street and it was too small to secure a flag pole. So Edwin attached a wooden plinth to run across the top of his property before he could attach some bunting. He had made his way up the ladder for the fourth time, about to hammer in another nail when a gust of wind blew the flags right out of his hand and the end of the bunting was left flapping furiously in the wind. In his haste to grab the bunting he almost lost his balance and toppled off the ladder. As he stood there at the top of the ladder, pale faced and open mouthed his family below burst into fits of laughter. Even eleven-month-old baby Lionel nestled in his mother's arms found it funny. Her baby's reaction made Mary laugh even more. Just at that moment another gust of wind blew down the rest of the bunting which Edwin had spent the last ten minutes struggling to attach. As it blew away down the street Teddy followed in quick pursuit.

"Mind out for the carts Teddy!" his mother shouted after him.

"Well, that was a complete and utter waste of time," moaned Edwin as he reached the bottom of the ladder.

"Never mind dear, if at first you don't succeed . . ." smiled Mary. "I'm sure you'll have it under control in a moment." Teddy returned with a bundle of tangled flags and handed them to his father.

"Thank you, Teddy," said Edwin, trying to keep his composure. He knew the boy was only trying to help but it took Edwin a further ten minutes to untangle them again. When he had finished Edwin held tight to the end of the flags as he repositioned the ladder and climbed back up. He attempted the task a second time. This time he used more nails and made sure that they were hammered deeper into the wooden plinth. Mary watched from the street below as her determined husband wrestled again with the bunting.

Suddenly a voice from behind Mary startled her and she spun round to see who was there. "Good morning Mary."

"Oh, good morning Mr Mason. How are you today?"

"I'm very well, thank you. I'd like to make a purchase if your husband can spare a moment."

"Edwin! You have a customer," called Mary.

Edwin didn't often swear but today he did, under his breath of course.

"Can't the bloody man see I'm busy," he muttered to himself. Edwin descended the ladder leaving half of the material flapping in the breeze and politely greeted the council clerk, Mr Mason.

"After you, sir," Edwin said, directing him into the shop. Edwin grumbled quietly to Mary as he passed her on the way into the shop. "Can't he see I'm doing this for his silly council?" Mary sniggered at her husband's sarcasm. "Right Mr Mason, what can I get for you?"

"I'd like your biggest piece of skate please and a couple of chickens."

"Certainly, sir."

"We have some members of the council coming round for dinner this evening and the wife wants to make a good impression." Edwin acknowledged the man's statement but didn't reply. He set about his task, wrapped the goods in paper and took the man's money.

Mr Mason thanked Edwin and turned to leave. As he got to the doorway where the flags were merrily flapping about above his head he turned back to Edwin and said, "You'd better make sure you secure those flags properly. We don't want an accident on Jubilee Day, do we?" Edwin really had to bite his tongue. He smiled and nodded politely at the man thinking to himself, well if you hadn't interrupted me they would be secure by now you silly old fool.

Mr Mason stepped out of the doorway and as he did so the bunting broke free once more and landed straight on top of Mr Mason's head, wrapping itself around his head and blocking his view. He stumbled, his fish and poultry flying in opposite directions. Inside the shop Edwin couldn't contain his delight and had to quickly go into the storeroom out the back where it was his turn to burst into hysterics. It was poor Mary who came to Mr Mason's rescue, removing the flags from around his head while Teddy picked up his purchases. A very red-faced council clerk thanked them both and quickly left.

It took Edwin and Mary another five minutes to compose themselves before Edwin was able to safely ascend the ladder again and complete the job. By the end of the day Downing Street was looking especially festive and the whole town was looking forward to its Jubilee celebrations planned for the next day.

There was plenty for the townsfolk to do the following day. At 1pm a dinner had been arranged for the elderly of Farnham. Mary had popped out on an errand with the children at the time and told Edwin she had seen the old folks flocking to the Corn Exchange in their droves. There was a special tea at 3pm for all the children who attended elementary school in Farnham. It was held at their respective schools and Teddy thoroughly enjoyed his. He had only attended the school for the past two months but thought this was great fun. Everyone was dressed in their Sunday best and Teddy had never seen so much food. He ate so much he was nearly sick but it was so delicious he couldn't stop himself. The meats, pies, sausages and cakes were irresistible to Teddy. He thought he had died and gone to heaven.

At 4.30pm Mary took the children to watch three trees being planted in Castle Street where they joined in with the national anthem and enjoyed listening to the military band. Previously supplied by the council, a number of Jubilee Day wooden benches had been placed along Castle Street and at various points around the town and at 5pm there were sports for the children and the old people in the park. The military band also played there to a large and excited crowd.

Edwin closed his shop early that day and joined his family in the park. When the sports activities and races were over, Mary and Edwin took the children to the Corn Exchange for something to eat and drink. It was an extra treat which the whole family enjoyed. Finally that night the town enjoyed fireworks and a bonfire and rounded it all off with the military band to close the proceedings. Edwin and his family retired to bed that evening satisfied and content that they had thoroughly enjoyed their day. Jubilee Day had given pleasure to many of the townsfolk and would stay in Edwin's and Mary's thoughts for many years to come as a principal celebration in their new home town.

*

Although life was hard work for Edwin and Mary, it was relatively good to them and on 26 July the following year things got even better when their fourth daughter was born. She was their first child to be born in Farnham and there was a big celebration for the new baby a couple of weeks later. A christening service was held for the child in St Andrew's where she was named Doris Mary. Then afterwards, back at the house a small party for family and friends was given. Mary had prepared a delicious spread which included home-cured hams, prime pickled pork, the best sausages and home-made bread and pickles. There was also salmon and crabmeat which Edwin had cooked and prepared and a small Christening cake which Mary had lovingly made and decorated. The family were now very settled and their business prospering. They wanted to share their good fortune and happiness with their closest friends and family.

Mary and Edwin were both thrilled to have Emily and Arthur attend. Emily had only recently added to her family and given Arthur his first son and the couple couldn't wait to show off their new addition. Baby Jack and baby Doris were placed side by side in Doris's brand new crib. Ever since the death of little Lillian Mary had wanted to replace the cradle but lack of funds at the time had prevented this and she had been forced to use it for Lionel. Mary was telling Emily how she had managed to find the beautiful second-hand, oak crib with rocking feet when Edwin overheard and couldn't resist teasing her, saying it had cost him a small fortune. "You tight, sod" Mary joked. "It's an investment for the future." Edwin just raised his eyebrows, shook his head and smiled.

Mary and Emily rocked their babies off to sleep and Doris and Jack slept peacefully together throughout most of the celebrations. This was possibly due to the fact that both had bawled almost continuously throughout the baptism service earlier. The celebrations lasted for most of the day with a steady flow of delicious food, drink and relaxing conversation.

Dorothy, nearly four years old, and her sister Margaret and cousin Lionel, both two years old, were enjoying themselves immensely under the buffet table, all hidden or so they thought, from their parents. Teddy, who was now six, after having polished off as much food as he could without his parents' knowledge had now become very bored. He asked his father if he and Mabel could go and play outside. "Yes, all right, but mind you don't get dirty," their father shouted after them. "You've both got your Sunday best on." The pair ran off without a care in the world and were soon into mischief. Teddy had recently become quite wilful. Many times of late Mary had been forced to threaten Teddy with his father. It had worked on most occasions. On one occasion Edwin had overheard Teddy giving his mother cheek and intervened, punishing him by making him stand in the corner of the room facing the wall for ten minutes. Teddy had later been forced to apologise to his mother but felt very humiliated. Now he was about to disobey his parents again and was encouraging his sister to misbehave also.

The pair returned to the house later that afternoon covered from head to toe in soot, rejoining the family celebrations looking like a couple of street urchins. Mabel who had taken her favourite doll with her was looking very sad and dejected as she carried the filthy thing under her arm. Edwin didn't ask his children where they had been or what they had been doing to get so filthy. Setting his eyes upon them he was so humiliated in front of his guests that he immediately frogmarched the pair down to the cellar where he told them they were to stay until everyone had gone home. When Mary realised what Edwin had done she thought the punishment too harsh but recognised it was her place to support her husband's decision. It was difficult for her as she believed his decision had been made in haste.

Edwin had known Teddy could be disobedient and felt things had been gradually getting worse. How dare he, thought Edwin. Today of all days he blatantly disobeys me in front of all our guests. He had felt embarrassed and this was why he acted hastily and with so little thought. Edwin blamed his son's recent behaviour on his schooling. When Teddy had first started school his behaviour had been good. After six months his parents had seen a distinct change in Teddy's behaviour which was not for the better. He always seemed to be getting into scrapes, fighting with the other boys or answering his teacher back. On numerous occasions he had been made to stand in the corner of the classroom with his hands upon his head and on a couple of occasions he had been smacked with a cane for being impertinent to his teacher. Teddy hated the restrictions that school placed upon him and detested subjects like reading, writing, poetry and sculpture, which he had to endure every morning. His favourite subject was arithmetic which he excelled in.

By the time Edwin and Mary's guests had left, Teddy and Mabel had been in the cellar for almost two hours. Mary had found herself willing her guests to leave so that Edwin would let the pair out. When they were finally released it was clear both had been crying. They had clean streaks down their checks where tears had fallen and upon seeing them emerge from the cellar Edwin couldn't help feeling a pang of guilt. He spoke to them with authority saying, "I shall say no more than this. I hope you both have learnt from this escapade and will think twice about what I ask you to do next time." Edwin could see the pair were clearly upset and regretted their adventure but couldn't help pushing his point. "If either of you try anything like this again I will not hesitate to put you back into the cellar as punishment. Do you understand?" Teddy and Mabel both nodded silently.

Mary was just as cross with them as Edwin when she was able at last to inspect the state of their clothes. Apart from being covered in soot, Mabel had managed to tear a hole in her underskirt and Teddy's trousers were torn on both knees. Mabel's doll was unrecognisable and Mary almost threw it away but later reconsidered. She eventually managed to clean it up although it was never quite the same again. Mary helped to clean the pair up and got them ready for bed. Bath night had been the night before in preparation for the christening. Now she would have to warm the water to fill the tin bath for a second night running. When the bath water was finally ready Mary undressed her children saying, "You both look as though you've been crawling up a chimney or at least amongst the coal heap."

"We have," jumped in Mabel without thinking.

"Shh," insisted Teddy.

"Teddy!" scolded Mary. "Where have you been?"

Teddy knew at this point it was no use lying to his mother. It would only get him in deeper trouble. "Down in Middle Church Lane at Mr Drover's smithy," he finally admitted as his mother scrubbed him rather vigorously. The children could tell their mother was terribly disappointed in their behaviour. "We're sorry Mum," they sang together. "We won't do it again," said Teddy. "We promise," said Mabel.

After their bath Mary used the same water to wash their soot-stained clothes and Mabel's doll. Then she tucked them up into their beds and said goodnight. In a couple of days the incident had been forgotten, at least by Edwin and Mary. Teddy on the other hand was not going to find his father's punishment as easy to forget. He had gained a fear of going anywhere near the cellar and this fear would remain with him until he was an adult.

Although life for the children was strict and their father was an authoritarian, they did enjoy a somewhat privileged upbringing. There occasionally was spare money for luxuries like toys, especially around their birthdays. Mabel had been the proud owner of a beautiful doll until the day she had become covered in soot. The doll had been given to Mabel complete with clothes her mother had hand sewn. She had named the doll Margaret and taken her everywhere she went. Teddy adored the clockwork train he had been given by his father. He also enjoyed playing with his glass marbles. Using a string circle, he and his friends would play for hours, trying to hit as many marbles inside the circle as possible. It was usually Teddy who ended up winning his opponent's collection.

Edwin would occasionally find time to assist in his children's play by threading conkers on a string or joining in with hide and seek. Often the children would raid his shop for a piece of chalk for their hopscotch game or a piece of string to make a cat's cradle. They were much loved and well cared for. Their mother always cooked them delicious, filling meals, kept them clean and taught them right from wrong with the help of regular church services and often read them passages from her Bible. Hoping to improve her ability as a mother and housewife, Mary regularly read articles in Edwin's paper about the home. She would search avidly every day for her favourite section of the paper *"Hints for the Home"*. Here it might inform her for example, on how best to care for her baby.*"Don't send baby out for his morning walk in a thick fog if the air is very damp, or the wind extremely cold. But on the other hand do not fall into the error of coddling a child too much. Frosty air is not harmful if the baby is well wrapped up."*

Mary took this advice seriously, often sharing it with Edwin. Another article she read was on how best to bring up her children. It read, *"It is not a wise thing for a mother to relate to friends or relatives in a child's hearing its little sayings and doings. The child will at once imagine it is an object for admiration and may become spoilt and forward. The prettiest ways and tricks are completely spoilt when self-conscious-ness is apparent."*

Edwin and Mary always put their family first, often going without themselves so that their children didn't have to. Their daily lives focused upon how best to benefit their children.

Chapter 5

1899

The summer of 1899 was warm and dry, not the type of weather one wishes to cook in for any length of time. Edwin had for some weeks been frying fish in the back room of his shop premises on Downing Street. He'd heard of other fishmongers trying out this new service which had proved successful in drumming up more trade, so Edwin had decided to try it himself. He had purchased a large cauldron in which to fry the fish. He filled the cauldron with cooking fat, heating it from underneath by burning coal, and coated his fish in a home-made batter before deep frying it in the oil. He had received interest in this dish locally and sales were increasing quickly, much to Edwin's delight. The process however, had caused his premises to emit a strong frying smell and smoke to accompany the odour. Unfortunately, in doing this Edwin had managed to upset a great many of his fellow townsfolk with his antics. One complaint had come from his adjoining neighbour in the coffee house. He had entered Edwin's shop one day to complain in person. He claimed that his customers were getting up and leaving his shop because of the horrendous smell drifting in from Edwin's premises, and threatened to take the matter to the council if Edwin didn't stop.

When Edwin discovered that some of his fellow shopkeepers and neighbours had objected to his new business, it came as no surprise. A petition had begun to circulate around the town against his offensive trade. The petition was signed by twenty-six residents and ratepayers and presented to the council. Edwin was reluctantly forced to attend a meeting shortly after to answer the claims made against him. He strongly protested his innocence.

During the council's proceedings Edwin expressed his willingness to do all in his power to stop the nuisance. He offered to only fry his fish between certain agreed hours but his offer fell upon deaf ears and he was fined ten shillings. Reluctantly Edwin paid the fine and put his fish frying on hold for a while until the fuss died down.

Edwin had by now cut all ties with Billingsgate and was doing business in Grimsby. The Great Central Railway had opened for passengers to travel to Grimsby in the March of 1899 and for goods to be transported from Grimsby a month later. Edwin had transferred his business there in the April of this year as it had made good business sense. He had managed to save enough money to acquire premises at the fish dock in Grimsby where he could buy, store and sell his fish and had also begun to sell wholesale as well as retail. These premises allowed him to run his business with professionalism and gave him more scope and control. This was what most fishmongers, who could afford it, were doing and Edwin knew he needed to follow suit if he stood a chance in competing for business.

He used the dock's premises for storage before he sold stock on or transported his merchandise. His stock was purchased on a daily basis at dockside auctions. Once caught and paid for Edwin had the fish packed in ice and displayed for wholesale. He also bought from other wholesalers at the dock. Good communication skills were important when dealing with people and bartering, as was the ability to handle cash and keep accounts. Edwin could boast all of these attributes. He was also supplying two other shops in Farnham with fish, as well as his own. Mary was impressed with her husband's business acumen. Edwin was always thinking up ways of how to improve his business and making useful contacts.

Grimsby was a seaport on the Humber Estuary in Lincolnshire. Its development as a fishing port was breathtaking. From the 1850s until 1891 its fleet had expanded from just one, to eight hundred vessels. Grimsby had a huge fleet of sailing trawlers and even a few steam vessels. Now that the railway had been built Edwin was able to make his long journey to Grimsby using this new line. This was also the mode of transport he used to transport his fish back to Farnham where it would be sold. The building of the railways had made it easier for people like Edwin to transport goods to and from the port.

Edwin could recognise when he was getting close to arriving in Grimsby as the amazing Grimsby Dock Tower would come into view. It was the focal point of the docks. Wherever you were or wherever you went around Grimsby you could see it from miles away. Grimsby Dock Tower had dominated the town's skyline since it was built and stood over three hundred feet in height. Edwin had been amazed to learn that it had taken around one million bricks to build it. As his train journey came to an end he smiled to himself as he thought about the bricklayers on that job. He found himself reminiscing about the time he had met Mary and all the things that had happened to them since. It had been ten years but it had gone by in a flash. It had taken him all this time to get to where he was today and to achieve his ultimate goal, to own his very own successful business.

Travelling to Grimsby earlier that year to set everything up had taken its toll on Edwin and he had begun to look quite tired. Mary couldn't help feeling he may have taken on too much. So by the summer of 1899 the couple had decided that Edwin needed help with his business in Grimsby. Edwin made the decision to visit Grimsby Docks main office to enquire about organising and employing a full time wholesaler to work for him. He and Mary had concluded that Edwin needed and wanted to spend more time in his shop because it was that side of things which he truly loved. They decided to invest some of their money in employing someone else to handle the orders in Grimsby. That way, Edwin would only have to visit Grimsby if and when he wanted to.

As Edwin waited to speak with the manager about his request

he started to read a notice which was inside a frame fixed to the dock's office wall. The notice told of the day, when on 18 April 1849 Prince Albert came to lay the foundation stone of the new dock walls. The story read that the Prince Consort arrived onto the dockside in a railway carriage pulled by teams of navvies employed in the docks construction. It went on to say that a public park, Prince Albert Gardens, was built at the docks entrance and was overlooked by a statue of the Prince himself. Then later, with the formalities dispensed with, construction of the central pier on which the Dock Tower stands, was begun.

He read on, how after two years of operation the docks and the tower were officially opened in the October of 1854 by Queen Victoria. The Queen was accompanied by Prince Albert and the Princess Royal who rode to the top of the tower on the wooden lift inside. Following The Queen's visit the tower became something of a tourist attraction and visitors could take the 225ft lift ride for 6d.

Edwin recalled the day that he had done just that. He had admired the building each time he had visited and promised himself he would one day climb up to catch the view. Edwin had endured the gruelling climb up the cast-iron spiral staircase where at the top of its main tower the building had flared out into a beautiful balcony. It was this which Edwin believed gave the building much of its character. Above this was the ornamental second tower and Lantern House which gave the building its architectural grace and symmetry. Edwin experienced excellent views from the top that day, with Grimsby town spread out beneath and the Lincolnshire Wolds to the south, and Spurn Point and the North Sea off to the North East. The Dock Tower was a landmark that was visible from as far away as twenty miles. It was also one of the first sights that fishermen saw returning to the Humber and Edwin was able to spot many little boats out at sea in the distance. Glancing to the ground below him he could see the four docks. There were the two fish docks, and the Royal Dock and

Alexandra Dock were used for transporting and storing coal and timber. Edwin held premises on fish dock number one.

Edwin came away from his meeting feeling both happy and relieved. It had gone well and he had managed to strike a good deal. He would now only have to telephone his orders through and his man on site would bid for the fish on his behalf. Edwin felt as though a great weight had been lifted from his shoulders. It had been well worth the trip he thought to himself and he knew Mary would be delighted. However, it was difficult not to feel a little sad. He would miss the chaos of the place.

On every occasion Edwin had cause to visit the docks, the first thing he would notice was the noise. It was the hustle and bustle of the men going about their work. Around the docks there was always a lot of shouting. It might be the auctioneer or someone shouting instructions. The docks were always a busy place. It was a thriving community and always packed with fish sellers on a market day. It was also a very smelly place but only to the unaccustomed nose. The men from the boats and those who worked on the docks dealing regularly with the fish rarely noticed the stench that was all around them.

Some of the fishing boats were fairly small; the larger boats tended to be trawling vessels. The owners of these vessels were usually skipper of their own boat. Edwin would enjoy watching the boats arrive. They lined up along the dockside, gently bobbing up and down on the water. The men quickly unloaded their catch by lowering a large basket held by a rope down through a central hatch and into the hold of the vessel. Down below there were a couple more men to scoop the fish up into the baskets. All of the fishermen were dressed in overalls with their trousers tucked into their boots. The baskets were hoisted back up to the surface where the contents were tipped into crates and this process continued until the hold was empty.

The fish were laid out in boxes, trays and tea chests along the dockside. Their lifeless bodies trailed over the edges of the crates which were haphazardly scattered across the floor of the dock. There was hardly space to walk between them. An auctioneer would move along the dockside stepping onto an upturned box and start the bidding for the crates of fish positioned around him. This could either prove successful for Edwin, if the price was right, or terribly frustrating if he was outbid for the produce he wanted. Once sold, a label would be stuck onto the box of produce displaying its new owner's name. The auctioneer would then move on to his next lot of fish.

There were very few members of the general public present at the docks. This was of course unless dealers had brought along friends or family members for the experience. There were usually only the fishermen, dock workers, fish merchants and other dealers. All the fish were sold in large quantities and then in turn sold on to the shops. Occasionally Edwin saw crew members carrying a fish supper home wrapped in a newspaper bundle and if you knew a dealer well you might get this special treatment. When the crates had been cleared away the area was hosed down, ready for a new day. The fish had to be sold on straightaway as it wouldn't keep. Dealers couldn't sell it if it wasn't fresh. The fish from the deep sea catch would be packed in ice to keep it fresh for as long as possible. Those boats might have been out at sea all week and brought fish to Grimsby from as far away as Iceland. They could bring back hundreds of tons of fish.

Edwin had listened to various tales on the docks related by the fishermen. Plenty of these tales involved the Dock tower, with some local fishermen believing the tower was "built on cotton wool" or that exactly one million bricks had gone into its construction or that the staircase within had a step for every day of the year. Edwin had heard about the local legend which suggested that the Dock Tower had been built on cotton wool a few times during his trips to Grimsby. The story went that when the foundations were laid there were problems when the excavations kept filling with water. Apparently no amount of bailing seemed to help and this was when someone suggested soaking the water up using bales of sheep's wool that were being kept in a dockside warehouse. The bales were positioned and found successful and some say the bales are supposedly there to this day beneath the hardcore footings. Edwin had heard other tales that had been handed down through generations of fisherman, about bricklayers who it was claimed had actually dived from the tower into the dock for no better reason other than for public spectacle.

During one visit to Grimsby Edwin was able to witness for himself an incident which occurred on the Dock Tower. A Manchester steeplejack collapsed on the scaffold during an inspection of work and subsequently died. The dock workers were used to dealing with accidents on boats, in the graving docks and in the filleting sheds and took this incident in their stride. Getting him in off the scaffold and down the tower seemed to take no time at all. There was a bit of shouting but within half an hour you would never have known anything had happened and so Edwin did as all the other merchants that day and continued with his work.

During his train journey home Edwin found himself thinking about his family back in Sutton and in particular his mother and father. It had been some years since he'd had contact with any of them and he wondered how his parents were and if they were both in good health. I really should write to them, he thought, and let them know about the business and my ever increasing family. It had been over a year since he had written to his mother and now on his journey home, when he was able to relax and allow his mind to wander, he had found himself speculating about them. He pulled from his pocket a spare piece of paper and pencil and began to put his few thoughts on paper. His letter was fairly brief and to the point. He asked after them both and his brothers and sisters and said he and Mary were well. He told them all about his family and his shop in Farnham. However, he neglected to mention what he had been doing in Grimsby that day, as he suspected his father would think he was getting ideas above his station.

*

When he arrived home much later that day, Mary had already gone to bed. She had recently discovered she was expecting another baby and she was exhausted after juggling the shop and the children. It was the following morning before Edwin was able to ask Mary for her approval of the content of his letter. "It's a bit brief, dear," she commented.

"Maybe, but it's to the point don't you think?" Edwin replied in his authoritarian manner. "Yes I'll give you that," responded Mary, giving up as she suspected he would send it anyway.

It didn't take long for Edwin's mother to reply. She talked about all the family in her letter including his father and it seemed to Edwin as though time back at home had stood still all these years. There was no news really. Everything was the same as it had been before. His brothers were all doing the same jobs, some may have had another child but having another mouth to feed was hardly news to Edwin. Towards the end of her letter his mother briefly mentioned that she had recently felt unwell. She hadn't gone into much detail but had assured him that she was feeling much better now and that he was not to worry. Of course, being a man he thought no more of it but when he showed the letter to Mary she couldn't help wondering if there may be more to worry about than Harriet was letting on. When Mary shared her feelings on the matter with Edwin he responded with, "Well what do you want me to do? It's not as if they live just across the street. Didn't she say there was nothing to worry about?" Mary thought her husband could be so supercilious at times.

Edwin and Mary now had five children and another baby's birth was imminent. Their youngest child was one year old. Evelyn had been born in the January of last year. It had been a very long and difficult labour for Mary. Edwin had been sent to fetch Dr Charles Tanner from down the bottom of Downing Street and the doctor had stayed with Mary until she had finally given birth. The doctor had later told Edwin that it was one of the most difficult births he had attended in a long while but Mary had been marvellous and he was satisfied that the baby was healthy. With plenty of rest Mary had made a full recovery. However, Mary was now seriously beginning to feel the strain and restraints that motherhood brings. She desperately needed some extra help. She was always tired. There never seemed to be enough hours in the day to do all the jobs she needed to do and things just seemed to get on top of her all the time. Mary thought Edwin had started to distance himself from her more and more and Edwin felt as though every time he went near his wife she would snipe at him about something. He thought it best to stay clear, get on with his job and let her get on with hers.

As she had reached the end of her tether, Mary fondly remembered the time when her niece, Alice had come to stay. It was now eight years ago, shortly after she had given birth to Mabel. What a delight the child had been and an enormous help to Mary. She recalled these memories and thought how nice it would be to see the child again. It had been over a year ago during a family gathering that they had last met. Mary knew Alice was still living at home because she was often mentioned in the letters she received from Emily. She must be sixteen by now, thought Mary, almost a woman herself.

Mary did not delay and put pen to paper and wrote a begging letter to her brother James, almost pleading for his help. She asked if she could have Alice to help as soon as possible and for her to stay until after her baby was born. She hoped her niece would accept her invitation, as she had the first time, but couldn't help worry that she would not want to visit now as she was older. Mary need not have worried. Alice jumped at the chance to visit and stay with her aunt again and arrived in Farnham a week later at the end of February. She was an instant help to Mary, immediately lightening the load and bringing a ray of happiness to the place. It was as though a large grey cloud had been lifted from over the house. Even Edwin felt relieved and things seemed to get back to normal pretty quickly. Mary couldn't get over how much Alice had grown and kept telling her so which just embarrassed her poor niece. After all these years Alice had retained the cheery and positive persona she had always had as a child and was still able to find the positive side to a difficult situation. Order and routine were restored to the house once more.

It was during the month of May when Mary received a letter from her sister Emily. The letter contained some distressing news about their father. It read,

My dearest sister, Mary,

It is with great sadness that I am compelled to write you this letter. There is no easy way to inform you about our poor, unfortunate father who has recently been taken ill. We are all greatly concerned for him. Father's health has quickly declined and he has been suffering with severe abdominal pains for some weeks now. They have recently become so bad that he was forced to see the doctor. You know Father, Mary, he is a very proud man and must have been despairing and in great agony to resort to such measures. Mother said later how he had been so terribly embarrassed by this affliction that he wasn't even able to describe to her what was wrong with him.

After some insistence from mother, all Father would say was that there was very little the doctor could do for him. I am afraid things are very bleak here. I heard Father and Mother crying together after the doctor's visit.

Father's health is deteriorating quickly but although he has asked me to write and tell you this news, he wishes you not to travel to visit him. He says he doesn't want you travelling in your condition, knowing you are due to give birth at any time. I suspect the truth of the matter is that he is excruciatingly embarrassed about his ailment and doesn't want either of us to see him like this. He has insisted I remain downstairs during my visits home and I am respecting his wishes. Oh Mary, dear Mary, what are we to do?

Your mournful sister,
Emily.

Mary was devastated both about her father's illness and that she was unable to travel. She wrote back to her father immediately but found the letter almost impossible to write. How do you write to your dying father and say all the things you want to say? Poor Mary didn't know where to start. "Just try to keep it short and simple darling," Edwin advised. And so she did.

My dearest, dearest Father,

The only reason I am not with you right now is because it is you that wishes it this way. You know that I have always only ever tried to do things which would please you.

No words can express the love and admiration I have for you. I cannot begin to contemplate my life knowing you will no longer be near. You have always been there for me, reassuring, encouraging and supporting me.

I will miss you so very much, Father, more than any words can describe.

I wish that the journey you now take is a painless one and that when you reach your destination you will feel peace and be at one with our Lord.

Your sorrowing daughter,
Mary.

Mary's mother appeared a tower of strength for her husband over the next six weeks. Inside she was trying to hold it together but slowly crumbling. For Jane, exposed to her husband's ordeal first hand, it seemed a particularly cruel way to end such a good man's life. Thomas's only crime was that he was hardworking, loving and generous. He was a kind, gentle man. He had only good things to say about others and would never have done anything bad to anyone. Jane nursed her husband as best she could although it broke her heart to see him in such agony. She was constantly washing soiled bed sheets and bathing her husband as one of Thomas's symptoms was terrible diarrhoea. His stools often contained blood and his stomach was badly bloated. Thomas didn't have to tell his wife he was in pain; she could see and hear this for herself. Thomas often cried out in agony and Jane could only stand by, looking on helplessly. The doctor had prescribed a drug to help with the pain but it seemed to be having little positive effect.

Thomas lost weight quickly and eventually became jaundiced. He had looked at death's door for some time and Jane prayed it would not take much longer before her darling husband would be allowed to die. She prayed daily that his end would come soon so that he could be released from the terrible pain and at last find some peace. As Thomas had requested, Jane kept her children from seeing their father during his last month. Although Emily visited the house daily she was never allowed upstairs. Jane was determined to protect her children from witnessing the hell and agony which their father was going through.

On 15 June Thomas passed away at his home in Edgell Road, Staines. At his side was his wife, Jane. His daughter Emily had been downstairs cleaning the fire grate when her father's end had come. It had upset the family enormously to know of Thomas's agony, but his death was a blessing when it had finally happened. Jane had been surprised at how quiet Thomas had been at the end. She had wondered if his last breath would come with a cry of pain but there was nothing. Later that day Emily sent a telegram to Mary and Edwin informing them of Thomas's death.

The funeral was to be in a few days' time but Mary knew she would be unable to travel with the arrival of her latest baby being so imminent so they decided Edwin would go alone, by train, and return the same day.

It had been an early start and Edwin had returned home later than he'd expected due to the train being delayed when a cow had escaped from its field and decided to take a walk along the railway track. Mary had tried to stay awake, waiting for her husband's return. Sitting in the armchair, her belly bulging out in front of her, Mary drifted in and out of sleep a number of times. She was suddenly jolted awake as she heard Edwin arrive home. How she wished she could have gone, but Edwin had attended on her behalf and done his duty by Thomas. Mary was sure this would have pleased her father.

On his return, Edwin filled Mary in on the day's events. He explained how well Mary's mother and sister had coped. They had both appeared strong during the burial and later put on a huge spread back at the house. Mary had sent gifts with Edwin for Emily's children. Her nieces Dorothy and Margaret were now aged six and five and her nephew Jack was three. Edwin described to Mary the scene back at the house after the funeral where Emily had depicted her girls as 'little women' and they had displayed extremely mature behaviour. Jack on the other hand illustrated he was an extremely lively lad and unable to be still for a minute. Mary managed a smile as she listened to her husband's account of the day. "It seemed more of a party than a funeral," said Edwin.

"I'm pleased," replied Mary. "I'm sure father would have wanted it that way."

"I think you're right," replied Edwin. Gently touching Mary's belly Edwin said, "If this one is a boy, how about we call him Thomas after your father?"

"That's a lovely idea," Mary said as tears began to fill her eyes.

Less than a week later, Mary gave birth to their seventh child. Edwin was soon made aware of the baby's arrival as he could hear its cries from downstairs in his shop. The birth had been fairly quick and not too painful for Mary but as the child had entered its new world, it had shrieked at the top of its voice. Down in the shop, one of Edwin's regular customers had commented on the noise. "It sounds as though your new baby has a fine pair of lungs on him."

"It does, doesn't it? But all this noise is putting me off my work. Look, I've gone and given you the wrong order." And as Edwin spoke the crying only became louder.

"What in God's name are they doing to the poor little mite?" Edwin's customer questioned.

"Sounds like they're castrating him," laughed Edwin.

"Another son then, Edwin? It must feel good to have things evened out again?"

"I'd agree with that," smiled Edwin handing his customer his correct order this time.

When Edwin was summoned upstairs a little while later he was surprised to discover he had another daughter. "It's a girl but I'm not sure what we should call her," were the words Mary had greeted him with.

"A girl? Blimey. By the noise it was making I was convinced it was a boy." He picked the baby up from out of Mary's arms to take a better look at her. "She looks more like a boy to me. Are you sure it's a girl?"

"You silly sod, of course I'm sure. I do know the difference. Check for yourself if you don't believe me."

And with that offer, Edwin gave the baby back to Mary and said, "No, no. I'll take your word for it."

Mary laughed, which made the baby start to cry all over again. "This one's going to be hard work I suspect."

"No harder than the others I suspect," smiled Edwin.

"So what are we going to call her?" Mary shouted over the child's screams.

"Something bold as she's not very shy," Edwin shouted back.

"Pardon," shouted Mary even louder.

"I said, something bold, as she's no shrinking Violet."

"I like that!" replied Mary.

"Like what? I haven't suggested anything yet," shouted Edwin.

"Violet," and with that the child stopped crying.

"Oh," said Edwin. "I see."

"What about Violet Louise, giving her my mother's middle name seeing as we can't name her after my father?"

"If that's what you'd like, it's fine by me."

"Violet Louise it is then."

Alice Clara had been a godsend and after baby Violet's birth she had more than proven her worth. Nothing was too much trouble for the girl and she kept Mary's younger children in check until Mary was strong enough to take over and do the job herself. Everyone was sorry to see Alice leave when she finally departed for home, six months after she had arrived.

Violet was four months old when Edwin received some unexpected news. It was a miserable, damp and windy day in November. The shop had seen very few customers that morning and Edwin was putting it down to the abject weather conditions. He had been feeling fairly low even before the telegram had arrived. Edwin could hear that Mary was having a pretty horrendous time upstairs with baby Violet who had been screaming continuously all morning, her cries echoing around the shop and rooms upstairs. Even little Alice whom nothing fazed had snapped at Teddy for teasing Doris, which just recently seemed to have turned into an everyday occurrence. Within the sanctuary of his shop Edwin opened and read the telegram. The boy from the telegraph office had handed it to him and Edwin had neglected to thank or tip the boy. The boy had hung around for a couple of seconds and when he realised he was not going to receive any thanks or coins for his trouble he left the shop disappointed.

The telegram was from his brother, John. It had been some years since Edwin had heard from any of his brothers or seen his mother or father. He was sending news of their mother. Edwin rightly assumed that his father would be too inebriated to send word himself. John explained he had been contacted by a neighbour who said their mother had been taken ill. She had been visited by the doctor and confined to her bed. Her prognosis was not good. She had deteriorated quickly and John was basically telling Edwin that if he wished to see his mother before she died, he should come quickly. Edwin wasted no time in telling Mary and in making the necessary arrangements.

Edwin left for Sutton the following day. His brother John opened the door of their parents' house to Edwin. It had been a long time since the brothers had seen each other. They hardly recognised one another. The two men shook hands very formally and neither of them really knew what to say to the other. Eventually John spoke first. "Father is down at the local ale house." This didn't surprise Edwin in the slightest. "I haven't seen him all week, but I know he's been back some nights, as the house is a complete mess in the morning. The doctor came this morning and is due to call round tomorrow lunchtime." Edwin nodded at his brother. "I have to go back to work now but will call in tomorrow afternoon. Mother is upstairs." He led Edwin upstairs to where their mother lay motionless in her bed. John spoke nervously to his mother. "Edwin's here to see you mother. I have to go to work now, but I'll see you tomorrow," and with that he bent down, kissed his mother's cheek and left the room before she was able to respond.

Edwin pulled a chair up next to his mother's bed, picked up and held on to her icy cold hands. She appeared very weak and in a great deal of discomfort. Edwin puffed up her pillows and tried to make her more comfortable. He talked and talked to his mother for the rest of the day, mainly because he didn't quite know what else to do. He talked about his life in Farnham and his ever-growing family and about Mary. He never asked after his father as he didn't wish to upset his mother. Edwin spoke to his mother with a gentle demeanour about everyday things and could visibly see his mother relax while she listened to him. She managed to smile a couple of times when Edwin told her stories about some of the funny things his children had been getting up to. He recognised when his mother had become tired and stopped talking, staying

...her, holding and gently rubbing her hands as she slept. He spent the rest of the day in her room leaving only for minutes to find a drink or have something to eat, returning to resume his vigil at his mother's bedside.

That night Edwin heard his father arrive home and falling over the furniture downstairs before collapsing into the armchair where Edwin found him the following morning. "Well, look who's decided to pay us a visit," slurred the old man as he set his bloodshot eyes upon Edwin.

"Hello Father. I'm here to see Mother, not to have an argument with you." The old man raised his eyebrows but said no more. He curled back up in the arm chair and closed his eyes again.

Edwin set about making three cups of tea. Leaving one on the table for his father he carried the other two upstairs for him and his mother. She stirred when he entered the room. He helped her to sit up in her bed, supporting her with the pillows. After it had cooled he put the cup of tea to her lips and she drank a little. Harriet seemed a little brighter and managed a few words. "Don't be too hard on your father. He just doesn't know how to cope with the situation. He doesn't like it when I'm not well. He's not a bad man really."

"I know Mum. Don't worry about Father. He can look after himself."

"I don't believe he can," she worried. "Will you look after him when I'm gone, Edwin? I don't think he'll cope too well on his own."

"Of course I will. Don't you worry about Father, Mary and I will see he's looked after." Although Edwin resented his father for his drinking he had meant what he said. He had made this promise to his mother and would stand by it. He would be doing it for her, not his father.

When the doctor arrived at lunchtime he was too late. Harriet had passed away at around ten thirty that morning. Edwin had been at her bedside, holding her hand as she had drifted away. Her body was completely exhausted from its ordeal. Edwin hadn't expected to cry but had been unable to control his emotions. He sat holding his dead mother's hand and the tears emerged as he remembered her unconditional love, which she had given him all of his life. She had died from breast cancer which had taken such a hold over her body that she had given up from sheer exhaustion.

John was inconsolable that afternoon when he arrived to visit his mother. Not being there when his mother had passed away was almost too much for him to bear. Edwin was eventually able to convince him to focus on making arrangements for her funeral. The two brothers did this without any input from their father who was once again too inebriated to be of any help to anyone. He had not reacted in any way to the news of his wife's death. When Edwin had informed him he silently plonked himself back into his chair and fell asleep. Trying to keep his father sober from then until his mother's funeral was near impossible. Edwin thought it was worse than having ten children. His father's tantrums and the arguments they had over the next two days were enough to drive anyone to drink. Edwin had no idea how on earth he was going to keep his promise to his mother and broach the subject of his father coming to live with him in Farnham.

Thankfully the funeral went smoothly and Edwin was pleasantly surprised at how well behaved his father was. He was also overwhelmed by the number of villagers who turned out to say their farewells to his mother. She had been a good friend to many people and all had wished to share their admiration for Harriet. They were keen to express how much his mother would be missed. When all the formalities were over and there were just a few members of the immediate family left clearing up inside the house, Edwin glanced out of the kitchen window and noticed his father alone in the back yard. No time like the present, he thought.

Edwin's father had always been the indisputable head of his working class household. He had always been the breadwinner, engaging in hard physical labour as a bricklayer and working in all weathers. He had done this job for over forty years and when times were more prosperous he had employed men to work for him. He automatically assumed the role of controller of the family's finances and decided when and how his wages should be spent.

Edwin remembered his childhood and how his father could be a bit of a handful, enjoying a drink after a hard day's work. His mother had taken responsibility for the purchasing of food for the family and the running of the house and it was not uncommon for her to go and meet her husband from work to relieve him of enough of his wages for her to feed her family before he spent it all down the pub. This happened fairly regularly in fact and on occasions it had been Edwin's job to meet his father after work. On more than one occasion he'd frequented his local ale house, walked home rather inebriated and given what he had left of his wages to the poor kids playing in the street. Harriet had been furious when she had found out and Edwin could remember vividly the arguments and shouting that seemed to continue for days afterwards.

It was also assumed without doubt that Edwin's father was the dispenser of any rewards and punishments. Edwin could remember receiving his father's belt on many occasions when he was growing up. Along with his brothers, William and John, he gained a form of terrified respect for his father. Understandably when his father returned home from the pub in the middle of the night and ordered all the children out of bed, lined them up on the stairs and demanded a "jolly old sing song" that was exactly what they did. None of them dare to disobey his wishes, however unreasonable. Members of the family did not challenge his authority, with the exception of Harriet on some rare occasions.

Edwin decided now was as good a time as any to approach his father for a chat. As he made his way outside he noticed his father take a swig of drink from a flask he had hidden inside his breast pocket. Edwin had considered many ways, over the last couple of days, to broach this subject with his father. But now that the time had arrived the words tumbled from his mouth in no particular order. "I'm going home tomorrow Dad. Are you coming with me?"

"Why would I want to do that, son?"

"I just thought you wouldn't want to be on your own in the house now that Mother is no longer around. Mary and I would be very happy for you to come and live with us."

"This is my home, son. I'm not going anywhere. Everything I need is right here."

"But how will you look after yourself?" Edwin could see in his father's eyes that he was becoming more and more agitated by his son's persistence. "I can manage well enough thank you. I don't need you interfering. I've managed for the last sixty-seven years, haven't I?"

"But you had Mother then," insisted Edwin but as he did he wished he hadn't. A change came about his father's face. He looked Edwin straight in the eye and said firmly, "I'm staying here and no more will be said about it," and no more was. Edwin had tried his best for the sake of his mother but left Sutton for Farnham the next day without his father.

With the arrival of another daughter and the deaths of both Mary's father and Edwin's mother in quick succession, it was hardly surprising that Edwin found himself comparing his own parentage with that of his children. Edwin's father had dictated his children's education, the family routines, their social relationships and how the family behaved outside the home. But it wasn't until Edwin's father came to live with his family in Farnham that Edwin realised just how alike he and his father truly were and that history really can repeat itself.

Since the death of his wife more than a year ago, Edwin's father's health had declined. Although he appeared a tyrant, his father had loved his mother and it had been a wrench to have lost her. She had been the only person who had ever stood up to him and he had respected her for that. Typically, with no thought than for himeself, he simply turned up on his son's doorstep one day announcing he had come to live with them. "I don't want to be on my own any more," he boomed as he marched into his son's fish shop. Edwin was understandably taken aback and at first lost for words. He turned to Teddy, now aged ten and said, "You had better fetch your mother, lad." Teddy obeyed.

Edwin and Mary had no real choice in the matter. They weren't about to throw their elderly father out onto the street, even if he could be cantankerous and most of the time, a drunk. They knew it was going to be difficult. They were under no illusion. Unfortunately at the time they had no idea just how difficult it was going to be. The family would just have to make the best of the situation.

The children's sleeping arrangements were altered to accommodate Edwin's father and this proved quite disruptive for the family. Teddy and Lionel had always shared a bed in the smallest room. Teddy had never liked this arrangement because he rarely got on with his brother, but he'd put up with it. The girls all shared a larger room which housed two double beds and they had always been more than happy with this arrangement. Now their grandfather had arrived on the scene and everyone was being moved around. No one was happy. Teddy and Lionel had been moved in with the girls, freeing up the smallest room for their grandfather. Baby Violet was in with her parents. Fights and squabbles now took precedence over calm family evenings between the children, until one night when Edwin had finally had enough and could take no more. He spanked the lot of them and they were told if it happened again their punishment would be more severe. From then on bedtimes were much more peaceful.

Most of the younger children were quite wary of their grandfather and as they witnessed him drunk most days were also frightened by his riotous behaviour. Teddy resented his grandfather, mainly because he had been made to move out of his own bedroom. He vented his frustrations by playing tricks on him.

During his day at school and on his way home, Teddy collected spiders, woodlice, worms and dirt, anything and everything nasty he could lay his hands on. He collected them in an old cigarette packet which he kept hidden under his bed. He waited until his siblings had fallen asleep before creeping into his old bedroom armed with his little box of creepy-crawlies. Teddy emptied its contents under his grandfather's covers, towards the bottom of the bed, and waited. He was surprised to receive no reaction from anyone the following morning and so repeated his actions for a second, third and fourth time. About a week later Teddy overheard his mother complaining to his father about the state of his grandfather's bed sheets. She couldn't understand how his sheets had become so dirty, unless he had been wearing his shoes in bed.

There was an almighty row later that evening when Edwin had broached the subject with his father. Edwin's father ended up storming out of the house and spending the night drinking in The Hop Bag situated a little further along Downing Street. When he had returned very much later and very much worse for the drink he had accidently entered the children's bedroom and urinated into the corner of the room soaking Teddy's school shoes. The next morning all hell was let loose when Teddy put on his shoes only to discover they were saturated and blamed his brother Lionel. Another massive argument ensued.

On one other occasion Edwin's father returned home in a similar condition and endeavoured to get into bed with his son and Mary. The shouts of surprise and confusion that night woke baby Violet and Mary had a terrible job to get her back off to sleep again. They were sure the child's screams could be heard right across the town. Later the following day Edwin and Mary were able to see the funny side but at the time Edwin was furious and embarrassed by his father's behaviour.

Edwin had been good friends with the landlord of the Borough Stores. He and William Hodges had shared many a deep and meaningful conversation, most recently the subject mainly being Edwin's father. In the bar one particular evening, William informed Edwin that he had decided to leave Farnham. William had recently become widowed and Edwin had recognised he was missing his wife greatly. William explained how he craved a fresh start and although Edwin would miss his friend, he understood and supported his decision. When the day of William's departure arrived Edwin was eager to see what the new publican of the Borough would be like.

Ambrose and Eliza Dann moved into the Borough Stores in the March of 1902, not long after Edwin's father had come to stay. Ambrose had previously been publican's manager of the Park Road Hotel in Finchley and before that publican of the Rising Sun in St Bartholomew, London. Ambrose and Eliza had been married for nine years and had two children, Roy aged seven and Victor aged two.

Ambrose was older than Edwin had expected but this didn't stop the two men getting along instantly. They had both proven themselves to be successful businessmen and therefore had a great respect for one another. Their relationship was reinforced some weeks later when they introduced their wives to each other. The women had their children in common, both were devout church-goers and they shared similar interests such as dressmaking. It was inevitable therefore that the families should become very close, spending more and more time in each other's company. Edwin and Mary saw their friendship with Ambrose and Eliza quickly blossom. Ambrose and Eliza were pleased to have found true friends in Edwin and Mary as moving to new premises as often as they did was always difficult.

Over the next couple of years the two families built up a solid friendship. The two women would shop together, enjoy walks in the park with the children and attend the Sunday service at St Andrew's parish church. Their main topic of conversation would usually be the children or what they were cooking for dinner that evening and any local gossip that was doing the rounds in the town. Edwin would see Ambrose when he visited the Borough

Stores some evenings and quite often on a Sunday. He would position himself at the bar, usually armed with his newspaper to read for the times when Ambrose was especially busy serving his other customers. Then during the quieter spells the two men would swap amusing stories about awkward customers or discuss business issues that were affecting them at the time.

During this period Edwin and Mary shared many personal experiences with Ambrose and Elizabeth. Edwin's father's antics would often come up in conversation and the two families came together to celebrate news of imminent births. Emily and Arthur announced the arrival of their fourth child, a son during the autumn of 1903. Mary was particularly happy for them when Emily announced she wanted to call the child Thomas after their late father. No sooner had she announced Thomas's birth than Emily was writing to Mary to say she was pregnant again. A couple of months later Mary was writing back with her own announcement.

The first half of 1904 held plenty of excitement and anticipation. Preparations took place in both sisters' lives. They stayed in continual correspondence with each other during this time and Mary shared her sister's letters with her friend Eliza. Sadly, Emily's fifth child arrived early and died when it was just a few hours old. Emily was devastated, as was Mary when she found out. It brought back all those painful memories of when she and Edwin had lost their beloved Lillian, ten years earlier. This time it was Mary who was unable to be with Emily which put a great strain on her emotions. They stayed in constant contact through letter writing during this difficult period and it was her friend Eliza who supported Mary during this time. Mary gave birth two months later to another daughter and named her Muriel Nancy. Her good friend Eliza was in attendance. It had been a much easier birth than her previous, which had surprised Mary under the circumstances and Mary put this down to Eliza's calming influence.

When baby Muriel was about two months old Mary transferred

her concerns to her friend Eliza. Every discussion Ambrose and Eliza had with Edwin and Mary was about their son, Victor. They were becoming increasingly concerned about his health. He was also the major topic of discussion at home between Edwin and Mary, taking precedence over Edwin's father as they were more concerned for their friend's child. The four adults had all noticed a recent decline in the child's well-being. It was of course his mother who had first spotted it. The poor child seemed to be losing weight at such a pace and feeding him larger portions as Mary had recommended seemed to be having little or no positive impact.

Victor was now five years old. He trailed behind his mother and Mary as they walked through the graveyard after the morning church service. The other children had run on ahead and were shouting and playing tag. Victor's little head hung down, his chin resting on his chest. It seemed to take all of his effort just to keep up with his mother. "He always looks so sad and his little face is so pale. He never has any energy to play with the other children any more," Eliza complained to Mary.

"I can see a change in him too," agreed Mary. "He always used to be such an active little boy."

"If he fetches me something from upstairs, he seems to become short of breath very quickly as though he's been out running," continued Eliza. The women turned to look at Victor who made no attempt to repay the glance. Instead he coughed, hawking up some mucus and spitting it out onto the ground. Mary could see the deep concern in Eliza's eyes. "Then there's that cough," said Eliza. "I've taken him to the doctor but I don't think he knows what it is. Nothing seems to be helping it. All the doctor could say was make sure he gets plenty of fresh air."

"Well, that's what he's getting right now," replied Mary, reassuringly. But it seemed all too familiar to Mary and the memories of Lillian's death came flooding back. The two women continued their chat for the duration of their walk, a concerned mother and a loyal friend trying to offer her support.

When the New Year arrived things were no better for little Victor. His cough had worsened and become very troublesome to him, distressing him and his mother terribly. His breathing had become more impeded. He was suffering from fevers which caused pains in his chest, like those of pleurisy, resulting in restless nights. He had lost a huge amount of weight for someone so little, caused by his failing appetite, so ultimately he had no strength or energy. It was February when the doctor finally diagnosed him with consumption. By then the most unpractised eye could have detected the ravages of this disease as it had altered the whole of Victor's appearance. His eyes were sunken, his cheek bones prominent. His head bent forward permanently on his chest and his arms and legs were terribly wasted.

Victor spent his last days propped up in his bed. His voice had been reduced to a mere whisper. He was having terrible difficulty breathing and was coughing up blood. His mother was beside herself, unable to do anything for her son. She was understandably failing to cope but her best friend Mary was there to support her. It was 20 March when his end finally came. Edwin was in his fish shop but Ambrose, Eliza and Mary were all in the little room above the Borough Stores when tiny Victor took his last breath. Ambrose and Eliza clung on to each other and sobbed as Mary pulled the sheet up to cover the boy's face. Ambrose and Eliza had been forced to witness their beloved son, who used to be so full of life, wither away to nothing. Their pain was unbearable.

Victor was buried at Abney Cemetery in Stamford Hill near to where he had been born and where other members of the Dann family lived. Edwin and Mary attended the funeral in support of their friends but found the experience very difficult. It was upsetting to see their friends so broken and distraught but it also brought back those distressing memories they'd also experienced ten years earlier when Lillian had died. Throughout the service and burial Mary was supported by Edwin as she held on tightly to a memorial card which Eliza had earlier slipped into her hand.

Eliza had arranged for some cards to be printed by E.W. Langham who was a printer, stationer and bookbinder on South Street, Farnham. On the front of the card was a picture of a wooden cross smothered in twisting ivy. Inside it read: *In Loving memory of Victor Richard Dann, the dearly loved boy of Ambrose and Eliza Dann, who fell asleep, Monday, 20 March, 1905 aged 5 years 7 months.* On the opposite side a poem read: *Only a little angel, gone to its heavenly rest: only a little lamb, safe on our saviour's breast. His end was peace.*

Upon returning home, Mary placed little Victor's death card safely inside a Bible she had entitled, The Life of our Lord and Saviour Jesus Christ. It had once belonged to her mother and within the Bible Mary had written, at the top of the first page, her wedding date and below listed all the names and dates of birth of her children. Lillian's death was also noted on the adjacent page and it was here that Victor's death card would remain, for a great many years to come.

It wasn't long before Ambrose and Eliza were drawn back to the London area. After the death of their son Victor, Farnham had held too many sad memories for them and by June they were making plans to leave. Edwin and Mary were truly sorry to see their friends move away from the town but understood why they must. The families promised to stay in touch and through her letters, Mary could tell the move had been the right step for Eliza. So in February 1906 Mary felt able to write to her friend to inform her she was expecting another child. She would be forty when this child was born and she stated in her letter to Eliza that she hoped that this one would be her last. She had written a similarly difficult letter to her sister, Emily who had not had a child since losing her baby two years previously. Thankfully both women replied positively to Mary's letters.

Mary gave birth to another daughter on 30 June 1906. Edwin and Mary named their daughter Hilda Nellie and almost immediately after the child was born, Mary firmly suggested to Edwin that she should be their last. Hilda was a small, pretty baby. She had the most endearing features and a personality that went with them. It wasn't long before Hilda became fondly known as 'Babe' to the rest of the family. She was, of course, the baby of the family and Mary hoped she would always remain the youngest. Emily was of the same opinion when she eventually gave birth to another child early in 1907. Emily and Arthur had been blessed with another boy and they named him George. At the time it was impossible for Emily not to experience thoughts of losing her baby again, but George appeared strong and healthy and after a few weeks, Emily's fears had subsided. She wrote to her sister with her news and considered herself blessed for being able to have another child at her age. She was after all 43 that year and believed George would be her last. The women's letters flew through the post at great knots while they tried to organise a trip to see each other.

When Mary finally took Babe, Nan (as Muriel was now known) and Violet with her back to Staines to visit Emily and Arthur, it was the summer of 1907. They were away for three nights. The journey by train was pretty stressful but Mary was looking ahead of that to when she could spend some special time with her sister Emily and her five children. The two sets of cousins instantly became friends. Mealtimes were noisy, as were bedtimes, but the grown-ups had as much fun as the children, going for walks in the park and catching fish in the stream. Arthur was incredibly understanding of his wife and sister-in-law's needs. Even after a hard day's work he allowed his wife the space she needed to chat with her sister after the children had all gone to bed.

Doris now nine and Evie aged seven were left in the care of a trusted neighbour who had volunteered to take them to school each day, along with Lionel. But eleven-year-old Lionel was not happy with this arrangement and protested on a daily basis. Teddy, fifteen, and Mabel aged fourteen were considered old enough to look after themselves and stayed at home. Teddy helped his father in the shop during the day and Mabel kept house, cooked the meals and looked after her younger siblings.

Chapter 6

1907

During the last five years the family had endured many difficult times with the added difficulty of having Edwin's father come to live with them. Just recently his health had deteriorated significantly and Edwin and Mary had become rather concerned. Winter and especially Christmas, had always brought plenty of hard work for the family, but this year it was particularly difficult for Edwin, who was trying to care for his ailing father at the same time as running the family business. With his health deteriorating gradually over the last five years, Edwin's father was spending more and more time alone in his bedroom, usually after a heavy drinking session down at the Hop Bag or The Bird in Hand.

To deter his father from frequenting the local public houses so often, Edwin had sometimes asked him to help out in the shop. He'd made sure on these occasions that he was always there to oversee proceedings to ensure the smooth running of his shop. On one particular morning, Edwin had been forced to ask his father to help out as Teddy was nowhere to be found. Teddy had vanished and Edwin had been unable to find his son. As a last resort Edwin had left his father alone and in charge of his shop while he carried out his son's deliveries.

Edwin had recently purchased a motor vehicle which he was using to deliver to his regular customers. He set off daily to deliver orders to places such as Churt, Frensham, Seale and Ewshot. It had been Teddy who had pestered his father for some time to buy the delivery van. "It's an expensive luxury we just don't need. We have a cart which does the job," had been Edwin's immediate reply, but Teddy had finally worn his father down, explaining that his customers would buy elsewhere if his father didn't modernise his business and move with the times. "I've seen at least two other fish and poultry sellers in the area and a greengrocer who deliver using a motor van," argued Teddy. "It's much quicker and more efficient."

Edwin had finally conceded, without allowing Teddy to find out that he actually agreed with him and thought it was a good idea. Edwin had justified his decision by explaining he would give it a go and if it didn't work out he could always sell the van later. Teddy was thrilled with the idea of being able to escape his father's shop to tinker on the van. He hated being stuck in the shop all day. He had recently felt very restricted and smothered by his father and the family business. There never seemed to be any time for him to do what he wanted to do. It was always the business which had to come first every time. So when his father had purchased the van, Teddy felt as though he had been given a new lease of life. He spent the early mornings cleaning the van in preparation for his father's deliveries and most evenings tinkering with its engine under the gas lamp outside his father's shop, until long after dark.

As Teddy seemed to have disappeared into thin air that morning, Edwin reluctantly departed with the van and his deliveries, leaving his father, briefed and ready to serve in the shop. Mary had been instructed to discreetly check on her elderly father-in-law at intervals throughout the morning and to severely reprimand Teddy when he eventually decided to turn up. The children had all been sent off to school except Mabel who had completed school last year and now helped her mother at home with Babe and the housework. Edwin had been gone about an hour when Mary popped downstairs to see how her father-in-law was coping. She was careful not to let him see her or hear her as she crept quietly down the wooden staircase. She didn't want him to think she was checking up on him, even though she was. Mary knew that the conversation which would follow, if that happened, would be very difficult and she had no intention of having it. As she peered through the crack in the door, everything appeared quite normal. There were no customers in the shop at the time and her father-in-law was just sitting on Edwin's stool, staring out into the street, watching the younger children wrapped up in their winter coats, playing hopscotch and tag. She didn't disturb him. She turned and made her way back upstairs to get on with her chores.

It was Monday, wash day, and she was always glad of Mabel's help on this day. Mary became quite engrossed in her work and quite forgot the time until a while later when her thoughts were interrupted by a loud commotion outside the shop. She glanced through the upstairs front room window to notice a large group of about twenty people, gathered around the shop entrance just as Edwin was returning down the street in his van. As she made her way down the stairs she could hear raised voices and above them all was her husband's. He appeared to be shouting at his customers. She flew through the door into the shop to witness the complete pandemonium that had broken out.

Edwin had turned into Downing Street after completing his deliveries and noticed a large crowd gathering around his shop. At first he thought something had happened to his father, maybe he had been taken ill. He parked the van as close to his shop as he could and when he climbed out, realised that in fact a disorderly queue had formed along the pavement and was now stretching back down the street and past the coffee house next door. Shouting at the crowd outside to let him past, Edwin arrived inside the shop at exactly the same moment as Mary. They realised within a split second of one another exactly what was happening. Edwin's father was giving away his son's livelihood for free. He was dishing out fish, poultry and game to anyone who wanted it at no cost to them whatsoever. He had become bored in the shop by himself. With no customers and nothing to do, he had started to hand out free fish to passers-by. The locals, of course, weren't going to waste this rare opportunity and were soon queuing to see what bargains were on offer.

Edwin's father was having a magnificent time. Unable to wrap the requests quickly enough, he was almost throwing the raw fish and meat at the hordes. Then he noticed his son and daughter-in-law. He was unable to comprehend why they appeared to be so distressed by the situation. Edwin was furious and ranted at his customers, insisting they leave his shop immediately unless they were going to pay for the items they wanted. "What's the problem son? The shop's busy, that's what you wanted wasn't it?" asked his confused father.

"Take him upstairs, Mary," ordered Edwin, "while I try to sort out this mess."

"Come on, Dad, I'll make you a hot drink," urged Mary, as she placed her arm around his waist and guided him through the doorway and upstairs. As Edwin's wife and father disappeared, the crowds dispersed and Edwin set about restoring some order in his shop and recounting his stock to see how much he had lost. He was still very angry about the situation when Teddy appeared in the doorway fifteen minutes later.

"Morning, Father," smiled an unsuspecting Teddy, who saw nothing unusual inside or outside the shop as he'd arrived.

"Where the bloody hell have you been?" boomed Edwin, causing Teddy to become rooted to the spot with shock. Teddy composed himself and was just about to explain, when his father's raised voice butted in before he could get the words out. "Don't bother explaining. I don't want to know. You have no idea what problems you have caused today, have you?" Edwin didn't wait for Teddy to answer but continued, "Well, son, you soon will when the money I've lost this morning comes out of your wage packet. Get out of my sight."

Teddy knew his father only too well and did as he was told. He was now seventeen, taller than his father, but didn't mind admitting his father could be pretty terrifying at times. Teddy retreated upstairs to where his mother filled him in on what his grandfather had been up to.

"Stupid old bugger," Teddy mumbled under his breath.

"Teddy!" his mother chastised.

"Well, how much is this going to cost me?" he demanded.

"If you hadn't stayed out all night celebrating your birthday with your friends, and been here this morning to help me, none of this would have happened." Teddy shut up after that as he knew his mother was right. "I haven't even told your father you didn't come home last night. He thinks you left the house early to go somewhere this morning. So make sure you keep it that way, or he'll be even more furious with you than he is now." And with that Mary left the room, slamming the door shut behind her.

That evening, Edwin was still reeling from the day's events. He and Mary finally got to sit down together at 9pm. The long and difficult conversation that took place between them that evening culminated in a decision that neither of them wanted to ever have to make. But it was clear to them now that they could no longer afford, cope with or care for Edwin's father at home to the degree that he needed and reluctantly they conceded that he would have to go into the workhouse. His mind now appeared to be letting him down and although Edwin and Mary hated having to make this decision, the workhouse was their only option. It was generally accepted that a family member with a serious illness, who was unable to work, was sent to the workhouse. But this did not make their decision any easier.

Edwin couldn't stop working to look after his father. The business was the family's only means of income and it would be impossible for Mary to look after the house, children and have time to care for an elderly drunk who was losing his mind. The couple also feared he might come to some harm. "He could wander off anywhere, at any time and end up in all sorts of trouble. Already he's returned, or has been brought home, the worse for drink. What if he was to turn violent towards us or even the children?" worried Mary. Once they had made their decision,

Edwin and Mary decided they should keep it to themselves for the time being. Edwin agreed he would speak to Dr Tanner the next day to organise a visit to the workhouse and fill out all the necessary forms.

Farnham had accommodated a workhouse since 1727 and at first it had been situated in Middle Church Lane, opposite to where Edwin now had his shop. When the little Farnham Workhouse became too small, a new Union Workhouse was built about a mile away on Hale Road in 1790, at a cost of £4,000. By the time Edwin and Mary had moved into Farnham, the Workhouse Infirmary had opened its doors to the general public as well as inmates and they had been forced to increase their numbers of staff to suit. Conditions had improved for patients, especially after the arrival of the new medical officer, Dr Tanner. Charles Tanner was forty-seven years old, an unmarried, well-spoken, polite gentleman. He lived at number four Downing Street and had run his practice from there for some years. More recently he'd started working at the workhouse. Edwin had often served the doctor in his shop and today asked his advice concerning his father's welfare. Dr Tanner kindly said he would arrange for Edwin to visit the workhouse and they could discuss his father's case.

Lionel had heard his mother and father whispering and also noticed how recently, their conversation would abruptly cease when he entered the room. He was both suspicious and intrigued about where his father could be going so early in the morning and why he was leaving Teddy to open the shop alone. Unbeknown to Edwin, as he walked the mile-long journey to the workhouse the following day, he was being followed by his son Lionel. Lionel managed to follow his father all the way without his father's knowledge. The workhouse was made of brick with high walls and small windows and Lionel thought it looked like a prison. He'd seen pictures of a prison in books at school. As his father disappeared through the large gates he knew he could go no further without being discovered, so he found a place to hide, crouching down beside a stone wall, out of sight of his father when he should reappear through the gates. He soon became bored waiting for his father, wondering what he could possibly want with the place, when his attention was captured by an unkempt vagrant walking along the road, pushing an old pram. The tramp had obviously been walking for some time and looked very tired. His clothes were filthy as though he had been working on a farm and sleeping amongst the haystacks. The old pram wobbled under the weight of his life's belongings which Lionel thought looked as though they had been pulled from a rubbish heap. Upon reaching the workhouse gates he stopped and looked around him as though searching to see if anyone was watching.

Lionel could not be seen from his hiding place and watched to see what the tramp would do next. He was surprised to see the man produce some coins from his pocket and place them carefully behind a leafy shrub growing beside the large workhouse gates. The man hid his coins knowing he would be refused food and a bed for the night if he was found to have more than a shilling on his person. Lionel waited for the vagrant to disappear through the gates before emerging from his hiding place and crossing over the road. He quickly retrieved the coins from their hiding place and, deciding to return home, soon forgot the reason for being there in the first place. He was pleased with his stroke of luck and skipped most of the mile home, stopping only twice to purchase sweets and cigarettes. He was never found out, as he was careful to dispose of all evidence. He had taken a huge risk as he knew his father would punish him severely if he ever did find out, yet somehow this made his deceit more exciting.

Meanwhile, Edwin was shown to Dr Tanner's office where he explained that his father's health had recently deteriorated and he felt unable to provide his father with the care he desperately needed. Dr Tanner showed Edwin around the ward. The workhouse appeared very busy, verging on becoming overcrowded.

The atmosphere inside the building felt very depressing and then there was the smell. It was a stale kind of odour, a musty smell mixed together with carbolic acid and bleach.

Edwin was shown around some areas of the workhouse. As men, women and children were segregated, Edwin's father would have a bed in an all-male dormitory and eat together with the other male inmates. It was explained that his meals would consist of morning porridge, a cooked dinner with pudding at lunchtime and bread and jam for tea. The doctor explained how cost was of huge importance in the workhouse and all meat that was purchased was carefully weighed. Edwin suggested he might be able to help with a small donation towards any meat or new equipment the Infirmary might need and Dr Tanner was most grateful.

When Dr Tanner had completed his tour he turned to Edwin and said, "Would you be able to care for your father for a little while longer? We are always so busy at this time of the year. I feel confident that once the Christmas festivities have passed we will have more than enough room to accommodate him."

"I'm sure my wife and I will be able to manage for another week or so," Edwin replied.

Together the two men made the necessary arrangements and agreed upon a date, and when Edwin had signed the papers he returned home to Mary with the news. She didn't need to ask her husband about the conditions inside the workhouse. Although she had never been inside it herself, she had heard many a tale of what life was like. "We should be able to manage for another week or so," Mary said trying to sound positive. "We'll try and make this Christmas extra special for him." Both Edwin and Mary realised that it would probably be his last.

On 28 December Edwin reluctantly took his father to the Union Workhouse in Farnham. The workhouse was truly the final resort. His father had deteriorated again during this last week and was becoming more frequently incontinent during the night and unco-operative during the day. Edwin knew he was doing the right thing for his father. Even if it was a place where his father would become confined to his bed all day and eventually die, he knew it had to be done. The two never spoke during the journey. Edwin carried his father's few belongings in the small bag which he had turned up with six years earlier, while his father struggled not to slip on the icy ground beneath his feet. Edwin knew, when he accompanied him to the workhouse on that cold winter's evening, that his father would never be coming home again. Edwin's father also suspected that his time left in this world was running out.

Edwin visited his father as regularly as he could. He forced himself to go as he detested the place. It wasn't a place he felt comfortable about being associated with. The very first time he visited his father, which was less than a week later, Edwin noticed a big disparity in his father's well-being. He seemed confused and disorientated about where he was and at first didn't recognise Edwin. It took Edwin a good ten minutes to convince his father he was who he said he was. During other times, his father would be asleep and didn't wake throughout the whole of Edwin's visit. On these occasions Edwin couldn't help feeling his visit had been a complete waste of time. His father appeared to have lost weight, displayed a pale complexion and suddenly appeared terribly frail. Edwin suspected he had begun to concede defeat.

During the visits when he was awake, it was impossible to hold a conversation with his father, as his concentration would just wander. Any conversation that did take place between them didn't make much sense. During one visit a young girl entered the room and approached Edwin's father with a plate full of supper. Her patient knocked the plate right out of her hands, causing it to crash to the floor. "If you think I'm eating that poison you can think again," Edwin's father shouted at her. The poor girl ran off and Edwin was left quite unsure as how to react.

"What did you do that for?" he whispered.

"They're trying to poison me you know, and I'm not falling for it," his father shouted.

"No they're not," Edwin whispered again, trying to calm the situation.

"Oh yes they are. What do you know anyway?"

"They're just trying to help you. No wonder you look so thin," Edwin concluded.

His father began to raise his voice even louder this time. "Who are you anyway? Are you after my money as well? Go away, I don't know you."

After that there was just no reasoning with him. Reluctantly, Edwin got up and left before his father became any more distressed. On the way out he met Dr Tanner who suggested he try to visit in another couple of days. "I'm sure your father will be in a cheerier mood then," he smiled reassuringly.

A reluctant Edwin entered the workhouse a couple of days later and it was then that he noticed the most significant change in his father's health. His father seemed very depressed and more argumentative than normal. It didn't matter what subject Edwin chose to discuss, his father found fault with it. His father's speech had become almost incoherent and Edwin was struggling to understand his father's ranting. He appeared to have no idea where he was or who indeed Edwin was. Edwin had been particularly agitated by this visit and hadn't stayed long. Mary had been surprised to see him return home so quickly. She hadn't needed to ask Edwin about his father. She could tell her husband was distressed and hoped and prayed this situation would not go on for much longer.

On 17 March 1908 Edwin's father died. Edwin was called to the workhouse only an hour before his father's death, when Dr Tanner recognised that his patient's time was close. Edwin was at his father's side as he passed away. The old man was seventy-four years old and a shadow of his former self, the man Edwin had always known as his father.

The following day Edwin informed George Murrell, the Registrar, of his father's death. The cause of death was recorded as Morbus Cordis and Delirium. "Morbus Cordis means he had a disease of the heart," explained Dr Tanner. "I must admit I use this term because I am unsure as to the exact cause of your father's death. However, I do believe it to be by natural causes." Edwin was aware that the delirium referred to his father's mental state, which had been characterised by confusion, disordered speech and hallucinations.

Edwin's father had no money saved to pay for his own funeral, and normally under these circumstances he would have been buried in the workhouse graveyard but Edwin didn't want this. To preserve the family's standing in the community and out of respect for his father, Edwin had to be seen to provide a decent funeral. Shortly after his father had turned up on his doorstep seven years previously, Edwin had had the sense and foresight to start making small weekly payments into a burial club. There was plenty in the fund now to pay for a funeral and transport his father's body back to Sutton to be buried next to his mother. Edwin knew this would have been what his father would have wanted.

The workhouse kept the body until Edwin had made the necessary arrangements for the undertaker to attend to his father. Edwin's shop remained open and was run by Mary, or Teddy and Mabel (much to their dislike), while Edwin was otherwise engaged organising the funeral arrangements. A couple of days later, Edwin travelled with his father's body by train to Sutton, where his family gathered to bury him in a grave alongside their mother. It was a sombre occasion and Edwin found it difficult to communicate with most of his close family. They had made no attempt to contact or visit the old man during the last seven years of his life. Even when Edwin had wired to let them know that their father's health was deteriorating, not one had visited. Edwin was only too aware his father could be difficult. He could understand they were probably glad to see the back of him when he had left for Farnham.

It is easy to forget about a person when they are no longer around to remind you. At least they had all made the effort to turn up for the old man's funeral, thought Edwin.

It was a small family gathering at the graveside while prayers were said and the coffin lowered. Afterwards, Edwin's eldest brother William spoke briefly to him. "He lost the house you know. He couldn't meet the rent and spent all his money on the ale."

"I hadn't realised he'd lost the house," said Edwin.

"The only reason you ended up with him was because John and I wouldn't take him in." And with that, William left, followed shortly by the rest of the family. There was no wake to follow and nothing to keep Edwin there, so he left to catch his train.

During his trip home Edwin considered his family's situation and concluded that he had very little in common with them. It was he who had wanted more from life while his siblings remained unchanged. He was pleased he had taken the necessary steps to break ties with his family all those years ago. They had never had the same aspirations as he. As he had buried his father earlier that day, he couldn't help feeling his father had never approved of the changes he had made in his life.

The first decade of the twentieth century had brought the family an assortment of emotions. By the end of 1901 both Mary and Edwin had lost a parent but Mary had given birth to two more daughters. This theme had continued with three more losses for the family to endure but only one more birth to counteract the balance. Now Edwin and Mary were to endure more sorrow before the end of this first decade.

In the summer of the same year that Edwin's father passed away, Edwin and Mary received more sad news. A very moving letter arrived from the Isle of Wight and as soon as Edwin noticed the postmark he suspected it was bad news. He thought it was going to be from Edward Hooper's son, who ran the family hotel in Ryde, informing Edwin that his father had died. It was not. The letter was from Edward himself, terribly depressed after the death of his beloved wife, Jane. Edwin and Mary discussed the contents of the letter and Edwin wrote back to his old employer and friend by return of post. He promised he would visit his friend as soon as was possible and had every intention of keeping that promise.

During these sad occasions the atmosphere within the household changed, and at times Edwin could become very sombre, communicating very little with the rest of his family. He tended to go about his daily life within a bubble, using his shop as an escape. Mary's disposition was less affected as the children kept her fully occupied, allowing her little time for reflection.

Six months later things were not improving for the family. Edwin had not been able to find the time to visit his friend in Ryde and just recently Teddy had become increasingly troublesome and difficult for his parents. Their son's behaviour was worring them terribly. Teddy had shown little interest in girls during the past few years, although on a couple of occasions had been seen walking out with a local girl from East Street, but this was not Edwin's and Mary's real concern. Teddy's passion was for motor cars, or any motor vehicle really. Over the years he had been pretty consistent in this area and Mary had often commented to her husband that she thought he would probably end up doing something in the motor trade. Edwin, however, had other plans for his son. He had always expected Teddy to follow him into the retail trade which Edwin loved and knew well. Edwin believed Teddy would eventually take over the running of his shop when he retired.

Teddy had other ideas, and recently Edwin had become more and more aware of his son's lack of interest in the family business. Any chance he had, he would disappear down the road to the local garage where he was allowed to work on the cars with the other men. With his son spending more and more time away from the family business and more and more time tinkering on other people's cars, Edwin realised that if he didn't act quickly he was going to lose him. Edwin had hoped that when Teddy had convinced him to purchase the motor van for the business's deliveries, he might show a little more interest, but he hadn't.

The situation was really bothering Edwin and he could sense Mary felt she was losing her son as well. Edwin hated to see his wife distressed in this way. Edwin and Mary had spent most nights during the last week discussing various possibilities that might make Teddy see things in a new light. It was Mary who came up with the idea of purchasing additional premises for Teddy to run alone. Edwin was reluctant at first. He felt his son had let him down recently and couldn't justify spending such an amount of money on anything that did not come fully guaranteed but the desire to make Mary happy and to have their son involved in the family business all but outweighed the risk he might be taking with this venture. Edwin liked the idea of having second premises which sold fish and poultry. The thought of expanding his business appealed but he was unsure whether he could trust his son enough to risk sinking such a large amount of money into a new business.

"What if I look for somewhere to rent rather than to buy?" Edwin said to his wife. "Think of it as a compromise."

"Could we afford to do that long term?" enquired Mary.

"We could short term and if it was working out we could purchase the property at a later date. If it didn't work out, for whatever reason, I wouldn't have to hang on to the premises, or have to find someone that I could trust to run it."

"I think that makes sense," agreed Mary. "Do you have anywhere in mind?"

"No. But when do I ever get out of this place to be able to notice anywhere up for rent?"

"Now I come to think of it, I noticed a place up on East Street the other day. Do you remember where that girl lived that Teddy was seeing for a while? It was a few doors away from her, on the same side. I'm sure there was a notice outside saying 'For Rent'. Shall I find out tomorrow?"

"Would you dear? But don't mention anything to Teddy at this stage, just in case nothing comes of it."

"I won't," and Mary paused for a moment, deep in thought. "Do you know dear, that is a weight off my mind."

"I know what you mean. It's a weight off mine as well."

By the time winter arrived, Edwin had been so busy setting up the new business for his son, all thoughts of visiting his friend Edward Hooper on the Isle of Wight had been unwillingly pushed to the back of his mind. So when another letter arrived from the Isle of Wight he assumed it would be from Edward again and felt terribly guilty as he opened it because he had still made no plans to visit.

Edwin was feeling particularly exhausted after having rushed backwards and forwards from his shop on Downing Street to the new one on East Street every day for the past week. He had been helping to sort orders and deliveries while Teddy was getting used to the responsibility of running his own shop. He had enlisted the help of Mabel and Lionel and even Doris at the weekends but Edwin felt completely drained when he finally got to sit down in his armchair around 9.30pm that night. He picked up the letter from the Isle of Wight and began to read.

Edwin read two lines of the letter unable to take in what had been written. The letter was not from Edward Hooper, but Edward's son, informing Edwin of his father's death. He read on in disbelief, tears stinging the back of his eyes. Edwin was obviously terribly upset as Mary entered the room. It took her some moments to understand just what Edwin was trying to tell her. He felt so dreadfully guilty for not having made more of an effort to visit his friend earlier and now it was too late. Edwin felt Teddy was partially to blame for the situation. If he hadn't spent all this time setting up another shop for his son, he may have found time to visit his friend. Now he wouldn't get that chance. Edwin spent a number of days composing a letter to Edward Hooper's son, expressing his condolences and sympathy. He wished him and his family well, offering his support should they ever need it, but did not promise to visit the hotel as he now suspected that would never happen.

During the following year when his son's new business was flourishing, things came to an abrupt halt when Teddy announced he had had enough of working for his father. Teddy's parents had been exceedingly generous in their offer to set him up in business. They had allowed him to live alone above the new shop for a minimal amount of rent and life had seemed to be getting better for Edwin and Mary. Edwin wandered down to his son's shop one day, as he did every so often, leaving Mabel and Lionel in charge, but when he got there it was closed. Edwin was furious. Always carrying his keys on his person he opened up the shop. You can imagine Teddy's surprise when an hour later he returned to find his father serving behind the counter.

"Where the hell have you been?" Edwin demanded. "You've had customers waiting." A terrible argument ensued, culminating in Teddy informing his father he no longer wished to work for him. Edwin was shocked by his son's callous attitude and called him indolent, self-centred and conceited. "You only care about yourself. No one else matters, do they?"

"You're a fine one to talk," Teddy retaliated.

"And what's that supposed to mean?" demanded Edwin.

"Look Father, there's no point in discussing it any more. I've made up my mind."

"Oh, you've made up your mind."

"Yes. I've even got another job lined up."

Edwin was taken aback. "And where might that be?"

"It doesn't matter. I'm just trying to explain. I'm not idle. I just want to make my own choices."

Not to be defeated, Edwin replied, "In that case you won't mind finding yourself somewhere else to live then." Now it was Teddy's turn to be taken by surprise. He was so angry that his father could be so intransigent, he stormed out of the shop, slamming the door so hard it almost came off its hinges.

One week later Edwin had given notice on the shop, Teddy had moved out and all communications between Edwin and Teddy had broken down. Mary was distraught at first and it took her some time to come to terms with what had happened. She would make special trips with the children that took her past where Teddy was working, just to get a glance of him repairing cycles. His job paid barely enough for him to be able to afford his board and lodgings with Mrs Marshall in Long Garden Walk. Mary insisted he visit home on Sunday afternoons which usually happened while his father was at the pub. She would always make enough dinner for him and leave it warming on the stove until he arrived. Edwin was aware this went on and said to Mary one Sunday evening, "As long as I don't have to see him, I don't mind." Teddy's feeling was precisely mutual.

With Teddy gone, responsibility fell to Mabel and Lionel to assist their father in the shop. Mabel had never enjoyed this task and was soon looking for her way out. She had witnessed Teddy breaking free from his family ties and wanted to do the same. Mary recognised her daughter was troubled and grabbed a rare opportunity one day for a chat when she found herself alone with Mabel. The rest of the children were in bed and Edwin was still clearing up in the shop with Lionel. Mary sat her daughter down in the front room to discuss her problem. Mary began to feel her age as she realised her eldest daughter was now a grown woman with her own opinions. It was agreed that Mabel could start looking for another job and that Mary would inform Edwin of this fact on her behalf. At first Mabel began to look for a job close by, one where she could still live at home to help her mother with the children and housework. But events never turn out the way you expect them to and within the month Mabel was packing a bag and getting ready to travel to Sussex.

Mabel had just turned eighteen and it was her mother who had seen the job advertised in the paper and had encouraged her. Mary felt it would give her daughter the freedom she craved, allowing her to develop into an independent woman through experience of the real world. At first Mabel was reluctant as she had little inclination to leave the security of her family home. It took some doing, but her mother was finally able to persuade her. "Lionel already helps your father in the shop. Doris and Evie are old enough to help me around the house after school and during the day I only have Babe to look after. She will be starting school soon anyway." Mabel was beginning to feel like a spare part.

"But I don't want to move away from you all," she reasoned.

Mary knew she would have to be cruel to be kind and spoke the truth. "Look darling, it would make life a lot easier on the family finances if you were to have a job where you could live in." Unconvinced, Mabel eventually agreed and was offered the job. She accepted the live-in domestic servant's job in Uckfield, Sussex. Her employer was a single woman, an inspector of midwives, who made Mabel feel immediately welcome in her home and Mabel was soon thoroughly enjoying her new-found autonomous life.

Early in the evening of Monday 3 April 1911, an enumerator entered Edwin's shop to carry out the England and Wales Census. Edwin finished serving his customer, washed his hands, cleared a space in his tiny office area and began to fill out the form. He wrote his surname first, and then named everyone in the household who had been sleeping under his roof the previous night. Teddy and Mabel were not included in the schedule as Teddy was now living in Long Garden Walk and Mabel was working and living away in Sussex. Edwin continued with his task and gave details of everyone's age. He was forty-two and Mary, forty-three. That was the easy bit. He then had to try to remember all his children's ages. He recorded Lionel as fifteen, Doris, thirteen and Evelyn eleven.

He rounded up his last few children's ages, Violet, ten, Muriel, seven and Hilda, five. The schedule then asked for how many years he and Mary had been married, just as Mary entered the shop to fetch some skate for the children's tea. Edwin looked over to his wife and asked for confirmation. "Mary, how many years have we been wed now?"

"Don't pretend you can't remember. You know it was twenty years last month."

"I'd best put twenty then," he said, and continued to fill out the schedule. The enumerator smiled. Next the form asked how many children they had had in total, how many were still alive and how many had died. Edwin needed no help with this question and quietly filled in 9, 8 and 1. In the occupation column he recorded himself as a Fishmonger and Poulterer with Lionel as his shop assistant. The rest of the children were recorded as attending school except for Hilda who wasn't quite old enough yet. Lastly Edwin filled in where everyone had been born and signed his name and address to the schedule. The enumerator checked Edwin's details, filled out the total of males, females and persons in the building and checked the number of rooms in the house. He thanked Edwin for his cooperation and left for the next property.

A dashing young man had recently moved into Downing Street and he too had given his details to the enumerator. His name was James Corpe, Jim, to his friends, new boss and landlady. He was twenty-one and had travelled to Farnham from Wandsworth, where he had lived with his family. He was boarding with Mary Newall at 52 Downing Street. Jim had managed to secure himself a job in Farnham, working as a butcher's assistant for Harry Baker, a pork butcher with premises at 18 Downing Street. Harry's family had been in the business for over one hundred years. He was a celebrated sausage maker and had an outstanding reputation for good quality and an excellent, prompt service. Harry had found

Jim very pleasant and hard working. He had no complaints about the lad and was pleased to have found him.

Edwin and Mary had welcomed Harry to Downing Street when he had arrived a few years after they. He had been no threat to Edwin's business and the family had since then always bought their meat from Harry. They had continually been delighted with the quality and taste of his meats and never had occasion for complaint. They knew they were guaranteed quality from Harry. Edwin and Harry had become friends over the years, and often straight swapped a decent piece of meat for a fine, filleted fish. Both had great respect for the other's trade. Now that Jim Corpe worked for Harry, the family had all grown used to seeing him also. Jim was always polite and courteous to Mary whenever she popped into the shop and he always made time to talk and joke with her daughters. Over the next few years, Jim would prove to make a big impression upon one daughter in particular.

In 1911 there seemed to be plenty of choice and variety of shops for the men and women of Farnham, especially when deciding where to have their hair cut. F. A. Mitchell advertised his high class ladies' and gentlemen's toilet salon as also having a private room for ladies and children. It was situated at 23 The Borough. He stocked all toilet requisites, including razors. Fringe nets and side combs were a speciality. He advertised wigs, transformations, combings, Marcel waving and electric treatment by a competent West End hand. H. Pullen advertised his premises as a Hairdresser and Perfumer, stocking all articles for the toilet and was situated at number 50 The Borough. He supplied ladies' combings and ornamental hair of every description, made in any design. He offered a separate ladies' hair-cutting room.

When a new hair salon appeared on West Street, Edwin was tempted to give it a try. He felt like a change from his usual. After leaving Mary and Lionel in charge of his shop, he walked through the doors of Lionel H. Smith's salon, never to look back. Lionel

Smith had completed his training and gained certificates and diplomas while at the International Academy of Hairdressing. He had moved to premises in Farnham after working at the Harrods store in London. His premises offered 'private salons for ladies and children' and a 'perfectly fitted hygienic salon for gentlemen'. Lionel made wigs on his premises, gave electric massages of the scalp and performed Marcel waving. He also provided all toilet articles and fringe nets at competitive prices.

Edwin entered the building and was greeted by Mr Smith who asked politely, "What can I do for you today, sir?"

"I'd like a wet shave please and a bit of a tidy up," answered Edwin ruffling his hair through with his hand. Lionel led him through into a back room. Here Mr Smith was careful to explain exactly what he was going to do. He did this for all his clients, throughout the process, to put them at their ease. First he placed some hot towels over Edwin's face. "I use fragrant hot towels to relax my clients and prepare their skin. It helps to soften the beard ready for the shave," he explained. After about thirty seconds Lionel applied lather to Edwin's face using a shaving brush made from badger hair. "Now I'm lathering up," explained Lionel as he applied the shaving cream from the pot and used the brush in a circular motion. "This will lift and moisten your beard and prepare it for shaving." Edwin had experienced shaves before at various establishments, but he could honestly never remember feeling as relaxed as he did at this precise moment.

Once the lather was complete, and he had warmed the razor in hot water, Lionel Smith began to skilfully shave Edwin with an open razor. He did this with ease and great precision, especially around Edwin's moustache and sideburns. Lionel shaved with the grain of Edwin's beard or moved the blade sideways across the growth when he came to more awkward areas such as Edwin's chin. "You should never shave against the grain as this pulls the skin in the wrong direction and can cause small cuts and grazing," advised Lionel.

"I will try to remember that, thank you," replied Edwin.

"I don't want to be sending my clients out on to the street with a shaving rash now, do I?"

"No, that would never do," agreed Edwin, remembering this man held a very sharp razor close to his throat. It wouldn't be the first time I've had one of those, thought Edwin. He could remember rushing home and having to cool down his stinging face with icy water on one occasion. Mary had thought he'd been in a fight when he had rushed through the door, all bleeding and covered in little cuts.

Lionel rinsed Edwin's face thoroughly with cool water to close the pores and patted his face dry with a soft towel. "Now, this final application of cold towels and lotion will leave your face feeling smooth and soft, just like a baby's bottom," he laughed. Edwin had enjoyed his first experience at Lionel H. Smith's. He had been able to completely unwind, and it had been a while since he'd felt that relaxed. In fact he wasn't sure he would be able to get back up out of the chair. He felt as though he could fall into a deep sleep. Lionel too had recognised his client was completely at ease with him and knew then that he had done a good job. "I believe a professional shave is a real treat and that every man should experience it at least once in his life."

"I couldn't agree with you more," smiled Edwin, easing himself out of the chair. "But I'll be back every week from now on," he said as he stroked his smooth face. "That feels amazing, thank you."

"No problem sir. I'll look forward to it."

Over the years Lionel and Edwin became firm friends. Edwin visited Lionel regularly for a shave and haircut and soon the rest of the family were also going to Lionel Smith's salon for all their hair-dressing needs. Even when Lionel moved his premises to Number One The Borough in 1920, Edwin and his family remained loyal to their friend and continued to give Lionel their business.

Edwin spent most Sunday afternoons catching up with male acquaintances down at his local pub or reading his newspaper quietly at home on the rare occasion when Mary and the children had gone out. The days when he had the house to himself were a delight. Six children and running the family business six days a week allowed Edwin little time for escape. It was now July and most of the country was perspiring in 80°F temperatures. Mary had decided to meet up with some of her friends at the local park where the children could play in the shallow stream while their parents stayed cool, chatting under the trees. Edwin took this opportunity to stay at home by himself. It was too hot for him anyway; he hated the intensity of the heat. He read his *Times* newspaper through from cover to cover and relished the tranquillity. During this month the *Times* had begun to run a regular column under the heading "Deaths From Heat". Edwin started to read about a schoolgirl, Amy Reeves aged 10, who took off her boots and stockings and left them on the grass beside a shallow pond at Longcross near Chertsey. She was discovered drowned later that afternoon, her head caught in the weeds beneath the water. A thought ran through Edwin's head and he hoped Mary was taking her responsibility as a mother seriously. He knew she could be easily influenced and inclined to get caught up in local gossip and hoped this would not distract her from watching their children near the water.

He read on: There had been twenty-eight consecutive days without rain and the weathermen forecast that temperatures would continue to rise. Fires had been reported as spontaneously breaking out along the railway tracks at Ascot, Bagshot and Bracknell, and the gorse on Greenham Common in Newbury had caught light. The lack of rain and scorching sun had resulted in a dangerous scarcity of grass for herds and flocks. Pastures had turned brown and farmers were being forced to raise the price of milk. Edwin recalled that earlier in the week Mary had returned home from shopping complaining about the price of milk going up. He had assumed she was just having another of her little moans. His peace was soon shattered as Mary and the tribe arrived home earlier than expected. "It's just too hot for the children," Mary surmised. "We had to come home. "Oh it's lovely and cool up here."

"Yes, and it was peaceful as well for a short time," retorted Edwin.

By August Edwin had resigned himself that while this heatwave continued he would get no peace at home. It was Sunday again and Edwin was at home sitting in his front room with his wife and his two younger daughters, Muriel and Babe, who were playing on the floor with their dolls. Edwin had flung open the windows desperate for a breeze, which was not very forthcoming, and a glass of cool beer sat upon the table next to him. Lionel, Doris, Evie and Violet had all gone down to Gostrey Meadows, in the centre of Farnham town, to swim in the river. Gostrey Meadows had been created last year as a recreational area for the residents of Farnham and was proving very popular during the heatwave.

Edwin read some more from his newspaper and shared some headlines with Mary, telling her that the royal party had arrived at Cowes, on the Isle of Wight, for the Regatta. He read, "'In the heat, an enchanting picture of gleaming sails and gently swaying masts could be seen and the King, George V, and the Prince of Wales, the future Edward VIII, had taken to cooling themselves with a pre-breakfast swim in Osborne Bay'". Mary smiled as she recalled their time on the island. It seemed a very long time ago now. Edwin continued, "It says here 'The press quickly discovered this secluded place. As cameramen jostled to get their shots of the sovereign and his heir in bathing dress, a statement was issued by Buckingham Palace: "If less objectionable behaviour is not observed by the photographers they are warned that steps will be taken to stop the nuisance."'"

"I should jolly well think so," replied Mary.

By late August the whole nation had become exhausted as the hot weather hung over England like a heavy curtain. The relentless

sunshine seemed to have bleached the colour from life, replacing it with an oppressive haze. Even by early September, summer was not quite ready to release its long hold on the year, but on the eleventh of September the average temperature suddenly dropped by twenty degrees and in Edwin's *Times* newspaper that day, they forecast good news: "The condition over the kingdom as a whole is no longer of the fine, settled type of last week and the prospects of rain before long appear to be more hopeful for all districts."
"Thank goodness for that," said Mary.

Along with the change in the weather, there came a change in Teddy. He had found the last year extremely difficult. Now nineteen years old and a man, he was eager to see what else the world had to offer him. Although he had found some freedom from his family ties, the job he had now was a temporary solution. It didn't pay well enough to allow him what he desired and was hardly taxing his mind.

As a young boy he had always shown an interest in motor cars. When the family had moved to Farnham, Teddy had been about eight years old. He enjoyed the thrill and commotion a car and its occupant could cause as it travelled through Farnham and up and down Downing Street passing his father's shop. People would stop as if paralysed and stare at the contraptions as they passed. Teddy and other boys of a similar age would run behind them shouting and waving. Even at that time Teddy recognised the connection between being well off and owning a car and he desperately aspired to owning one himself. As he grew up, he would hang around the garages more and more, watching the mechanics at work. He much preferred to do this than play in the street with his friends.

The mechanics became so used to seeing Teddy they found little jobs for him to help with. Teddy had started by washing and polishing the cars and as he grew older he learnt about the engines and how they worked. He would harass the mechanics with endless questions and was soon learning how to clean plugs, change the oil and strip the engine, making sure all working parts were put back in good order. As a teenager he became terribly frustrated because he was desperate to drive. An opportunity presented itself one day when a customer's car needed to be moved inside the garage from the forecourt and Teddy was told that under supervision he could help with this. He was only thirteen at the time and thrilled to be given the responsibility. Fortunately for the mechanic who had involved Teddy in this procedure, Teddy had preformed proficiently, as though he had been driving for many years. If there had been an incident involving a customer's vehicle, the mechanic would, without a doubt, have lost his job.

On occasions Teddy might spot a mechanic from John Henry Knight's place testing cars in the town, and would hound the poor man until he allowed him to look under the bonnet. When Teddy had convinced his father to purchase a van for the family business it had allowed him some of the freedom he craved, but that hadn't lasted very long. Soon, that freedom had been replaced with the responsibility of running his father's second business and all the limitations that went with that and now he was feeling stifled by the constraints of the cycle repair shop. Teddy felt as though he had just moved from one restriction to another.

Then, one Sunday afternoon when Teddy was visiting his mother, an advert in his father's paper caught his eye. An owner of a fine house in Wiltshire was looking for a chauffeur. It didn't take Teddy long to decide this was the opportunity he had been waiting for. He applied for the job immediately by telegram, without consulting his family. He was surprised but delighted when two days later he received a telegram offering him the position.

It came as no surprise to Edwin, when Mary told her husband Teddy was leaving Farnham. Looking up from his paper he said, "Maybe it's for the best."

"Do you really think so, dear?"

Edwin thought for a minute. "I don't know, Mary," he replied, shaking and folding his paper noisily, placing it on the arm of the chair. Edwin was conscious not to upset his wife and decided to keep his thoughts to himself, believing his son would tire of his new venture and return to Farnham in less than a year.

At the beginning of 1912 Teddy was thoroughly enjoying his life and his employment, working as chauffeur for his employer who owned a manor house in Wiltshire. The moated manor house was small but grand. Beautiful oriel windows jutted out from its walls and rooftop soldiers decorated the house. Within the grounds was a gatehouse, extensive gardens and tiny parish church. Teddy lived in one of the small, labourers' cottages which stood at the bottom of the garden, behind a stone wall. All he wanted was to be able to save a decent amount of money each month from his wages and have enough to do whatever he wished on his days off. Teddy had really fallen on his feet this time. He was able to drive his employer's numerous motor vehicles, expected to service them, clean them and keep them in good working order. He cleaned and polished them daily with great love and care. Teddy couldn't have been happier in his work. His employer was happy with the service he was getting and more importantly Teddy now knew what he wanted for the future and was determined to save until he got it. The one thing he hadn't planned for though was to fall in love.

He met Eva as she was working at the manor as a domestic servant. Her family had lived in the area all their lives. Her father, uncle, brothers and cousins were all quarrymen. They all worked at the local Bath Stone Quarry and had varying jobs from picker to gaffer. Men had been quarrying the hills on this site for hundreds of years, but only in the last thirty years had they begun to quarry under the ground.

As this was no job for women, it was assumed Eva would work at the manor as her older sister had done before her, and her younger sister would, after her. Eva had never aspired to doing any more than this, until the day she met Teddy. She had spotted him as he had approached the house in his employer's car. She had been impressed by his stance and the way that he carried himself with importance. She might have thought him to be a visitor to the manor if it had not been for the chauffeur's uniform he wore. Eva had been upstairs cleaning the bedrooms and happened to glance out of the window at the moment Teddy had arrived. She had quickly ducked out of sight when he had glanced up at the big house to admire its beauty. Eva had blushed at the thought of the handsome chauffeur spotting her watching him, but he had no idea she was there and that he was being watched. Their relationship developed over the next few weeks as Teddy became well acquainted with all the staff that worked at the manor. He was always made to feel welcome, especially in the kitchen. Cook had taken an instant liking to Teddy, allowing him to participate in the delights of whatever she was baking that day. She reminded him a little of his mother.

There had been an instant attraction between Eva and Teddy which seemed inexplicable as they actually had very little in common. They managed to snatch the odd quiet moment together before one of them would have to return to their work, and every time they did, the passion and desire inside them both multiplied until it became almost unbearable. Their desire became too strong to ignore. On their occasional days off, Teddy would take Eva out for picnics or for a drive in his employer's car. His employer had no idea Teddy was using the car for his own purpose. Teddy sometimes used the excuse that he needed to take the vehicle for a ride to check the engine was operating correctly and his employer never questioned this. His employer believed he had found himself a dependable and conscientious employee in Teddy.

Things took an abrupt and unexpected turn one day when Eva discovered she was going to have a baby. Very frightened and with no mother to confide in or advise her, as she had passed away some years previously, Eva decided she must inform Teddy first. She knew her father would insist Teddy marry her and Eva was uncertain that Teddy wanted that. She was very confused and didn't really know what she wanted, either. Eva had no idea how Teddy was going to react. At first he denied the baby could be his. "It's not mine. It can't be. You must have had relations with another boy from the village," Teddy accused her.

Eva was terribly hurt by his cruel words and shouted back at him. "When could I? Every spare day I have off I spend with you. My father is always moaning that he never sees me. You are the only man I've ever been with. How can you say that to me?"

Teddy was reluctantly forced to accept and admit that he must be the father. "I'm sorry," he eventually conceded. "It's just come as a bit of a shock."

"How do you think I feel?" Eva replied.

"Well I suppose we should get married," said Teddy, with little emotion.

"Yes, I suppose so," said Eva as she breathed a silent sigh of relief. It would certainly make telling her father a lot easier.

There was a change in Teddy after that day. He seemed to mature in many ways and recognise that he needed to face up to his responsibilities. At the back of his mind though he was still determined that one day he would make his father proud.

So Teddy's fun was over and reality had set in. A wedding was planned quickly and when the preliminaries of publishing the banns were complete, Teddy married Eva on 9 June in the local parish church. Eva was slightly older than Edwin, not unlike when his own parents had married. The day was not a particularly happy one for the couple, but they both believed it was the right thing to do. Eva's family attended the ceremony and her father laid on an impressive spread for his daughter afterwards, back at their home.

Teddy had chosen not to inform his family of his marriage to Eva. He had never been terribly good at staying in touch with them. In the two years he had been absent, they had received just the one letter. That had arrived shortly after he had left and only described his job and accommodation in the briefest of details. A couple of months after his wedding he did decide to write and tell his parents about his marriage and the child his wife was expecting. It was not an easy letter for him to compose, but he did it. Unfortunately, two weeks after writing the letter he was forced to contact them again with the difficult task of explaining that Eva's baby had died. By the end of the year, Teddy's marriage was teetering on the edge of a precipice. His relationship with his wife had become extremely strained and almost broke down completely after the death of their baby. It was now evident that the only reason they had married one another was because of the baby. So it almost came as a welcome release for Teddy when war was declared the following year and although he didn't have to, Teddy enlisted.

Chapter 7

1914

When the First World War started in August 1914, no one believed it would last very long. Most of the people in Farnham and in the rest of Britain believed it would be over by Christmas. The customers in Edwin's shop spoke about the war as something that was carried on 'over there' in France and Belgium. It was not important to the people of Farnham in the beginning as it caused very little change to their daily lives. There were no threats of bombings of factories, ports or railways, schools continued to open and life remained unchanged for many people. Edwin read his newspaper daily to keep abreast of affairs; it was always useful to have up-to-date knowledge of the war as many of his customers chose to discuss this subject with him on a regular basis.

The government had anticipated shortages of many food supplies and made bulk purchases, stockpiling many items such as wheat and sugar. This meant that early on in the war the people of Farnham and other towns across England had plenty to eat and shops were well supplied. Although there was a plentiful supply of food, this hadn't stopped people in some parts of the country from behaving in an un-British manner. One of Edwin's customers had told him how she had family in the North, where there had been panic buying and hoarding which had caused food shortages. "I guess we're a little more sensible down here in the South," had been Edwin's tactful reply.

The most significant difference for the people of Britain was how the war played havoc with the country's workforce, as many young men rushed to recruiting offices to join up. This had a knock-on effect when many jobs previously done by women, such as operating sewing machines, making confectionery and gutting and scaling fish, were axed as they were not considered essential to the war effort. Edwin soon found he was working harder than ever. He now had to gut and descale all the fish he sold, where previously much of this had been done for him by women before the fish had left Grimsby. Many women suddenly found themselves without paid jobs and it was some months before the situation was resolved. Women were soon encouraged to undertake jobs such as shoe making, printing, baking and as bus conductors and guards on the railways.

Mary and her older daughters did their bit for the war effort, as did many of the women in Farnham. They spent much of their spare time knitting scarves, gloves and socks for the soldiers, or making up parcels with tinned and dried food and tobacco. Mary also involved her younger children in making up the parcels. They enjoyed this activity and would add little notes to their parcels to raise the soldiers' spirits. Mary often took advantage of the situation, turning it into more of a social occasion and inviting friends and neighbours for tea and knitting sessions in the family's front room. Many a time raucous laughter could be heard emerging from the upstairs' room as Edwin worked in his shop below. During these occasions it was easy to forget there was a war on.

One week, posters went up in prominent areas around Farnham to advertise a recruiting rally to be held in Farnham on 2 October 1915. When that day arrived Mary took her four youngest daughters with her to Castle Street where many had assembled to listen to speakers and the Cavalry band playing. Afterwards the recruits were to march through the district. There was great support for these courageous young men.

Doris had remained behind to help her father in the shop but after Edwin had received no customers for over an hour that afternoon, he decided to shut his shop for an hour and the two of them went to watch the parade. Most of Edwin's daughters enjoyed listening to the band of the 1st Reserve Cavalry but while nine-year-old Babe marched on the spot to the beat of the drum her big sister Violet stood with her hands over her ears. Many volunteer training corps had turned out. Evie and Nan made sure they got a good look at the boys from the Scouts and Farnham Grammar School Cadets. Evie couldn't wait to tell Doris about them when they returned home. "You missed all the handsome lads," she boasted as soon as she walked through the shop door. Their father had disappeared downstairs to get more ice from the cellar.

"Actually, I spotted a few myself," taunted Doris.

"How could you? You've been stuck in here all day," mocked Evie.

"Father and I nipped out for a while to watch the parade. I had a very good view thank you very much."

"What? He actually shut the shop?" Evie asked sarcastically in disbelief.

"Yes he did!" boomed her father's voice from behind her as he returned from the cellar carrying a bucket of ice, at which point Evie made a quick exit upstairs with the excuse she had to help her mother, much to Edwin's and Doris's amusement.

Across the country, young men rushed to rallies and recruiting offices in their thousands to join up, believing they were volunteering for a war that would be over by Christmas. This was the first indication of the seriousness of the war, brought home to Edwin and his family after the rally when an ever-increasing number of local men in uniform could be seen wandering around the town. Farnham's railway station was one of the busiest places during the war as endless men in uniform, many of them terribly young, left for the front. Many would never return.

Edwin had missed the initial Army call up, as he was too old. As there was no conscription at first, Lionel had chosen not to join up straight away, believing the war wouldn't last. When Christmas was over and the country was still at war, he decided to join up and fight for his country. It was soon after Christmas, when the war showed no signs of slowing, that Mabel returned home to be with her family. She was surprised to find very little had changed at home, even with the war on. Although she disliked the work, she kept herself busy in her father's fish shop during the day but her evenings were her own to do with as she pleased and so she and her friends often frequented the local dances, usually in search of suitors. In wartime you might think this would prove difficult, but Farnham was not far from the Aldershot Army base and many soldiers would turn up at the dances whilst on leave, looking for escapism and the possibility of romance. Mabel and her friends were more than happy to provide this.

Mabel was twenty-four now and blamed the war, solely, for the reason she was not married. It wasn't for want of trying. Tonight was another opportunity where she might meet her future husband and nothing and no one was going to get in her way. Ever since returning to the family home Mabel had felt desperate to leave again. Life with her parents felt stifling. She wanted a home and a family of her own and felt her time was running out and that her choices were being limited daily by this unfortunate war.

Doris was not yet eighteen and had only recently begun to show an interest in boys. Most of her time while her sister had been away had been spent helping her father in the shop. She had often felt too exhausted in the evenings to go in search of boys. Today, however, Doris had decided she wanted to go along with her sister to the dance. "Can I tag along?" Doris asked as Mabel was putting on her make-up in the mirror. "I've asked Mother if I can go and she said it was all right."

"All right then, if you must," Mabel replied unsympathetically. "But don't get in the way."

"I won't," Doris replied, exasperated by her sister's lack of compassion.

Mabel and Doris had always shared a love-hate relationship. There were five and a half years between the pair and it had often showed. Mabel could be very protective of Doris, standing up for her if anyone was mean or picked on her but she could also be quite callous and spiteful towards her younger sister. Doris loved Mabel and looked up to her but relished every opportunity to wind her big sister up. This had often proved easy to achieve and Doris had guessed correctly that Mabel was warning her tonight, for that very reason. The sisters walked the short distance together to the top of Downing Street without speaking to one another. It was here that Mabel's friends met up with them and walked the rest of the way to where the dance was being held. Not one of Mabel's friends acknowledged Doris's presence, much to Mabel's delight.

By the end of the evening Doris felt the whole night had been a disastrous experience. It was clear both girls had experienced very different evenings. Doris had not enjoyed her first proper taste of socialising with men. She had watched shyly as the other girls had danced with the soldiers and subsequently convinced herself that she couldn't. She was painfully shy and inexperienced and on the two occasions she had been asked to dance that evening, she had quickly declined, making up some poor excuse, her miserable face putting off many other prospective suitors.

Mabel on the other hand had met a soldier named Fred. She had thought him terribly good-looking in his uniform and had been literally swept off her feet by his fancy footwork and his charming manners. They spent most of the evening together, dancing, talking and laughing. She had, for the best part, forgotten about the friends who had accompanied her there and completely neglected poor Doris. As Mabel and Fred got up to leave, Mabel suddenly remembered her younger sister. She discovered Doris sitting in exactly the same seat as she had left her earlier on that evening. Everyone around her was gathering up their belongings and getting ready to leave. Doris was sipping the last drop of drink from her glass, which she had managed to make last for well over an hour, when she noticed Mabel walking towards her with a soldier. "You ready to leave?" enquired Mabel.

"Oh you haven't forgotten me then?" Doris replied sarcastically. Mabel glared at her sister, ignoring her comment. "Are you going to introduce us then?" continued Doris, mustering some confidence from within her frustration.

But before Mabel could, Fred had leant forward and outstretched his hand. "I'm Fred, how do you do?" Doris, suddenly feeling shy again took the soldier's hand and shook it.

"This is my sister," butted in Mabel. "Come on, let's go."

Fred walked the two women back home to Downing Street. Very little conversation ensued except for some polite conversation from Fred to Doris. So as soon as they reached home, Doris politely said goodnight and quickly disappeared through the back door off Ivy Lane. Mabel stayed and chatted some more with Fred. She was out there for another hour, in the Lane, under the stars with Fred. Amongst many other subjects they discussed Fred's leave and agreed to see each other again. Then they kissed for the first time and it was everything Mabel had hoped it would be. When Mabel finally entered the house that evening she felt as though she was walking on air. She was determined this would be the start of the rest of her life and Fred and Mabel saw each other as often as they could after that night, war and leave allowing.

Eighteen months later, volunteering had not provided the British Army with the huge numbers of fighting men that it needed to win the war and conscription with a few employment exemptions was introduced. This applied to all men between the ages of eighteen and forty-one years. Once again Edwin found himself exempt, as he was over forty-one. During the war Edwin and Mary heard very little from their eldest son Teddy who wrote only occasionally and never spent his leave in Farnham. They understood Teddy's commitments were to his wife and hoped one day soon they would get to meet their daughter-in-law. Lionel on the other hand wrote regularly and spent all of his leave at home.

By the spring of 1917 the cost of living had increased dramatically.

In particular, bread cost twice as much as it had the year before and Mary was complaining to Edwin that her housekeeping wasn't going as far as it had done. "The price of bread and potatoes is ridiculous and we're the lucky ones," she said. "It cost me one shilling for a 4lb loaf of bread this morning. It's daylight robbery. When will this bloody war end?"

"Soon, I hope," Edwin replied. "But I am worried it may not be as soon as some people are hoping. On a positive note though, my newspaper today has reported that the government are at last going to intervene and the price of bread will come back down to 9d. I suspect potatoes will do the same eventually. I'm just not sure it's going to be enough though for all of those who are less well off than us. There seem to be many people struggling all across the country. I feel rather guilty as I have just treated myself to another a new 78rpm for the phonograph. They're not as easy to get hold of at the moment which was why I bought it when I saw it. But I can't help feeling it's rather extravagant," concluded Edwin.

"Well I suppose it is dear, but we all enjoy listening to it so much. You know how much it means to the girls and it always manages to lift all of our spirits."

This was true. The family had always enjoyed listening to music, whether it was a brass band in the park, tinkering on the family's piano or listening to their father's wireless or gramophone records. The younger children had always enjoyed the job of winding the handle attached to the side of the gramophone's wooden cabinet and would edge closer to it as they waited for the record to stop. But it was always their father who turned the records over and carefully placed the needle onto its grooves.

During the war it was music which seemed to bring the family closer when they found themselves together on most Sunday afternoons. Edwin would forgo time spent down his local in favour of spending it with his family and his children were surprised to find themselves looking forward to these events. Mabel and Doris took it in turns to play the piano, with Mabel being the more accomplished player. When Evie and Violet were allowed their turn, they enjoyed playing a duet together while the rest of the family listened and clapped. Occasionally Edwin and Mary would treat their girls to a display of their dancing ability. This amused the girls immensely and usually resulted in their father tripping up over his own feet, often on purpose and much to Mary's amusement, enabling her to hear her children laugh, something which seemed to happen far too infrequently these days. The afternoon would always have the desired effect, to escape their thoughts on the war and give them a sense of hope for the future. No one looked forward to these afternoons of frolicking more than Hilda. Now aged ten, she would dance around the room in her stockinged feet, the furniture pushed back especially for the purpose. Her older sisters all took a turn to waltz or foxtrot with her to the music playing on their father's gramophone. This usually shy, quiet little girl came out from her shell on these occasions and thought these days were the best.

Up until now Edwin had been able to access a steady supply of fresh fish and keep his shop well stocked, although he had at times had to call in a few favours from various contacts. This was a time when people pulled together and friendships were cemented. Suddenly Edwin's livelihood looked uncertain when German U-boats threatened food supplies by perpetrating constant and prolonged submarine attacks upon fishing and other vessels. No ship or its cargo was safe. These attacks caused great disruption to Edwin's supply, some days leaving his shop almost empty of fish, but he and Mary had experienced difficult times before and saw it as yet another challenge. As long as they had each other and their family, they knew they would get through these hard times.

During the summer of that year when the country was almost on its knees, Fred was on leave and asked Mabel to marry him. They were soon married at St Andrew's Church in Farnham. Mabel had made the decision quickly, needing little time to consider her answer. The couple managed to arrange their big day during one of Fred's leaves of absence, a common occurrence for many wartime couples. Mabel and Fred were very happy about the situation; Edwin, however, had reservations. He did not wish to see his daughter widowed before her marriage had even had a chance to begin and had tried not to interfere, but just one week before the wedding he felt unable to remain silent any longer. He had to speak to her about it. Edwin and Mary asked their daughter to join them in the front room, upstairs, above the shop. Mary already knew what the outcome of their discussions would be, but needed to show her husband that she supported him, while she greatly empathised with her daughter.

"I'm just suggesting you wait a little longer," Edwin proposed.

"But we don't want to. We want to get married now. You just don't understand," complained Mabel as she became more and more frustrated with her father's outlook.

"But have you thought about what it would be like if Fred was seriously wounded or even killed?" Edwin persisted. Mary sat silently as Edwin's and Mabel's dispute escalated.

"Of course I have. I think about it every minute of every day and every time he has to go away. But it makes no difference. It doesn't change the way I feel about him."

"But it might do."

"No it won't," Mabel insisted.

"You don't know that for sure," reiterated Edwin.

"Yes I do!" Mabel shouted this with such clarity that Edwin was finally forced to accept he had lost the battle. Mary breathed a sigh of relief as the discussion reached its conclusion.

On their wedding day, a week later, Mabel and Fred could not have been happier. Most of Mabel's family attended but unfortunately her brothers had both been forced to send their apologies as they had been unable to gain any leave, but this had not perturbed Mabel.

Edwin proudly gave his daughter away, accepting that the war was the reason for such urgency in her getting married. Doris was overjoyed to have been asked to be her sister's chief bridesmaid and considered her role extremely important. She enjoyed organising her sibling bridesmaids. Earlier that morning though, Mabel had been ready to lock her chief bridesmaid in the wardrobe and leave her at home for the day. Doris had driven Mabel mad for most of the morning, fussing and making sure everyone was fulfilling their assigned roles. Then suddenly she disappeared, tearing off around the house looking for something old, something new, something borrowed and something blue. "I can't find something new!" Doris screamed as everyone was just about ready to leave. "It doesn't matter," said Mabel calmly. "I don't believe in all that stuff anyway."

"But it's unlucky if you don't have them," Doris screeched back. Luckily their mother stepped in and came to Mabel's rescue. "Aren't you wearing the new pair of stockings I bought in Elphicks, Mabel?" she asked, winking at her daughter. Mabel nodded. "Oh, thank goodness," groaned Doris. Peace was resumed and the wedding party were able to leave for the church. Fred and Mabel spent their wedding night under Edwin and Mary's roof, which wasn't an ideal situation for the couple but it didn't prevent Mabel from conceiving their first child that night, just as her mother had done, all those years earlier.

When the New Year of 1918 dawned and the country was still at war, the British people began to fear that food would soon run out and started panic buying. It was then the Ministry of Food introduced rationing in some areas and Edwin and his family had to make the best of it, like everyone else. It was only now that the people of Farnham began to realise that the war had changed things. Human life was suffering and not just with countless young soldiers dying in battle. Each day, the average person was becoming more and more affected by the war. Some had turned incredibly selfish as they queued for meagre rations to supplement their daily menu of tea, bread and dripping, potatoes and scraps of fish or meat. Arguing over the amount or the cost of food and pushing and shoving were becoming commonplace up and down the country. However, Edwin would stand for none of this inside his shop, and was happy to escort any customer whom he considered was being unreasonable from his premises.

The people of Farnham had felt unsafe now for some time because of the threatened increase in attacks from the air. Many had read in their newspapers and seen pictures of the damage which the Germans had caused in London and they no longer felt safe in their home town. All around Farnham posters had been displayed, usually at the gates of larger houses, offering the townsfolk protection in a cellar from air attacks. Edwin had displayed a poster outside his shop which read: *This property contains a fairly good sized cellar. In the event of an air raid, customers and passers-by are welcome to what shelter it affords.*

Edwin's property had a large cellar. He had been forced to move things around in order to accommodate the number of people who may be in his shop at any given time and whom needed to take shelter. It was rather cold, damp and smelly as this was where Edwin stored his ice and some of his fish. He had placed a few chairs down there, with some candles, blankets and of course a couple bottles of his favourite tipple. (For medicinal use, of course, not knowing how long they might have to stay down there.) To date he had only had to use his cellar once and had been able to shelter safely with his family and those customers who happened to be in his shop at the time of the air raid. Thankfully, this time huddled together in the cellar had not lasted long nor had there been any damage to his property when they had all resurfaced later.

Mary's visits to church had become more frequent during this troublesome time, as had those of many of Farnham's parishioners. The church gave Mary and others hope, through a difficult period. The loss of human life had been tremendous and was increasing all the time. A whole generation of eighteen- to twenty-five-year old men had died in the war, leaving behind them countless widows and fatherless children. Mary would frequently pray for her two sons and for their safe return and so far, her prayers had been heard. Mary's Bible had never received such regular use as it did during the years between 1914 and 1918. As her visits to church increased so too did her reading of the Bible, strengthening her belief. Mary found an inner peace through these activities, which made her feel calmer and more able to cope, when all around her seemed disconcerted and ill at ease.

As the war reached its conclusion it was Evie who surprised everyone when she announced she was getting married. She had turned eighteen earlier that year and begun a relationship with a man who was ten years her senior. Her father would most likely have forbidden such a thing if the family had not known this man so well and for so long.

Evie had often been a customer in Harry Baker's butcher's shop and over the last twelve months frequented it more and more. She had started working for him, serving his customers every Saturday morning for which he had paid her a small sum of money. It somehow made her feel more connected to the man she thought she loved, while he was away fighting for his country, for they had met in that very shop many years earlier when Jim had first started working for Mr Baker as his assistant. Jim and Evie had always got on well. He had always admired her bubbly personality and positive outlook on life, but as she was so much younger than he, he had been forced to push back any feelings of desire he might have felt, until now that was. He had joined the war at the same time as Evie's brothers and while away had gained new skills and interests. Evie's family and Harry Baker had missed him but it was Evie who missed him the most. She was always writing and sending him 'happy parcels' as Jim's colleagues had started to call them and Jim would always find time to reply to her letters. Evie's father also paid her a small wage for helping in his shop during the week and so she was able to save enough money to fill her parcels with treats as well as practical things. They would usually contain cigarettes, writing paper, a pair of woolly socks she had knitted herself, matches, tinned meat, tea, salt biscuits and plenty of chocolate as she knew Jim loved it. She felt a little guilty as she rarely sent a parcel to her brothers and on the rare occasions she did, they wouldn't contain the same treats.

It wasn't until Jim returned to Farnham on leave during the February of 1918 that their relationship had taken a romantic turn. It had hit them both suddenly without warning. One minute Jim had been serving with Evie in the shop and chatting about how much leave he had left, and the next they were walking through the park arm in arm, Evie's head tilted to one side, resting on Jim's shoulder. It was a cold but beautiful Saturday afternoon. The sun shone and the winter crocus was out in full bloom. The park looked stunning. Jim turned to face her and pulled her close, kissing Evie passionately for the first time. That kiss changed everything for Evie, for she now knew he felt the same about her as she did about him. Upon Jim's return to duty, the pair had written to each other almost every day and it was in one of his letters that Jim had promised they would marry as soon as the war was over.

When the time came and the war ended on 11 November, Jim was true to his word. As Jim's parents were unable to travel to Farnham, the couple decided to marry in his home town, Wandsworth. Jim went along with Evie to inform her parents of their decision. Neither Mary nor Edwin were particularly against the idea, but they would have liked to have had more warning to enable them to be part of Evie's special day. It appeared that Evie was in too much of a rush to have considered their feelings but in truth she was just not prepared to wait any longer, knowing for sure it was exactly what she wanted. They were married the next day with only Jim's family as witnesses at the registry office, but the pair could not have been happier. They returned to Farnham a week later where they moved into rented accommodation on Ivy Lane. After the couple returned home married, Evie's parents accepted Jim into their family and no more was said about it.

The end of the First World War brought families together again as soldiers returned home to their loved ones. Farnham tried to return to its pre-war habits but there was a growing desire among the young for independence and freedom from the ties of home. Already three of Edwin and Mary's children had married and were living their own lives elsewhere but Edwin and Mary considered themselves very blessed. They had not lost their two only sons in the war and neither had been seriously injured. Teddy wrote to inform them he had arrived home safely to his wife in Wiltshire. He mentioned in his letter how he was thinking of moving back to the Farnham area with his wife. This news delighted Mary; however Edwin was a little more sceptical.

Lionel made a brief visit back to the family home after the war to ask his father to loan him some money. Lionel, like his brother, had tasted freedom and wanted to cut his ties with home. Reluctant at first, but later persuaded by Mary, Edwin helped his son financially the best he could and Lionel promised his father he would pay him back, every last penny. He moved away to live and work in St Marylebone, London. Here, Lionel managed to secure himself a job working as a fishmonger and within a couple of years had worked his way up to the position of manager. He lived in a five-storey block of flats called Wharncliffe Gardens, which was where he met his future wife, Gladys.

Although Mary did not have her sons living at home with her any more or see them very often, she could only consider herself blessed, for at least they were both alive and safe, unlike thousands of other soldiers whose families would never see them again. When the war was declared over, only a fraction of Farnham's young men returned. Anxious relatives could be seen packing the station platform, meeting their loved ones as they arrived wounded, dishevelled and exhausted. Many soldiers returned disabled. Some had limbs missing; others had been hit by shrapnel. Then there were the soldiers affected by shellshock. Ironically, the soldiers who returned home to their loved ones were labelled the 'lucky ones'. It was a shame that many of them didn't consider themselves very lucky.

No soldier could have been happier than Fred when he stepped off his train at Guildford station and saw his wife, Mabel, clutching their young daughter in her arms. Fred had not met his daughter before. She had been born at the couple's home in Guildford while he had been fighting abroad. To begin with, when Fred had returned to the war after their marriage, Mabel had lived with her parents, but soon found a three-bed semi-detached house to rent on a quiet street minutes from Guildford town centre. It was here, eight months later, that Mabel gave birth to their first child, a daughter. Shortly after his return from the war, Fred secured himself work in Guildford as an engine tester, at an aeroplane works. In the February of 1920 the couple had their second child, a son.

Edwin and Mary's two youngest daughters, Hilda and Nan, were still at school but nearing the end of their education. Both were very different girls but had always got on well together. Hilda was always quiet but happy, nothing ever seemed to get her down and she was always pleased with her lot. She was content to spend time with her father in his shop when her schooling allowed and had no other expectations to tempt her away. Nan displayed much more determination and was very independent like her father. She expected everyone to have the same high standards that she exhibited and looked down upon them if they didn't. It was obvious from an early age that she too craved more from her life, like her eldest brother, and that working for her father in the family's fish shop was not going to be enough for her. It had also been obvious to Mary for some time now that her two older daughters Doris and Violet, who were both unmarried and living at home, craved the ability to lead their own lives. This was proving impossible as they did not have the earning power to achieve this goal and so their home above the fish shop remained the base in which these two young women struggled to establish themselves.

Violet was now nineteen and although she enjoyed helping in her father's shop she would much rather it were her own business. She had always had a head for figures and craved an independence she did not have whilst living under her father's roof. They would often clash over ideas for the shop, Edwin over-ruling his daughter every time, and Violet was becoming very frustrated. "He never, ever listens to me," she often complained to her mother. "I hate him. I'll show him one of these days."

Violet had always been different from her sisters. She had always been the tomboy as they were growing up, with her short hair and slacks, and more recently had been mistaken for a young man when first-time customers had entered the fish shop. She was very masculine looking and would prefer to wear trousers than the "silly dresses my sisters prance around in" as she thought them. She thought trousers much more practical for the work she and her father did and thought nothing of the heavy lifting and loading of stock that was involved. In fact, Edwin had come to rely upon his daughter more and more now for the heavier lifting, as he was gaining in years.

Doris was slightly older at twenty-two, and was more like her mother. She had a strong belief in family values and morals and didn't like conflict. Only too often she would give in to something she had believed, for fear of upsetting someone. She too craved change and hoped it would come in the form of the young man she had recently met. It had been in April when she had attended a dance with a friend and met Sydney.

She had spotted him chatting to friends and noted he was smartly dressed in a high-waisted jacket with narrow lapels, which he kept buttoned up throughout the whole evening. His trousers were relatively narrow and straight and rather short so that she could see his socks. One of the first things Doris noticed about Syd was his limp and she was intrigued to know why he had it. She suspected it would have something to do with the war. This made for a great deal of speculation that evening between Doris and her best friend Muriel, whom she had known since school. Muriel was quick to realise her friend found this stranger very attractive and intriguing.

Syd had also noticed Doris, but not had the courage to approach her and ask her to dance. Instead he had hovered close by for some time, eventually moving towards Muriel (who was not so good looking, so Sydney thought) and asking her to dance. Muriel accepted much to Doris's disgust and Doris spent the whole dance glaring at her friend. As the dance finished Syd didn't know what to do and asked Muriel if she would like to dance again. "I think my friend would like to dance now," she smiled. That had been just the excuse Syd had been looking for and together they made their way over to where Doris was sitting. Doris pretended not to see them and looked the other way. "Would you like to dance?" asked Syd, holding out his hand. "Pardon?" replied Doris, pretending not to hear.

"I asked if you would like to dance?" repeated an uncomfortable Syd.

"Oh, no thank you," answered a stubborn Doris. Before Syd shrivelled with embarrassment, Mabel grabbed her friend's arm and pulled her from her seat, saying "Yes she would." Whispering in her friend's ear before she pushed Doris and Syd together, she said, "Can't you see, he didn't want to dance with me in the first place? He was just too embarrassed to ask you first."

That evening Doris gently interrogated her dance partner and discovered that Syd lived in Woodford, Essex, and was in Farnham visiting some army pals. He had joined up in 1914 when he was twenty-one and had been a groomsman in the 15th Hussars. While posted to France in 1916 he had been injured by shrapnel in his left leg and had spent some time in a military hospital in Sheffield for his nervous disability. Now he worked in his home town as a milkman and lived at home with his mother.

After their initial meeting their interest in each other increased over the next few months. The issue of such distance between their two family homes failed to cool their desire and one way and another they continued to see each other regularly. Doris married Sydney on 28 March 1921 at St Andrew's Parish Church, Farnham. Doris was eight months pregnant at the time. She had been sworn to secrecy when her parents had discovered her predicament and her father had summoned Sydney to the house insisting he did the right thing. Both Doris and Sydney were more than happy to oblige and the marriage was arranged, for a little later than Edwin would have ideally liked.

Doris carried a large bouquet of flowers in front of her belly to hide her indiscretion on her wedding day and again, so as not to cause her family any embarrassment, during the few photographs which were taken afterwards. With only one month to go before the birth of their first child, Doris and Sydney were encouraged to move away and stay with Sydney's mother immediately after their wedding. It made sense as Sydney was already working there as a milkman. It was here that their son was born less than a month later. He was named Thomas, after Sydney's father who had passed away only a few years before the couple had met.

Eleven days earlier, on 17 March, Lionel had married his sweetheart, Gladys Russell, at the Register Office in St Marylebone, London. The pair had known each other for a couple of years as Gladys's family lived in the flat below Lionel's. Gladys's father worked as an omnibus conductor for the London General Omnibus Company. It was his job to collect fares from the passengers but he would often allow Gladys and Lionel to ride for free whenever they stepped onto his brightly painted, red omnibus. By now Lionel was manager of the fishmongers where he had worked for the past three years, and had managed to pay back the money he had borrowed from his father. Lionel moved his new wife into his flat where they began their married life together.

Completely out of the blue, one Sunday afternoon, Teddy appeared at the family home in Farnham with his wife, Eva. Edwin and Mary were surprised to see them as they had received no warning but delighted as they were able finally to meet Teddy's wife. "It's just like Teddy to turn up out of the blue," complained Edwin to Mary, quietly, in the kitchen as Mary buttered some scones she had baked earlier that day.

"Well I'm just so pleased to see him and to meet Eva at last. I was wondering if this day would ever come." Mary looked towards Edwin as she placed the last of the buttered scones onto the plate. "She seems very nice, don't you think?"

"I suppose," replied Edwin, nonchalantly. "Don't expect to see them too often though, will you." Mary frowned at Edwin. "You know Teddy. There's bound to be a reason for their visit."

"Maybe they have an announcement to make," said Mary, hopefully.

"It's more likely he wants to borrow some money."

"Edwin!" scolded Mary.

They returned to the sitting room and as the four of them chatted over tea and home-made scones it transpired that Teddy and Eva were now living just down the road in Guildford. His parents listened, Mary astonished that her son had not been in touch sooner now that he lived so close by, and Edwin waiting for his son to reveal the true reason for his visit.

Teddy had always had the intention and determination to do something more with his life than just working in his father's fish shop. He had hated every minute in the Army, even though he had gained plenty of experience as a mechanic, doing what he loved best, but once demobbed he was determined to make damn sure he enjoyed his new found freedom. Unbeknown to his parents and with some outside financial help he had set up a garage business. It had been a big day for Teddy when two months earlier he had opened his very own business on Guildford Road in Pirbright.

As Mary listened she realised why he had not called round sooner and thought his news was wonderful. Teddy knew she would be pleased for him. His father however was a little more reserved with his congratulations. "You will have to put the hours in, lad, to make it work you, know," advised Edwin.

"I'm well aware of that, Father," was Teddy's reply. "Eva and I have worked hard to set this up. We already have many customers, a large part of who are ex-servicemen, including some military officers. The garage is always busy and already we are looking to employ another mechanic. Eva and I have some interviews to conduct tomorrow," continued Teddy confidently.

"That sounds just wonderful darling," Mary said proudly.

Edwin was impressed with his son's news and by his determination and enthusiasm but too proud to tell him. Edwin couldn't help wondering how Teddy had been able to afford to set up his business and was interested to know more, but he was too stubborn to ask. Edwin was convinced his son would not be able to make his business a long-term success. He believed Teddy would lose interest in the business before too long as he appeared to do this with most other things.

When Teddy and Eva had left, Mary asked her husband what he thought. "I give it a year, two at the most," was his reply.

"I meant, what do you think about Teddy and Eva?" replied Mary, crossly.

"I give them about the same."

"Oh Edwin! I give up with you sometimes. Can't you just be happy for them?"

"I'm sorry, Mary, but you did ask." Mary saw no point in continuing with the conversation and made her excuses, saying she was going to wash up.

It would take Teddy and Eva several years to build up their clientele and to save enough money to make some substantial improvements to their service. Word of mouth soon spread about the facilities at Teddy's garage. Teddy installed a special room on his premises which contained a small cinema. He had come up with the ingenious idea of entertaining his customers while they had their cars serviced and repaired and it had proved a big hit. In the late spring of 1920 Eva gave birth to a daughter and they named her Eileen.

By 1922 Evie and her husband Jim were also running a successful business together, in Farnham. They had, with a little financial help from Edwin, been able to purchase the small property on Ivy Lane where they lived, just off Downing Street. Here they had set up home and, below, were running a garage, where they ran and maintained a small fleet of taxi cabs. The couple worked hard at their business. Together, they were a good team. Jim worked in the garage, maintaining the engines and sometimes driving the taxis while Evie spent most of her day in the office catching up with paperwork or manning the telephone. This way of life continued for them for the next five years.

By 1926 Doris and Sydney had moved back to Farnham. They had managed to find a small terrace house on St George's Road which they could afford and Syd had secured a new milk round. He had worked with horses regularly, before, during and now after the war. He delivered his milk using a horse and cart and he and his horse were now very well known around Farnham. Syd attached a nosebag to his horse's head and the horse would be content eating its way through the bag as Syd distributed his milk. It would walk freely along the street, keeping pace with his master, and occasionally, as Syd delivered his last bottle of milk, he would have to turn and glance back in search of his horse that had fallen asleep halfway back up the street. He whistled loudly at the creature causing him to wake and walk on to where Syd was waiting. He stabled his horse opposite to where he and Doris lived, in St George's Road, where there was also a field for the horse to graze in. Doris and Syd's second son, John, was born this year and both Mary and Edwin were delighted to have their grandchildren living close by.

The following year, Nan was preparing to pack her bags and leave the family home. She had seized the opportunity to experience pastures new after being offered a house-keeping job in Devon. It had taken her longer than she had anticipated finding this job, as she had been scouring the adverts in her father's paper for months and written endless letters applying for many different positions. Eventually she had achieved success and now couldn't wait to get settled into her new life. She was going to be working for a Lieutenant Colonel whose wife had recently died, leaving him to fend for himself in a lovely big house. Nan's many roles would include cook, laundry maid, cleaner, secretary and companion and although she didn't know it at the time, over the next twenty years she would also become this gentleman's confidante.

Jim and Evie's business was prospering and their marriage was very happy. They thought their lives couldn't get much better until the day Evie discovered she was pregnant. It had been eight years since they had married and although they had never discussed the subject, they had both assumed they could not have children. When Evie and Jim shared their unexpected news, the whole family was thrilled for them.

Evie's pregnancy was normal and gave her little cause for concern. She took to it like a duck to water. It seemed to suit her and she was a picture of health during her second and third trimesters. Evie gave birth to a baby girl on 21 February 1927. Jim and Evie named their daughter Joy because she had brought them so much, and thought she was the most beautiful baby they had ever seen. It should have been the happiest time for them both, but the following day Jim and Evie's daughter died. She had been born with a heart defect. The couple had been informed by their doctor immediately after Evie had given birth that their daughter would most probably only live for a few hours. It was impossible for them to digest this news. Neither one of them wanted to believe they were going to lose the daughter they had waited so long for. Their little bundle had given them one whole day of joy but the pain which followed was unbearable. The child slipped away quietly in her mother's arms twenty-four hours after she had been born. Neither Jim nor Evie could function properly for months afterwards. Their marriage almost fell apart as Jim threw himself into his work and Evie moped about at home. Eventually, after many weeks, something snapped inside Evie and she was forced to confront the situation. The couple finally discussed their future. They had been advised by their doctor at the time of Joy's birth that the same thing could happen again with any subsequent babies and consequently they chose never to have any more children. Jim and Evie were never able to fully come to terms with their loss but the experience did eventually bring them closer together, cementing a strong and lasting relationship.

The Great Depression of 1929 broke out at a time when the United Kingdom was still far from having recovered from the effects of the First World War. Edwin had always considered himself extremely lucky, for it was only on a few occasions that the war itself or the war effort had ever had a direct effect upon his business. Now, with the Depression, he also appeared to be little affected.

Edwin was aware that some of his neighbours had been hit harder. Some were seen making regular weekly visits to the pawn shop. Wives hocking their husband's clothes or family possessions and redeeming them at the end of the week on pay day was not an unusual sight to be seen around the town.

The effects of the Depression were uneven. Like Edwin and his neighbours, some parts of the country and some industries fared better than others. Both the motor industry and the electrical goods industry fared better during this time. Although these British products were not usually sufficiently advanced to compete in world markets, they did well in Britain's domestic market. Mass production methods brought new products such as electrical cookers, washing machines and radios into the reach of the "middle classes".

It was during this time that Edwin felt financially able to treat himself to his first crystal radio set with earphones. It was a little later than planned as he had wanted one for several years. He had put it off, again and again, usually because the needs of his family came first. Crystal sets had by now been around for over twenty years, used at first to receive Morse code, for example when the *Titanic* had sunk. Later, around 1920 when electronics had evolved, the ability to send voice signals by radio had caused a technological explosion and they had become extremely popular.

Factory-made radios were very expensive and rather large. Edwin could not justify spending that amount of money and they didn't really have enough space to house one. He had always been cautious with his money and insisted Mary and the children should be like him, and he felt he must, even now with only two of his children remaining at home, set an example. A crystal radio needed no battery or power source, but ran on power received from radio waves along a wire antenna and more importantly would take up very little space, so Mary would have less to complain about.

Edwin could have made the radio himself, if he'd had the time or inclination to, but he decided to purchase one which had already been assembled for him. It wasn't expensive, even with the extra cost to have it pre-assembled. It was well worth it in Edwin's opinion. He was pleasantly surprised at the quality of sound it emitted. He was able to tune in to the weather and news and keep up with special events, finding the times for these and other music programmes in his newspaper. And it was Hilda, especially, who enjoyed listening to her father's new wireless. She would often slip upstairs into the front room and sit quietly listening to plays or quizzes or when she knew no one was around she'd dance around the room to the jazz tunes of Louis Armstrong, Al Jolson and the like.

The motor industry prospered during the early 1930s and that was great news for Teddy. At last he was able to show his father that he was successful at something. Manufacturers such as Austin, Morris and Ford dominated the motor industry and the number of cars on the roads doubled within the decade. Teddy's motor garage business had started out small, but had proved a gold mine and over the years Teddy was able to extend his business and built up a select client base which included many military officers. He would encourage his more important customers to wait and relax in his cinema while their vehicles were serviced or repaired. As he became complacent about his successful and prosperous business he would often instruct his mechanics to invent repair work on some cars, usually those belonging to his wealthier clients. When Eva realised what her husband was up to it widened and deepened the fracture that had already begun to appear in their unhappy marriage.

At around the same time, Evie and her husband Jim were expanding their garage business in Ivy Lane. Although it was orig-inally set up as a small taxi business, Jim now had a growing number of mechanics working alongside him and plans to expand even further, but to do this he would require larger premises. Recently he and Evie had been able to afford to purchase a house in East Street, where Jim's sister Doreen lived with them. Doreen also helped out at the garage and got on very well with Evie. Both women had no children and so were able to put their enthusiasm and energy into the taxi business, which they had running like clockwork in no time at all, enabling Jim to start looking for larger premises.

With the war years now over and a new era of the 1930's just beginning, the family from 37 Downing Street were thriving, within the varied roles which they had chosen for themselves. The future seemed optimistic.

Chapter 8

1932

During the October of 1932 when Mary was sixty-five years old, her health took a turn for the worse. She had for some years noticed subtle changes in her body but had never felt the desire to seek medical advice. She had just simply put these symptoms down to growing old. Mary had always kept herself busy. She enjoyed helping out in the shop as well as fitting in her household chores but she had begun to feel so tired a lot of the time. Although her children were all grown up and she did not have them to care for in the same way any more, they were still a worry to her at times. Some of them lived some distance away while others were close by. Some had children and businesses of their own and there always seemed to be something or someone for Mary to worry about. Then of course there was Edwin and his business. Edwin had been complaining just lately that things were rather slow in his shop. That evening, after listening to her husband complaining for the last half hour, Mary thought, is it any wonder I'm always worried and tired.

Recently Mary had noticed that during the day she would often feel thirsty. "Too much gossiping with my customers," had been Edwin's helpful response, on a rare occasion when she had complained. She began to drink more and this was why Mary believed she had to get up two or three times in the night to use the lav, which in turn disturbed her night's sleep and made her feel even more tired. Another symptom which Mary had just put down to her increasing number of years was the deterioration in her eyesight. Some days were worse than others. Her vision could blur without warning causing her terrible distress, rendering her unable to continue with whatever it was she was engrossed in at the time. One evening she was sewing a button back onto her favourite winter coat. The weather had taken a turn for the worse recently and Mary wanted to make sure she would be able to ensure the cold breeze which had savaged her the day before would not get another chance. "I reckon it's all because of the length of time you spent sewing by candlelight when we were first wed," Edwin replied in response to Mary complaining she couldn't see well enough to thread her needle. "No it's not Edwin, it's just my age. And I don't remember hearing you complaining when your shirt or trousers were made good as new by the next morning."

Edwin had been secretly logging his wife's various complaints for some time now and as he had also noticed that she seemed to have recently lost some weight, he began to feel rather concerned about her health. There was one occasion when Mary's vision went blurred while she was in the town, shopping. She had just popped out for a handful of groceries and had said to Edwin she would be gone only a few moments, when in reality she returned home over an hour later and Edwin had started to become a little worried about her. Fortunately, Mary had completed most of her shopping when the unpleasant attack had occurred. She had walked along The Borough into East Street where she had purchased meat for the family's supper, back down South Street into Union Street almost forgetting to take Edwin's boots into the cobblers for re-heeling, and finally stopping at Hone and Sons, the greengrocers at the bottom of Downing Street for the last few items she needed. She purchased apples, potatoes, carrots, and a nice big cabbage she was planning on steaming for supper. Inside the shop were a few customers waiting to be served and as luck would have it, as she was about to leave, her neighbour Mrs Lloyd, who owned the coffee shop next door to Edwin's fishmongers, walked in. They were briefly chatting about the empty premises up for rent opposite their shops and deliberating who would move in and what their business might be, when a sharp shooting pain in Mary's head caused her to come over all faint. She leant heavily on Mrs Lloyd's arm, dropping her groceries to the floor.

Thomas, the greengrocer's boy, fetched a chair for Mary in a flash, which later George Hone, long-time proprietor of the greengrocers commended him for. Between the boy and Mrs Lloyd, they managed to help Mary into the chair as Mr Hone rushed to finish serving a customer. "Fetch a glass of water lad, quick now," boomed his employer as he rounded the counter into the shop. Mrs Lloyd began to pick up Mary's shopping, replacing it in the basket. "You all right, Mary?" enquired Mr Hone, but before she could answer the boy had returned with the water. "Here's your water Missus," said the boy, stretching out his arm. "Thank you," responded Mary, rather weakly.

Mary's eyesight was blurred. She was struggling to find the position of the glass. Mrs Lloyd noticed her plight and guided Mary's hand to the drink. Mary took a sip while the remaining customers within the shop had come to a complete standstill, distracted from their purchases by the disturbance. It was quite rare for anything exciting to happen in the greengrocers, so all eyes were on Mary. She took another sip of the water. "How you feeling Mary?" enquired Mr Hone, concerned not only for his neighbour's plight but also for his shop's unblemished reputation. "Oh, not too bad," lied Mary. She turned to where she sensed her neighbour to be standing. "Would you mind walking me home Mrs Lloyd?"

"Oh course I will dear. Here, take my arm." And that was just what she did. Mrs Lloyd guided Mary safely back up Downing Street. Edwin and Violet were working in the shop while Hilda was upstairs going about her chores and listening to her father's radio at full pelt. Both were unaware of the events which had just taken place. Edwin was understandably worried and greatly concerned when he looked up from his fish guts to see his wife being helped through the doorway by their neighbour. Violet was terribly professional and appeared impervious, continuing to serve her customer, but inwardly she was both agitated and anxious by her mother's behaviour.

"What on earth has happened, woman?" Edwin enquired, noticing his wife's pained expression and pale complexion.

Mrs Lloyd spoke on Mary's behalf. "She came over all faint while we were in the greengrocers, didn't you dear?" she said kindly, as she helped Mary to sit down on the chair which Edwin kept near to the counter for his more elderly customers.

Violet's customer exited the shop so she quickly closed the door behind him. "You all right Mum?"

"I'm fine love, just a bit tired, that's all," replied Mary.

"I think she'll need some help to get upstairs," continued Mrs Lloyd.

"You can leave her with me now," insisted Edwin, sufficiently embarrassed. "I'll see to her." He took control, thanked Mrs Lloyd for her assistance and ushered her out of the door, closing it again behind her. Then he helped Mary upstairs. Just before disappearing upstairs he turned to Violet and said, "You can open up again Vi, once we're upstairs."

"Unbelievable," muttered Violet under her breath.

Once upstairs and after briefly explaining to Babe that her mother was tired and could she please switch off the wireless, Edwin helped his wife undress and climb into bed. He made sure she was comfortable before returning to his shop and allowing Hilda to take over any of his wife's other needs. Hilda fussed over her mother, enquiring if she needed a drink or anything to eat, could she get her a book to read or did she need to use the lav, until eventually, Mary was left alone and allowed to drop off to sleep. It wasn't long before Violet ventured upstairs to enquire after her mother's health. The two concerned sisters spoke briefly. Later when the shop had closed and their father was clearing away, they went together to speak to him about their mother. It took some convincing from them, but eventually their father agreed to call out the doctor. Edwin kept saying their mother wouldn't want it but they had insisted and he was pleased they had, for he hated to admit it but he felt the same way. He hadn't wanted to upset his wife any more than was necessary and he knew that calling out the doctor would result in this. He had been worried about Mary for some time now. Obviously he hadn't wanted to alarm his children by mentioning this, nor had he wanted to distress Mary, but when the doctor arrived at the house Edwin felt relieved that finally they were doing something about it.

When the doctor eventually gave his diagnosis, he was vague. He did say however that Mary should get as much rest as she could and advised her to do as little as possible. "No more working in your husband's shop or any heavy housework," he warned.

"But I'll go mad if I can't do anything," she complained.

"Well a little light cleaning around the house then and only if you really must. You have your daughters to help you. You really need to get plenty of rest," he insisted.

"All right doctor, you know best," conceded Mary and with that he left her side to reiterate to Edwin exactly what he had just told Mary.

"There'll be no more helping me out in the shop," Edwin told Mary that evening after he had locked up his premises for the night. Mary was not impressed with her husband's orders, feeling they all were ganging up against her, but seemingly didn't have the energy she required to argue.

All she could manage to say was, "I'm sure I'll be fine tomorrow after a decent night's sleep."

Mary never did regain her complete strength after her experience in the greengrocers. She and her family hadn't paid much attention over the last few years to her weight loss as it had been gradual and therefore hardly noticeable. As with most women, losing a bit of weight can be a bonus and if Mary had been concerned she would probably have put this symptom also down to her age. As the weeks went by, Mary's health deteriorated and by Christmas the family was very worried about her. She had now seen the doctor on a number of separate occasions and he had reluctantly prescribed various drugs, none of which seemed to have had a positive effect on her. On the last occasion, the medicine had made her so violently sick that Mary had refused to take any more.

Christmas that year was pretty miserable. Violet had disappeared on Christmas Day, at the risk of upsetting her mother, saying she was spending it with a girlfriend. It was her way of dealing with her mother's illness and the tensions which were developing between her and her father, as Edwin realised his wife's health was deteriorating. He didn't blame Violet for Mary's ill health. It was just unfortunate that it was usually Violet who was around when Edwin felt the need to vent his frustrations on someone. Her father always seemed to be getting at her for something or other these days. It seemed to Violet that she could do nothing right in his eyes. She had left it to the very last minute before letting her father and sister know that she would not be spending Christmas Day at home and neither of them had been terribly impressed when she had made her announcement.

Mary spent her Christmas Day in bed as she did most of her days now, so Hilda and Edwin were forced to make the best of each other's company. Neither of them enjoyed the day very much and to make matters worse the dinner was a complete disaster. During the day Edwin had endured his wife's various well-wishers, while Hilda had been glad of the extra company. Evie, Jim and Jim's sister had called at the house in the morning, along with Mr Hone, who had brought Mary a lovely basket of fresh fruit. Later, as Hilda prepared her special dinner, Doris and Syd arrived with their two overexcited boys. Doris could sense her sister's relief at having them visit yet at the same time picked up on her father's agitation towards her two energetic sons. Unfortunately for Hilda, Doris cut their Christmas Day visit short and after she had spent some time with her mother, made her excuses and the family left. Hilda's attempt at the dinner had been ill-fated from the start as she had made the mistake of preparing too much of everything. When the cooking was complete, the pots and pans of vegetables were soggy, with the potatoes still hard in the middle and the turkey was burnt on the outside and almost raw on the inside. She had, however, managed to save grace with a trifle for afterwards. Neither she nor her father liked the traditional Christmas pudding and so had agreed the previous day that she would make a trifle.

Edwin commented during the meal that he felt Hilda had been fussing around her sisters and their families too much that morning to take notice of what was happening in the kitchen. "Maybe if you had paid a little more attention to the dinner it might not have proven such a disaster," grumbled her father. This comment really hurt Hilda's feelings but when Edwin realised that his harsh words had upset her he restrained himself from further negative comments and tried to praise his daughter's efforts more. After all, it was her first attempt and it was usually Mary who cooked on Christmas Day. Hilda and her father left most of their main course as it had been so bad, moving on quickly to the dessert. "This is delicious Babe. You've excelled yourself with this trifle," praised her father.

"I'm glad you like it," smiled Hilda. She threw away a lot of food that day, something her mother never did, and was glad her mother was not aware of this fact. She'd hoped she would be able to tempt her mother into joining them for lunch but Mary had declined. Hilda took her a sandwich later in the day. Both she and Edwin had tried to encourage Mary to eat something but she had only nibbled at things briefly. Mary had no appetite and no energy. As Hilda sat on her mother's bed later that day, recalling the disastrous lunch, she couldn't help feeling her mother was giving up and slipping away from her. "I'm sorry the day wasn't as successful as you would have liked Babe," Mary said weakly.

"Don't worry about that," replied Hilda. "We just want you to concentrate on getting better."

"I'm trying, dear, but you must prepare yourself for the worst."

"What do you mean, Mother?" Hilda asked naively.

"I need my rest now, dear," Mary said, exhausted.

"Of course, Mother. I'll pop in later to see you." And with that she kissed her mother's forehead and left the room.

One month later, on Wednesday 25 January, Mary died in her bed at her home in Downing Street. She had been suffering terribly over the past few weeks. It had been so upsetting for Edwin and his children to witness her demise in this way. She had deteriorated significantly over the last year and suffered more so in the last month but during this last week, right in front of Edwin's eyes on a daily basis, her ailment was particularly displayed through her once beautiful skin. Now unusually dry and pallid in colour, her drained face was the most noticeable difference for Edwin. Over the last month, Mary had intermittently suffered with headaches, muscular twitching, drowsiness, temporary blindness, ringing in her ears, dizziness and sometimes even deafness. When the end had finally come for Mary, Edwin had been nursing his wife in his arms. He held her tightly on the bed where they had shared their love-making, newborn babies, disagreements, reconciliations and plenty of important discussions during the many years they had been together. Mary had been surrounded by five of her six daughters and her husband when she had died, but she hadn't really been aware they were in the room with her. When her time had come all she felt was a huge sense of release from her pain and she drifted away peacefully. When Mary had departed, although surrounded by his family, Edwin had never felt more alone in the whole of his life. He had lost the one most precious thing belonging to him and knew he could never get her back.

The doctor was called and a death certificate issued. Mary was placed in an open coffin in the downstairs back room for anyone who wished to pay their respects. Numerous people came and went from his house continuously for the next two days but Edwin could not bring himself to see or speak to anyone or to even visit Mary. His shop remained in darkness, displaying the closed sign on the door.

It was Doris's husband, Sydney, who volunteered to inform the registrar of his mother-in-law's death. Edwin could not bring himself to leave the house. On her death certificate, Mary's cause of death was recorded as "Uraemia", which is a term used to loosely describe the illness accompanying kidney failure. This disease does not show many of its symptoms until there is quite a lot of damage already done. Mary's kidneys would have been terribly inflamed and the doctor was understandably distressed as he was aware of this fact but unable to help his patient or prevent the disease from progressing so rapidly. Mary was buried two days later. The cemetery of St Andrew's had been full for some years so she was buried in Green Lane Cemetery, on the outskirts of Farnham, after a small family service was held in its chapel. Edwin and his children attended but he had requested it remain just the immediate family, which Mary's many friends and neighbours adhered to.

Edwin would never get over the death of his beloved wife. In the days and weeks that followed he longed to be transported back in time to live their dreams all over again, to start their life together again on the Isle of Wight, to enjoy their first born child, to spend Christmas at Mary's parents' house, to build their successful business together and watch her sewing all night, endless garments for the children. He longed to hear Mary's voice, even if it were to hear her moan that he hadn't done something she'd asked him to do, or that she was worried about one of the children. He missed her smells, the perfume she always wore, the smell of her baking drifting downstairs and into his shop and that clean smell just after she'd had a bath, as she climbed in bed next to him. He missed the little signs that she was around: her underwear drip-drying in the bathroom, her hairbrush on the dressing table or purse left out on the mantle after a trip into the town.

He had no idea how he was going to cope without her. The pain he felt at times in his chest was unbearable and could only be the feeling one has when one's heart has been broken. He always knew his feelings for Mary were special. He had tried over the years to show her how strongly he felt for her and believed in his heart that Mary knew how much he really loved her.

Nothing could have prepared him for how he would feel when she was no longer around. He felt depressed, desolate and despondent. He had no future if it were to be without Mary. Had she not realised that it was he who was supposed to go first and not her? Did she not recognise that it was she who had held the family together like glue all these years? God only knows what will become of us all now, thought Edwin.

And so it transpired that over the next few years there were to be many transformations which would take place at number 37 Downing Street. In life itself, very little stays the same for very long. The young of today are never satisfied and always wanting something more, was Edwin's thought, but in truth didn't this happen with every generation? Didn't Edwin himself want exactly that and strived until he'd achieved it? The next generation will always want something additional to the last and so it perpetuates on and on. Progress and change go hand in hand, for without progress there would be no change and without change, there would be no progress.

The first change became apparent within a few months of Mary's death. Edwin was soon to discover his daughter Violet had been secretly squirrelling money away and had managed to save herself a tidy sum. In her head Violet knew exactly what she wanted to do with her money. She had bided her time but the death of her mother had given her the push she needed. Now was the right time to fulfil her dream.

The problem was that Violet couldn't see herself living with and caring for her elderly father for the rest of his days. In fact, that thought alone sent chills right through her. It wasn't working in the fish shop for the rest of her life that frightened her. She had always rather enjoyed that. It was her father with whom she had found it difficult to live all these years. Maybe they were just too alike. She recognised they both had very strong opinions and both refused to budge on anything they felt passionate about, so consequently they were always disagreeing with one other.

Since the death of her mother their incompatibility had heightened. Her mother had always played the go-between and peacemaker between her father and many of her siblings at various times throughout her life. Recently it seemed that Violet and Edwin's frequent disputes were never resolved. They were allowed to build up almost to the point of eruption. It was poor Hilda who repeatedly felt like piggy in the middle of their many disagreements.

Violet had chosen not to disclose her plans to anyone until everything was in place. She had dealt with the bank manager and property agent all by herself and managed to find a property close enough so that she had been able to nip out and meet with fitters and suppliers without her father becoming suspicious. She put off notifying Edwin of her plans until everything had been finalised as she suspected he would not react positively to her news. When she finally plucked up enough courage to approach him, he allowed her to explain her situation without criticism or interruption. He managed to surprise her with his response. The only detail that seemed to concern him was whether or not she would be in direct competition with him, so when Violet explained she would be selling cooked fish and chips, her father breathed a sigh of relief. He then asked where she was hoping to source her fish supply. Both astonished and relieved not to receive his disapproval, she boldly answered, "Well, I was hoping that's where you'd come in."

"I'd be delighted," was his response.

After some further discussion, Violet was finally congratulated by her father for having so much determination to carry out her dream. Edwin was surprised to discover he actually admired his daughter for her resolve and for her astute investment of her earnings. It wasn't until much later after their conversation that Edwin had realised how alike he and Violet were. How could he have missed it all these years? And it wasn't until then that he wondered if he would have been better off sharing all of his expertise and wisdom over the years with Violet, rather than trying to coax Teddy into the family business. But there was no point in dwelling on that now. What was done was done.

At the end of 1933, Violet left the family home where she had lived for the last thirty two years and set up the "Sea Lion" fish and chip shop at 34 Downing Street. She lived above her business in very comfortable accommodation and thoroughly enjoyed her new-found independence. By the spring of 1934 her business was thriving.

It soon became apparent that it was Hilda and not her father who had been hit the hardest when Violet had left. Coupled with the loss of her mother the year before, Hilda found she was looking more deeply at her own life achievements. She quickly realised she had no job prospects, apart from the work she did in her father's shop, no spare money and more importantly no man interested in her. In fact, she couldn't even remember the last time she had been out anywhere she might have had the opportunity to meet one. All her time now was spent with her father, working in his shop, cooking, cleaning and caring for him. She had been forced to take on this role without any consultation. It had been expected of her and for the first time in her life, Hilda realised her future looked pretty bleak.

Hilda began to lose interest in just about everything. She had always had such a positive look out on life and was usually very happy. Now she hardly ever left the house. When she did it was only to shop for herself and her father, spending the rest of her time working in the fish shop or reading quietly in her bedroom. During the last five months she had begun to feel very isolated. Edwin too was suffering inwardly with his own depression. He was still trying to come to terms with his wife's death and therefore too distressed to notice his daughter's plight.

It was Violet who first noticed the change in her sister and became concerned. Violet's business had been a success from the start and she was now able to employ enough reliable staff to run things in her absence, enabling her to leave the premises whenever she wished. She hadn't seen her sister properly for weeks and decided to call in on her. It was early evening. Edwin was working in his shop, so Violet slipped in through the back and upstairs expecting to find Hilda in the kitchen. Instead, she found the rooms upstairs empty and terribly neglected. Mother will be turning in her grave, she thought. The front room was untidy with newspapers left scattered on the floor and dirty cups and plates on the table. The fire grates had not been cleared, curtains left closed, beds unmade and day-old pots left soaking in cold stinking water in the kitchen sink.

Violet found Hilda sitting alone in her bedroom, reading a book. Hilda looked up and seemed pleased to see her sister. After an exchange of pleasantries, including Hilda enquiring after how the Sea Lion was doing, Violet piped up, "I know what you need. A night out with the girls," she suggested cheerfully.

"Oh I don't think so," replied Hilda.

"Come on Babe, it'll do you the world of good," continued Violet. "Some of us are off to the dance on Saturday. Why don't you come with us?"

"No, it's not for me."

"Well, do it for me then," insisted Violet. "I promise you'll enjoy it."

"I'll think about it."

"I tell you what," she persevered. "Let's go and get our hair done at Lionel's. Let's treat ourselves," she giggled.

"But I don't have any money."

"No matter, it'll be my treat."

"But I thought you liked to do your own hair." This was true. Violet had never liked anyone messing with her hair. Even as a child, when her mother had attempted to brush it Violet had wriggled profusely and it had taken a long time for her to allow Lionel Smith, the family's hairdresser, to even touch it. Many times the family had left his salon embarrassed by Violet's behaviour but Lionel had refused to give up and eventually managed to win her round with a little bribery and distraction.

"Well, if I promise to get my hair done, will you promise to come to the dance?" asked Violet. Hilda thought for a moment. "Please Babe," pleaded Violet.

"Oh all right then, if you insist," replied Hilda, accepting defeat and smiling.

The family had always gone to Lionel H. Smith's to have their hair cut. Edwin had been the first to make Mr Smith's acquaintance and over the years they had become very good friends. Later when Lionel had adapted his salon, Edwin had introduced his wife and children to the delights of the salon and over the years Lionel had become more like a son to Edwin.

Lionel was the kind of son Edwin would have liked Teddy to have been. He was the same age as Teddy, hardworking, honest, caring and reliable and an excellent friend, as well as a good hairdresser. Lionel, in return, saw Edwin as a father figure. His own father had never really supported him in his chosen career. He had wanted Lionel to follow into his own trade as a grocer and had never been able to see what the attraction was with hairdressing. Edwin had become a good friend over the years and helped Lionel when at times he had struggled with his business accounts. Edwin had shown him where he could make cutbacks to save money and also improve his service. Lionel had always listened to Edwin and usually taken his advice.

During the spring of 1934 a new hair salon appeared just across the road from Lionel's. It seemed to pop up overnight and turned poor Lionel's world upside down. He was well aware there were other salons in Farnham and the surrounding areas but it was a little off-putting when a larger and more modern one opened up opposite and was so obviously in direct competition with his. Edwin had noticed it as well. The next time he called in for a shave and cut, Edwin asked if Lionel had been to have a look yet.

"No. Why, do you think I should?" replied Lionel.

"Have I not taught you anything boy? If it had been a fish shop opening opposite to me, I'd be round there like a shot. You've got to suss out the competition lad. You don't want to be losing your customers."

Lionel looked worried as he stared out of his shop window. "I think I already have."

"What makes you say that?"

"Well, I know of at least two regulars who have been over there this week and cancelled their appointments here. I saw them both coming out, bold as brass."

"Don't fret about it lad. Do something about it."

"How? What would you have me do?"

"There's plenty you could do. Special offers are always a good way to get customers back, or give away a product with every haircut. People will soon get fed up with going over there. At the moment it's just a novelty to them."

"Do you think so?"

"You've been here a lot longer. People know you and what you can do. They trust you and know you're reliable. If they do wander, I'm sure they'll come back with their tails between their legs. It's just curiosity. It won't last."

Lionel looked a little happier. "Thanks for the advice, Edwin."

"That's what friends are for," smiled Edwin. "Now, where's my free cigar?" And both men laughed.

Edwin had gone home that night and mulled over his conversation with Lionel. He was glad to have something new to occupy his mind instead of sitting and moping about Mary all the night. I must have a word with the girls and make sure none of them are tempted to stray into that new salon, he thought. They're very fond of Daddy Smith so I'm certain they wouldn't. He smiled to himself as he fondly remembered that when his girls were younger they had given Lionel this pet name. The phrase "Daddy Smith" had always made Edwin laugh. He'd almost forgotten that Hilda, to this day, still used it.

The weather recently had been drier than normal, not much rain at all but this hadn't stopped the landscape and streets around Farnham looking fresh, luscious and green. There seemed to be a spring in the step of most people and on the whole, the townsfolk of Farnham were pretty content with their lot considering the state of the economy after the crash of 1929.

Farnham town council along with other councils did their best to cheer up their people by holding band concerts and dances at various times during the year. These were primarily for the young and it was to one of these dances that Violet had convinced her baby sister to go along to that Saturday night. If the truth be known, Violet was not at all interested in attending the dance and had been persuaded by her friend Nancy, but she had realised it would be the perfect opportunity to allow Hilda to escape the confines of their father's home. Her friend Nancy worried about being left on the shelf. She had convinced herself that if she didn't find a decent man at the dance, then she would end up a spinster for the rest of her life. Although having Violet's baby sister tag along might vastly reduce her chances of finding that special man, Nancy knew she couldn't say no to her friend and went along with Violet's wishes. It didn't matter to Violet that she didn't have a man to walk out with. She found men rather dull. She much preferred the company of women. She had decided a long time ago that she would never marry – it just wasn't her thing.

Violet and Hilda were off to the hairdressers in preparation for the evening's dance, a treat that would be paid for by their father. Violet had at first declined his generous offer and said she preferred to pay for herself but their father had an ulterior motive. When he had discovered they were planning a trip to Lionel's, he asked his daughters if they would visit the new salon across the street instead. Edwin was aware Lionel's salon was suffering due to the new one opening and believed he had come up with a tactic to help his friend.

"But why do you want us to go there? We like Daddy Smith's place. We've always gone to Daddy Smith," complained Hilda. Edwin smiled at that phrase again.

"You'd be doing it for Lionel," answered their father.

"And how will that help him?" asked Violet.

"Because you will be able to report back to me about the sort of things they do in there. I want to know about the facilities they have and the kind of service they offer and of course, their prices. Then I can let Lionel know. He's losing an awful lot of his clients to this new salon."

"We hadn't realised, had we Vi? Of course we'll help," agreed Hilda, concerned for her "Daddy Smith".

"Good girls. I knew I could rely on you. Just remember to get exactly what you want done to your hair and don't leave until you're completely happy."

"We won't," Violet and Hilda replied in unison, hardly believing their father was agreeing to pay for them to have their hair done at the newest, most trendy salon in the town.

Edwin's daughters left for their appointment with some trepidation. Hilda was feeling quite nervous and very guilty about using the new salon. It felt quite strange crossing over at the bottom of Castle Street. As they approached the modern salon's shop window, an array of merchandise displayed for sale and advertisements for hair and beauty products met their eyes. Hilda was struck by the well-dressed window. It was not too overcrowded; certain products caught her eye and for a second she was distracted by them, until Violet yanked her by her arm. The shop belonged to a Mr Lawrence, who had moved into the Town Hall buildings situated on the Borough after his last business premises in Kingston upon Thames had been sold. He had been unable to afford to buy that building and been forced to search for new premises. He had worked in Kingston with his loyal employee, George, and when he had found new premises for rent in Farnham he'd asked George if he would like to continue to work for him there. George had accepted. He had no family ties in Kingston and only rented a room, so leaving one place for another made no difference to him. He was a hard worker, putting in long hours, sometimes without extra pay, and Mr Lawrence had appreciated his commitment.

Violet pushed open the door to the salon and Hilda followed, nervously. The salon had a bell that dangled from the door frame and jingled when knocked as the door was opened to attract attention to the customer entering. Stuart Lawrence's right-hand man George looked up and smiled as Violet and Hilda walked in.

The salon inside was very modern. The girls entered into a space which was the reception area, with desk, telephone and comfortable-looking seats. It incorporated streamlined display units and a glamorous-looking mannequin. Leading from this area was the main ladies' salon, where they could see George working inside one of the cubicles, and further behind that was another area, presumably for men. Everywhere they looked, surfaces were shiny and clean and the salon appeared to be organised and smoothly run. Between the cubicles was a frosted glass partition, creating a light and airy feel to an efficient and hygienic space.

"It's very different from Daddy Smith's," whispered Hilda to Violet.

They sat down on the big comfortable sofa positioned in the

waiting area. It made them feel very relaxed, as though they were at home in their own sitting room. Then a young woman came over to them from her desk and, whispering quietly, asked them if they had booked in advance. "Sorry love, we didn't know we had to," spoke up Violet.

"That's not a problem," replied the girl, smiling politely. "I'm sure we can still accommodate you." Violet raised her eyebrows at Hilda. The girl returned to her desk as the telephone rang loudly. She began a conversation with the person on the line and started to write something down in her book, presumably an appointment but Hilda couldn't quite catch the conversation as she was speaking so quietly.

On the walls of the salon there was wallpaper, which looked as though it was washable, and, every so often, panels of Formica. Strips of gleaming metal were inlaid at intervals and concealed lighting backlit mirrors to provide a wash of light that appeared like magic to light up the work space.

The owner, Mr Lawrence, was with another gentleman in a separate room beyond the main salon, which Violet and Hilda could partially see into through a glass panel in the wall. There was a woman sitting under some sort of hair-drying machine that looked like a metal jellyfish on a stand and the place just seemed a hive of activity.

The two sisters watched George as he went about his work. He was very handsome, clean-shaven and immaculately dressed. He wore a crisp, clean white coat over the top of a suit. Hilda admired his glossy, well-groomed, dark brown hair and was struck by his masculine beauty. His shoes were exceptionally shiny. He suited his surroundings as they both were immaculately clean and very modern.

George was standing behind a middle-aged woman sitting in a salon chair and he had just completed her hair. He held up a hand mirror for her to admire his excellent work. Neither Hilda nor Violet recognised her as one of Lionel's regulars.

"Thank you George, that's wonderful," said the woman. George smiled as he pulled out her chair to allow her to stand.

"That's a pleasure Mrs Trodd. Please call again soon."

"I will. I will indeed," she replied.

"Miss Stevens will be happy to sort out your bill," he said pointing in the direction of where the quietly spoken young woman was seated behind her desk. Mrs Trodd paid while George swept the floor quickly and effortlessly. On her way out Mrs Trodd went back over to George and pressed a coin into his hand. "Thank you again, George," said Mrs Trodd. Before returning home to her husband she turned and admired her hair in the large wall mirror one last time. George then turned his attentions to Violet and Hilda. "Now, what can I do for you two young ladies?" he grinned. Perfect teeth as well, thought Hilda. Her observational skills were excelling themselves today. Unfortunately her feet appeared to be glued to the floor and her bottom to the chair, and she had suddenly found that she had been struck dumb. Inside, her stomach was doing somersaults. She felt herself go all hot and knew she must be blushing.

Why do I feel like this, she wondered? I wonder if it's because I haven't been in this salon before. But she knew it was more likely to have more to do with this attractive man who was speaking to her. All Hilda could manage to do was stare at George while Violet took the lead and started to explain what the two sisters wanted doing with their hair, ready for the dance that night. "Off to the dance are you? Well, we'll have to get you both looking your best then, won't we?"

In the few seconds it had taken Violet to explain, Hilda was completely smitten by this man she had never met before and didn't know. George however, wasn't a stranger to this type of reaction and took it all in his stride. From his late teens George had become more and more aware of his good looks. He had endured many admirers, the first of whom had been when he was just seventeen years old. The girl in question, who was only sixteen years old herself at the time, had become completely obsessed with George.

Elsie and George had grown up together and lived in the same street. They had attended the same school and Elsie had been infatuated with George from a very early age. She would follow him around the playground like a lovesick puppy but, unfortunately for Elsie, George hadn't noticed her at all back then. He had been too engrossed in playing marbles or tag with his friends and hadn't bothered with girls. Girls were boring to George when he was young and he only really began to take an interest in them after he had left school. He would often see Elsie at the local corner shop where she worked part time. He'd call in for cigarettes on his way home after work or he'd bump into her as he was leaving his house in the morning. At the time George thought nothing of Elsie. She was just a friend and he was always polite and kind to her.

Secretly he felt sorry for the girl. He thought she must be very lonely. She was the eldest of six children and her father had left the family home when Elsie was just ten years old. Nobody had known where he had gone but one day he had just never returned. George's father had joked that Elsie's mother had probably done away with her husband because she was built more like a bloke than he was and was probably stronger than him too. George's father could recall her dragging her husband out from the pub, in front of all his mates, on more than one occasion. Sadly, Elsie's mother wasn't very well liked in the community. She had a deafening voice and a sharp tongue and wasn't afraid to use them both. George had always been pretty frightened of her when he was younger.

So when George was seventeen and had finally begun to take notice of girls, he was flattered yet nervous when he realised Elsie was interested in him. At first he played along with it. His feelings for her were not the same, but he didn't want to upset her. He didn't want to lead her up the garden path but found it hard to disappoint her and so felt bound to spend time with her. After a few months things became more serious as Elsie wanted to take the relationship further but George didn't and was forced to put an end to their friendship. After a few days he started to receive letters and small gifts through the post. Sometimes they were hand delivered but when he answered the door no one was there. On occasions he felt as though he was being watched and sometimes followed. Once he caught Elsie following him home and confronted her about it. She made up some excuse about how she just happened to be walking the same way and suggested they walk together. George wasn't one for a scene and so he'd agreed. As they reached their destination she shocked him by kissing him forcefully on the lips. George was cross with her and told her to never do it again. Elsie marched off and that was the last he saw or heard of her for a while.

About two months later he started to sense that some of his neighbours were looking at him strangely and some seemed to be whispering about him behind his back. It came to a head one day when his father arrived home from work and demanded to see him. George came down from his room and walked into the kitchen where his mother and father were sitting at the table. As soon as George's father caught sight of his son, he launched into his attack. "Do you have anything you wish to tell us boy?" he boomed.

"No Father," replied George, a little stunned by his father's behaviour.

"Are you sure?"

"Yes, why? What's happened?" enquired George.

"Apparently Elsie is having a baby and apparently the baby is yours."

Shocked by this news, George was at first lost for words but as he could see his father's anger building, he knew he must speak quickly. He told his parents all about his and Elsie's friendship, if you could call it that, and how he had ended it and how she had started to behave strangely towards him. He promised them that he had never done anything to dishonour her or his family. George's father took some convincing but eventually believed his son was telling him the truth.

George was instructed to leave it with his father, who would sort it out. It eventually transpired that Elsie had slept with another boy from the town in an attempt to get back at George for rejecting her. But when she had discovered her pregnancy, she had stupidly believed it might help her to win him back and ultimately end in marriage to George. But things did not go according to her plan and she eventually confessed all.

George moved away shortly after the incident and started training as a hairdresser. He'd heard via his mother that Elsie's mother was helping to bring up the poor mite that Elsie had given birth to. He was glad the child had nothing to do with him. The whole experience had scared and frightened George. Ever since then he had kept his distance and not become emotionally involved with any woman. He made sure his relationships were purely professional and had a rule never to get involved with his clients. This had not been easy because of his good looks and charming personality. He had been made plenty of offers over the years but George had remained modest, trustworthy and genuine throughout.

When George and Violet's discussion had reached its conclusion, George showed each sister to their own salon chair within individual cubicles. Mr Lawrence, who had finished with his gentleman, came out from the back room, thanked his client and left him in the capable hands of Miss Stevens. "Is this lovely lady my next client, George?" asked Mr Lawrence, smiling at Violet.

"She certainly is. She'd like her hair cutting a little shorter and some waves putting in," said George.

"Righto my dear. Let's make a start then," said Mr Lawrence as he held out a gown to cover Violet's shoulders.

George grabbed one for Hilda and wafted the small piece of pink material in front of her, tying it gently under her chin. "Now, what would you like me to do for you?" asked George.

Hilda just wanted the floor to open up and swallow her but as she knew that was unlikely to happen, she would just have to bring herself to speak to this god-like, handsome creature. "I'd like some waves, please," she whispered nervously, "and a little taking off."

"Like your friend?" asked George.

"She's not my friend, she's my sister," replied Hilda nervously. "Well she is my friend, but ..."

"I think I understand," said George, trying to relax Hilda. "You'd like it the same as your sister's."

"Yes please," replied Hilda, relieved he understood. What is the matter with me? she thought.

George could tell just from looking at the shape of Hilda's face what would suit her best and what style would accentuate her beauty. "May I suggest some finger waving? I'm sure it will complement your features and really suit you." Hilda nodded with approval. The smile upon her face told George she knew she was in capable hands, so he set about his task.

During her time in the salon, George was surprised by the thoughts and feelings that this woman was stirring up inside him. He suddenly became conscious of how very nervous he felt in her presence. He had been doing this for many years, skilfully and confidently and couldn't understand why he felt so anxious. He unexpectedly became very aware of his every move, thought and action, and couldn't understand why this particular woman was having such an effect on him. George had learnt his lesson early on in his life, to never get involved with the wrong woman. Mr Lawrence had also drummed into him about upholding a strict professional conduct and George had always adhered to this rule. But there was just something about this woman which tempted him.

While waiting for George to gather the equipment he needed to perform his finger wave, Hilda recalled how one day her sister Violet had offered to cut her hair for her. When Hilda had been in her early twenties, it had been fashionable to wear your hair very short, and the Bob cut was all the rage. Things had gone wrong and Hilda had ended up with an Eton crop, losing a little more of her hair than she had anticipated. Her parents were horrified, as were plenty of her father's customers when she served them in the shop later that day. The following day Lionel had tried to put right the horrendous hairstyle her sister had inflicted upon her but unfortunately had made little progress as he had so little hair to work with. Hilda had been so distraught about her look that she had worn a hat almost consistently for three months until her hair had reached a more acceptable length. Hilda was now wondering if, when George had finished with her, she and her father would feel the same about her hair today as they had back then. She wanted it cut but not so drastically. Somehow she instinctively suspected she was in good hands.

"Would you like it parting in the centre or at the side?" enquired George.

"At the side please, where it is now," replied Hilda.

First George dampened Hilda's hair with water, combed it out straight and cut it to the required length. Next he sponged it with the curling lotion. He began the first wave about an inch from her scalp, pressing down her hair with his left hand, drawing it up with a comb towards her brow, making a sharp edge. He pressed the comb upwards, grazing her scalp, making sure he included every single hair in the first wave. Hilda was almost driven to the edge of ecstasy by the movements of his fingers through her hair. He didn't release the comb until the ridge was held firmly in place between his first and second fingers of his left hand and then he drew it through her hair to the ends.

For the second wave he used the comb and drew it sharply away from her brow, while the first wave was held firmly in place. He continued this process again and again, waving around her head. When George reached Hilda's ears he curled the ends in front into a flat ringlet and as the hair over her ear was curled, he explained that when he had dried it he would comb it over her ears to cover them.

Next he placed a net over her head and sat her under a dryer until her hair was thoroughly dry. He gave her a few magazines to look at while he started work on his next customer. Hilda glanced briefly at *Cosmopolitan* magazine but couldn't resist having a closer look around her cubicle. After all, they were there to check out the competition for Daddy Smith. The cubicle contained built-in cupboards which held different products and equipment and a hidden hatch for waste disposal.

George returned to her every few minutes while her hair was drying to check her curls and press them in more deeply. She felt as though he was really looking after her and couldn't help wondering if he was giving her special treatment or whether all his clients were treated in this way.

Meanwhile Violet was feeling pretty relaxed. Mr Lawrence had made curls in her shoulder-length hair by tightly winding strands of her wet hair around his index finger in an overlapping curl, then smoothly brushing it with a stiff brush, followed by securely pinning it to her scalp with wire hairpins. He had parted it in the middle and divided it into squares, but Hilda could only see Violet's silhouette through the frosted glass and couldn't help wondering if Violet's curls looked as beautifully sculptured as hers did. I hope she likes it, she thought.

Violet, too, was now at the next stage where her hair was being dried under a dryer which was gently blowing out artificial heat. She had almost drifted off to sleep, left alone with her thoughts and the warming air around her face. Mr Lawrence was seeing to another gentleman in the back room who was having a haircut and shave, and who had brought in his son to have his hair cut also. By the time the two men had finished with their other customers,

Violet's and Hilda's hair had dried and they were ready for the next part of the process. The precision timing within the salon was a credit to the men.

Mr Lawrence started to remove the pins from Violet's hair. There were many of them. When they were all removed he began to comb out her curls, and then formed them into waves using his fingers and a comb. George combed Hilda's hair back from her face and then pushed her hair upwards into waves using a comb and his magical fingers.

George and Hilda, after the initial few minutes, had found it fairly easy to talk to one another. The pair both appeared very relaxed in each other's company. Hilda had almost forgotten she was there to discover information that might help Lionel and his business until George had left her alone under the dryer and she was able to take a good look around. Violet on the other hand, when she wasn't dropping off under the dryer, was making plenty of mental notes that she thought might be of use to her father and Lionel.

Both Mr Lawrence and George finished their clients' hair within seconds of each other. They held up mirrors for their ladies to admire their new look, back and front while new clients waited for their turn in the waiting area. "I hope you like it?" asked George.

"I love it," replied Hilda.

"I'm pleased. I think it really suits you," smiled George.

"Thank you."

"I'll look forward to seeing you again soon," said George, but he didn't quite know why he had said that. The words just escaped from his mouth before he could stop them and until that moment he had no intention of attending the dance that evening. He relaxed as he realised Hilda thought he meant seeing her again at the salon.

"I'll look forward to that too," replied Hilda, blushing again. She was overjoyed with her new look. It was everything she had wanted and more. She felt a million dollars and hoped her sister did too. She paid Miss Stevens her father's money and met Violet outside where she had been waiting some five minutes.

"What took you so long?" Violet was not so happy. "Your hair looks gorgeous," she said. "What do you think of mine?"

"Turn around then, let me get a proper look," said Hilda.

Violet turned quickly. "Well?"

"It's not bad, but I can see why you're not so happy."

"I look more like Shirley bloody Temple," Violet hissed.

Hilda laughed. "No you don't, it's not that bad. Come on, let's go home and show father."

Edwin had been waiting for his daughters to return and was in his shop when they arrived. Violet entered first, closely followed by Hilda who was daydreaming and almost walked into Violet as she stopped to speak to their father. "Well, what was it like?" he asked, eager to know all the details.

"Not a patch on Lionel's," replied Violet.

"It was wonderful," replied Hilda dreamily.

"It was too posh," continued Violet.

"No it wasn't," argued Hilda. "It was perfect."

Her father raised his eyebrows and Hilda realised that she was close to upsetting him and insulting Daddy Smith, so she quickly followed this up with, "Well, it wasn't too bad."

"Vi, what was it really like?" Edwin asked again, almost exasperated with his daughters' differing opinions. "Well, it was very comfortable and they made us feel very welcome. Everything was extremely modern, clean and tidy. It was a bit like walking into a posh hotel like the Bush, but newer. Everything was properly displayed and you could tell that careful attention had been paid to the arrangement of furniture and goods within the salon. They somehow managed to make us feel as though we were getting a better service there. Don't you think so Babe?" Hilda nodded approvingly.

"So you were happy with everything then?" asked Edwin.

"Yes," replied Hilda.

"No," replied Violet. "I'm not happy with my hair."

"Why, what's wrong with it?" asked her father.

"It's not how I wanted it."

"Well, did you tell them that? Did you tell them you weren't happy with it?"

"Not exactly," replied Violet quietly. "I …"

"Why ever not?" demanded Edwin.

"I don't know. I suppose I just wanted to get out of there as soon as possible."

"Well, I bet that's what those scoundrels rely upon," replied her father. He had begun to raise his voice and this was just the ammunition he needed.

"They were very nice people and only wanted to do a good job," Hilda added in their defence. "I'm very happy with mine. Violet is just far too fussy."

"No I'm not," Violet retaliated.

"Anyway, you two, how much change do I get?" enquired Edwin. Violet and Hilda handed over the few coins of change they had left. "Is that it? Blimey. Well, you won't be able to afford to go there again, even if you wanted to. I think I have plenty to tell Lionel." And with that, their father returned to his work in the shop.

Chapter 9

1934

The final preparations for the evening's dance began around seven o'clock. The girls all met at Violet's place and started to get ready together. Violet's friend Nancy was taking longer than anyone to get ready. She was feeling left out as she had not been able to afford the hairdressers and now was desperately trying to improve her hairstyle. "How much longer are you going to be?" enquired Violet, one hour after they had begun to get ready. Violet was in no hurry to get there but she was rather bored with sitting and watching her friend fuss and preen herself so much.

Nancy felt disappointed to have been left out. Working part-time at the greengrocers on East Street she struggled to save any money, mainly because she had an uncontrollable passion for shoes and couldn't pass any shoe shop without going in and adding to her ever-increasing collection. Violet often made fun of her friend because of her shoe fetish. "Reckless spending is supposed to be a thing of the past. Didn't anybody tell you about the Wall Street Crash?" Violet jested with her friend. "There is a depression on you know."

It was unplanned but Hilda and Nancy had both unwittingly chosen to wear similar dresses, patterned, but in different colours. The dresses, although quite long and almost touching their ankles, accentuated their feminine qualities. With a low neckline they sensuously moulded their torsos beneath squared shoulders and three-quarter length sleeves, gathering in at the waist and minimising their hips. Then a moderately full skirt dropped almost to the floor. Hilda's dress was a little plainer and royal blue.

She had purchased hers especially for the dance from a shop called "Sisters" on Downing Street, mostly because she had liked the name. Her shoes were brown and rounded at the toes with a moderate heel. She wore her best Sunday coat over the top of her outfit and carried a matching royal blue beaded bag.

Nancy had bought her dress from Vivienne Frocks situated in the Lion and Lamb yard. The bodice of Nancy's dress incorporated inset pieces and the neckline had a wide scallopededge. At the back was a low V-shaped opening leading down to a bow. Nancy's dress was a deep red with coordinated shoes with ankle straps. She was also wearing a fur cape her mother had bought for her last birthday and carrying an enamelled mesh handbag. Both girls were very pleased with the way they looked when Nancy had finally accepted there was nothing more she could do to improve on her hairstyle.

Violet was less bothered about her look. If she could have, she would have chosen to wear her comfortable trousers. Violet wore trousers all day at work and felt quite uncomfortable in a dress or skirt. Tonight, however, she was making an effort for her sister and her friend. She had decided to wear her grey two-piece. The skirt went straight to the floor, designed in a V-shape, extending from her hips and meeting in the centre at the floor. It was full and pleated. Her jacket was long and rested below her hips. She wore a white shirt underneath. Her slip-on style flat shoes were black and she didn't need a handbag. She carried her money in a little purse which she kept in her jacket pocket. Violet, unlike her companions, hadn't been out especially to buy a new outfit. She had owned her suit for some years now but was determined to get full wear out of it and her money's worth.

Hilda felt a million dollars as she entered the Memorial Hall on West Street where the dance was being held that night. She had been to dances here before and remembered how overcome she had felt the first time she had entered the hall. It was a fairly strange looking building from the outside. She thought it looked as though they had built a rectangular hall with a pointed roof and then someone had decided it wasn't large enough, so extra little bits had been added to both sides. From the outside and parts of the inside it reminded her of a church.

The building inside appeared new and pristine and incorporated a symmetrical design. The walls were painted white and the floor was wooden. The extra bits to the sides had low ceilings which were held up on the inside by strong looking, square white pillars which lined the edge of a dance floor. This central area, left clear for dancing, displayed a high beamed ceiling where little curtained windows had been added. Spotlights were positioned to highlight the dancers and single pendant lighting ran along the middle length of the dance floor.

Scattered around the edges of the hall and just in front of the stage with its heavy swagged curtains were white painted wicker or wooden chairs positioned around metal and wooden tables. This stage area where the band played was directly opposite the entrance, with steps giving access to it and two large displays of fresh flowers on either side.

Safety was paramount when dealing with the general public so, to the left were steps giving access to the under-stage area and positioned at each side of the stage a pair of curtains covered two doors which might at any time allow access to an emergency exit. There were also cone shaped fire extinguishers which adorned the four corners of the main hall.

One entered the hall through a door whose upper panel had been glazed. Over this main entrance a clock hung and above that was a balcony area where more freshly cut flower displays had been attached to the balustrades. Off to the right was the bar and to the left was a more secluded area. This area contained comfortable seating and a large mirror. Four light pendants hung from the ceiling, creating a completely different atmosphere from the main area. It was a section where, if one wished, one could gain more privacy.

The three young women found themselves a table halfway down the hall and it wasn't long before some of their other friends joined them. Violet offered to go to the bar and get the three of them a drink. In fact, Violet assumed that role for the majority of the evening, making sure that Hilda and Nancy paid their share. Both sisters had friends who commented upon their hair that evening and once again, Nancy felt quite left out. Their friends wanted to know where they had had their hair done and Hilda found herself stretching the truth a little, to protect her Daddy Smith. "Well, we've always gone to Lionel Smith's on West Street," she found herself saying. "Well it looks fabulous," commented one of her friends. "I will definitely have to try there next time." Hilda found she allowed her friends to wander off again before she had time to explain.

The place was buzzing with people determined to have a good time. Although Violet, Nancy and Hilda felt that the vast majority of the women who were there that night were at least five years younger than they were, they didn't let it put them off having a good time. It was one of those rare occasions when they could really let their hair down and forget about their everyday mundane lives.

A live band began to play and Hilda commented to her sister about how good she thought they were. They played all sorts of tunes throughout the evening, some that Hilda had heard before and others she had not. The band had opened the evening with a few tunes from Tiger Ray which were quite fast to dance to but which had produced the desired effect and drawn many people up onto the dance floor. Hilda and Violet had found it much more entertaining at first to sit and watch, than to join in. The band had then moved onto ballroom dances and guests enjoyed a foxtrot, waltz and quickstep.

By the middle of the evening, Hilda was feeling rather disappointed. She had not been asked to dance once and was feeling quite neglected. She had rather secretly hoped there might have been a chance for her to make a new acquaintance during the evening. Violet recognised her sister's descending mood and asked her if she would like to dance. A smile appeared on Hilda's face and Violet knew she'd asked the right thing. "You never ask me to dance," moaned Nancy across the table.

"Oh what it is to be in such demand," laughed Violet. "I'll dance with you next," she said, winking at her friend.

Violet and Hilda started to dance a quickstep together and it wasn't long before they noticed Nancy had got up and was dancing with a rather older, rounded-looking gentleman. "Poor old Nan," Violet whispered to Hilda and the pair giggled together which then caused them to lose their rhythm for a moment. The music changed and the dance turned into a Waltz. Violet was finding dancing increasingly difficult because of her outfit. Her skirt was really annoying her and kept getting in the way, almost to the point of tripping her up. She kept flicking her leg out to the side to allow her feet to move more freely and in doing so, kicked Hilda in the shins, twice. "Do you have to keep doing that?" Hilda complained.

"Sorry," replied Violet. "It's this damned skirt."

Much to Violet's relief the tempo of the music changed again and the band began to play some jazz. Violet and Hilda took this opportunity to sit back down at their table. They both reached for their drinks and took a long gulp. It was a good job Hilda had swallowed hers or she might have spat it out, for as she glanced up she noticed the good-looking gentleman from the hairdressers entering the hall through the main door. Her hand began to tremble as she replaced her glass down on to the table. "What's he doing here?" Hilda whispered to her sister, tilting her head in George's direction. Violet looked over to where George was standing. Hilda couldn't resist and had to take another look. The hairdresser looked even more handsome tonight than he had when she had met him earlier that day. "Oh no, he's looking this way," she muttered to Violet. "Please don't come over, please don't come over." Hilda was muttering so loudly under her breath that Violet dug her in the ribs.

It was too late, George had spotted them. "Oh no, he's coming over," she whispered again. George was heading straight for their table. I just want to die, thought Hilda. Please God, make me invisible. Please! ... But of course he didn't.

"Hello again ladies," George said smiling, confidently. "You're both looking very glamorous tonight." Violet managed half a smile, turned, and started talking to Nancy. "Who's that?" Nancy asked Violet with interest.

"No one special," replied Violet.

"Oh I wouldn't say that," replied Nancy. Violet ignored her remark.

"Hello again," said Hilda politely and as casually as she could. "It's George isn't it?" George nodded and grinned. "I don't remember you saying you were coming here tonight," enquired Hilda, bravely.

"No, I didn't. I'm not supposed to discuss things like that while I'm working you see."

"Oh, I see."

"Can I get you another drink?" asked George, changing the subject.

"Oh, yes please, that's very kind of you."

"Martini was it?"

"Yes, thank you."

"What about your sister and her friend?"

"Oh they're both happy to get their own," replied Hilda. Nancy overheard the conversation and threw Hilda an unimpressed glance.

"What did you say that for?" moaned Nancy to Hilda when George had left for the bar.

"Well we are happy getting our own," butted in Violet. Then it was her turn to do the staring, this time at Nancy. Turning her attention to her sister, Violet then asked, "Why are you encouraging him?"

"Because I like him," responded Hilda. "I think he's a very polite gentleman."

"And handsome," added Nancy.

"That helps," grinned Hilda.

"Lucky devil," spat Nancy. "Pass him this way when you've had enough," she giggled.

Violet elbowed her friend in the ribs. "Please be careful Babe. Don't be so taken in by those good looks and charm. Remember, you haven't had much experience in that area."

"Yes, thank you Vi. I'm very well aware of that," replied Hilda. "That's why I'm just going to talk to him." Violet didn't respond.

It felt like an age before George returned to the table with Hilda's drink, but when he did, he was full of apologies. "Sorry about the delay. I bumped into a bloke I know and we got talking. You know what it's like." Hilda smiled and said thank you for her drink. George sat down, next to Hilda, the opposite side to Violet.

"Are you enjoying the evening so far?" he enquired.

"Yes, thank you. I'm afraid you've missed most of it," replied Hilda.

"I had to work late. We usually work later on a Saturday. It can be a bit of a pain sometimes." The band changed tempo and started to play a Foxtrot. "Have you done much dancing?" enquired George.

"A little," replied Hilda.

"Would you like to dance now? With me?" enquired a nervous George.

"That would be lovely. Thank you," replied Hilda. George took Hilda's hand and led her to the dance floor.

The pair spent the rest of the evening on the dance floor or chatting to one another. They appeared to be getting on extremely well. Neither had the need to engage with anyone else nor did anyone else seem to matter. They were totally engrossed in each other's company and conversation. Hilda was both surprised and relieved at how easily the conversation had flowed. She felt completely at ease in George's presence and he in hers, so much so that she eventually felt comfortable enough to explain to George the circumstances behind her and her sister's visit to the new salon.

Violet kept a discreet, watchful eye on her baby sister while Nancy was more perturbed that it wasn't her whom George was giving all his attention to. What had also upset Nancy was the fact that no other man had asked her to dance that night. The older, more rounded gent, whose name she had discovered was Alf, had approached her later on in the evening for another dance but she had declined. Alf had left the dance hall soon after that so Nancy and Violet had ended up dancing together for the rest of the evening. By ten o'clock, Nancy's feet and shins were battered and bruised from being trodden on and kicked most of the night and she and Violet were no longer speaking to each other.

When the music stopped and the band were starting to pack up their instruments, Hilda and George were so locked in deep conversation that they didn't notice everyone around them was leaving. It was Violet who interrupted their intimate discussion. "Time to go, Babe, everyone's leaving."

"I hadn't realised what time it was," said Hilda glancing at her watch.

"Can I walk you home?" George asked.

"Only if you walk us home too," interjected Violet, pointing to herself and Nancy.

"What a terrible chore, having to walk home three beautiful women," grinned George.

Hilda giggled. She was getting used to George's sense of humour. Violet on the other hand raised her eyebrows and tutted. She found George rather irritating. Nancy blushed, as she was referred to as a beautiful woman.

The four left the Memorial Hall together, dropping Nancy off at home first. Hilda and George wished Nancy goodnight and Violet kissed her friend on the cheek and continued on, walking ahead of Hilda and George. For the next few minutes, on their way back to Downing Street, George and Hilda chatted continuously. Although

Violet tried to listen in to their conversation she was unable to hear anything of any interest as she was too far ahead of them. As she crossed over Ivy Lane, Violet shouted back sarcastically, "Goodnight then. I think I can find my own way from here."

"All right then Vi. Goodnight," shouted Hilda, as Violet continued on towards her home at the bottom of Downing Street. "Goodnight," echoed George, but there was no further response from Violet. "I go in through the back entrance, it's down here," explained Hilda, leading George down Ivy Lane. They stopped outside the back gate. "It's a bit late to come in with you I suppose?" asked George.

"I'm not sure that would be such a good idea anyway," said Hilda, "given that you are the enemy at the moment."

"Oh yes, of course. I forgot." There was a pause and then George asked, "Can I see you again?"

"I'd like that," smiled Hilda.

"I'm not working tomorrow," continued George. "Shall we go for a walk, if the weather's nice?"

"That sounds lovely. I'll be going to church first thing, so after lunch, say about two o'clock?"

"That's great," replied George.

Suddenly the thought of George calling for her and her father finding out caused Hilda's stomach to start doing somersaults. "I could meet you at the bottom of Castle Street if you like?" Hilda suggested.

"I'll look forward to it," replied George. He took a step closer to Hilda and gently pressed his mouth to hers. They kissed for a brief moment. The kiss took Hilda a little by surprise, but the feelings she experienced in those few seconds she wanted to last forever. George noticed Hilda's stunned expression and stepping back, apologised. "Sorry, I think I was a bit presumptuous."

"No no," Hilda blushed. "I don't mind. I rather enjoyed it." George stepped towards her once more and they kissed again. He wrapped his arms around her this time and she emulated his actions. This kiss was more passionate and lasted longer. Hilda began to feel lightheaded and dizzy, but it was a nice feeling, one of elation. When George finally pulled away, Hilda tried not to show her disappointment. She had wanted him to continue forever.

"Goodnight then, Hilda. I'll see you tomorrow."

"Goodnight, George," Hilda managed to reply as he left her fumbling for her key. Once inside, she dreamily made her way upstairs to bed.

The following morning at breakfast Edwin asked his daughter how her evening had gone. "Did you enjoy yourselves?" he enquired.

"Yes, it was all right," she replied vaguely. Edwin sensed he was going to get very little more out of his daughter on the subject and suspected, incorrectly, that the evening had been a bit of a disaster. So he pressed her no further. Changing the subject and trying to cheer his daughter up, he asked, "Shall we go to church together this morning?" Hilda was more than a little surprised by her father's question but answered, "That would be nice. I don't really like going on my own any more."

"That's sorted then," exclaimed Edwin.

Since her mother had died and Violet had moved out, Hilda had continued attending St Andrew's Sunday service every week on her own. She had found it very difficult but she had kept going for the sake of her mother's memory. Edwin hadn't visited church since his wife's funeral and then it had only been to make the necessary arrangements.

He had only really attended church services during Christmas, on Easter Sundays or when the children had been christened, while Mary was alive. He maintained Sunday was his day off and he wasn't prepared to "waste it" praying. He and Mary had often had words on this subject but over the years Mary had learned to accept her husband's point of view and relented, no longer trying to persuade him to attend every week.

So, understandably, Hilda was taken aback by her father's offer and Edwin was now regretting his decision. Nevertheless, he was a man of his word and went along to church with Hilda that morning. The service was exactly the same as he had remembered and at one stage, when the vicar was preaching his sermon, Edwin had found himself nodding off. He had managed to wipe away the drool which had formed in the corner of his mouth quickly enough before anyone noticed.

Hilda appreciated her father's company that morning or at least she did until she spotted George in a pew almost parallel with where she and her father were seated. George had gone to the service with the hope of seeing Hilda sooner. He simply hadn't been able to wait until that afternoon. When he noticed Hilda and her father as they sat down, he knew she would never forgive him if he spoke to her. For now he would have to be content with just being able to look at her.

Hilda sat nervously throughout the service, willing George not to come over. When the service was over, George remained in his seat and nodded discreetly to her as she and her father got up to leave. Edwin did not notice. Hilda's stomach turned a somersault as she realised she would have to tell her father about George one day, if they were to continue seeing one another.

After the church service Edwin and Hilda enjoyed lunch together and then Hilda made her excuses and left the house to meet George. As she was leaving she heard her father switch on his gramophone. This was the first time she had known him do this since the death of her mother. He'll be sitting in his armchair reading his newspaper and listening to his music for the rest of the afternoon, she thought.

George was already waiting at the bottom of Castle Street when Hilda arrived. "Am I late?" she asked.

"No. I think I'm a little early," laughed George.

"I've never seen you in church before," she enquired.

"No. I was rather eager to see you again and couldn't wait until this afternoon."

Hilda was flattered and felt herself blushing. "Thank you for not coming over to speak to me while my father was there."

"I thought it best not to. At least, not until you've told him about us."

"Us?" questioned Hilda.

"Well, I'd like there to be an 'us'. Wouldn't you?"

"Very much so," smiled Hilda.

"Us, it is then." George found he couldn't explain the feelings he had for Hilda. He had always been so careful after the accusation from Elsie and now his feelings just seemed to be running away with themselves. It seemed he had lost control but it wasn't an unpleasant feeling, in fact, since their first meeting George had felt somewhat released.

George and Hilda thoroughly enjoyed each other's company that afternoon. It was a perfectly romantic first rendezvous. The sun was warm and there was only an occasional gentle breeze that brushed past their faces every now and again. As they walked through the park, the scents from the blossoming flowers only added to their enjoyment. They strolled together linking arms or holding hands as if they had known each other all their lives. They were both surprised at how at ease they felt with one another. Nothing could have been more natural. As they walked, they shared a bag of toffees which George had bought on his way home after the church service.

They stopped for a while and sat on a park bench, kissing and cuddling, oblivious to anyone else around them, risking if anyone were to see them. After another walk they sat on the grass making daisy chains, laughing and joking together, discussing their likes, dislikes and their hopes and fears for the future. They found each other's company both stimulating and exciting. The hours flew by and before they knew it, it was time for Hilda to go home. She always had her father's tea ready for him and he would worry if she wasn't home soon.

"Can I see you again, tomorrow after work?" asked George.

"I'd like that," said Hilda. "But I'm just a bit nervous that my father doesn't know about us yet. I really should tell him. Could you give me a few days to pluck up enough courage and find the right moment?"

"Of course, but don't leave it too long," George said, impatient already for their next meeting. "The longer you leave it the more difficult it will become."

"I know you're right," Hilda said. She was deep in thought about the best way to break the news to her father.

"Tell you what," said George. "You drop by the shop in a few days when you have spoken to your father and then we will go out again."

"That sounds like a plan. Thank you for being so understanding."

"Don't be silly. Just don't leave it too long."

"I won't," promised Hilda.

George walked Hilda as far as Castle Street before she asked if he would mind leaving her there in case anyone was to see them together. George understood Hilda's concern and when he didn't kiss her goodbye, she only felt relief.

"See you soon," he shouted after her. She waved back to him.

The next few days were torturous for Hilda. There never seemed to be the right moment to speak to her father. He was always too busy, too tired or too miserable for her to broach the subject. By Wednesday Hilda was desperate to see George again but the only way that was going to be possible was if she could manage to tell her father about him. She'd gone over in her head many times all the different ways she might announce her news, but not one seemed right. This is crazy she thought. I'm entitled to a life of my own and to choose my own friends. I shall just have to tell him and if he doesn't like it, then tough.

It was late afternoon when the shop suddenly became free of customers. Standing at his counter, Edwin was gutting two fish on his wooden chopping board for his and Hilda's dinner later. Hilda muttered to herself under her breath. "Do it now, while you've got the chance."

"Sorry dear, what did you say?" asked Edwin.

"Oh, nothing, Father," she replied. A voice inside her was shouting in despair, *Just tell him*! "Well, actually, I wanted to speak to you about something," she finally blurted out, then hesitated.

"Spit it out then," Edwin insisted. There's no going back now, Hilda thought.

"It's just that I've met someone," she tried to say casually.

Edwin had his back to his daughter, but for a split second Hilda noticed he had stopped what he was doing. "Go on," he said, continuing to gut the fish, his back still to his daughter. She had to go on now. "Well, you remember when Vi and I went to the new salon on Saturday ...?"

"Yes," recalled Edwin.

"Because you asked us to ..." she added. Edwin was silent. "Well, there was a hairdresser there called George, whom we met again at the dance on Saturday night. He and I rather hit it off and ..." Hilda stopped talking when she noticed her father had once again stopped what he was doing, put down the knife and was now facing her.

Edwin was struggling to take in what he was hearing. Now he understood her reluctance to discuss how her Saturday evening had gone, and to think he had thought it was because she'd not enjoyed herself. And then he'd even given up his Sunday morning to accompany her to church because he had felt sorry for her.

"Go on," he said, in a much firmer voice.

Hilda thought her legs might give way under her at any moment and that it might be better not to mention their Sunday meeting and the wonderful time they'd spent together in the park.

"Well I'd like to see him again. He's very nice and—" but before she could finish, her father's voice boomed across the shop.

"Out of the question. How could you be so disloyal to Lionel, and me? How can you possibly trust the man? I forbid you to have anything more to do with him."

"But I've explained the situation to George about Daddy Smith's place and he said—" But again Edwin stepped in before his daughter could finish.

"You did what? Have I not taught you anything? I forbid you to ever see this 'George' person again and I don't want to hear another word about it."

There was just no point in Hilda trying any more. It was futile. She knew her father could never be swayed on something like this. When Edwin felt strongly enough about something the only person who had ever been able to persuade him otherwise had been Hilda's mother. As she was no longer around, Hilda didn't stand a chance. She ran from the shop, upstairs to her room, tears stinging her eyes. She had never in all her life felt this way about anyone and now, because of her father, she was going to have to give up these new and exciting feelings she was experiencing and go back to her dull mundane life. As she silently sobbed into her pillow, the reality of her situation and the thought of being a spinster all her life finally hit her. It terrified her. However, at that moment going against her father's wishes terrified her even more. Hilda remained in her room all night, crying herself to sleep.

When she woke the following morning her eyes were sore. She lay in her bed going over and over in her head the events from the day before. She was desperate to see George again and for him to wrap his arms around her, and to experience that over-whelming feeling of joy that rushed through her body every time he pulled her close. It wasn't long before Hilda's need turned to anger. How dare her father treat her as if she were still a child? She was an adult and should be allowed to make her own decisions, be allowed to see whom she wanted and not have to answer to anyone. She knew it would be different if her mother were still alive. Her mother would understand Hilda's feelings and allow her to explain what had happened. Her father was impossible. He had changed since the death of her mother.

Although Edwin had always been the indisputable head of the family, since his wife's death he too had felt something change. He feared he had lost control over his life. His family had all gone their separate ways. His future was uncertain. Now he was fighting back the only way he knew how. He must hang on to his youngest daughter, his last hope.

Edwin rarely saw his sons. He hadn't heard from them since their mother's death and it hurt him that they didn't care enough to share any part of their lives with him. Mabel, Doris and Evelyn were all married and had their own families or businesses to look after and, although they lived close by, Edwin didn't see them very often either. They certainly didn't have time to help him in his shop. Mabel lived the furthest away in Guildford with her growing family. Doris was only around the corner but she was always too busy with her two boys. Evelyn and her husband had just expanded their business, purchasing new premises on Downing Street. Their "Central Garage" was taking up all their time and money, with its expensive gadgets and equipment, such as the stylish fuel hoses which swung out over the pavement on long arms.

Then there were Edwin's three youngest daughters. Violet now had her own Fish shop to run. Edwin had known for a while that Violet wasn't the marrying type and this had only made it even more difficult when she had left home. Although she was literally just down the road Edwin recognised how hard she would have to work to make her business a success, so it just wouldn't be fair to ask for Violet's help. Nan was living and working in Devon. She had a well-paid job, working as a housekeeper for one of the Army's Lieutenant Colonels. Even if Edwin had wanted her to come home, he knew she wouldn't. Nan wrote to her father regularly, but rarely visited. She had become very attached to the Lieutenant Colonel and her life in the South. Then of course there was Hilda, the baby of the family. After Mary had died, Edwin believed it was Hilda's duty to stay with her father and care for him into his old age. He had just assumed she would fall into that role after the death of her mother. Now it appeared he was wrong. He hadn't anticipated Hilda falling for a hairdresser. He had thought she would remain a spinster all her life, like her sister Violet, as neither had ever shown any real interest in being courted by a man. Now it appeared she wanted to see more of a man who would be the ruin of his good friend's business. He just could not allow it to happen, at any cost.

Hilda forced herself to get up and dressed. The thought of spending all day in the shop with her father was not one she relished. She just had to see George again, but how on earth was that going to be possible now? She simply must, if only to tell him how disastrous and futile the whole situation was. When she finally left her room that morning and greeted her father, she was surprised to find he spoke to her as if yesterday had never happened. She reciprocated his mood. They ate breakfast together with no mention of the burnt fish, still lying in the sink from Edwin's attempt at cooking his own dinner last night. They worked in the shop together throughout the morning as if nothing had happened. Around midday, Edwin asked Hilda to go and make the lunch, eat hers first and he would have his when she returned. Now's my chance, thought Hilda and she made the excuse to her father that she would need a couple of things from the grocers. "Could you call into Lionel's for me while you're out and get some more tobacco?" asked Edwin.

Doing well to disguise the delight she felt that he did not suspect her motives, she replied, "Yes. Just the one packet is it?"

"No. I think I'll have two," Edwin replied.

"See you shortly then," shouted Hilda, after retrieving her purse from upstairs and leaving through the shop.

Hilda headed to Lionel's place on the Borough, but upon noticing through the window that he was busy with customers, she crossed over at the bottom of Castle Street and headed for Mr Lawrence's new salon. She couldn't be too long or her father might become suspicious. She flew through the door of the salon making a noisy entrance, tripping over the doormat and disturbing the customers who were getting their hair done at the front of the salon. George looked up, surprised, yet delighted to see her.

"I won't be a moment," he explained to his female client, placing the roller and comb he had in his hand back into their compartments on the trolley. He rushed over to Hilda where the pair spoke in whispers. "Hilda. Oh it's good to see you. I must admit, I was beginning to wonder if I would again."

"I can't stop long George. My father doesn't know I'm here. I've told him about us, but it's going to be impossible for me to see you again."

"Why? What do you mean? What's happened?"

"He's forbidden me to see you. It just won't work George." Hilda was doing her best to fight back the tears and to keep her voice down, but her emotions were getting the better of her.

"Come through to the back," said George, recognising her distress and also aware that Mr Lawrence was watching them.

"I can't. My father will be wondering where I am."

"Well, meet me tonight then. I finish around six. I could meet you in the park? We could discuss it there?"

"You know I want to George, don't you? I just don't see how we can."

"Please, try your best for me. I'll be there, just after six. OK?"

"I'll try," promised Hilda, fleeing from the shop as quickly as she had entered.

As Hilda stepped back out onto the street, she glanced over to Daddy Smith's place and saw him opening the door for a customer who was leaving. Hilda quickly turned in the opposite direction and began walking along the Borough towards East Street. When she was sure she would be out of sight, she crossed over the road and walked back down towards his shop along the opposite side.

When she was parallel with Lionel's salon she crossed back over the road and went into his shop.

"Hello, Babe," Lionel said in his cheery voice. "What a surprise. What brings you in here?"

"Father would like some tobacco please."

"I think we can manage that," he smiled. "Are you all right? You look a bit flustered."

"Oh, I'm just running a few errands in my lunch break."

"You're lucky to get one," he joked. Hilda didn't acknowledge his comment; her thoughts were elsewhere.

"One or two?" asked Lionel.

"Sorry?"

"Do you want one or two packets?"

"Oh, two please." Lionel handed Hilda two packets of tobacco for her father. She fumbled in her purse and handed Lionel some coins. "I must dash. Thank you," she said as she struggled to open the shop door with her purse and the tobacco in her hands.

"Take care now. Give my regards to your father," Lionel shouted after her.

"I will," Hilda shouted back.

Hilda had almost reached her father's shop when she realised she had forgotten to go to the grocers. They didn't actually need anything, she had just made it up as an excuse to leave the shop but if she returned without groceries, her father might suspect. It was too late. She spotted her father in his shop doorway at the same time that he spotted her. He greeted her with, "You took your time."

"Yes, sorry. Everywhere was really busy and then I bumped into Doris doing her shopping and I couldn't get away," lied Hilda. She was surprised at how easily the lies flowed from her mouth.

"Where are the groceries?" asked Edwin.

"I'll get them tomorrow. The queue was far too long today," replied Hilda.

"Did you get my tobacco?"

"Yes, here you are." She handed her father the two packets Lionel had given her.

"Good girl. At least you managed that. Was Lionel all right?"

"Yes, he sends his regards," smiled Hilda, relieved to be telling the truth at last.

"He's a good chap," said Edwin and with that he started to roll himself a cigarette. "You'd better go and get yourself a bite to eat my girl before I take my break."

Hilda nibbled at her lunch, feeling nauseous and wondering how on earth she was going to find an excuse to go out later and meet George. Then she had a flash of inspiration. She could tell her father that Doris had invited her round for tea. He wouldn't doubt her. She had already mentioned she'd seen Doris earlier. What could be more normal than seeing one's sister for tea? When Hilda returned to the shop to release her father for his lunch she mentioned her plans for the evening. Edwin told her not to be home too late and that was all he said. She was relieved he hadn't questioned her further. Now what concerned her was the ease with which she appeared to be able to deceive her father.

At six o'clock Hilda was waiting by the same park bench where she and George had kissed only a few days earlier. She was fondly recalling their conversation and what they had discovered about each other, when she noticed George walking towards her. He seemed a little agitated. "Sorry I'm late," he puffed, a little out of breath.

"You're not," Hilda replied.

"Some people expect you to work all night."

"Mr Lawrence?" enquired Hilda.

"No, he's a decent bloke. Unfortunately it was one of his best customers. She'd insisted I do her hair for her, tonight, now, after we had closed."

"What happened?"

"Mr Lawrence very kindly made my excuses for me and offered

to do it himself. When she still insisted I do her hair, Mr Lawrence had to make it completely clear to her that she didn't have a choice. It was very embarrassing."

"Oh dear, poor George and poor Mr Lawrence," said Hilda as she forwardly placed her arm around George's waist. "Well, you're here now."

"Thanks to Mr Lawrence." George reciprocated Hilda's gesture by placing his arm through hers and they began to stroll through the park, their arms wrapped around each other's waists. "He's a right proper gent really. I hope you don't mind but I told him about our predicament."

Hilda pulled away sharply from George. She was a little surprised. "What did you do that for?"

"Don't worry; he's a man who respects certain values. If you tell him something in confidence he won't share it with a soul."

"I hope you're right George. If this gets back to my father, there's no telling what he might do."

"What are we going to do about your old man? Would you like me to go and see him? Talk to him? Do you think that would help?

"No George!" Hilda shouted. "I don't think that would help, not at the moment anyway."

"All right, calm down. We'll just have to think of something else then, won't we?"

That evening, George took Hilda to the station hotel where they ate a meal and chatted until late. The minutes flew and before they were ready, it was time for them to part.

Many more secret meetings between George and Hilda took place over the next year, and Hilda often dragged Doris into her deceit when she used her sister as an alibi. Hilda hated lying to her father but he had given her no option. On occasions she would broach the subject with him but no matter how good a mood he was in, as soon as he realised she was about to bring up the subject of George, he cut her dead, changing the subject and making it impossible for her to continue.

George couldn't quite believe that Hilda's father would not be persuaded. No one is that unreasonable, thought George. So one day, he decided he had to meet Edwin for himself. Without informing Hilda of his plans, he walked into the shop late one afternoon, hopeful for a positive outcome. Hilda was out the back boiling up crabs. It was a job she really hated. She felt as though she'd been doing it for hours. She was wringing wet with perspiration. Her father had asked her that morning whether she wanted to smoke the kippers or boil and dress the crabs and she had opted for the latter. Now she wished she had chosen the first option.

Edwin turned as George entered his shop and greeted his unfamiliar customer with "Good afternoon."

"Good afternoon," replied George, politely. As Edwin didn't recognise the young man he assumed he must be visiting some relations in the town.

"Yes sir, what can I get for you? I have a nice piece of salmon on special offer today or the smoked kippers are always popular. I've smoked them myself, out back this morning."

George thought quickly and nervously answered the fishmonger's enquiry. "Actually, I was just after two cod loins please."

"Certainly sir, no problem," said Edwin and he set about the task. It took him mere seconds to fulfil the order and as he was wrapping the cod into a small parcel for his new customer, Hilda appeared from the back room carrying a tray of dressed crabs. She froze like a statue at the sight that met her eyes, almost dropping the tray. At that moment Hilda found she could neither move nor speak. Both men had noticed her enter. Her father remarked mockingly, "What took you so long. I thought you'd gone to the coast to catch the damn things." He handed George the small parcel of fish. "Can I interest you in some delicious dressed crab, prepared by my daughter's own fair hands?"

George managed to find a smile from somewhere deep inside

but was momentarily lost for words, as he witnessed the sheer terror on Hilda's face. He was never more aware than during that instant of her love for her father and just how torn she must be feeling between the two of them. He had unwittingly put her in an impossible position. She looked petrified at the thought of what George might do next. George recognised her anguish and was forced to abandon his plan. "No thank you, not today," George finally replied. He reached into his pocket and paid for his purchase. Edwin took the money from George and thanked him. As George turned to leave he glanced over at Hilda who was still rooted to the spot.

"Your change sir," called Edwin as George was about to disappear out the door.

"Oh yes, thank you," replied George and he made a quick exit.

"Well don't just stand there woman," teased her father, releasing Hilda from her temporary paralysis. "Pass me those crabs."

It was the following day before Hilda could get to see George. She made him promise never to put her through something like that again. George apologised over a fish supper and promised he would never again attempt to speak with her father unless she had asked him to. It was pointless trying to explain that he was just trying to help. Hilda was aware of why he had done it, but she just had to sort out the situation with her father in her own way.

More weeks and months passed and finally Hilda reached the end of her tether. She had tried everything to get her father to listen to her. She had been patient, understanding and sympathetic to his needs and feelings but it had got her nowhere. Hilda and George were sitting in the kitchen at Doris's house. Doris had known about George for some time now and having invited the pair over on numerous occasions had got to know and like George very much. Over a pot of tea Doris had suggested Hilda put down her feelings on paper.

"What good will that do?" moaned Hilda.

"In a letter I mean. Tell Father exactly how you feel about George. He'll read it all and he can't interrupt you. He'll have to listen to you then."

Hilda looked at her sister and then at George, who shrugged. Hilda looked back at Doris.

"I suppose it couldn't make things any worse."

Hilda spent days over her letter, writing and rewriting it. When she was finally happy that she could not improve on it any further, she sealed it inside an envelope marked "To Father". She decided it was best not to hand it directly to her father but just to leave it by the side of his chair in the front room. Hopefully he would spot it later and read it while she was out. She was very nervous that evening. George took her to the picture house hoping to take her mind off things but she was unable to relax all night. She didn't enjoy the film. It was *Mutiny on the Bounty* staring Charles Laughton and Clark Gable. The story was about the HMS *Bounty* which was captained by a tyrannical, harsh disciplinarian, Captain William Bligh. All Hilda could think about when he made his entrance was her father and his unrealistic points of view. By the end of the film Hilda was wishing she had never written the stupid letter to her father and she was dreading what might be waiting for her when she arrived home.

On the way home she said to George, "You do realise I may be setting myself up for a mutiny of my own." George just nodded and smiled, understanding the irony in Hilda's comment. She asked George to walk her just to the top of Downing Street and that was where they kissed goodnight and went their separate ways. When Hilda entered the house via Ivy Lane, the place seemed very quiet. There was no sound coming from the upstairs front room, nor from her father's bedroom. Why was her father not waiting up for her? She crept as silently as she could into the front room, hoping the letter would be where she had left it, that her father had not read it and she could retrieve it. But it was not there. Hilda made her way back along the hallway to her bedroom and eventually fell into a rather restless sleep.

The following morning everything seemed normal. Edwin appeared to be in the same mood as he was most mornings. He'd breakfasted and was preparing his shop for his early customers. He greeted Hilda with a pleasant, "Good morning," as he always did when she brought him a cup of tea into the shop, first thing. Hilda did not know what to make of the situation and decided it was safer to go along with her father's good mood. But little did she know that the previous evening Edwin had found his daughter's letter on the arm of his chair, but not read it. He had no desire or need to read it. He knew exactly what it would contain. He knew his daughter wanted to be somewhere else and with someone else and it hurt him enormously to have to consider and acknowledge that fact, so he had destroyed the envelope and its contents. He knew only too well that he was burying his head in the sand, but he desperately hoped Hilda would change her mind.

Chapter 10

1935

By the winter of 1935 Edwin's relationship with his youngest daughter had completely broken down. Although the pair continued with their day-to-day lives as though nothing was wrong, neither of them wanted to face up to the truth. Both of them knew that soon they would have to. It was inevitable. Hilda had changed over the last few months. She had hardened towards her father. It had transpired that the whole situation with Daddy Smith's business losing custom to George's salon was nonsense. Lionel's business had soon picked up again when he had advertised and given products away along with a haircut. His business hadn't been affected long term. This situation only fuelled Hilda's opinion that her father was being unreasonable and she was old enough to make her own mistakes. She had reached the conclusion that no one, not even her own father, was going to prevent her from seeing George.

The problem was Edwin believed he was doing what any caring father should do to protect his daughter. However, his ulterior motive to keep his last remaining daughter at home to care for him into his old age was seen as purely selfish from Hilda's point of view. Both parties believed the other was being completely unreasonable in their request and so the pair had reached a stalemate. There was nothing for it; Hilda recognised that the only way she could be with George was if they were to move away from Farnham, her home, her family and, especially, her father.

A secret rendezvous was set up with the couple arranging to meet at the coffee room in Elphicks department store on West Street. Elphicks had an excellent reputation in the town. George

Elphick had opened his drapery business back in 1881. The business had gone from strength to strength and Hilda had always bought clothes and hosiery from the store. She had, on more than one occasion, used shopping as her excuse to meet George here. On this particular morning it wasn't too busy in the coffee room. Hilda guessed the weather was putting a lot of people off today as it was so cold. She didn't mind. It meant the pair could enjoy their time together without being overheard and the conversation soon turned to Hilda's father. "I don't really want to discuss this again," sighed Hilda. "Can we please talk about something else?"

"I'm sorry, Babe, but I can't go on like this for much longer. All this sneaking around is no good for anyone. At first it was exciting and dangerous. Now it just seems totally unfair. We aren't doing anything wrong. We're both adults."

Hilda placed her cup of coffee back down on the table in front of her. "I know, I agree with you completely. It's just that I can't see any way out of this situation."

"Well I might just have a solution," grinned George.

With nervous apprehension Hilda enquired what solution George was referring to. "Marry me," he blurted out across the table, almost too loudly. Hilda was stunned.

Whenever she had imagined this moment she had pictured herself in a more romantic setting, such as lying side by side in a field of bright red poppies or sharing a romantic meal in a very expensive restaurant. Her imagined proposal had always been tender and passionate, under very different circumstances. Here, she had the man of her dreams but he had been forced into a proposal of marriage in an attempt to save her from her over-possessive, selfish and controlling father. This was definitely not how she had imagined it. "I can't, not like this," Hilda said taking hold of George's hand across the table. "It's not that I don't want to. It's just that we'd be doing it for all the wrong reasons."

"I just thought it might solve the problem," said George, disheartened. "I thought your father might realise just how serious

I am about you, if we were to announce we were getting married. Wouldn't he have to listen then?"

"You obviously don't know my father as well as you think you do," replied Hilda who was now even more concerned than before. "I'll tell you something George. I'd much rather run away with you and marry in secret than tell my father. Then, I'd tell him later after the event, when there would be nothing he could do about it." George was surprised by the determination in Hilda's statement. He realised she was serious and that she too had reached the end of her tether with her father. George suddenly realised that Hilda had just confirmed to him that marriage was not out of the question and he secretly smiled within.

"If that is truly how you feel, then let's do it. Let's move away from Farnham and your father and get married," said George.

"What about your job?"

"I should be able to find another job fairly quickly. We both could and then we could rent a bigger place together. What do you say?"

"You make it sound so easy George."

"There's no reason why it shouldn't be. But we won't know unless we give it a try. What do you think?"

Hilda stared into George's eyes and could see that they sparkled with excitement. Am I really going to do this? Am I really going to be able to share the rest of my life with George? she thought.

Hilda needed little time to answer. "All right, George, let's do it."

The first thing George needed to do was speak to Mr Lawrence. He wondered if his employer would have contacts or know of a salon in another town that might be looking for new staff. It came as no great surprise to Mr Lawrence that George wanted to leave his establishment. George had kept Mr Lawrence pretty much in the picture about Hilda and her father. This being said, George couldn't help feeling he was letting Mr Lawrence down. It had, after all, been extremely generous of Mr Lawrence to ask George to accompany him to his new shop in Farnham two years ago.

George had found Mr Lawrence tidying up in the back room and reluctantly explained to him the difficult situation he now found himself in. George made it clear that he had appreciated all of his help and thanked his employer for his initial encouragement and the continued support he had given him over the years.

Mr Lawrence accepted and supported George's decision. "I wouldn't have been able to set up in Farnham without your help George. You owe me nothing so you have nothing to worry about. I'm just sorry I'm going to lose a damn fine hairdresser, but I understand why you have to leave."

The two men joked together for a moment, reminiscing about difficult clients and then Mr Lawrence said, "Right, back to business. I'll get in touch with a few colleagues and see what I can find for you. I can't guarantee where you might end up though."

"Oh I don't think that really matters to Hilda or me," said George, who was grateful for any help.

"I'm sorry I can't do more. It's a pity I don't have another salon. You'd be ideal to run it if only I could afford another one. I'll give you a glowing reference of course."

"Well that's very good to know and I appreciate your confidence in me."

"I can honestly say it isn't going be easy finding a replacement for you George."

"I'm sure you will in no time."

"If I'm lucky I'll find a decent hairdresser, but I doubt I'll find anyone with the same integrity and regard for their clients that can equal yours."

"Oh you'll have me blushing if you don't stop," smiled George, who not for the first time felt choked during the conversation. The two men shook hands and pulled each other close, patting one another on the back.

"I'll miss you George."

"I appreciate that and I'll miss having such a considerate boss."

"I wish you and Hilda all the happiness you deserve."

"Thank you Mr Lawrence. I promise to keep in touch."

"That would be great George, really great."

George let Hilda know as soon as possible how it had gone with Mr Lawrence. She was both relieved and excited. The next few days were some of the longest in Hilda's life. Keeping this secret was almost impossible; she thought she was going to burst waiting for news. During this time Hilda and George made many plans for their future together and couldn't wait for them to reach fruition. Finally on 13 December Mr Lawrence informed George about a chain of salons across London owned by the Sorensen family. "The owners are looking for a new, more senior member of staff to oversee their salon in Battersea. The role may possibly involve some travel to the other salons on occasions but I'm sure it will suit you George," he said with some enthusiasm. "I met one of the owners during a business conference in London some years ago. We enjoyed each other's company and swapped ideas and have stayed in touch. He now owns quite a modern salon in Battersea which I believe also employs beauty therapists." George was lost for words. "If you take the job you would be in complete charge of the salon and have full responsibility for sorting out any staffing issues with the added responsibility of some input into the other salons."

George thought this sounded an incredible opportunity, although he was a little daunted by the amount of responsibility that went with it.

"Are you sure you think I could do it?" he asked Mr Lawrence.

"I have no doubt in my mind at all. I have complete confidence in you, George. I just wish you were going to be doing it with me."

"I should like to accept then," smiled George, "but I would just like to run it past Hilda before we contact Mr Sorensen to confirm. Would that be all right?"

"No problem, George. Don't leave it too long though. Busy people don't wait for ever."

"I'll be as quick as I can," and with that George flew out of the salon.

George almost bumped into Hilda as he dashed around the corner of Downing Street. Hilda had been on her way to deliver an order for her father. She of course was pleased for George, but a little apprehensive. Now that the impossible finally seemed credible and it looked as though she was at last going to get to spend the rest of her life with George, it scared her. She suddenly felt like the changeling who had been set free from its gilded cage in the book she had read as a child.

"I've never been to Battersea before. I'm not sure I know exactly where it is."

"Neither have I," said George. "But I do know where it is," he continued, trying to reassure her. "It will be an adventure for us both."

"I'll have to find a job," she said. "And where will we live?" Hilda was starting to panic. "When do you start this new job? When do we leave?"

"All these questions," laughed George. "Don't worry. I'm sure everything will work itself out."

"How do you manage to stay so calm about everything George?"

"I don't know really. I just do. What's the point in worrying? Why do you always worry about everything?" he asked Hilda.

"I don't know. I just do," replied Hilda and the pair of them laughed together.

George pulled Hilda in close, right where they stood in the street and they embraced. "Hey, careful someone might see us," Hilda said, jumping away from him quickly.

"I don't care now," replied George and he grabbed her again. "It doesn't matter any more."

George was right, and from then on everything moved very

quickly. Mr Lawrence let Mr Sorensen know that George had accepted the job offer and George travelled to Battersea a week later to meet Mr Sorensen and look around his salon. He found the salon with little trouble. It was situated on Battersea Park Road, a fairly main road in Battersea town centre. It was a much larger shop than the one he was used to in Farnham and had many more staff which was a good thing as it appeared to be very busy. George didn't allow this to put him off. I bet it's because of the Christmas period, George thought to himself. He rose to the challenge, appearing competent and efficient. All of the salon staff seemed very friendly and understandably surprised to meet a much younger man who was to be their new boss. The two Mr Sorensens who owned the chain of salons were much older, about the same age as George's father would have been. The two brothers made George feel very welcome and showed him around the salon, introducing him to all the staff before conducting a short interview. George sailed through the interview, able to answer all the brothers' questions with confidence and accuracy. A starting date was arranged and George left the modern salon with a spring in his step. He had enjoyed his visit. He had been able to get a proper feel for the place. He had been pampered by the women staff and brought numerous cups of tea and coffee during his visit, although he wasn't quite sure whether this was for his benefit or the Mr Sorensens'.

That afternoon George set about his next task. His visit to Battersea gave him the opportunity to search for somewhere for him and Hilda to live. By late afternoon, he felt as though he had been walking the streets of Battersea all day. He finally stumbled upon a property which might suit their needs. It was an empty basement flat, about a fifteen-minute walk away from the salon. It had just come on to the market for rent. He was able to arrange an appointment to look around it early that evening. George was pleasantly surprised as he was shown into every room. It was more than big enough for the two of them and although the flat was situated in the basement, it appeared bright and airy. The building sat opposite Battersea Park and he knew Hilda would love its position and outlook. He agreed to take it there and then and paid a deposit to the agent. They could move in straightaway.

George arrived home late that evening, so was unable to meet with Hilda until the following morning. She popped out of her father's shop saying she was going on a couple of errands which was true but also an excuse to leave. She couldn't wait to see George but her first errand on that Saturday morning before Christmas was to deliver an order to her sister Doris, who lived on St George's Road, which she did in record time. The other was to Mrs Wren on Tilford Road. Mr Wren had The Auto House on St George's Road. From here he ran a haulage contracting business. As Hilda passed his place she called out to him. "Morning Mr Wren. I have your dinner here. I'm just taking it round to your wife."

"I'll look forward to that love. Thank you."

"No problem Mr Wren." Hilda had always thought they were a lovely couple. She ran all the way from St George's Road to Tilford Road and then all the way back into Farnham town without stopping. She made herself slow down to a brisk walk when she got to South Street as she didn't want to attract unnecessary attention to herself. She just had to get to see George as quickly as possible. She couldn't wait to hear his news.

She burst through the door of Stuart Lawrence's salon, breathless and perspiring. The two men turned suddenly to inspect the commotion.

"What took you so long?" enquired George, comb and rollers in hand. His customer looked surprised but George and Mr Lawrence both laughed. Hilda scanned the salon's customers for anyone she knew. She was fortunate, there was no one.

"I'll take over here George, if you would like to see to the young lady," insisted Mr Lawrence, relieving George of his comb and roller and promptly and politely beginning to strike up a conversation with George's customer.

George led Hilda into the back room where he filled her in on the previous day's events. "I'll need to get a job now," Hilda said excitedly.

"Well yes, but we can sort that out once we are settled into the new flat. It shouldn't be too difficult."

"I don't mind what I do, as long as it isn't working in a fish shop," she said smiling.

They embraced in the back room for quite some time, completely relaxed in each other's company, not noticing the customers coming and going in the front of the shop. Now it felt very real for Hilda. She was going to leave her home town to be with George. Her life was about to change for ever. Although she couldn't have been happier, she also felt much sadness. The feelings she had in the pit of her stomach made her want to retch. It would be some time before they would subside.

George and Hilda spent the next week making the necessary plans and arrangements which would allow them to move to Battersea. It was difficult as this week fell right over the Christmas period, her father's busiest time in the shop. On some occasions during the day Edwin's customers seemed to be queuing for miles down the street. The two of them were rushed off their feet. Hilda found little time to nip out and see George, and on the few occasions when she was alone upstairs in the house she used her time wisely for packing away items of clothes and keepsakes she wanted to take with her when she left, hiding things in a suitcase under her bed and boxes in her wardrobe.

Christmas Day was strained to say the least and she thought the day would never end. Her father did nothing but complain about the food she had prepared and seemed to delight in recounting the disastrous food she had prepared the previous Christmas. The back door didn't stop opening and closing all day as family members and neighbours visited to share their tidings of joy, bearing small gifts of food and sweets and tobacco or cigars for her father. Inside, Hilda felt ready to burst. As the day continued she was finding it more and more difficult to keep her secret hidden. What she wanted to do was to shout it from the roof tops: "I love George and we're going to run away together," but she couldn't. She mulled over in her head the various scenarios that might happen when she informed her father of her decision. They all scared her. She knew that none would give her the positive outcome she so desperately wanted. When her sister Doris had called in that afternoon with her two boys, Hilda finally succumbed. After her father had left the room she informed her sister of her plans and made Doris swear not to mention them to anyone. Hilda asked Doris to only let the others know after she and George had left. She wanted to leave nothing to chance, for nothing to go wrong and for no one to try to persuade her to change her mind.

How she longed to see George, but he had gone to spend a couple of days with his family, just outside London. George was taking this opportunity to inform his mother and sister of his plans. They both responded positively, saying they couldn't wait to meet Hilda. "You'll love her, I know you will," said George. "She's so sweet and kind and she makes me so happy."

"That's wonderful George," his mother had replied.

"I'm sure we'll have lots in common and I'll be able to tell her how horrible you were to me as a child," teased his sister Wyn.

"Don't you dare," laughed George. As George was leaving, his mother and sister promised to visit the new flat in Battersea as soon as he and Hilda were settled. George was relieved to have told them his news and that they had taken it so well.

By the time he'd returned to Farnham, the day after Boxing Day, Hilda had finally made up her mind and decided how she was going to tell her father she was leaving. She informed George first of her plans, knowing he would support her in her decision.

"Would you like me to be with you when you tell him?" George asked.

"Thank you George, but this is one thing I have to do by myself."

"Well, I'll be waiting for you afterwards, right outside, just as you've planned, and we'll catch the last train together."

"Thank you. I love you George."

"I love you too Babe. Stay strong."

Edwin wasn't stupid. He knew his relationship with his daughter was in shreds. He had noticed little trinkets going missing from around the house and some of the smaller pieces of furniture were no longer in Hilda's bedroom. She had been careless and left hand-written shop receipts for purchases in the bins which Edwin had spotted and read. She had purchased numerous household items and Edwin suspected she was likely storing them at a friend's house. He knew she was preparing to leave him and he was incapable of stopping it. He had given up because he had realised he couldn't do this any more to his beautiful daughter, his Babe. He had realised he must let her go, but he was unable to let her know that he had reached this decision. He secretly hoped that if he didn't tell her, there might be a possibility she would stay.

The train to Waterloo wasn't until 4pm. George had promised he would be waiting outside the shop, down Ivy Lane at half past three. Hilda had no idea how she was going to get through the day with her father until that time. The day was like any other, even though it was New Year's Eve. They had plenty of satisfied customers and Hilda's father spent time with each of them making sure they were more than happy with their purchases, suggesting recipes and discussing the best way to store their fish. Edwin gave the impression he was fairly cheerful and appeared to be making more of an effort today with his customers. He had spoken to Hilda more today than he had in a long time, which just served to make her feel even more guilty about what she was about to do to him.

Hilda had finished packing her small suitcase the night before and hidden it back under her bed, out of sight. At around twenty past three she made an excuse to her father, which he didn't query, and went upstairs to her room. She retrieved the case from under her bed and nervously made her way down the back stairs, grabbing her coat off the stand by the back door. She placed the case down onto the floor and laid the coat over the top of it. She then re-entered the shop. Her legs felt like jelly and her hands were shaking. A customer was just leaving the shop and her father was clearing away the fish guts from his fish board. Hilda saw her opportunity and decided to take it.

Glancing at her watch she walked over to the shop door and pulled it shut, turning the sign to closed. Her father looked up. "What are you doing?" he enquired. It's now or never, she thought to herself. Time to put into practice the speech you have rehearsed over and over again, so many times in your head. Hilda attempted to sound confident and determined.

"Father, I have something I want to say." Her father stood directly opposite her, his eyes staring straight through her. His body felt numb, his soul knew exactly what she was about to say.

"I'm leaving. I'm going to live with George and you can't stop me. Our train leaves in half an hour and George is right outside waiting for me." She said this, hoping it would deter him from trying to stop her. Her father made no attempt to speak. Hilda found it impossible to control her strong feelings of guilt which were taking over her whole body and making her tremble. This was the hardest and cruellest thing she had ever had to do, but there was no going back now.

"When we are settled, I will write to you." She had thought about telephoning but didn't know if when the time came she would be able to bring herself to pick up the receiver and dial. She had concluded that a letter would be more appropriate. This way, it allowed her not to have to face any difficult questions he might ask.

Hilda waited a few seconds for a response from her father. When she didn't get one, she turned and left the shop to retrieve her suitcase and coat from the hall. Upon her return, her father hadn't moved. She placed her case on the floor and put on her coat. She left the buttons undone as her trembling hands would not allow her to do them up. She picked up her case and walked towards the shop entrance. She turned the sign back around and opened the door. Hilda couldn't quite believe that her father was making no attempt to stop her and no attempt to speak. Had he given up? Was he letting her go? Had she really won?

She stood in the doorway and turned to look at her father one last time. "Bye then Dad." The words choked her and still he said nothing. Hilda, by some means – she didn't know how – managed to make her legs, which felt as heavy as lead, move forward and guide her through the shop doorway. As she stepped out onto the street, a tall woman brushed past her and entered the shop in rather a hurry. She heard the woman say, "Oh thank the lord, you're open. I must have some kippers for my husband's tea. He'll kill me if he doesn't get his kippers." Without looking back, Hilda turned the corner into Ivy Lane and almost fell into George's arms. He held her as the tears came, uncontrollably.

Inside the shop, Edwin was spirited into action by the arrival of this brash woman. His mind was temporarily taken off his daughter while he served this customer, who appeared to be in somewhat of a hurry. As soon as she had left, realisation hit him and he flew out of the door hoping to catch his daughter. He was disappointed. Hilda was nowhere to be seen. If he had managed to see her he didn't know what he would have said to her but now he had missed his chance. Edwin spent New Year's Eve in his local, drinking rather more than he should have. He returned home before the stroke of midnight. He had anticipated this day would come. And so with the New Year there would come many changes for Edwin.

The thought of sharing a house with a man terrified Hilda yet at the same time gave her little butterflies of excitement in the pit of her stomach. For George, this same thought gave him a sense of achievement. It had been over a year since the pair had first met and in all that time George had remained a gentleman. Although both parties had been tempted on many occasions to take their relationship to another level, they had both resisted the temptation. Whenever Hilda had spent any length of time alone with George in his flat in Farnham, she had always felt nervous and uncomfortable. It wasn't because she didn't trust George; she had been more concerned about what other people might think. She had been brought up "properly" and knew that if her mother had been alive and aware she was entering a single man's home without a chaperone, she would have felt very disappointed with her daughter. Hilda dare not even contemplate what her father's reaction would have been.

The journey by train was fairly easy. Bearing in mind it was New Year's Eve, there didn't seem to be many people about so Hilda and George were able to share a compartment of the train without being interrupted. Once away from Downing Street Hilda had pulled herself together and by the time they had reached Farnham station George and Hilda were already discussing plans for their future. "I can't wait for you to see the flat and decide where you want all the furniture to go in it," said George, trying to take Hilda's mind off leaving. "And the park across the road, I know you'll love it. Mother and Wyn say they'll visit as soon as we are settled and maybe you could invite Doris, Syd and the boys over sometime."

"I'd like that," replied Hilda.

Once inside London, they took another train from Waterloo to Battersea Park. Although it seemed as though most places across London were accessible via the underground, Battersea could only be reached by rail or bus. It was Hilda who suggested they change trains at Waterloo and catch another to Battersea Park station. "I don't fancy struggling with this case on the bus," she complained to George. "It's beginning to feel rather heavy."

"No problem," replied George. "The train sounds good to me; it should only take about ten minutes."

They stepped onto the platform at Battersea Park station at around quarter past five. They then had a short walk along Prince of Wales Drive which ran along the south edge of the park, until they turned right into Albert Bridge Road.

"Nearly there Babe," said George. "Are you tired?"

"I am a little." Hilda was trying not to complain, but her suitcase felt as though it was getting heavier with every second she walked and she had to keep stopping to swap hands.

"Doesn't the park look nice?" said George gesturing with his head, as his hands were full also. They had already passed one set of fancy wrought-iron gates leading into the park when they had turned into Albert Bridge Road. Now they were approaching another set. Just inside this set of gates, set off to the left, was a lovely little house, named Albert Gate. There were originally four of these lodge houses when the park had been built, for use by the park's employees. But not long after they were completed, Chelsea Gate lodge house had burnt down and so there now remained only three. George noticed Hilda admiring it. "We could look around the park tomorrow if you'd like."

"That sounds good George."

"That's it Babe" exclaimed George. "We're here. We just need to cross the road."

They crossed over the busy road and Hilda set eyes upon their new home for the first time. It was a tall, very grand-looking house which had been built during Queen Victoria's reign. It was truly elegant and shouted character and style. It stretched four floors high with an attic room slotted into the roof. On the second floor was a small balcony which Hilda thought must hold great views of the park opposite. Their flat was in the basement and Hilda couldn't wait to see inside.

While Hilda waited with their bags, George climbed the steps to the flat above to retrieve the key, as instructed to do by the landlord. He introduced himself briefly to its occupant, a rather tall and robust-looking woman, probably in her late forties, who was wearing an apron covered in flour and carrying a pair of oven gloves, which she slung over her left shoulder as she opened her door. "I'm George" said George holding out his hand for the woman to shake. She obliged. "And this is Hilda, George continued, waving his arm to where Hilda was waiting. Hilda felt the woman look her up and down and then she smiled. Hilda smiled back. "We're the couple moving into the basement flat today and believe you've been holding the keys for us."

"Oh yes. Hello, I'm June," said the woman patting her rather large chest and attempting to put on a posh voice.

"It's very nice to meet you June," replied George politely as Hilda attempted to stifle a giggle.

"Here you go," said the woman, producing two keys on a piece of string from her apron pocket. "If there is anything you need, don't hesitate to ask. You know where to find me."

"Thank you very much," said George and then he turned to go back down the steps to rejoin Hilda.

"Your furniture arrived just after two this afternoon and I let them in," June called down to them. Rather snootily she added, "It didn't seem to take the removal men long to finish their work."

"No. We haven't managed to acquire very much furniture as yet," replied George. "Nosey parker" whispered George under his breath so that only Hilda could hear. She nudged George's arm.

"I'm sure you'll furnish it in no time," said June. "In my opinion, it needs a woman's touch."

"Well, I'd best leave that to Hilda then, hadn't I dear?" smiled George, grabbing Hilda around her waist and pulling her tightly into him. Hilda blushed.

"My buns!" screeched June and dashed back inside her flat, slamming her front door.

Giggling to each other the excited couple accessed their new home via a couple of steps which led down to their front door. They entered the flat and switched on the lights. It felt large and airy. It had been freshly painted and appeared clean. The flat consisted of a fairly large living room at the front, where the removal men had left George's one armchair, a small, folding, wooden table and two dining chairs. Then to the back of the property was a large bedroom and communal garden area. The separate galley kitchen was basic, but would serve its purpose and Hilda loved it. In fact, she loved the whole flat.

George's few pieces of inexpensive second-hand furniture, such as his table, chairs, wardrobe, double bed and armchair he had purchased when he had moved to Farnham, did little to deflect from the sparseness of the rooms in the new flat. Hilda had brought even less with her, but the one, most important thing which Hilda had managed to acquire from her old life in Farnham, was her father's old wireless. It had arrived with the other furniture and boxes earlier in the day. Edwin hadn't listened to the radio since the death of his wife and Hilda knew her father wouldn't miss it. She had carefully packed it into a box and left it at George's flat with the other things she had collected over the past couple of weeks. Now she was glancing around the living room, looking for a special place to put it where she could listen to it every day. She decided the mantelpiece would be as good a place as any for the time being.

"What do you think of the place?" asked George who had started to search through another box of household items that had been carefully wrapped in newspaper.

"It's perfect. I love it," replied Hilda.

By seven that evening both George and Hilda were starving hungry and George suggested they visit The Prince Albert public house which was literally two doors away and served food. "I'd like to eat in on our first night, George, if that's all right. Besides I'm sure it will be a bit busy in there tonight with it being New Year's Eve."

"That's true. I keep forgetting we're on the edge of a new year."

"Well, we've both had a lot on our minds."

"How about I fetch us some fish and chips from down the road and we spend our first night in together?"

"That sounds good to me. I'll unpack a few more boxes and see if I can find some plates and cutlery while you're gone."

George popped into the Prince Albert for a bottle of beer to go with his meal and it was busy and extremely noisy in there. He had to fight his way to the bar and shout out his order to the landlady. He bought two bottles, one for Hilda. By the time George returned, Hilda had made a start on the boxes. She had found sheets and pillow cases and had made the bed. Then she'd found some of George's clothes, badly folded and creased, which looked as though they had been packed in a hurry. Shaking out the creases and placing them on coat hangers, she hung them up with care in the wardrobe. From her suitcase she took her few items of clothing and placed them beside George's. This task had given her an animated feeling of pleasure and a strange sense of belonging.

By the time George returned Hilda had found a number of kitchen utensils but had been unsuccessful in finding the plates and cutlery she had packed. "Never mind, we'll eat them with our fingers," George said helpfully. "They taste better that way and it will save on the washing up." The pair enjoyed their meal of fish and chips, eating them straight from the paper with their fingers. Hilda felt quite naughty. At home they had always been expected to use a knife and fork and here she was eating her food with her fingers and drinking straight from a bottle of beer. "Here's to us Babe, to our new home and new life together," said George, raising his bottle of beer up into the air.

"Happy New Year George," replied Hilda, clanking her bottle together with George's. They laughed and chatted over their meal, both careful not to spoil the moment by mention of the problems they had left behind.

They were so tired after their exhausting day that they didn't manage to stay awake long enough to see in the New Year. Hilda fell into a deep relaxing sleep after George had made love to her, waking only once to the sound of fireworks at midnight. George moved over, cuddled her and whispered Happy New Year in her ear. Hilda had never experienced anything quite like this. When George had made love to her that night it had been her first time, and George's first time in a long while. She had surprised herself. She hadn't felt self-conscious about getting undressed in front of him. If anyone had been nervous, it had been George. She hadn't suppressed her feelings or actions during their love making and had managed to enjoy it without feeling guilty. Perhaps it hadn't lasted as long as Hilda might have hoped and George had ruined the moment slightly when he had apologised for finishing sooner than he'd anticipated, but Hilda knew they had the rest of their lives together, to practise as many times as they desired in order to get it right.

Chapter 11

Hilda and George spent New Year's Day arranging their flat just as they wanted it and finding out about the immediate area to which they had moved. Battersea wasn't a huge place but it felt big because it was on the outskirts of London. Hilda had never lived on the outskirts of a city before. Battersea was a bustling place with plenty of people passing by the flat at all times of the day and night. The area never really seemed to go to sleep.

That morning Hilda and George discovered a row of small shops nearby on Parkgate Road, where the Prince Albert pub sat on the corner. The shops were open so Hilda purchased some basic ingredients to stock her kitchen cupboards. "Do we really need all this?" George moaned to Hilda on the way back to the flat, as he struggled with a box and two bags.

"Yes, we do, George, if I am going to look after you properly," replied Hilda. "Now be careful with that. Don't drop it."

"You're quite bossy really aren't you?" George retaliated, trying unsuccessfully to disguise his amusement. Hilda just smiled.

After making a drink, Hilda busied herself filling her kitchen cupboards with her purchases and cleaned the kitchen thoroughly in preparation for cooking her first meal for George, later that day. Following a light lunch of sandwiches and fruit, Hilda spent most of the afternoon unpacking and sorting the rest of their belongings. She disappeared into the kitchen occasionally to prepare and cook the meal while her father's old radio played in the background. George helped sometimes, when Hilda couldn't reach or move something, but spent most of his afternoon relaxing and reading the paper he'd purchased that morning. The pair didn't object to staying in. It had rained hard all afternoon so they couldn't have gone out for a walk even if they had wanted to. They were just enjoying being around one another and not having to worry about what other people might be thinking or feeling. Hilda felt so relaxed in George's company. She knew she could talk to him about anything and he would approve and go along with it. Hilda was beginning to feel more at ease about what they had done. She was starting to believe that she had done the right thing. George was the one for her and they were going to be so happy together. How she hoped her father would soon realise this and come round to her way of thinking.

George and Hilda enjoyed their evening meal together and listened to a music programme on the radio while they ate and chatted. Hilda had spent hours in the kitchen and George was obviously impressed by her culinary abilities. "Blimey Babe, you've hidden talents," he commented as he devoured his toad in the hole. Hilda had used spam instead of sausages in the meal and served it with potatoes, carrots and turnip. "This is delicious. Where have you been all my life?" George teased.

"Wait until you taste my apple pie, it's my mother's recipe," retaliated an amused and satisfied Hilda.

That night Hilda and George retired to bed to practise their love-making some more. They were now more relaxed in each other's company and tonight George was much more attentive to Hilda's needs than to his own. Afterwards they both felt more fulfilled than they had the previous evening. They fell asleep in each other's arms, content they were the only people in the whole world that mattered.

It was Thursday afternoon when George suggested a walk around the local area. He felt as though he needed to get some fresh air and Hilda jumped at the chance of exploring their local park together. It was a chilly winter's day outside. The day had started damp although it hadn't rained and the sun was out now but it still felt cooler than it had done previously during the last week. Once outside their flat, they crossed the road and entered the park, stopping briefly to admire Albert Gate lodge on their left. They read from a plaque about the park's history and were surprised to learn that most of the land had previously been a marshy wasteland which had been reclaimed from the River Thames in the sixteenth century. "It's quite incredible what man can achieve," commented George as he surveyed his surroundings. Hilda read on about a famous duel which had taken place between the Duke of Wellington and the Earl of Winchelsea in 1829. She couldn't quite get the image out of her head of her father and George charging towards each other on horseback armed with lances, jousting to save her honour.

"You all right Babe?" enquired George, noticing a look of anxiety on Hilda's face.

"Yes, sorry George. I found myself thinking about my father, that's all."

"Were you thinking about contacting him?"

"No, I'll write, in a few days, as we planned."

"Well, if you're sure, Babe."

"I'm sure," replied Hilda. "Thank you for being so understanding about everything."

"Come on," said George trying to lift her sudden, doleful mood. "Let's carry on exploring." George led Hilda off to their right to a wide tree-lined road with evenly placed street lamps along the right-hand side which led them directly to a bandstand, standing at a crossroads, almost at the centre of the park. "Which way now?" asked George.

"You choose," replied Hilda. As there was no band playing today to stop and listen to, George decided to head south. "Let's go this way, I think it takes us to a lake where you can hire boats." George had heard a woman in the shop the previous morning, relaying the fun she and her friend had on one of the boats the day before. George had thought it might be something Babe would like to do. "But I can't swim, George," worried Hilda.

"Neither can I," smiled George. "So we'd best make sure we don't fall in then."

Holding hands they continued to walk along a narrower path where they took a left turn at the next fork. This walk took them to Battersea Park lake. The lake appeared large and twisting so that one was unable to take it all in without having to walk further around it. A grass verge followed the lake's curves and led their eyes down to the water. In parts a low fence had been erected to discourage anyone from entering the water as in some places it appeared quite deep. A number of islands, some larger than others, had been constructed at various intervals on the lake. These gave shelter to the wildlife which inhabited the park, mainly varieties of water fowl such as ducks, geese and swans. Other birds like gulls and herons did visit occasionally. Nests had previously built in the reeds which lined the edge of the lake and these were easy to see as the foliage had died back and exposed them.

Hilda thought the park was a beautiful place. It included a variety of plants and many species of trees. She could see that plenty of thought had gone into their planting. Even in the winter with the trees all bare and most of their greenery gone, Hilda thought the place looked appealing. "I bet this place is beautiful during the spring and summer months," she said, "really colourful when all the flowers are in bloom."

"Yes. I bet it's a bit busier here then too," replied George. They passed the odd person out for a walk. Some were walking their dogs and George and Hilda watched and laughed as one dog chased a squirrel up a tree, barking and circling the base of the tree, willing it to appear again. A number of women pushed their babies in prams or were out with older children for some fresh air before teatime. "I guess it's the cold weather which has put a lot of people off coming out today," continued George.

They proceeded to walk around the lake until they reached the area where the boats were for hire. There was only one other mad couple already out on the lake in a rowing boat. The man was rowing while the woman seemed to be enjoying the view.

"Do you fancy it then?" asked George, turning to face Hilda.

"All right then," said Hilda, "as long as I can have a turn with the oars."

"As you like," replied George.

"It will give me something to concentrate on and might take my mind off falling in."

"You won't fall in, my darling. I shan't let you," grinned George and he kissed Hilda on her forehead.

George paid a man who was hidden inside a small kiosk beside the lake. The elderly Londoner cheerfully informed them they had half an hour before he closed for the day, so they quickly made their way to the water's edge where George climbed into a blue coloured rowing boat. He held out his hand for Hilda's. "Climb in Babe."

"I can't, my legs have suddenly turned to jelly," Hilda said nervously.

"Come on, just grab hold of me," said George still offering his hand but growing impatient. Hilda eventually did as George advised but instead of stepping ladylike into the boat she stumbled and lost her footing, causing the boat to rock back and forth rather quickly. Hilda let out a little scream as she fell into the boat, landing abruptly on her bottom. George couldn't help but laugh at his beautiful, clumsy Babe. Hilda was very embarrassed and looked around to see if anyone had witnessed her antics. Thankfully it appeared no one had, except for George, who was still grinning, so she pulled herself together, straightened her skirt and shot George a look of disapproval. This only served to make him laugh all over again. Hilda decided there was nothing for it but to join in and the pair of them giggled like children from the moment George pushed off from the edge of the lake until they reached the middle. Their antics had given the bored old man in the kiosk some well-deserved entertainment, breaking up what had been a rather monotonous day before his last customers had arrived.

"Can I have a go at rowing now, George?" enquired Hilda as they reached the middle of the lake, nearing an island.

"With pleasure," replied George.

George pushed the oars over towards Hilda. "There you go." Hilda grabbed the oars and began to push them through the water. Her strokes were uneven and no matter what instructions George gave her to try and help her to master the oars, Hilda could not manage to get a basic rhythm going with them.

After five minutes all she had managed to do was send the boat round in a complete circle and nearly run them aground on the island. George had tried his hardest not to laugh at her again but it was impossible and at last he gave in. Tears started to stream down his cheeks. "You made it look so easy," complained Hilda.

George had to bite his tongue, smiling at her as she handed the oars back to him in defeat.

George proceeded to steer the boat across the lake, passing the other couple, who were by now making their way back, weaving around ducks and other obstacles with ease. Hilda observed the gentle ripples their boat left behind and eventually relaxed enough to enjoy the ride. The couple discussed George's new job which was to start on Monday and Hilda's plans to search for work. Hilda was just telling George that she thought she might take a bus into Piccadilly and start looking there first as they ended up where they had first begun and it was time to climb back out of the boat. This Hilda managed to do with a little more decorum than when she got in.

Once back on dry land George and Hilda thanked the old man from the kiosk who had come out to secure their boat and continued their walk through the park. They joined the East Carriage Drive and walked south, passing the Rosary Garden which included rose beds and was surrounded by paths. Sadly they were unable to benefit from the sweet scents of the roses as they were not in bloom. Hilda thought the area looked very sad and sparse. They followed the drive around, passing Rosery Gate lodge as they turned into South Carriage Drive. About halfway along they decided to take a right turn which took them past the subtropical gardens. This was an area of island beds, which in the summer months were richly planted with exotic and tropical plants including ferns, India rubber trees, banana plants from Ethiopia, papyrus from Egypt and large-leaved tobacco plants. Many of these were planted out in pots, making them easier to transfer into the large Victorian-built greenhouses during the winter months.

When George and Hilda found themselves back at the bandstand they decided to retrace their steps to their flat. Becoming colder now and in need of something hot to eat, they decided the park would have much more appeal for them in the summer months. As they reached the Albert Gate exit George suggested they try the Prince Albert's food and hospitality.

The next day was Friday and it rained again, continuously all day, but George and Hilda didn't mind. They were together now, able to enjoy each other's company and that was all that mattered. To be able to spend these few days alone together, doing exactly as they wanted with no one else to consider, was Hilda's idea of heaven. This time together was very precious to them both. They had never properly experienced this kind of relationship before and used the time to get to know each other better, for tomorrow George would start his new job and on Monday Hilda intended to go in search of one too. But for now all they wanted to do was to make the most of their time together.

When Hilda had woken that morning, she had experienced a sense of peace which had swept across her whole being. It had given her such a sense of pleasure to know that today she would again be able to cook, care and clean for her man. The simplest of things gave Hilda enormous pleasure and the feeling of setting up home with someone as special and as loving as George created a feeling of wholeness within Hilda that was quite different from any emotions she'd previously experienced, which had left her feeling so downhearted.

Once again Hilda excelled herself and cooked George a fabulous dinner. She spent most of the morning in the kitchen preparing the food and had impressed George so much with her culinary skills that he had given her the biggest compliment she could have wished for: "You know, Babe, I think this is better than my mum used to make." Hilda blushed with pride as George devoured the meal.

The couple thoroughly enjoyed another day together. Although they had remained inside their flat all day, they had laughed together about silly things and discussed more serious issues such as job-hunting and Hilda's father. George had provoked feelings within Hilda during their conversations, and later that afternoon Hilda put pen to paper, having decided to write to her father. She found it extremely difficult trying to get her words to sound right, many attempts ending up in the waste-paper bin, before she was finally satisfied with her letter. Hilda made her letter brief and to the point and she hoped her father would realise that she was happy and that George was good for her. George had read it through for her when she had finished and agreed she would succeed in making herself understood.

Early on Saturday morning George left for work as planned. Hilda thought he seemed a little nervous. He had woken before the alarm clock had gone off and was washed and dressed smartly before seven o'clock. The night before he'd polished his shoes with such enthusiasm, she thought he would wear a hole in them, and when he'd come back into the bedroom at quarter past seven to see if she was getting up, he'd tripped over the rug in his haste.

They sat together and ate breakfast, and George said he wondered if he should start to make tracks. "It's only a quarter to" said Hilda. "I thought you didn't have to be there until eight thirty."

"I don't," replied George, "but I thought I'd try to make a good impression on my first day and show willing."

"You'll make a good impression anyway," smiled Hilda.

"Thanks Babe. You always manage to make me feel better. Do I seem a little nervous to you?" asked George.

"Not enough that anyone will notice," replied Hilda, kindly.

"Good," said George and with that he pulled Hilda to him, kissed her on her lips and said, "Wish me luck." Then he was gone through the front door in a flash. Hilda ran to the basement window just in time to see him disappearing up onto the pavement above her. She smiled to herself knowing that funny, lovely man was all hers.

There were many times throughout the day when Hilda wondered how George was getting on. To take her mind off worrying about him, she kept herself busy with shopping, cleaning and a little washing. Hilda also took the opportunity to write to her sister Doris, letting her know how they had settled in and what the area was like. She warned Doris in her letter that she had also written to their father and was unsure as to how he might react and apologised for having to leave Doris with the conse-quences of her actions. She later walked to the post office, purchased two stamps and posted her letters.

Upon receipt of his daughter's letter, Edwin chose to throw it straight into the bin, without a thought or glance. He believed his daughter could have nothing to say to him that would be of any interest. She had defied him and gone against his wishes with little regard. She was on her own now and she would have to deal with the consequences.

Doris suspected this would happen. She had no proof, but she knew how stubborn her father could be and that he had probably not even read the letter. She had no choice but to respect her father's decision and knew it was pointless trying to persuade him to do otherwise. In a return letter to her sister, a week later, Doris tried to reassure Hilda that their father would eventually come round and that if he could be honest with himself, he was missing her greatly. Doris prayed that what she wrote to Hilda was the truth and that one day the situation between her father and her sister would change for the better.

George's first day had flown by and Hilda was surprised to see him walk through the door when he did. She hadn't realised the time. The pair chatted about George's day while Hilda prepared their dinner and George was still filling her in on his various clients as they sat down to eat. They laughed together as George admitted he was the first to arrive that morning and had to wait a good half an hour before Mr Sorensen had turned up with the keys and let him in.

"Very good, George, I'm pleased to see you're so eager. Let's hope your attitude will rub off on other members of my staff," Mr Sorensen commented.

"It's good to see you again sir," George said as he shook his new boss's hand. "Thank you for giving me this opportunity. I can't wait to get started."

"Yes, I can see that George."

Mr Sorensen waited until the rest of his staff had arrived and suggested to them all, during a brief meeting, that George spend the day chatting with them individually to understand their place within the salon and to work out if he need make any changes.

This was exactly what George did. It wasn't unlike his previous job. The salon appeared to be run in a very similar, efficient way. It was just on a much bigger scale and now he alone was responsible for running the show. To his staff, George appeared to take everything in his stride. He had soon learnt about the salon's structure and who played which role. He had also been able to gauge which of his staff might be more prone to causing him problems. Later George announced that he could see no reason to make any changes for the time being as the day had visibly gone smoothly, and his decision had obviously relieved his staff.

The many customers that had visited the salon during George's first day appeared delighted with the friendly and efficient service. George told Hilda stories about well-to-do ladies leaving large tips and men who entered looking like tramps and left feeling and looking like wealthy gentlemen. He explained to Hilda that there were two other male members of staff, William who was about the same age as him and an older man who had worked for the Misters Sorensen at one of their other salons. Then there were four female hairdressers, three fully trained and one apprentice, and a beautician.

During his first day he had got to know Margaret, the receptionist, better than anyone else. She had been very kind to him, supplying him with a steady flow of tea and information about the business side of things, and of course, plenty of gossip about staff members and clients.

"I'm really looking forward to going back to work on Monday morning," admitted George.

"Well, that's good, George. You must think we've done the right thing then?" replied Hilda.

"Definitely," smiled George, "but I have to admit I'm pleased I have tomorrow off to digest all the information that's been thrown at me today."

"I'm sure," agreed Hilda.

Monday morning arrived and it was Hilda's turn to look for work. Both George and Hilda were up early, washed and dressed smartly and breakfasted by eight. George walked Hilda the short distance to the bus stop, kissed her goodbye and wished her luck then continued with his short journey to work. "See you later," he shouted, waving back at Hilda as he walked off down Albert Bridge Road in the direction of the salon. His journey would only take him around fifteen minutes

Hilda really had no idea where her journey would lead her today or how long it would take. After the Depression, unemployment had fallen modestly in 1934 but much further by 1935. She had recently read that employment levels had now increased and that this tended to be mostly in the South and the London area, where lower interest rates had spurred the house building boom. She was hoping this recovery may assist her in finding work. Hilda travelled by bus and on foot and later that morning eventually ended up in Piccadilly Circus, where nearby, she managed to find herself a job at the Regent Palace Hotel.

The Regent Palace Hotel was located on a triangular site close to the north side of Piccadilly Circus and had been completed in 1915. It had nine floors above ground level, with a lower ground floor, basement and sub-basement. The main entrance faced towards Piccadilly Circus and immediately caught Hilda's attention. She entered through a vestibule into a circular lounge, with marble floor and domed ceiling. The vestibule opened into a reception hall, where on one side there was a marble staircase and three lifts and on the other, a staff counter and office. Hilda made an enquiry and the smartly dressed receptionist made a telephone call to someone upstairs. Hilda was surprised to be offered an interview there and then.

A smartly dressed and well-spoken woman appeared and escorted Hilda through a set of large swing doors into a room named the Rotunda Court, en route to the interview room. Hanging in the centre of the Rotunda Court was a large domed light stained – and leaded glasslight. The room was filled with chairs and tables which were mainly occupied by patrons enjoying afternoon tea. Hilda was politely but decisively informed that it was not in here where she could offer her work. Upon passing through this room Hilda had glanced at the other waitresses realising they were somewhat younger than she. This made Hilda very nervous during her interview. The middle-aged woman introduced herself and asked her numerous questions, some very personal, which made Hilda feel quite intimidated. Hilda gave details of her true address and marital status, that of being single, but left out the fact that she was living with George. She had also felt compelled to lie about her age. Hilda knew she could get away with the deceit as she had always seemed younger than her years because she was so petite and pretty. Hilda knocked five years off her actual age and her interviewee noted it without query. During her interview she was asked endless questions to check her suitability for the job and was told in no uncertain terms that married women were not employed as waitresses.

After her interview, Hilda was escorted around the building and to a flight of stairs. From the first floor upwards, the whole of the hotel was occupied by bedrooms, sitting rooms and bathrooms. The woman led Hilda downstairs to the apartments on the lower ground floor. Here she showed Hilda an immense Grill Room, a smoking and reading room, a small palm court and a billiard room. In the Grill Room she explained, "This is where you will work as a waitress. Our waitresses are commonly known as Nippies, so called because they are forever nipping here and there and our service is quick and reliable. You will be expected to start tomorrow morning at eight o'clock sharp." Hilda nodded to acknowledge the woman's instructions. Then she was handed a bundle. "You will have to wear this uniform and it is your responsibility to see that it stays in the same pristine condition it is in today." Hilda thanked the woman for her time and promised she would return for work tomorrow at eight.

Later, at home, Hilda unpacked the bundle of clothes and found she had been supplied with a black dress incorporating a white collar, a white apron and a matching hat. George teased Hilda when she tried it on for him, later that evening. The clothes were a perfect fit. The woman had judged Hilda's size remarkably well, and George thought Hilda looked very grand in her uniform. "There'll be no more waiting on for me then," smiled George. "I wouldn't be able to afford you a tip. You're far too grand for the likes of me."

"Nonsense," blushed Hilda. "I don't know how I'm going to keep it so clean."

Although the hours were long and she was on her feet for much of the day, Hilda adored her new job. She enjoyed the banter between the other girls, behind the scenes in the kitchen with the chefs and the play-acting for the customers in the Grill Room. She worked hard and got to know her regulars well and received plenty of tips and male attention. The tips she accepted gracefully but the male attention she always declined politely. It wasn't long before Hilda was asked to work some shifts in the Rotunda Court also.

Hilda's confidence grew as she was given more responsibility and learnt how to deal with difficult customers. She was always pleased to see George pay her a visit for his tea on the days when she worked late, although it was difficult at times not to disclose to the other waitresses that they knew each other. On other days George would discreetly wait outside for Hilda until she finished work and then they would travel home together to their Battersea flat.

Since starting work, Hilda had made new friends, but there was one girl in particular with whom Hilda got on well and liked more than any other. The two women had been moved from the Grill Room to the Rotunda Court at the same time. Quite often their shifts would coincide. On occasions they had eaten out together after work if they had been on the same shift, or met for a coffee before their shift had begun.

Hilda found she was able to confide in her new-found friend. Ruth was a little younger than Hilda but you would not have known it. She had short dark hair and a pale complexion, great teeth and a tiny body but looked and appeared older than Hilda.

Feeling confident that they had got to know one another well, they disclosed some of their deepest secrets to each other. Hilda informed Ruth about how she was living with George and the problems she had experienced leaving her father, and Ruth told Hilda how she had recently become divorced after a very short, abusive marriage. Ruth was a true friend and wanted to help Hilda wherever she could. The pair would swap many stories and experiences with one another over the coming months.

On her way to work on Tuesday morning, 21 January, Hilda's eyes were drawn, as were those of every passer-by, to the newspaper headlines which were splattered across every front page. Sellers shouted at the tops of their voices the devastating news of the King's death. Along with the rest of the crowd Hilda felt compelled to purchase a newspaper. Her *Daily Mirror's* headline read "The King Dies – his hand clasped by the weeping Queen". Hilda was overwhelmed, as was the rest of the population. She had not switched on the radio that morning as she had been running late and so had missed the inevitable announcement. She read as quickly as she could, while being jostled by the crowds, reading how King George V had been ill for some years with breathing-related difficulties. His son Edward had taken over many of the King's duties during this time. The report read that on the evening of 15 January, the King had taken to his bedroom at Sandringham House, complaining of a cold. He had never left that room. He had gradually become weaker, drifting in and out of consciousness. His physician, Lord Dawson, admitted hastening the King's end by giving him a lethal injection of cocaine and morphine, both to prevent further strain on the family and so that the news of his death could be announced in the morning edition. It was stated that the King died at 11.55pm and would be buried at St George's Chapel, Windsor Castle.

This sad news had an impact on Hilda's customers at the Regent Palace that day and for a good many weeks thereafter. The business was affected as many people appeared to stay away and the ones who did call in were understandably in sombre mood. The only subject of quiet discussion that took place that day and for many days thereafter, between customer and waitress, and amongst the staff themselves, was the sad news of the King's death.

One week later, when it was the day of the King's funeral, the Grill Room to the Rotunda Court closed its doors for a couple of hours, as a mark of respect. As the funeral cortège made its way from Westminster Hall, where the King's body had lain in state, to St George's Chapel, Windsor, Hilda and Ruth were amongst the thousands paying their respects. Desperate to get a glimpse of the royal procession they unashamedly pushed their way to the front of the crowds of onlookers.

From Westminster Hall, where for the previous four days the King had received the homage of thousands, his coffin, draped with the Royal Standard, was carried on a four-mile procession through the streets of London to Paddington station. Here, the King's body was placed in the funeral coach for Windsor. Immediately behind the gun carriage, which bore the King's coffin, walked King Edward VII followed by the Queen Mother. Crowds of silent mourners lined the route of the procession, bowing their heads as the procession passed. Hilda and Ruth both managed to get a momentary glance of the coffin and King Edward's head before the sea of people engulfed them once more. The solemn silence which fell upon the waiting crowds left a deep impression on the pair, one they would remember for the rest of their lives. It was broken only by the tolling of Big Ben in the distance and the boom of the minute guns in Hyde Park.

That evening at home, Hilda relayed her experience to George, who sat listening intently to her every word. Unlike Hilda's employers, Mr Sorensen had insisted the salon stay open for business that day. He had explained to his staff that some of their clients had booked many weeks in advance and he felt unable to disappoint them.

Not for the first time since the King's death, Hilda found herself thinking about her father and wondering about his thoughts and feelings on the matter. She knew he would be finding today particularly difficult and wondered if he too, as many others, had closed his shop, out of respect.

The news of the King's death had reached Edwin that very same morning. His first customer had entered the shop and enquired if he had heard the news. As Edwin was always up very early to prepare his shop, he had not heard or read of the King's demise. After his initial shock, Edwin had shut the shop for an hour over lunchtime, which just also happened to be his quiet period. He had used this time to read the details of the King's death in the local *Farnham Herald*. He had previously known about the King's ill health and had expected his death to have come sooner, but it was still a shock to Edwin, now that it had finally happened. Edwin's customers talked of nothing else all day. Most were sorrowful and mourning the King's death, so by late afternoon Edwin had had enough and took the unusual step of shutting up his shop early. That evening he had sat alone in the upstairs front room listening to his gramophone records.

On the day of the King's funeral Edwin found himself strangely drawn to thinking about Hilda. No matter how he tried to direct his thoughts elsewhere they kept coming back to Hilda. He knew she lived somewhere in Battersea, and that Battersea wasn't far from where the funeral cortège would process and he couldn't help wondering if she might be among the many mourners.

Edwin did not shut his shop on the day of the King's funeral as he felt he had already paid his respects to the King. Besides, he felt he couldn't afford to close again so soon and lose yet another day's takings. As it was, business was slow that day and his mind kept slipping back to Hilda. He missed her and considered for a split second if he should write. He knew Doris would have an address for her; they were bound to have stayed in contact as they had always been close. But as quickly as he contemplated the discussion it might generate between him and Doris, he obstinately pushed the ridiculous idea from his mind.

It was the end of February when Hilda discovered she was pregnant. She had suspected nothing when her period had been late, as this was not unusual for Hilda, but over the past couple of weeks and usually in the mornings while at work she had experienced a strong feeling of nausea. At first she had wondered if it had been something she had eaten, some food that hadn't agreed with her. She had discussed it with George and the idea that Hilda could be pregnant hadn't crossed either of their minds. But after a week or two of feeling this way it had been her friend Ruth who had suggested the possibility to Hilda. Without consulting George, Hilda arranged to visit a doctor for confirmation. The doctor hesitated little in giving his professional opinion of Hilda's condition. He was adamant she was with child.

On the way home all Hilda could think about was how George would react when she told him, for she would have to tell him. It would be unfair to keep the news to herself, besides, George would want to know. He would want to share the responsibility, wouldn't he, and he'd know what to do? As Hilda thought about the new life she was carrying, little fizzes of excitement bubbled up inside her. She couldn't wait to share her news with her best friend, Ruth and then there were her sisters. The baby of the family was having a baby! Oh dear God, what would they all say? How would they all react? Her father would go mad. She wasn't even married to George. Feelings of panic started to fill the spaces where the fizzes of excitement had previously been. Then the story of Elsie, which George had shared with her not long after they had first met, leapt into her mind. Hilda desperately hoped George would not see any comparisons between past events and those of which she would soon be sharing with him. She now realised she would have to pick the right moment in which to tell George as her news may prove difficult for him to accept. She would also have to tell George first, before anyone else, even her best friend Ruth. But over the next week, she could never seem to find the right moment.

During that week at work, the girls at the Regent could talk of nothing else but who was brave enough to propose to their boyfriend, as this year was a leap year. It appeared to be an acceptable thing for a woman to do during a leap year but Hilda disagreed. "I must be old fashioned," Hilda whispered to her friend, Ruth during their lunch break. "I think there's something much more romantic about a proposal of marriage if it comes from the man."

"I would have to agree with you there," replied Ruth. "You wouldn't find me proposing to a man. It all sounds a little desperate to me."

Later, at home, when Hilda recalled the conversation she had had with Ruth, it dawned on her that the situation she now found herself in was desperate – living in sin, as well as being pregnant. Her poor, dear mother must be turning in her grave. Was it any wonder her father wanted nothing to do with her? Hilda concluded there was nothing else for it. She could put it off no longer. She would have to tell George, tonight, and hope he took her news positively.

George arrived home around seven. He gave Hilda a big kiss and a squeeze as he did every evening when he arrived home. Hilda had been on the early shift that day, so had the dinner all ready for them and they sat down to eat straightaway. The time had come to share her news with George, but suddenly she found herself unable to string together the right words. She sat picking at the food on her plate, deep in thought.

"Are you all right?" asked George. "You've not eaten much."

"Yes, I'm fine." There was a pause, and Hilda continued. "Actually George, I have something I need to tell you."

"Oh yes," he smiled looking up from his plate. "That sounds

ominous," he said thinking she might have splashed out and bought something that perhaps she shouldn't have.

There seemed to be no other way and the words rushed out uncontrollably from her mouth. "I'm pregnant."

Silence fell between them, as George took in her news. Hilda thought she saw him turn a little pale. After a few seconds George asked, "Are you sure?"

"Yes, I've had it confirmed," said Hilda calmly.

George looked a little surprised. After another few seconds he asked, "Well, how do you feel?" Now it was Hilda's turn to be surprised. "I don't know really. I don't actually feel any different at the moment, just a little queasy sometimes."

"No, I don't mean physically," said George a little abruptly. "I mean about having a baby, with me?"

"Oh I see." Hilda thought for a second. "Well I think I'm happy about it."

"You only think you're happy?" enquired George with a smile, touching her hand and putting Hilda immediately at ease.

"OK, I'm over the moon really, except that I wasn't expecting things to happen quite as quickly as they have."

"No, neither was I," George admitted honestly. "But now they have I couldn't be more happy." He got up from the table and walked around to Hilda. Taking her into his strong, safe arms he held her close, pondering his impending fatherhood. His thoughts were interrupted as he realised Hilda was crying.

"What's the matter, Babe?" he asked, cupping her tear-stained face in his hands.

"I wasn't sure how you would take the news," she explained. "I guess I'm just relieved."

"How did you think I would take it?"

"Well, I wasn't sure, knowing that something like this has happened to you before."

"Nothing like this has happened to me before. I'm in love with you and totally committed to you. It's nothing like last time."

"So you don't feel trapped?"

"Please don't ever think that way."

The pair embraced again and savoured a lingering passionate kiss. George then gently took hold of Hilda's hands and, holding her away from him but looking directly into her eyes, said, "I'm afraid I am totally unprepared for this." Still holding her hands he bent down to kneel on the floor. He looked up at his Babe with a deep desire in his eyes and spoke with a shaky voice. "Babe, would you do me the honour of becoming my wife?"

Hilda was temporarily stunned, but soon managed to gather herself. "Nothing would make me happier," she replied, tugging at him to stand up.

"I'm sorry I don't have a ring for you," he explained as he stood up.

"I don't need one George. It's not as though I'll be able to wear it anyway."

"What do you mean? You should have an engagement ring."

"I won't be able to wear it at work, so it seems a little pointless. Besides, we could probably do with the money now."

George looked a little dejected. "Who made you the sensible one all of a sudden?"

"I tell you what, George, once we've set a date, how about we just spend the money on two wedding rings."

"Oh all right Miss Practical, if you are really happy with just a wedding ring."

"I am," reassured Hilda.

"Well I guess all that remains is to set a date. Do you have any preference as to when?" asked George.

Hilda knew she couldn't leave it too late as she didn't want to be showing on her wedding day. She also knew they would have to marry in a register office rather than a church. She would not feel right about a church wedding under the circumstances. "How does early June sound, maybe around my birthday?"

"Sounds like you have it all planned."

"No no, I don't, honestly, George," replied Hilda nervously. The last thing she wanted was for George to feel trapped. "I just thought it would allow me to work for as long as possible, giving us more time to save up."

"I'm only teasing you," he said, pulling her towards him for another cuddle. "You take life too seriously sometimes. June sounds lovely, and you're lovely, and I can't believe how lucky I am."

"Stop it, George, you'll have me in tears again."

George and Hilda spent the next three months working hard and trying to save as much money as possible. They had been unable to book Battersea Register Office for Hilda's birthday, but secured 13 June, the Saturday after.

It was late April before Hilda wrote to her sister Doris to share her news. She had chosen to wait till then to tell her sister as she wanted to make quite sure that everything was all right with the baby. (And somewhere very deep down inside she needed to be sure that George wasn't going to change his mind.)

Hilda's sisters had written regularly each month since Doris had informed them of her move to Battersea. It had been difficult for Hilda not to be tempted to share her good news with them and especially Doris. On many occasions she had almost written phrases like, "and when we get married George hopes to visit the new Simpson's store in Piccadilly and get himself a new suit" or ask her sister Doris questions about pregnancy. But she had managed to stop herself in time.

Hilda's correspondence from Evelyn told her all about a small cottage she and Jim had recently purchased in East Street. They had sold their property on Ivy lane and moved the business into premises at 43 Downing Street, just doors away from their father's fish shop. She was very excited about their new venture, explaining, how when the "The Central Garage" sign had gone up over the front of the building, it had been a very proud moment for both of them. According to Evelyn the business was going from strength to strength as she explained how hard she and Jim were working to ensure it was a success.

Violet had also sent Hilda a couple of letters. Hers were always filled with funny stories about her fish shop, the Sea Lion on Downing Street, or gossip about other Farnham residents. Whenever Violet's letters arrived they always seemed to lift Hilda's spirits. When reading one of them Hilda could almost picture herself back on Downing Street, during the days when her life had been less complicated.

Hilda had even received one letter from her sister Nan, telling her all about where she was working and how wonderful her employer was. He was a retired Lieutenant Colonel in the British Army and had in his time been posted to many countries. He had been made a Lieutenant Colonel in 1920 and during his time in the army had been shot at on more than one occasion. Nan had been employed by him now for some years, ever since the death of his wife in 1927, and he had always allowed her free rein of his grand house in Devon. It appeared he was a very kind and generous man.

Receiving these letters from her sisters served to make her father's lack of contact with her even more apparent to Hilda. It hurt her terribly to feel as though her father had disowned her and wanted nothing more to do with her. She so desperately hoped he would change his mind. If he knew that she and George were to be married and that she was going to have a baby, then maybe, just maybe, he might, but she doubted it.

Having waited all these weeks to break her news to Doris, Hilda sat at the table in the front room unable to think of what to write, or rather how to write it.

She began with, "My dear sister Doris." That bit was easy. Then she was stuck. After some time and many pieces of writing paper later, she managed to produce a letter which she was finally satisfied with.

My Dear sister Doris,

I have wanted to share this news with you for some time now, and I am sure you will understand why I have chosen to wait until now. George and I are getting married on 13 June at Battersea Registry Office. I am of course thrilled at the prospect and couldn't feel happier. We would love for you, Evie and Violet to be there, but understand you all have other commitments at home and therefore would not ask this of you. But if you could find it in your hearts to give us your blessing, I could ask for no more.

My dear sister, you have always been very supportive of my decisions, even though some, I'm sure, have not always been ones that you yourself would have made. I know how you must have felt when I left Farnham to set up home with a man to whom I was not married, but I have not regretted that decision and I appreciate you did not try to prevent me. I am afraid then, that I must shock you further, by letting you know that George and I are expecting a baby in September.

Although at first we were both surprised that it had happened so quickly, we are both extremely happy with the notion of becoming parents. I plan to finish working at the Regent before I begin to show, so as to avoid any scandal. My best friend, Ruth, has been so supportive and has agreed to be a witness for us at the wedding.

Well then, now you know. Please be happy for me Sis. I am so content with George. I couldn't wish for anyone more caring or giving.

I would ask you one small favour and I'm sure you can guess what is coming next. This news would probably destroy Father if he ever found out and for that reason I am sure you will agree that there is no need for him to be told.

I trust that you, Sydney and your lovely boys are all in good health. I miss you all greatly and send much love.

Your devoted sister, Babe.

Doris wrote back in record time. "Must have been delivered by carrier pigeon," George exclaimed as he picked it up from the doormat on Saturday morning. Hilda snatched the letter from George's hand, ripping it open eagerly. Doris had obviously been shocked to hear of her sister's news and began her letter by telling Hilda so. She worried greatly for her sister and couldn't help feeling things were moving too fast, but kept those thoughts to herself. Later in her letter, Doris tried to put Hilda's mind at ease by reassuring her that her sisters would support her in her decision and that their father would not hear anything on the matter from any of them. Doris ended her letter by saying that she didn't think she would be able to make the wedding, but would arrange for a wedding gift to be sent nearer the time.

Over the next couple of months the pair continued to write regularly to one another. The contents of these letters now had more to do with the arrangements and outfits for the wedding or guidance and information on the subject of pregnancy and child-birth. Hilda was amazed at how much her sister knew about both subjects, but of course she had the advantage of already having done both. There also seemed to be very little that Hilda could ask that would faze her sister. Doris offered an answer for everything, but they both realised that it was up to Hilda to choose if she took that help and advice.

Chapter 12

Doris had never blamed Hilda for leaving their father and Farnham or for the decisions she had made later. She admired her sister's determination and independence and as a joint wedding gift from Nan, Evelyn, Violet and herself, Doris had purchased a new radio to replace Hilda's old one, the one she had rescued from her father's house. The girls were all aware of how their youngest sister enjoyed listening to the radio, so they had clubbed together and chosen her a Philco People's Radio. It was Doris who arranged to have it delivered the week before the wedding and Hilda arrived home from work to find a delivery boy on her doorstep, looking for somewhere to leave his parcel.

Hilda was delighted with her gift and gave it pride of place on her mantelpiece, removing the old one and relocating that to the windowsill in the kitchen. "Why don't you just throw it away," George had complained later that day.

"I don't know. I just can't," explained Hilda. "Not yet."

She had previously informed Doris, in one of her letters, about how she had accidentally dropped their father's old radio while carrying it under her arm to take it to another room, so that she could listen to it while she continued with her chores. Since that day it had never sounded quite the same. Now she would be able to listen to her favourite programmes wherever she was in the flat. The Philco had a much clearer sound compared to her father's old thing and could go much louder. Hilda loved it.

Saturday, 13 June was a warm muggy day to begin with, which soon clouded over and produced much rain. Around 11.30am the rain briefly stopped and a gentle breeze rustled through the leaves in the park trees as George and Hilda left their flat for the short walk to Battersea Town Hall. George was thirty-two and Hilda twenty-eight, both old enough to marry, both able and willing to make the commitment, but it had crossed both of their minds whether they would be doing this if it wasn't for the baby Hilda was carrying.

They arranged to meet their work colleagues outside the Town Hall at a quarter to twelve. When Hilda had asked her best friend, Ruth, if she would be a witness at her marriage, Ruth had cried. The two friends had become very close over the past six months and had shared many secrets together. At first, Hilda thought she must have said something to upset her friend, but later they had laughed about Ruth's oversensitive emotions. "I'll try not to do this on the day," Ruth promised. "Well, if you do it will only start me off," Hilda replied. "Any little thing seems to set me off at the moment."

When George had asked his work colleague William to be his witness, he'd replied, "It's about time you made an honest woman of her," then concluded he would be honoured to be their witness. The two men had always got on well, ever since their first meeting back when George had first been introduced to everyone at the salon. George had confided in Will when Hilda had told him she was pregnant, but as with most men, it had been mainly business issues which were discussed between the pair and rarely personal ones.

As they left their flat, Hilda thought George looked incredibly handsome, dressed in the dark suit which he had purchased second hand. He wore a Navy tie which he had borrowed from Will and shiny black shoes which he had spent ten minutes polishing that morning. His hat, he wore with a slight tilt making him appear even more attractive, if not a little intriguing. He'd placed a cream-coloured carnation, delivered earlier that morning along with Hilda's bouquet, into his buttonhole and was very sensibly carrying a black umbrella over his arm. He had planned to purchase his new suit from Simpsons but unfortunately discovered they were a little out of his price range and what with the baby on the way it was an expense they could do without. So when he had spotted an advert for a second-hand suit in the post office window he wasted no time in contacting its previous owner. Luckily for George the man was a very similar height and build and the suit had fitted beautifully. "Who needs Simpsons," joked George as he strutted around the flat, showing off like a peacock for Hilda, in his new two piece.

Hilda was wearing new stockings and shoes, a cream silk and lace drop-waist dress and a matching hat. Ruth had organised for Hilda to borrow the dress and hat from her older, slightly larger, sister, who had recently married and now lived in London. By now, Hilda was five months into her pregnancy and just about showing. She had a tiny protruding bump in front of her which appeared to Hilda to be growing on a daily basis. She was very conscious of it, especially at work and it was becoming increasingly difficult to disguise it. Today however, she was doing a good job of hiding her shape as she held her small bouquet of flowers permanently in front of her little bump.

As they approached the Town Hall, it suddenly began to rain heavily. George put up his black umbrella and held it over Hilda. They spotted their friends Ruth and William waiting outside, dressed in their Sunday best and struggling to put up their umbrellas.

"Well, our witnesses have turned up," said George.

"I guess we had better go through with it then," smiled Hilda.

"Looks that way," grinned George as he leaned over and kissed her on the cheek.

When they reached their friends, the women embraced one another and the men shook hands. Umbrellas danced in all directions as George moved to hug Ruth and William dodged George to kiss Hilda.

"Come on! I'm getting wet," shouted George as he indicated they should all go inside. The grand looking building they entered was little more than forty years old. It had been built in 1893 and used as council offices ever since. Built in a "Modern Renaissance" style, it displayed red Suffolk brick and Bath stone elevations, along with a green Westmorland slate roof. "Do you know it took them less than two years to build this and it cost around £42,000," Will informed everyone as they entered. "It was designed by Edward Mountford, the same architect who designed the Old Bailey," Will continued and then abruptly ended his guided tour as he realised no one was paying him much attention. Once inside there was a grand staircase opposite the main door, with a half-landing and then curving wings sweeping up on each side to the first floor. The small party of four ascended the staircase and waited where they had been directed to by a stuffy-looking woman, until it was their time to be called to enter the registrar's office room.

After what seemed like an age, their names were called and they were invited into the room. It had a high ceiling with huge high windows and a marble floor. Once inside, it was all over in no time at all. A short ceremony was conducted after which George kissed his new wife, there was more hugging and shaking of hands and then the small wedding party added their signatures to the register. Hilda was a little subdued afterwards because she had expected the ceremony to be somewhat more special. As the party was leaving the building and reached the bottom of the steps George said, "Now the formalities are over, can we all go and enjoy ourselves?"

"Enjoy a drink or two, is that what you mean?" replied Will.

"Well, it is a special day," said Ruth, rummaging inside her handbag for something.

"Actually I didn't mean that," said George. "I just meant we can all relax now and enjoy a nice lunch together."

"Might have known you'd be thinking of your stomach," laughed Hilda.

"Oh I can't win, can I?" George looked dejected.

"Poor George," smiled Ruth as she threw a large handful of rice up into the air above Hilda's and George's heads. The tiny pieces scattered to the floor all around the newly married couple as Will and Ruth cheered. George and Hilda laughed as they shook themselves free of the rice. Ruth pushed a bundle into Will's hand and said, "On the count of three, Will. One, two, three," she screeched and they both released another handful of rice, together this time. George and Hilda were showered with the grains as they tried unsuccessfully to dodge the cascade. When the merriment had subsided it was Hilda who spoke first. "Come on then *husband*, I'll treat you to lunch."

"I like the sound of that," said George, "and I don't mean the word lunch."

"I know what you mean. It sounds strange doesn't it?" said Hilda.

"Yes my darling *wife*, it does. But I know I will soon get used to it."

As they left the Town Hall it started to rain again. Hilda linked arms with her husband and took shelter under his umbrella while their friends followed closely behind. Above them there were rumblings of thunder and in the distance this was preceded by flashes which lit up the sky. "I had imagined that on my wedding day it would be gloriously sunny," Hilda said, turning to speak to Ruth. "Not a bit like the weather is today."

"No, but don't you think there is something curiously romantic about thunder and lightning?" asked George. Hilda, Ruth and Will all looked at one another, then at George, shook their heads and laughed. It never ceased to amaze them how George could always see the positive side to things.

Hilda had previously arranged for the four of them to have lunch at the Prince Albert pub. She and George had got to know the landlord and his wife quite well since they had moved to Battersea. The landlady had said they could use the bridge room upstairs for their reception if they wished, but knowing there would only be the four of them, Hilda had politely declined and decided they could enjoy lunch quite happily together in the main bar area. She didn't want any fuss. The landlady had promised she would make sure the food was a little more upmarket than normal as it was a special occasion and had asked if there was anything they didn't like. "No no, just whatever is on the menu," Hilda had replied.

The landlady couldn't resist a celebration and had excelled herself throughout the afternoon and early evening with a steady flow of food and drinks. The girls had laughed together about how she would make a good "Nippy". The wedding party enjoyed their afternoon together, supplied with good food, a little alcohol, great friendship and plenty of laughter. They hadn't noticed the time slipping away as they swapped funny stories about their workplaces and discussed their futures. They didn't part company until around 8pm that evening and it wasn't until then that George noticed his new wife looking a little tired.

"What a day!" George said as he fumbled to turn the key in the door to their flat, a little the worse for drink.

"Yes, I'm exhausted," sighed Hilda. "Ooh!" she exclaimed as George unexpectedly bent down and scooped her up into his arms, staggering slightly as he carried her over the threshold.

"Blimey, Babe, you're getting heavy," spluttered George as he gently placed his wife back down onto the floor inside their flat.

"That's your son, not me," replied Hilda.

George stared at his wife. "What makes you think it's a boy?" he asked.

"Just a feeling I have," smiled Hilda.

The pair grinned at each other, and then embraced for some time before George suggested they have an early night. It had rained almost continuously all day and that night as they lay together in their bed, content and happy with their lives, they fell asleep listening to the rain bouncing off the roofs and pavements outside.

Thoughts of their unborn child whizzed around inside their heads and they wondered about what the future might hold for them all.

It wasn't long after her wedding day that Hilda was forced to give in her notice at the hotel. It came as a relief. Recently she had started to feel very tired by the end of her shift and worried that being on her feet all day might not be good for the baby. Knowing that she was breaking the rules of her employment by being married and pregnant made her feel uneasy. She hated lying. If she and George hadn't needed the money she would have packed it in months ago. As it was they desperately needed the extra money so she endured the pretence for as long as was possible. Hilda was relieved to be leaving on her own terms and not to have had her secret discovered by her employer or one of the girls. She hadn't been worried about Ruth spilling the beans, she trusted her completely, but she had been convinced ever since her wedding that somehow, someone would soon find out. A feeling of relief washed over Hilda as she left the hotel after her last shift that day. All she had to concentrate on now was George and their baby.

Hilda had the radio on all the time now that she was at home every day. Often she would leave it on when she had to pop out to the shops. Turned down low, on her return it made her feel as though she was not coming home to an empty house. If the sound of a familiar voice or cheerful tune greeted her as she entered the empty flat, it allowed her to cope better with her loneliness when George was at work all day.

Being in the basement flat, the sound of her radio often travelled up through the building allowing the other residents to hear snippets of programmes and often Hilda singing along to favourite tunes. Mrs Wootley, a woman who cleaned the flat upstairs for "posh June", as George and Hilda had nicknamed her, had started to call Hilda "the singing bride" soon after her new radio had arrived because she could be heard singing at all times of the day in her flat. Hilda had many favourite radio programmes. She liked *The Fred Allen Show* which was a variety show, and *Shadow*, a mystery drama, but *Gangbusters* was her most favourite radio programme. It was a police drama with ear-splitting sound effects such as loud car engines, screeching tyres, crashes, explosions and sirens. This was Hilda's time to escape. Sitting in her front room in the armchair by the window with her eyes tightly shut, she could almost believe she was one of the cast.

Hilda also enjoyed the radio as it kept her up to date with current affairs. Earlier in March she had listened intently to her father's old crackly radio and heard most of the information being broadcast about the construction of the Hoover Dam and how it was at last completed. During April she had listened with concern about the tornadoes which were striking Mississippi and Georgia which had killed over 400 people, and at the end of May, Hilda heard only part of a piece about how the RMS *Queen Mary* had just left Southampton on her maiden voyage across the Atlantic, as the radio had kept cutting out after she had dropped it. In June, listening to her new, crystal clear radio given to her by her sisters, she had discovered how thousands of people were dying in North America because of a heatwave. She found it incredible that two countries could be so very different. We were all soaked on Saturday outside the Town Hall, she thought. I can't begin to imagine what it must be like for those poor people, dying in such heat. As Hilda pondered their situation, she thought she might like to visit another country in the future with George and their child, but listening to current affairs programmes like these made her realise the world was both an enormous and dangerous place and she couldn't but feel worried for her unborn child. She realised she had little control over what was ahead for her, George and the baby.

These anxious feelings had become more pronounced since she had handed in her notice at the hotel. Now that she was stuck at home alone for most of the day, she often found her mind wandering towards negative feelings and thoughts. She missed her little chats with Ruth and the fact that she had always been rushed off her feet all day. That feeling of exhaustion at the end of the day had allowed her no time to fret over her situation. She had been simply too tired. Now she found she had all the time in the world to worry about the "little things".

Sometimes her days felt endless, especially when George was working late. It was quite normal on a Thursday and Friday evening for him to be home late. He had agreed to this because he felt they could do with the extra money. He would often be travelling home from one of the other salons. As Hilda's pregnancy advanced she became more and more tired and on some occasions she would have gone to bed before George arrived home, so the pair were seeing less and less of one another.

Sundays, however, were still very precious to the couple as it was the only quality time they spent together. Sometimes they would go for walks in the park or for a trip up the Thames. Other times they would stay at home together and listen to the radio or play cards in the evening. Occasionally they would enjoy a visit from Ruth or Will or call at the Prince Albert for a drink or meal.

Today, as Hilda neared the end of her pregnancy, she sat alone in the flat on a Saturday afternoon while George was at work, waiting excitedly for her sister-in-law to arrive. George's sister and mother had both visited in early April as they had promised to do once the pair were settled. Before their visit, Hilda had been very anxious. George had decided to take the opportunity to tell his mother and sister the news about his impending marriage and the baby. Hilda had been worried about how they would respond to his news. She need not have worried as she hit it off with George's sister straightaway. Onlookers would have thought that it was Hilda and Wyn who were related, not George. Wyn was a few years younger than George and not unlike Hilda's big sister, Doris. The two women giggled together, teased George and talked weddings and babies for most of the duration of the visit.

"I knew you would get on all right," George had announced smugly after their visitors had left. "You're very similar really."

"Wyn is so kind and understanding," Hilda said.

"And very supportive of what we are doing," replied George.

"Yes," agreed Hilda. "Your mother was a little more difficult to impress though. I don't think she trusts me George. All those questions she asked. Did you hear her?"

George explained. "She was just doing what any mother would do for their son. She was just trying to protect me and make sure I'm doing the right thing."

"I don't think she likes me that much, George," continued Hilda.

"Nonsense, how could anyone not like you? She's a worrier, that's all. She's anxious that we have so many changes in our lives to adjust to and so quickly. It's nothing personal. Just give her time, you'll see," reassured George.

At the time of their visit, George's mother and sister had discussed the wedding plans in detail and promised to be there on the day. However, as the time had approached George's mother had become ill and on the day of their wedding was confined to her bed with her daughter taking charge of her care. It was not a life-threatening illness, she would make a full recovery, but she had been strongly advised by her doctor to take it easy and to get plenty of rest as her recuperation would then prove much quicker.

George's mother had returned to good health but said she would prefer to wait until after the baby had been born to visit her son and his wife, so Wyn had travelled alone across London to Battersea to visit her brother and Hilda. The two women were delighted to be in each other's company again. Hilda greeted Wyn with a big hug on the doorstep, struggling to get her arms around her sister-in-law as her baby insisted on keeping them apart. The pair laughed at being unable to greet each other properly and Wyn made do with patting Hilda's bump with gentle affection.

When George arrived home later Wyn noticed a certain unease between her brother and Hilda. George looked tired and was very much preoccupied with his work, explaining he had to be in early all next week as he had individual appraisals of his staff to oversee and a stocktake of all the salon's products. She noticed Hilda go very quiet whenever George's workplace was mentioned, showing little interest in it or George's role within the salon. Wyn was relieved when Hilda later confided in her, explaining she was seeing less and less of her husband as he was working longer hours. Hilda explained, "George is worried we won't have enough money when the baby arrives and so he's trying to save as much as he can now. Trouble is, he's working himself into an early grave. Have you noticed how tired he looks?"

"I understand how you must feel Hilda dear, but this situation won't last for ever. Things will improve for you both, I'm sure."

"I hope you're right," responded Hilda.

Wyn stayed overnight that Saturday evening. They all enjoyed a fish and chip supper which Wyn treated them to and later the three of them played cards and chatted. It wasn't a late night. Both George and Hilda appeared tired, so around ten o'clock Wyn suggested they all have an early night and her suggestion was received with little resistance. George and Hilda seemed more relaxed in each other's company the following Sunday morning as the three of them enjoyed a stroll around Battersea Park followed by a light lunch in the Prince Albert. Then it was time for Wyn to leave. "I'd better not miss my train or Mother will not be pleased. She reminded me as I was leaving that she expected me home in time for supper and that she was cooking a roast dinner."

"Well, we'd better let you get off then," smiled George, remembering how particular his mother could be. "It's been so great to see you Sis," he said as he grabbed his sister for a hug.

"Mother and I will be back to see you both as soon as the baby is born. You take care now and don't do too much," Wyn said, directing her comment at Hilda.

"I'll try not to," replied Hilda.

"Give our love to Mother," George shouted as he watched his sister climb the steps and walk out onto the pavement.

"Take care both of you," shouted Wyn, frantically waving goodbye and rushing off to catch her train.

Hilda's pregnancy hadn't been too traumatic, or so she kept telling herself. After all, she had never been through this experience before and hadn't really known what to expect. The sickness had stopped after about three months and for a while she had quite enjoyed being pregnant, especially around the time before and immediately after her wedding. She had had a lot of attention from Ruth, Will, her sister-in-law Wyn, her neighbours and of course from George. But for some reason towards the end of her pregnancy Hilda had become more and more worried and unhappy. As the imminent birth approached, she couldn't really find anything that should be making her feel this way, but was unable to free herself from her feelings of anxiety. Thoughts of her father would creep to the forefront of her mind but she would push them away again as quickly as they had arrived.

Hilda couldn't fault George. He was being so supportive, running here and there at all times of the day and night, fetching, carrying and collecting second-hand baby clothes, blankets, napkins, a Moses basket and other equipment from work colleagues and second-hand shops in preparation for their baby's arrival. Working mainly with women did have its advantages, he thought. And at the same time he was still working the long hours at the salons. There was actually very little left for Hilda to do and she couldn't help feeling, by the end of her pregnancy, a little bit, or rather a big bit, of a spare part.

Similar to that of her mother's first experience of giving birth, Hilda's labour was long and difficult. It continued for most of the day. It was late September. She and George had gone to the hospital when the contractions had started early on Thursday morning. They arrived at the hospital around 6am and it was still dark. Hilda appeared to be in a lot of discomfort and so George had decided going to the hospital was the safest option. They did not receive a very warm welcome. After about an hour they were directed to a waiting room on the labour ward. From here, within minutes of arriving, a nurse entered and escorted Hilda onto the ward. Here she was briefly examined, while George nervously passed the time flicking through magazines in the waiting room. A stern-looking matron approached the waiting room and flung open the door. George looked up in surprise. "It will be some time before your child puts in an appearance," she reliably informed him. "So you might as well go to work and call back around 5pm, when it's visiting time."

"Right," agreed George, standing up quickly and accidentally knocking into the table of magazines. "I'll just go and say goodbye to my wife then," said George, trying to pass the corpulent woman in the doorway. She tutted with disapproval as he passed her but George ignored it and went to find Hilda. Hilda was reluctant for George to leave but didn't fancy taking on the matron, so after a brief kiss and George promising to return around five, he left his wife in the capable hands of the hospital's medical team.

Hilda was soon assigned a doctor and midwife who introduced themselves and checked on her a couple of times during the morning. At 2pm Hilda was taken to the delivery suite. Joining her in the room where she was to give birth was Dr Rowland and the midwife, Jean, both of whom she had met earlier, and a stern-looking nurse. The doctor was very kind and patient with Hilda. He made her feel a little more at ease, although she was in a great deal of discomfort. When the pain became too great for Hilda, she was given morphine. The midwife and nurse busied themselves, finding plenty to do around Hilda. They were obviously trying to impress the doctor, the nurse almost neglecting her patient as she tried to impress him with her knowledge and expertise. At times, Hilda felt as though she was in her way.

Some hours later, as the labour approached its climax, the nurse became quite agitated with Hilda. She accused Hilda of not trying hard enough to push, when in reality Hilda was absolutely exhausted from her lengthy labour. "Just visualise yourself walking up a hill, and when you get to the top, push," advised the midwife.

"There are an awful lot of bloody hills!" shouted Hilda. "It's too difficult."

"You can do it Hilda, I know you can," reassured the midwife, calmly.

Dr Rowland took Hilda's hand and looked at her caringly, almost pleading with her. "Right Hilda, on the next contraction I want you to push with all your might."

Hilda managed a nod but inside she felt drained and unable to continue. I can't do this any more, she thought. I've no strength left. She found her thoughts drifting to her mother. I wish Mother was here, she thought. Dear God, I wish my mum were here. "Oh God, here comes another one," she shouted.

The officious nurse went in for the kill. "Right, PUSH you stupid girl," she spat at Hilda.

Both the doctor and midwife were taken aback by the nurse's approach but it made Hilda angry, and appeared to give Hilda the extra strength she needed to finish the job. Hilda gave another massive push and in doing so the baby's head appeared.

The baby's head was facing the wrong way and Hilda's perineal area had torn. The doctor and midwife looked at each other and knew what they had to do. Quickly they jumped into action. As carefully as they could, they attempted to turn Hilda's baby around. If they were unable to do this they knew Hilda could bleed to death and the baby might possibly die also. All the nurse could do was to look on powerlessly. After a few minutes of uncertainty the doctor and midwife were finally successful in their attempt and the child was turned. Hilda was blissfully unaware of what had just taken place and of the danger she and her baby were in.

She was too overwhelmed with the pain to consider her baby might be facing the wrong way. The effect of the morphine was beginning to wear off and she was in agony.

"One more push, Hilda," instructed Dr Rowland again.

Hilda did as she was told, gathering all the strength she could muster, and this time her baby was born. It was a boy. She was shown her baby briefly before he was whisked away to the other side of the room by the midwife to be weighed and cleaned. The placenta followed almost immediately enabling Dr Rowland to stitch Hilda quickly and stop the excess bleeding. When he had finished he said, "The nurse will clean you up and get you looking presentable. It's visiting time now, are you up to it, or would you like to rest?"

"I'd really like to see my husband if that's all right?"

"Well, not for too long though, OK?"

"All right," agreed Hilda. "Thank you, Doctor." She was relieved it was all over.

The nurse wasn't the gentlest of people as she cleaned Hilda up. Hilda was relieved when she'd finished and when she had finally left the room. There had been no conversation between the pair. As the nurse disappeared, the midwife returned with Hilda's baby boy, wrapped up in a hospital blanket. Hilda was able to hold her baby boy finally, for the first time. All the hideous pain, ghastly contractions and horrendous pushing were put to the back of her mind and a feeling of euphoria took over her whole being. She, as her mother before her, cradled her beautiful baby boy in her arms, soaking up the joy, pride and achievement she felt inside.

George dashed back to the hospital for five o'clock, finishing work early to be there for visiting time. He was completely unaware of what his wife had just been through and how close he could have come to losing them both. He had been asked to stay in the waiting room again while his wife was being prepared.

During all her hours in labour, Hilda had given little thought to

George. Now she was back on the ward with her baby she couldn't wait to see him.

George was filled with emotion when he was eventually allowed on to the ward. He moved across the room to Hilda's bed and plonked himself down next to his wife and their new baby. When he realised Hilda had given birth to a boy, as the child was wrapped in a pale blue blanket, he burst into tears. He hadn't expected to feel so moved by the scene before him and his emotions had taken him completely by surprise. This in turn moved Hilda to tears. She had never seen George cry before and didn't quite know what to say. But it didn't seem to matter to either of them as the tears were purely ones of joy, nothing else. Handing their son to her husband, Hilda asked George, "Have you thought about what we should call him?" George looked down at his son. He was perfect and so tiny. George slipped his left index finger into the palm of his baby's hand and his son, in turn folded his fingers around his father's. "How about George William, after his old dad?" grinned George.

"Perfect," answered Hilda, oozing with pride.

Hilda and baby George stayed at the hospital for about a week which was quite normal. George found time to visit the hospital every day in his lunch hour and rushed back in the evenings as well. During his evening visit on the second day, Hilda's mood had changed. By late afternoon that day, Hilda found herself feeling very tired and emotional and the smallest of things upset her. She kept bursting into tears for no apparent reason and no matter what she did, she just couldn't cheer herself up. To make matters worse, Hilda was having trouble breastfeeding her baby. When she tried, baby George just didn't want to latch on, which distressed Hilda progressively more after each subsequent attempt. Eventually, after many attempts and the baby becoming increasingly hungry and distressed, the midwife suggested Hilda try him with a bottle. She suggested Hilda use evaporated milk which was widely available at a low cost. She reassured Hilda by telling her that studies had shown that babies fed evaporated milk formula thrive just as well as breastfed babies.

Baby George took his bottle straightaway but Hilda was leaking so much milk from her breasts and they were so swollen and sore, she couldn't help wonder if she had done the right thing. She tried to breastfeed her baby again just before George arrived but the child screamed the place down. Once she replaced her breast with the bottle again, he quietened down. Hilda felt the other mothers on the ward staring at her as if to say, "Can't you shut him up or he'll wake up mine.

When George arrived Hilda burst into tears and having tried to console his wife without success, George went to seek advice from one of the nurses. "You mustn't worry sir, it's very normal. We call it the 'Baby Blues' and usually about half of all woman who have just had a baby experience these feelings a couple of days after giving birth."

"Oh I see," said George. "I hadn't realised. So it's nothing to worry about?"

"No sir, it's nothing to worry about."

George returned to his tear-stained wife and tried to reassure her. "It's a difficult time for all of us darling. We all need time to adjust, Babe, especially you."

"I just want to come home with you and the baby," complained Hilda. "I hate it in here."

"Just a few more days and you will be coming home," reassured George. "That's when the fun will start," he smiled.

"What do you mean?" asked Hilda.

"Well, the sleepless nights and nappies drying all over the place," grinned George. "Secretly, I can't wait for you both to come home either," he whispered, leaning forward and kissing Hilda on her cheek. They discussed all the things they wanted to do together and the places they wanted to visit with their son and by the time George left, Hilda had cheered up and was feeling more positive.

Hilda put on a brave face during her next few days in hospital. She was still very sore and it was difficult to move around easily, but she was relieved when she was eventually allowed home with George and their new baby son, one week after his birth. Financially George and Hilda were now secure. George's hard work and long hours had paid off but he still had to put in some long hours at the salon. George had been able to buy everything Hilda needed for the baby. The fact that most of the baby's things were second hand didn't matter. George had even managed to acquire the most beautiful pram from a friend of one of the girls at the salon. He'd pushed it home from work one day while Hilda was still in the hospital and received some funny looks when passers-by had realised it was empty. He hadn't told Hilda about the pram. He had wanted it to be a secret. So when they had arrived home from the hospital with the baby Hilda had wept at the sight of the pram, saying it was beautiful and it must have cost a fortune.

With George still working long hours, Hilda hardly saw anyone throughout the day. Mrs Wootley knocked on the window a couple of times on her way past to clean upstairs and called in to see the baby once and "posh June" had dropped by with a small gift, but apart from that, Hilda had received no other callers.

On her first morning at home, Hilda was immediately thrown in at the deep end as George left early for work and she was left alone with the baby. She hadn't realised, until then, just how much help she had been given by the nurses while in the hospital. By lunch time she was exhausted from the feeding, winding, changing, washing, cleaning and everything else that goes with having a newborn baby. After lunch, Hilda fell asleep on the bed next to baby George. It felt like only minutes, but in reality it was an hour and a half later when the baby woke his mother up with his cries. He was letting her know he needed his napkin changing. In an attempt to stimulate her mind, cheer herself up and relieve the feeling of loneliness she was experiencing, she turned on her radio.

Thankfully this had the desired effect. Hilda pulled herself together and completed the smelly task, then made up another bottle for her son. She hummed and sang quietly along with the music while she held him in her arms and he emptied his bottle.

Over the next few days things did not improve for Hilda. She was forced to pay a visit to her doctor when her wound became infected. It was agony to walk and sleeping was nearly impossible. She felt very embarrassed and downhearted over her situation and unable to discuss it with anyone. Everything seemed to be getting worse, not better. Every time her baby stirred, whimpered or cried, it made Hilda feel anxious and tense. She had no idea that motherhood could be like this. She was completely unable to relax and enjoy her new baby. She wasn't sure she was doing anything properly. Was she washing and dressing him correctly? Was she feeding him at the correct times and changing his napkin properly? What would she do if he became ill? She was on her own with the baby all day and sometimes in the evenings. This feeling of isolation Hilda was experiencing continued for the next few weeks. She managed to muddle along and, most of the time, keep her feelings hidden from George. On Mondays the week seemed to stretch out in front of Hilda and she longed for Sunday again when George was at home with her and their son. These were the days she wished could go on for ever. Things like a simple walk in the park with George pushing the pram and she linking his arm, were the happy times. But it would only last for a day and the following morning she would go back to feeling lonely and isolated again. George was blissfully unaware of the feelings his wife was experiencing. He believed she had made a good recovery after the trauma of their son's birth and although at times she appeared tired and a little irritable he thought nothing of it.

It wasn't until early November when the situation started to unfold and become more obvious to George. The baby was now six weeks old. Hilda's anxiety had amplified during the past week when she had discovered baby George was poorly. It appeared he had started with a cold. He had a runny nose, was sneezing a lot and struggling to take his bottle, and his sleeping routine had gone completely out of the window. Hilda hadn't slept properly for days either and felt completely exhausted.

It was Sunday morning and George was reading his paper with a coffee after his breakfast. He noticed Hilda becoming frustrated with the baby because it was refusing to take its bottle. "He probably doesn't feel like it Babe, if he's got a cold." George suggested.

"Well he needs to drink it, to keep his strength up," replied Hilda, unimpressed with her husband's "helpful" comment. Hilda tried once more and the baby pulled away from his bottle again, squirming on his mother's lap and protesting loudly.

"Should I have a try?" enquired George helpfully.

"If you like," glared Hilda, thrusting the baby and his bottle into George's arms.

"I think I'll go for a walk George, if that's all right with you? The fresh air will do me good." Not waiting for her husband to reply, Hilda grabbed her coat and left, slamming the door behind her. George fed his son, who took his bottle after a little encouragement and before he'd finished, had fallen asleep in his father's arms.

Hilda crossed over the road and headed for the park. She couldn't understand why she felt as though everything and everyone was against her. Why did she feel so tense all the time? Was she really such a bad mother? At that moment in time it seemed to Hilda that her baby and her husband appeared to think so.

Hilda wandered around the park for about an hour. It was quite busy. There were plenty of people who had decided to brave the cold weather, as it was dry and sunny. There were a few families out for a stroll, a number of people walking dogs, some young boys kicking a football around and a few courting couples, and for a time her mind was taken off her situation.

When Hilda saw two mothers pushing prams and chatting, she changed the direction in which she was walking so she wouldn't have to walk past or acknowledge them. She was angry. These mothers had reminded her of her own circumstances and of how alone she was feeling. As she walked further into the park, unthinkable dark thoughts started to enter her head. She wondered if her husband and baby would be better off without her. After all, she wasn't doing a very good job now was she? Things were just not working out as she had imagined they would. Would they really miss her if she wasn't around?

She plonked herself down onto a solitary wooden bench positioned just across from the bandstand. It was then that she realised she had tears streaming uncontrollably down her cheeks. She pulled a handkerchief from her coat pocket and wiped her face. You must try to pull yourself together, she told herself. This is helping no one. After a few more moments of contemplation she stood up, brushed down her coat and decided to make her way back home.

Upon her return, George was waiting in the window, visibly relieved to see his wife return. He moved to open the door for her, as she had neglected to take her key when she'd left in a hurry. Hilda fell into her husband's waiting arms and sobbed uncontrollably. "Whatever is it?" asked George.

"I don't know. I can't help feeling this way," she sobbed. "I just don't think I'm cut out to be a mother."

"Nonsense, you're doing incredibly well. You're just understandably exhausted."

George was a tower of strength to Hilda. He calmed her down and reassured her. He just had a knack of always being able to make her feel better. "It can't be easy looking after a young baby by yourself every day, especially when he's not very well," George said reassuringly.

"Where is he?" Hilda suddenly asked, looking around the room, concerned.

"He's fine. He's sleeping in our room. He was so exhausted after his bottle that by the time I'd changed his napkin, he'd gone to sleep."

"You changed him?" Hilda asked, surprised.

"Yes. I did have a little difficulty at first, trying to get the pin in. That's probably why he fell asleep. The poor boy was probably sick and tired of me battling with his napkin." Hilda managed a smile. "That's better," said George. "Now, sit down and I'll make us both a cup of tea." Hilda did as she was told and sat down in their one comfy armchair in the front room which the couple shared.

"I love you George," she said.

"I love you more Babe," said George, winking at his wife before he left the room to make the tea.

Over the next week Hilda tried her absolute hardest to remain more positive and cheerful. In herself she was feeling better. Whatever the doctor had prescribed her for the infection had done the trick and she struggled not to let the baby's illness worry her too much. She enjoyed taking him for walks in his beautiful pram, she bathed him with love and attention, she established a routine with his feeds and generally she made an effort to try to enjoy her son more. Sometimes it was a little difficult to know what he wanted or how he was feeling but she did seem to be coping a lot better. She had George's tea ready for him when he arrived home from work, the cupboards in the kitchen were well stocked and she was managing to keep on top of the housework and the huge amount of washing baby George was creating.

"I was getting a little worried about your wife," Mrs Wootley commented to George early one morning on her way into the upstairs flat. "I hadn't seen her for a couple weeks."

"She's been a little tired lately, Mrs Wootley," replied George.

"Oh, I see. Yes, babies can do that to a person."

"Yes, they certainly can," smiled George.

"Only I hope you don't mind me asking, it's just that I never hear her singing along to her wireless any more, while I'm doing my cleaning."

"Oh I think you will again soon. She's feeling much better now," said George. "Got to go I'm afraid or I'll be late for work."

"Yes, me too," laughed Mrs Wootley, glancing down at her watch. Later that morning Mrs Wootley's mind was put at ease when she heard Hilda's tuneful tones as she sang along to her radio and later she saw her leaving the flat with the baby in the pram and watched as she crossed the road, disappearing into the park. The woman was relieved and left for home later that morning with a spring in her step.

Later that week, Hilda bumped into Mrs Wootley leaving the upstairs flat, as she was arriving home with the baby. They stopped and chatted for a moment, both cooing over the baby in his pram. "I wouldn't mind looking after him for you, if you ever need to go out for any reason," offered Mrs Wootley, at which point the baby started to cry.

"I think he's hungry," said Hilda. "I best get him in, but thank you for your offer. It's very kind of you."

"That's all right dear," and they parted company.

By the end of that week, baby George was poorly again. Hilda had been concerned about him on the Sunday as he had vomited a couple of times after his feeds and she had voiced her concerns to George. George had tried to reassure her and said he didn't think it was anything too much to worry about. That night the baby had woken them a couple of times, appearing distressed for no apparent reason but on both occasions Hilda had eventually managed to get him back off to sleep.

When Monday morning arrived George and his son woke at exactly the same time. Hilda woke, bleary eyed, made the baby a bottle and fed him while George got dressed and prepared the breakfast. George left for work just after eight o'clock, kissing both his wife and child goodbye before he left. He had only been gone half an hour when Hilda noticed the baby's health decline rapidly and the child become very agitated. It seemed nothing Hilda did would pacify him. He was obviously in some discomfort but no matter what Hilda tried, she couldn't get him to calm down. She checked his napkin, tried him with another bottle, which he refused, winded him again thinking that was the problem and even tried singing to him to try to quieten him, but nothing worked. His little face had become quite flushed and as Hilda paced the floor of the flat's front room, with the baby in her arms wondering what on earth to do, she realised he was terribly hot. She panicked. She put him into his pram, covering him with plenty of blankets, grabbed the bottle he had just refused and a clean napkin and hurried out of the flat.

Hilda was almost running as she made her way down Albert Bridge Road and on to Battersea Park Road. The baby was yelling loudly as he was bumped and bounced about in his pram. She was heading for Bolingbroke Hospital, about two to three miles away, which she knew to be a small general hospital with an accident and emergency department. All she could think about was getting a doctor to look at the baby and she assumed this would be the quickest way. The doctor's surgery was always too busy and it was further away so her best bet would be the hospital. She had almost reached George's salon before she realised where she was. She halted abruptly and seeing George through the salon window, hammered loudly upon it to get his attention. In doing so she startled George, his staff and customers and George came rushing out to see what was the matter.

"The baby's unwell. I think he has a temperature. Nothing I do settles him," she yelled at George. "I'm taking him to Bolingbroke," she continued.

"Is that really necessary? asked George, a little baffled by his wife's behaviour.

"Well look at him George!" Hilda exclaimed.

"All right Babe," George said trying to calm the situation.

"Look, don't worry; I'm sure he'll be fine. You get him to the hospital and get a doctor to check him over. I'm sure they'll be able to put your mind at ease." George was concerned by his wife's behaviour. "Where's your coat? You'll catch your death."

In her haste to leave the flat she had neglected to put on her coat and it was rather a cold day. "I'm fine George."

"Wait there," he barked at Hilda. He hurried back inside to find his coat. He returned in seconds. "Here, put this on," he said to Hilda, placing his coat around her shoulders.

Hilda slipped her arms into the sleeves, which were rather too long for her, and raced off down the street, shouting "Thank you."

George went back inside the salon to a crowd of concerned faces. "Is everything all right George?" asked Joan. Joan was Mr Sorensen's daughter. She was a beauty specialist and her father had recently arranged for her to start working at George's salon. She was a pretty, petite girl, not unlike Hilda in many ways and she and George had always got on well together.

"Yes thank you, Joan. That was my wife. She's a little concerned about our son. It appears he's not well again."

"Do you need to go with her?" Joan enquired, concerned.

"No, I'm sure it's something and nothing. The little mite will be fine. Once a professional has taken a look, I'm sure my wife's mind will be put at ease."

"Well if you're sure George."

"I'm sure," said George turning back to face his staff and their clients.

"Everyone back to work," shouted George, as he noticed his staff had downed tools and been distracted since the interruption.

Meanwhile, still rushing, Hilda crossed over and turned left into Latchmere Road. This was a long, straight road which crossed over the railway twice and Hilda wondered at this point if she would ever get there. She was by now quite exhausted and her pace had started to slow. In her haste to reach the hospital she hadn't noticed her baby had fallen asleep. The next part of her journey took her left into Lavender Hill, then she cut through Lavender Walk and across onto Laithwaite Road, turning left into Wakehurst Road, where after another mile and climbing a small gradient, she finally reached the hospital, exhausted.

The hospital building was made from red brick with stone dressings and a tiled roof. It displayed timber sash windows and had been built in phases since 1901 and was only recently completed. On one side it overlooked Wandsworth Common allowing splendid views from the upper floors.

Hilda gently lifted the baby from his pram, leaving the pram parked outside next to the railings. She climbed the few steps to the entrance and walked in through the main doors. Quickly she explained her situation and within no time at all was shown through to an examination room where a doctor agreed to examine her baby.

Baby George was still asleep in her arms as she undressed him to be examined. He only woke when the doctor took him from his mother. The doctor examined George for some time, using a stethoscope, listening to both his front and back, then shining a light into his ears. Finally the doctor spoke. "I'm not sure what's wrong with him," he finally offered, unhelpfully.

"What do you mean? Why don't you know? But you think that there is something wrong with him?"

"I'm sorry. Children are not really my area of expertise. I suggest you take him to the Victoria Hospital for Children in Kensington."

"What? Where's that?" asked Hilda.

"It's about four miles away on the other side of the Thames. If you go over the Albert Bridge onto Chelsea Embankment, it's just down there on the left," the doctor explained, trying to be helpful at last.

The realisation of where this hospital was hit Hilda hard. I should have taken him there first. I'm so stupid, thought Hilda. She grabbed the child, finished dressing him and left immediately. Once outside she placed the child back into his pram. He looked up at his mother with big round eyes and smiled. She moved her hand to gently touch his cheek, which was on fire. Hilda began to push the pram at speed. "We'll be there before you know it, Georgie," she comforted.

Hilda arrived home that night, exhausted and pushing an empty pram. As she entered the flat around 7pm, George rushed up to her clearly concerned as to where she had been all this time. "Where's the baby?"he asked as he glanced down into the empty pram. As Hilda sobbed on his shoulder, George tried to understand and make sense of what had gone on that day. At the hospital, after many different doctors had given their opinions, it had been decided that they should keep the baby in overnight to monitor him. Hilda had been inconsolable, pleading to be allowed to stay with her child, but staff there would not allow it and she was informed that she could return in the morning after the doctor had completed his rounds.

After very little sleep George and Hilda woke to the sound of silence in their flat. They discussed if George should accompany Hilda to the hospital and Hilda told George, "I'll be fine."

"Don't you want me to come with you?" George asked, concerned.

"They will need you at the salon, George. I'll telephone you at work if there's any news."

"Are you quite sure?"

"Georgie will be much better today, I'm sure of it. He's in the right place."

"I know," said George. "You did the right thing, Babe."

And so, a little reluctantly, George left for work.

Hilda had not known what to do with herself all morning. She had wandered around the flat, glancing at the clock every five minutes. Around mid morning Hilda left for the hospital. She crossed the bridge over the Thames, turning right for Chelsea and walking alongside the river on her right. Then she turned left into Tite Street for the hospital. When Hilda was eventually allowed into the ward to see her baby, she was warned by the doctor that the baby's condition had worsened. Hilda's baby boy looked very poorly. He was pale, yet flushed with colour, and discoloured crusty mucus had formed below his nose. "It's nothing to worry about," said the nurse next to her. "We have everything under control and we are confident your boy will make a full recovery." With tears in her eyes, Hilda picked up and held on to her son's hot little hand. "You'll see. He'll be as right as rain in a few days," reassured the nurse.

Baby George was in hospital for five, very long days. It seemed like an eternity to Hilda and George. Every hour Hilda was allowed, she spent it at her son's side. Most of the time she felt tired and lethargic and had to force herself to stay awake. She was having difficulty sleeping at night and would wander around the flat during all hours, often disturbing George's sleep.

While his baby was in hospital, George tried to continue with his normal life, going into work every day but taking long lunch hours to meet up with Hilda at the hospital. Mr Sorensen had been very understanding when he had been informed of George's troubles by his daughter, Joan. It was during this week that George received a letter from his mother, asking for a convenient date when she and Wyn could visit. George reluctantly wrote back, hoping his mother would understand that he wished to postpone their visit until a time when things were a little more settled.

When Hilda was finally able to bring her baby home from the hospital, she couldn't have been happier. He was bright and cheerful. A healthy colour had returned to his face and he had his appetite back. George was relieved to see his son safely home again and that evening when he returned home from work he swung him round gently in his arms. The baby smiled as he recognised his father's face and gentle voice. Both parents helped to bathe their child that night, getting immense pleasure from having him back home with them.

For the next couple of days Hilda appeared happy and at ease with her baby but slowly, Hilda began to worry again. She worried about his health and whether she was a good mother. The baby seemed to be crying more and more often and this in turn caused Hilda to worry more. She rarely left the flat at all, resulting in her going for days without seeing anyone, except George and that might only be for a couple of hours a day. George noticed the change in his wife and asked for advice from friends. One of his friends was Joan from the salon. She had been so supportive and easy to talk to that George had opened his heart up to her one day after work. He explained his wife's behaviour, revealing how she never went out and the state of their flat and Joan tried to reassure him, saying she believed it was not uncommon for some women to go through this sort of thing after having a child. She was sure everything would get back to normal again soon and that George shouldn't worry.

Later that week, Hilda was sorting through the washing, checking trouser pockets before she soaked them in water, just as her mother had taught her, when she found a crumpled piece of paper inside a pair of George's work trousers. She opened up the paper, straightening it out with her fingers as she read. At first the words on the paper meant nothing, but then they settled somewhere heavy inside her heart and her chest started to pound. She read it again to make sure she had read it right.

George, I'm popping home. I will see you after work. J.

George had found Joan's note that day on the reception desk at work. He'd read it, put it into his pocket and forgotten it was there.

Hilda confronted George when he arrived home that night, holding up the note in front of his face. "It's just a note," was George's defence.

"Who from?" demanded Hilda.

"It's from Joan at work."

"Why were you meeting her after work?"

"I wasn't."

"Don't lie to me George," Hilda demanded loudly.

"I'm not. I'd asked her to stay later, after the salon had closed, so that I could talk to her in private." At this point, George realised that if he told Hilda that he had talked to Joan about their situation she wouldn't understand or appreciate the concern he had for her, so he had to think quickly.

"What about?" asked Hilda.

"We've been having a few staffing issues and I just wanted to go through a few ideas with her. She's Mr Sorensen's daughter you know."

"No, I didn't," said Hilda, lowering her voice.

"It's all very innocent," replied George. "You really have nothing to worry about."

Hilda thought for a moment. "I'm sorry George. I think I've jumped to the wrong conclusion."

"Yes, I think you have." George moved to give Hilda a hug. "I could never do that to you Babe. I love you."

"I'm so sorry George." Hilda felt her eyes sting as they filled with tears.

"Don't be sorry, I can see how you might have thought …" He stopped. "Well, you know."

"I'm so silly. I don't know what's wrong with me at the moment. I don't seem to be able to do anything right."

"Nonsense," said George and he pulled her close for a second cuddle. When they parted again, George asked tentatively, "Hilda, do you think you should see a doctor about the way you're feeling?"

"What do you mean?"

"Well, they might be able to give you something to make you feel better."

"I don't know George. I've had more than enough of doctors recently. I'll see how I feel in a few days." At this point the baby started to cry. "I think he's ready for his bottle. I'll go and warm it," said Hilda.

"Shall I give it to him?" asked George.

"Yes, thank you, and I'll get the supper started."

Another month passed and Hilda's situation did not improve. Christmas was rapidly approaching. George was busy at work and Hilda and the baby still spent most days alone together. Baby George's cold had resurfaced, coming and going intermittently and now he also had a terrible cough a lot of the time. On some days he would cough up his milk followed by thick phlegm. Hilda couldn't help feeling as though it was something she was doing wrong. She was sleeping less and less. On the rare occasion she got a full night's sleep she would wake in the morning, not feeling refreshed but exhausted, longing for more sleep. Her friend Ruth had visited a couple of times after George had contacted her concerned for his wife's health and Ruth had suggested Hilda try sleeping during the day. "When the baby has a sleep, why don't you?" So Hilda tried this, but it didn't work. She felt tearful all the time and would burst into tears at the slightest thing. Only the other day when she had just finished changing baby George's clothes because he had been sick down them, he was sick again all over his clean clothes and tears poured uncontrollably as she slumped to the floor feeling completely defeated. In the past this would have been something that would have made her feel frustrated but she would have laughed about it. Now she only felt utter despair.

Hilda began to wonder if she was losing her mind when time started to disappear from her day. She used to be quite good at planning her day and fitting into it all the jobs she needed and wanted to do, but just recently she seemed to be getting very little done. While George was at work the hours dragged and when he finally arrived home it seemed as though the day had passed quickly as Hilda realised she had got nothing done. She couldn't understand where her days had gone.

George recognised things were difficult for his lovely wife and knew she was struggling. He helped where he could, but it was impossible for him to be with her all day, every day. He took the opportunity, when it arose, to speak again to Hilda's friend Ruth, and disclose to her his home circumstances. He explained Hilda was finding it difficult at home on her own all day with the baby and Ruth mentioned that she had noticed the change in her friend and it worried her too. Ruth was very understanding and said she would help where she could. George arranged for Ruth to pop in every now and again, dependent upon her shift at work, to help Hilda and to keep her company.

George also spoke to Mrs Wootley who was eager to help, saying she had offered to have the baby once before. "I could call in when I've finished upstairs and take the little mite for a walk in his pram. I wouldn't mind. I love babies."

"That would be very kind, Mrs Wootley. I'm sure Hilda would appreciate that, but I'm sure she'd like your company as well. If you just wanted to call for a drink and chat, I'm sure you'd get to see the baby as well."

"That sounds great, love. Leave it with me," replied Mrs Wootley.

Hilda didn't mind Ruth calling round as it wasn't that often on account of her job. Ruth never outstayed her welcome and always seemed to understand just what her friend needed to hear. Mrs Wootley, on the other hand, in Hilda's opinion was nothing more than a gossip. At first she had seemed very friendly and Hilda was glad of the company but it soon transpired she had an alternative motive, that of being incredibly nosey. The woman would follow Hilda into the kitchen while she made them both a drink and she would talk nonstop from the moment she entered the flat until the time she left. After a while her constant chatting got on Hilda's nerves and Mrs Wootley began to irritate her. The problem was Hilda couldn't fault Mrs Wootley where her son was concerned. Although past the age for having children of her own, she seemed to have a natural flair for getting the baby to take his bottle and could change his napkin much quicker than Hilda ever could. On one occasion Hilda left Mrs Wootley, or Sarah as the woman had now insisted she call her, in the front room cooing over the baby while she had gone into the kitchen to make the tea. Upon her return, the drawer to a cabinet where she kept her personal letters looked as though it had been opened and not closed again properly afterwards. Hilda was sure the drawer had not been open when she had left the room and so after that she had been reluctant to allow the woman back into the flat. Hilda would time it so that the baby was ready in his pram for a walk just as Mrs Wootley rang the doorbell and this seemed to work, as Mrs Wootley appeared none the wiser to Hilda's motives.

On one occasion Mrs Wootley hadn't turned up at the flat when Hilda had expected her. Hilda knew she was upstairs cleaning as she had seen the woman arrive earlier. She allowed her another twenty minutes and then went to find her. Hilda had hoped to nip out while Mrs Wootley took the baby for a walk. There were a few things she needed for Christmas and she wanted to get them early before the shops got too busy. She rang the doorbell to the flat upstairs and Mrs Wootley answered. "Hello dear, what can I do for you?"

"Hello, Mrs Wootley," replied Hilda.

"It's Sarah, dear, I've told you that."

"Yes, sorry."

"What is it, dear?"

"I was just wondering if you could have the baby for me while I pop out to do a bit of shopping."

"Yes. I will dear, but I'm running a bit late today. I'll be another half hour. Is that OK?"

"Thank you Mrs Wootley, sorry, Sarah," Hilda quickly corrected herself. "I'll have him ready for you."

"All right dear, see you shortly." And with that Hilda returned to her flat.

Later that day, Sarah Wootley returned from the park with the baby and found that Hilda was not at home, so she took herself and the baby back to her house where she and her mother fussed over him all afternoon, discussing their concern for his nasty cough and cold. Sarah Wootley had wanted to do some of her own shopping that day but was forced to postpone it to another time on account of the baby. Finally, when Sarah Wootley returned to the flat with the baby for the third time that day, Hilda was at home. Hilda offered no apology to the woman who had looked after her child all afternoon but seemed very quiet and subdued. "I should think he'll be ready for another bottle soon," advised Sarah Wootley.

"Thank you Mrs Wootley," Hilda replied quietly and closed the door.

Hilda's feelings of hopelessness and inadequacy were increasing fast. To only hinder her situation, four days later on 11 December, the abdication of King Edward VIII was announced. Hilda had turned on the radio particularly early that Friday before George had left for work and not long after he had, she heard the King's announcement. The broadcaster announced the King and for those brief moments during his broadcast Hilda was transported back to her family home in Farnham, imagining the whole family huddled around the radio set as they all listened intently to the sad news, just as they used to when important news stories broke at home. Sadly, this only gave her a moment's peace in amongst her troubled thoughts and confused feelings. She listened intently as the King began and seemed to go into a trance as he spoke.

At long last, I am able to say a few words of my own. I have never wanted to withhold anything, but until now, it has not been constitutionally possible for me to speak. A few hours ago, I discharged my last duty as King and Emperor, and now that I have been succeeded by my brother, the Duke of York, my first words must be to declare my allegiance to him. This I do with all my heart.

Hilda felt the powerful connection the King had with his brother, similar to the one which she had shared with her father and sister, Doris. Now, everything seemed different, just as the King's life would now change for ever.

I want you to understand that, in making up my mind, I did not forget the country or the Empire, which, as Prince of Wales and lately as King, I have for twenty-five years tried to serve. But you must believe me when I tell you that I have found it impossible to carry the heavy burden of responsibility and to discharge my duties as King as I would wish to do without the help and support of the woman I love.

Hilda too, had been forced to make a difficult decision, the one to leave Farnham and the home and father she had known all of her life. Hilda, not unlike the King, believed it would have been impossible to stay in Farnham and to have her father accept her relationship with George.

And I want you to know that the decision I have made has been mine and mine alone. This was a thing I had to judge entirely for myself. The other person most nearly concerned has tried up to the last to persuade me to take a different course. I have made this, the most serious decision of my life, only upon the single thought of what would, in the end, be best for all.

It had been entirely Hilda's decision to leave Farnham with George. Her father had tried to prevent it for as long as he could and ultimately pushed her into making the most difficult decision of her life.

I now quit altogether public affairs and I lay down my burden. It may be some time before I return to my native land, but I shall always follow the fortunes of the British race and Empire with profound interest, and if at any time in the future I can be found of service to His Majesty in a private station, I shall not fail.

The despair in the King's voice could not outweigh Hilda's own despair. She wasn't coping as a wife or mother and desperately missed her family, craving her father's love and approval. Suddenly, her thoughts were interrupted by baby George who had begun to cry rather loudly.

Edwin too, had found himself listening to the King's announcement that morning and like Hilda had remembered earlier, happier times with his family. For no more than a moment did he allow himself a brief thought about his youngest daughter. He wished her no harm and hoped she had found the happiness she desired in her life. He truly hoped to hear from his daughter one day and to be able to overlook what had happened between them. Just for the moment though, his wounds had not had enough time to heal properly and he felt it was too early to make contact with her. Things would just have to remain as they were, for the time being.

Chapter 13

For the next ten days Hilda struggled on. It was now 21 December and Monday morning again. Hilda said goodbye to George and secretly wished he didn't have to go to work. They had benefited from such a lovely day yesterday, just the three of them; she hadn't wanted it to end. The previous Sunday had been wet all day and they had been confined to their basement flat with a very fractious baby but yesterday had been a dry and surprisingly mild day for the time of year. They had taken baby George out in his pram and enjoyed a long afternoon's stroll around Battersea Park, chatting comfortably, observing the seasonal transformations and stopping to rest on a bench while the baby slept peacefully, wrapped up warmly, under his blankets. That evening things had deteriorated again for Hilda. She lay in bed, unable to sleep, worrying about the week ahead and feeling guilty for earlier rejecting George's amorous advances. The night lasted for what felt like for ever as she quietly paced the floors in their flat, careful not to wake her husband or son. When Monday morning finally arrived she had managed only two hours of sleep, something which was becoming an all-too-regular occurrence.

Although Hilda knew she would have George home on Friday this week for Christmas Day, the next four days loomed ahead of her like a heavy grey cloud and she knew they would drag terribly. She had plenty to do to keep her occupied. She still had presents to buy for George and the baby and of course their meals to plan but these chores would only prove to be minor distractions from her ever-increasing feelings of isolation and loneliness.

The last letter she'd had from her sister Doris had been weeks ago, wishing them the best for the holiday season ahead and explaining that she would try and arrange to see her sister and the baby in the New Year. Hilda had not seen her friend Ruth for over two weeks, as she had been taking advantage of the extra shifts offered to her at work, but Ruth had found time to write to Hilda and in her letter insisted they meet up for a coffee after her shift today and had asked Hilda to make sure she bring the baby along.

Hilda had been excited when she had received Ruth's letter last week but as the day had approached Hilda had become more and more alarmed at the prospect of their meeting. She desperately wanted to see Ruth again, but now that that time had arrived she suddenly felt terribly anxious about leaving the flat and about taking the baby with her. Thoughts of how staff at the hotel might react or judge her whizzed around in her head, causing her to feel dizzy and nauseous. As the time for her to leave drew closer, she began to suffer with terrible stomach pains. I can't do this, she thought, her heart starting to thump faster in her chest. She ran from the flat, flew up the steps and hammered on the door to the flat above. Mrs Wootley answered. "Is there a fire?" she asked.

"Oh, Mrs Wootley," puffed Hilda.

"Its Sarah, I've told you."

"Oh, yes, sorry."

"What is it dear? Is something wrong?"

"No, no. I just wondered if you could mind the baby for me this afternoon while I visit a friend."

"I would dear but I have to work until 3pm today." Mrs Wootley noticed the disappointment on Hilda's face. "You could take him round to my mother. She'll look after him until I get there."

"Are you sure?"

"Yes, it's no problem. You know where we live don't you? On Howie Street?"

"Yes I know it."

"Mother would love to have him to herself for a couple of hours. He's never any trouble."

"Thank you, Mrs Wootley, I'll make sure I'm back by five o'clock."

"All right dear, see you later then," and with that she closed the door and Hilda returned to her flat to get ready. Being able to leave George at Mrs Wootley's house was a weight off her mind.

Ruth, surprised to see her friend Hilda without baby George, nevertheless was relieved she had turned up. Once away from the flat and having dropped off the baby Hilda felt released from her duties and enjoyed her time chatting and catching up with her friend. Ruth noticed a further change in Hilda that day. She met a very different Hilda to the one she had known from their days working in the hotel together. Her friend seemed anxious and despondent during their meeting. She spoke negatively about her ability to care for her son and was over-emotional about her husband, needing reassurance from Ruth that she thought Hilda made him happy. Her friend appeared distracted for much of the time and Ruth found it difficult to discuss anything important with her, yet endeavoured to reassure Hilda and give her hope for the future. When it was time for the friends to part, Ruth hugged Hilda for perhaps longer than she would have done previously. When Hilda left, she did not turn back to wave to her friend, in case she were to notice the tears which were streaming down her face.

True to her word, Hilda arrived at Mrs Wootley's house just before 5pm to collect her son. "Is it time for him to go already?" complained Mrs Wootley's mother.

"He's been a delight. Only a few sniffles today," reassured Mrs Wootley.

"Thank you very much Mrs Wootley," Hilda said as she placed baby George into his pram which had been left outside the terrace property. The two older women waved to Hilda as she left for home with the pram.

George's week at work was hectic and busy. Even though he knew he would return home late every night with aching feet and feeling exhausted, he normally loved this time of year when everyone was in the mood for a party and the whole world seemed to be making plans for the future. This Christmas was more special than any other Christmas had been before and George would be spending it with the two people he most cared about. It was his first Christmas as a married man and his first Christmas as a father so George should have been feeling jubilant but instead he found himself constantly worrying about his wife and child.

His son had been poorly for weeks now. He just couldn't seem to shake off his cold and George couldn't help wondering if Hilda was doing something wrong. Of course, he didn't dare mention this, as he recognised his wife had been struggling to cope anyway, so she could do without his negative remarks. He had pretended for her sake, for weeks now, that everything was all right and that he was happy with their life but that was very far from the truth. He had noticed the subtle changes in Hilda's behaviour, for which he had sought advice, and he was assured by friends and colleagues that Hilda's condition would improve with time. At first it was a concern, nothing more. However he felt the situation had worsened and he was unsure as to how they were going to get through Christmas. Hilda would occasionally have good days, usually on a Sunday when George was at home all day, when he could help with the baby and the housework, but these were always followed by bad days. During the bad days she could be irritable and pessimistic, questioning her capabilities as a mother and wife or would just sit alone, looking downcast and detached from everything. On these days chaos would reign in the flat. When George arrived home after a long day at work, he might find clothes strewn across the furniture, the baby's bottles dirty in the sink, no food cooked for him or in the cupboards and the baby crying for his next feed or because he needed changing. George would often find Hilda sitting in the armchair, staring into space, with a blank expression on her face as the wireless played to itself quietly in the background. He never knew which Hilda he was going to wake up with. He didn't know what more he could do for his wife. He had no idea how anxious, lonely and despondent she could feel. He couldn't possibly have imagined how trapped, over-whelmed, detached and distressed she felt at times. He had no concept of how desperately she missed contact with her family and craved acceptance and love from her father. Hilda had all the ingredients for happiness yet it seemed she could only feel an all-pervading sadness, bursting into tears at any time for little reason. Her behaviour was beginning to put a real strain upon their relationship. George prayed the situation would improve and believed he would just have to ride it out.

When Christmas Day and Boxing Day arrived Hilda's mood slightly improved and so did baby George's cold. On the whole the family enjoyed most of this time together and when George noticed his wife slipping back into one of her quiet moods he jollied her out of it by suggesting a game of cards, a walk or a visit to their local pub. This took her mind off her troubles. She had just finished washing up after their lunch and sat down in the armchair with a drink, when terrible feelings of loneliness and regret suddenly consumed her. George noticed her eyes glaze over and asked her what was wrong.

"Nothing," was her reply eventually, as she tried to protect him from her thoughts.

"Are you thinking about your family?" asked George, making an educated guess. Reluctantly, Hilda admitted she was. "Why don't you take a walk to the phone box and give them a call?" he suggested. "It is Christmas Day after all. Doris has a phone now doesn't she?"

"Yes, but ... no I'm fine, really. Let's do something," she almost shouted back at him.

"Game of cards?" suggested George.

"Sounds good," agreed Hilda.

During the game George tried to cheat on more than one

occasion which lifted Hilda's spirits and she temporarily stopped thinking about her family back in Farnham.

It was Boxing Day when George suggested they visit the Prince Albert for a drink with the baby. "They won't mind, we can leave the baby in the back room. It'll be good to get out and see people, don't you think?" asked George. Hilda just smiled at her husband, while inside her stomach turned somersaults as she worried about having to mix with and chat to people she didn't really know. It was also the noise inside the pub and having to cope with the baby that terrified her. "Would you mind terribly if we didn't go?" she asked. "You go George, if you want to. I'll stay here with the baby. I don't mind," she lied.

"No, I'm not going without you. Why don't we go for a walk then instead? It's lovely and sunny today. The park might be closed but we could walk along the Thames."

"I'd like that George."

Hilda and George enjoyed their three days together and on the Sunday when Will called round, Hilda insisted he and George call into the Prince Albert for a drink. George was careful not to be away for too long and when he and Will returned, Hilda had prepared some supper and they all enjoyed the evening, listening to Hilda's radio playing in the background as they ate, played cards and chatted.

Having George at home for the last three days had improved Hilda's mood and George was less concerned about his wife when he left for work on Monday morning.

Back in Farnham, Christmas was a happy time for Doris and her family. Her two boys now aged ten and fifteen waited expectantly for Christmas morning to arrive when they hoped they would receive all that they wished for. Doris had been busy helping in her father's shop and making all the necessary preparations for the season's festivities while her husband Syd worked hard to deliver the residents of Farnham their milk every morning. Teddy, Mabel, Lionel and Nan rarely visited Farnham now. They all had their own busy lives to lead elsewhere and had little time for contact with their father or siblings. Although Evie and Violet were both still living and working in Farnham they too had little time to spend with their family as their businesses took priority. As for Edwin, this was to be his first Christmas without one or more of his children living at home. He'd got used to the house being empty and quiet and rarely spent much time in it, using the upstairs only to eat or sleep in. He spent most of his time in his shop or down at his local.

It hadn't occurred to Edwin to wonder where he would spend Christmas Day until Doris had broached the subject with him three days before Christmas. He had been so busy in his shop lately that he had little time to worry about or deliberate over where he would spend Christmas or who with.

"Dad, it's all sorted. You'll be spending Christmas Day round at our house," Doris informed her father without even looking up from arranging a display of prawns on the shop's marble slab. "It's not up for discussion. Everything has been arranged," she continued. Edwin had learnt that when Doris had got something into her head like this there was no point in arguing with her. Edwin thought she was very like her mother in that way. "Thomas will come over and help you tidy up on Christmas Eve and you can stay over, ready for Christmas morning." Edwin looked bemused. "And don't worry about presents, I have already sorted those out," reassured Doris.

Dozing in Syd's armchair on Christmas Day, after an enormous meal, Edwin listened to his grandsons as they argued over their Christmas presents. Edwin's thoughts once again briefly drifted to Hilda. He knew exactly where the rest of his children were today, including Teddy, and what they were all doing. Doris had made sure she'd comprehensively notified him of the details. Mabel had called in earlier with her brood and Evie and Jim were calling in later. The only person who had not been mentioned was Hilda. Pushing all thoughts of her out of his head, he turned to Doris and demanded, "How long is that cup of tea going to take that you promised me half an hour ago?" Doris hotfooted back to her kitchen.

George left for work on Monday morning with a spring in his step while Hilda's day deteriorated quickly. Over the last three days she had become used to having George around all the time and now he'd gone back to work she was alone again with the baby, with no one to talk to, no one to help her and very little to occupy her mind. The next four days loomed ahead of her again, the dark cloud above greyer than ever and threateningly oppressive. She knew George would be working late most nights and that she would hardly see him all week. This time he would only get New Year's Day off, which was Friday, and he would have to go back into work on the Saturday. Hilda saw no end to this monotonous routine. She felt trapped and wretched and by Tuesday when she felt things could not possibly get any worse, the baby's health deteriorated once again. Although he seemed to have got rid of his cold, a cough persisted and was now causing him to vomit after every feed and mixed in with this vomit was nasty thick phlegm.

By the time George arrived home in the evenings, had tidied the flat, washed up, changed and fed his son and found something to eat for himself and Hilda, he was completely exhausted. Hilda picked at the food he prepared for her and appeared to show little interest in him or their son. She was forgetting to eat during the day and wasn't sleeping properly at night. She had lost interest in the way she looked and was becoming more and more unaware of her baby's needs. There was nothing to motivate her and she thought no one cared about her. Then she would feel guilty for feeling this way when George tidied up or cooked them a meal. She hated herself and what she had become but didn't know how she could alter her situation. She saw no way out. All she knew was that she just couldn't go on like this.

New Year's Eve started the same as most of her days had done now for a number of weeks. As she lay there in her bed, having hardly slept again, listening to her husband breathing slow and regular next to her and her baby boy stirring in his basket, Hilda couldn't help wondering why she felt so unhappy. Why did she feel that she just couldn't be bothered to do anything? What was it all for anyway? She had turned out to be a terrible mother. Her baby was sick all the time and she was making him worse. She was even failing at being a wife, unable to keep up with the housework and caring for her husband. She was useless.

Hilda had to force herself to get up and get dressed. It took all her strength just to do this. But she had to try, for the sake of her husband and son. She somehow managed to put together something that resembled breakfast. She burnt the eggs and it was that smell that stirred George from his slumber. He pulled on his clothes, lifted the baby from the Moses basket and carried him through into the living room.

"What's for breakfast, love? You've got two hungry boys here who want feeding." George had meant this to sound light-hearted and was surprised when Hilda flashed him a look that could kill.

"Eggs and bread," came her sharp reply.

"Lovely," replied George trying to stay positive. "Shall I give Georgie his bottle?"

"If you want to," she replied, placing the bottle down on the table next to George. A feeling of despair took over Hilda's whole being. "He's still not well George. He just doesn't seem to be getting better and he never wants to take his bottle from me."

"He's just feeling a little under the weather, that's all."

"Don't go into work today, George," Hilda pleaded. "Stay at home with me and Georgie, please."

"You know I'd love to Babe, but it's going to be really busy at work today, with it being New Year's Eve an' all. We've got so many extra bookings. I can't let the poor folk down now, can I? They all want to look good for the parties they're going to tonight."

"Please George," Hilda begged.

"I'm sorry Babe, I just can't."

Hilda knew it was pointless. George would never let his clients down.

"Isn't Ruth calling in later today? That will be some company for you and the baby."

"Yes, I suppose so," Hilda agreed reluctantly. So George left for work at the usual time with an extremely busy day ahead of him and Hilda was left with the baby and her thoughts.

The baby didn't stop crying all morning, but finally dropped off in his pram and was now snoring through his restless slumber. Even the radio couldn't raise Hilda's spirits this New Year's Eve. Every discussion or tune she heard reminded her of home and her father, so she switched it off. How had things with her father got this bad? Where had it all gone wrong? Now that the flat was enveloped in silence, Hilda felt the need to escape her home. It felt unbearably suffocating. She had seen Mrs Wootley arrive earlier to clean the flat upstairs, so leaving the baby asleep in his pram and forgetting Ruth was due, Hilda disappeared to ask if Mrs Wootley would mind looking after the baby while she popped out.

"It's not very convenient at the moment dear. I'm a bit busy," said Mrs Wootley.

"I promised I'd visit some friends," Hilda lied desperately. Recognising Hilda's agitation, Mrs Wootley suggested, "Take the baby to my mother's again and she'll look after him until I've finished work."

"Thank you Mrs Wootley," said Hilda, shivering in the frosty air.

Hilda returned to the basement flat. As she sat herself down at the kitchen table to write a note, the baby started making strange little noises in his sleep, but it didn't put her off. It only took a matter of minutes and when she had finished writing, she folded the paper and placed it inside her handbag. She grabbed her coat from the stand, placed another blanket over the baby, put on her gloves and walked out into the street with the pram.

As Hilda shut the door to the flat behind her, she was set on an irreversible course. Long before the fresh December air outside hit her face, something had happened to Hilda which made her feel completely detached and isolated from everyone and everything. All she knew now was that she couldn't continue to feel this way.

She completed the five-minute walk to Howie Street where she left the baby with Mrs Wootley's mother. Once again the woman was more than pleased to look after Georgie and Hilda knew he was in good hands. She left Howie Street, and walked and walked and walked. She had no idea where she was going. She just kept walking, feeling more and more alone, inadequate and depressed. She didn't notice the time. One hour passed, then two, then another. Hilda hadn't even noticed it had gone dark. The temperature was dropping but she couldn't feel the cold any more. She felt very little. There were plenty of people passing by, going about their business, preparing for the last evening of the year and the celebrations they would enjoy, but Hilda didn't notice any of them. And not many noticed her.

George arrived home around 8.30pm after an exhausting day. He had completed no less than eleven customers' hairstyles during the day, a record even for him. He was surprised to discover no one was at home as he entered the flat and then an uneasy feeling washed over him. Where were Babe and Georgie? It was a bit late to be out with the baby. It suddenly struck him that Georgie may have been taken ill and that Hilda may have taken him to the hospital again. His eyes scanned the room for clues and he spotted Hilda's handbag left on the armchair. Wouldn't she need this if she had gone out? Reluctantly, but in search of clues, he opened his wife's handbag and looked inside. Amongst her keys, purse and some tissues, he found the piece of paper that Hilda had written a note on earlier that day. George read the note, but before he had reached the end his whole body had started to shake, involuntarily. Please God, don't let this be what I think it is. Flinging the note onto the chair, he rushed from the flat. Suffering from shock, he raced as quickly as he could to Howie Street, where he knew Mrs Wootley lived. He hammered on the door with such urgency that the neighbours might have thought the place was on fire. Sarah Wootley opened the door.

She greeted George with a pleasant smile and said, "I thought you'd forgotten about the little mite."

"What?" George looked confused. "Is Hilda not here?" he enquired.

"No love, I've not seen her since this afternoon."

"Do you have any idea where she might be?" George shouted, the urgency in his voice beginning to distress the woman.

"No. Sorry love. She just said she wanted to visit some friends."

"Friends? What friends?" George's voice was sufficiently raised now that a few curtains had begun to twitch as the neighbours tried to discover what all the commotion was about.

"I don't know, George. Hilda didn't tell me their names or where they lived." George was bewildered. "Don't look so worried. I'm sure she'll be fine. I think she just needed a bit of a break from the baby." Not wishing to disagree with the woman but wanting to get home as soon as possible to see if Hilda had returned, George asked, "Can I have the baby?"

"Of course you can love, I'll just fetch his things. We brought the pram in as it was so cold," she shouted from inside the house. Realising the urgency, Mrs Wootley returned quickly, pushing George in his pram through the door to his waiting father. "Thank you, Mrs Wootley," shouted George as he snatched the pram and wheeled his son away at speed.

"He's probably ready for another bottle now," she called after George, but he and the baby were already out of earshot.

George rushed back along Parkgate Road and as he rounded the corner of Albert Bridge Road he could just make out the figure of a woman in the dark, waiting on the pavement outside the flat. Relief swept over him and as he approached he said, "Am I glad to see you, where have you been?" The woman spun around. It was only then that George realised the woman was Ruth and not Hilda.

"Hello, George."

"What are you doing here?" asked George rather rudely.

"I just called in to apologise to Hilda for not getting here this afternoon. I had to work later than expected. Where is she?"

"I think you'd better come in," said George.

George showed Ruth Hilda's note and explained what had happened since. "Would you mind staying with the baby while I go and look for her?" asked George.

"Of course not, George, anything."

"He's due his last bottle and then he'll need changing and putting in his basket for the night."

"Don't worry George. I'll take care of the baby. You go and look for Hilda."

"Thank you Ruth. I don't know what I would have done if you hadn't have been here."

George grabbed his coat and was on his way out of the door when Ruth said, "Do you think we should let the police know?"

This stopped George dead in his tracks as he didn't want to believe the situation was as serious as that. "Let me see if I can find her first," he answered.

It was just after eleven when George returned to the flat, alone. As he entered he so desperately wanted to find that Hilda had returned home and was waiting for him but that was not to be. Ruth was sitting in the armchair, having just woken as George walked in. She sat bolt upright. "Have you found her?" George shook his head sombrely. He was exhausted. "What do we do now, George?"

"I don't know," was his reply. "I think I should ring for the police." George left the flat again to contact the police, using the phone box positioned just across the street from the park. He had never had to dial 999 before.

At first the police sergeant tried to reassure George and said he was sure his wife would turn up by the morning. "People do funny stuff on New Year's Eve. They usually turn up though, the next day, a little worse for the night before, if you know what I mean."

"My wife isn't like that," insisted George. "She left me a note." George retrieved the note from his coat pocket and read it out loud, down the phone line. It wasn't until then that the policeman began to take George more seriously. "We'll send someone round to you as soon as we can sir," said the gruff voice on the other end of the line. "It's rather a busy night tonight, so I can't promise a time."

"Thank you, Sergeant," replied George and he hung up the receiver.

Hilda had wandered into London and around its chaotic streets for hours, stopping nowhere and speaking to no one. If partygoers shouted their New Year wishes to her, she disregarded them. Hilda eventually completed a full circle and ended up only a short distance from her home, across the road in Battersea Park. It was almost midnight on New Year's Eve as she sat upon a wooden park bench, under the moonlight, thinking only about how unhappy she was feeling and what she was going to do next. There was no one else in the park. Hilda wasn't sure how she had even come to be there. The park gates had been locked earlier that evening by the head park keeper. His timekeeping was impeccable. Hilda had in fact squeezed through a tiny gap in the hedge, previously made by some children playing and not yet spotted by any of the park keepers.

As midnight struck, cheers and shouts of joy could be heard entering the park from all directions. These were followed by fireworks. Hilda sat as still as a statue on the park bench, only jumping intermittently when there was a particularly noisy firework. She tilted her head back to watch the array of spectacular colours lighting up the night sky. She was unmoved by the event. It meant nothing to her.

When the celebrations had all died down and the park was once again silent, she walked over to the boating lake. The pond was surrounded by a low picket fence about fifteen inches high, except in one area where there was a small shrubbery. Hilda stepped over the little fence that had no real purpose and stood at the water's edge, staring deep into its darkness. The moon shone brightly in the clear night sky and reflected off the water's surface, blinding her as she happened to glance over to it.

Hilda began to slowly unbutton her coat. Six buttons in total. She slipped it over her shoulders, releasing her arms. She folded the coat neatly and placed it on the grass beside her. Then she removed her gloves and laid them on top of her coat. Leaving her shoes on, she walked forward and entered the water. She couldn't feel the piercing coldness of the water or its harshness that shocked her body. She stepped out deeper and deeper, allowing the water to embrace her body. And then she disappeared. She hardly felt the agony as her lungs filled with pond water. Her last moments were peaceful, as she experienced a release from her misery.

After speaking to the police, George made his way back to the flat and waited. It was two in the morning before there was a knock at the door. A police constable, younger than George, stood there smartly in his uniform. "Evening, sir, I understand you want to report your wife as missing."

"Yes, come in," replied George. Ruth made them all a hot drink while George told the policeman what he knew and showed him the note Hilda had left. He gave a description of what Hilda looked like and what she was wearing. "Try not to worry sir. I'm sure she'll turn up," the constable tried to reassure George as he was leaving.

George and Ruth stayed awake all night. Ruth supplied them both with a steady flow of hot drinks and made some sandwiches, which neither of them touched. "I should be out there looking for her," said George.

"But you've looked everywhere you can think of. It's best we let the police do their job now," replied Ruth. "Anyway, she'd want you here with the baby, when she gets back." George managed a small smile for his wife's best friend. She was a true friend.

Chapter 14

1937

The baby woke early on New Year's Day morning, so Ruth dressed and fed him. She wrestled somewhat with him to get him to take his feed and after a coughing fit he brought some of it back up. She also noticed he seemed a little warmer than usual but didn't bother George with this news as she felt he had enough to cope with. George was pacing the floor of the flat again, undecided as to what to do next. Amongst the many other feelings that buzzed around in his head, he was now beginning to feel quite cross with Hilda for putting him through what had been the worst night of his life. She had made her point and he just wanted her home. He expected she would turn up very soon now.

At seven o'clock Ruth made them both a drink and some breakfast but again George hardly touched his food. Ruth spoke first. "We've heard nothing from the police." George didn't acknowledge her comment. His mind was elsewhere. "I thought they would have found her by now and brought her home. Still, no news is good news," she said light-heartedly. More minutes of silence passed between them and then Ruth spoke again. "George, I could do with going home for a change of clothes. Georgie was sick on me earlier. Would you mind?"

"What? No, of course not, you go."

"I'll be back as soon as I've washed and got changed."

"Yes, that's fine. You go."

When Ruth had gone, George placed his son in his pram, wrapped him up warmly and left the flat. Struggling to push the pram while holding onto an umbrella as it was beginning to rain, he walked back to the telephone box he had used the previous night and dialled his mother's house. His sister Wyn answered. George briefly explained that Hilda was missing. "I'll be there as soon as I can. I'll catch the next bus," said Wyn. "Oh, I can't. There won't be any, with it being New Year's Day." There were a few seconds of silence. "I know!" Wyn shouted down the phone. "Leave it with me. I can be there in no time," and with that she hung up.

True to her word, Wyn pulled up outside the flat less than an hour later. She'd dashed round to a neighbour who happened to own a car and asked for a favour. A good friend of her mother's, he was more than happy to help. Wyn stepped out of the car, went around to the back, opened the boot and produced a small suitcase. "Give George my best wishes," her neighbour called after her as she moved away from his car. "I will," she called back.

George had just returned from visiting Mrs Wootley who had neither seen nor heard from Hilda and was now just as worried as George. George was surprised to see his sister arrive so quickly, yet relieved to have her there. They hugged one another for some time. George was almost moved to tears. "Right, what can I do to help?" asked Wyn, before she'd even taken off her coat. "I don't know," replied George. "I don't even know what to do myself."

"How long has Hilda been missing?" Wyn asked gently.

"Since about yesterday lunchtime, I think."

"Could she have met up with a friend, maybe had a drink and decided to stay there the night?"

"I don't think so. I don't know. Look, I went through all this with the police."

"Yes, I'm sorry George."

"I think I need to go and look for her again. I can't just sit here. It's driving me mad. Will you stay here with the baby?"

"Of course I will," replied Wyn. George put on his coat. "Let me know as soon as you have any news won't you?" she shouted after him.

"I will," replied George, closing the door behind him.

Soon afterwards, Ruth returned to the flat. Wyn invited her in and the two women chatted over a cup of tea. It was decided that as Wyn was staying, there was very little point in Ruth being there. As Ruth left for home, Wyn promised she would let her know as soon as they had any news.

George spent many hours looking for Hilda that day and covered many miles, although possibly not quite as many as Hilda had done the previous day. He returned home terribly depressed, hungry and tired. Unable to eat or sleep, George spent a second restless night in the armchair while his sister slept in his and Hilda's bed.

George woke with a start the following morning, shaken from his troubled sleep by the baby stirring. For a split second he thought it was Hilda whom he could hear getting up to see to their baby but then reality hit him and he realised it was Wyn. Hilda had not returned to him while he had slept, as he had so longed for and urgently desired. He still had no idea where she was but desperately wanted to believe she would come home to him soon.

Under Wyn's instruction, George forced himself to start the day by washing himself and putting on some clean clothes. Together they dressed the baby and gave him his bottle and all the time George was wondering where next he should look for his missing wife. Suddenly blind panic struck him as he remembered he should be starting back at work today. "I'll telephone them and tell them you're ill," said Wyn, helpfully. George looked confused; he wasn't ill. "I'll telephone Mother at the same time," she added.

"No, I'll do it. I'll let Mother know what's happening and I'll ring Joan Sorensen at home to explain."

"Who's Joan?" enquired Wyn.

"She's the boss's daughter and I know I can trust her to be discreet."

"All right George, as you like," agreed Wyn. George had left the flat before she could say another word. It was just after seven. I hope they won't mind him phoning so early, Wyn thought to herself.

Meanwhile, the people of Battersea and the rest of the world were heading back to work, full of the hope and aspirations one has at the beginning of a New Year. Like clockwork, James Berry unlocked the gates to Battersea Park and set about his duties of head park keeper. His first job was to inspect the condition of the park, which appeared secure and to have suffered no vandalism during the New Year celebrations. The park itself was eerily quiet yet peacefully calm and he liked this time in the mornings.

It was around 9.30am when he approached the boating lake. Everything appeared completely normal around the pond, except for an area near to the water's edge which caught his eye. His sight was obscured at first by the low picket fence and he couldn't quite make out the small pile of clothes at the water's edge until he advanced closer. Strange, thought James and stepped over the fence to take a closer look. Upon examination James Berry realised they were a woman's coat and pair of gloves that had been neatly discarded at the edge of the boating lake.

He immediately jumped to the right conclusion. "Oh dear Lord," he said out loud, raising his hand to his mouth. Looking away from the now disturbed pile of clothes he focused his attention out onto the water. There was nothing obviously visible to give him concern but James felt drawn to investigate further. He obtained a small wooden rowing boat which had been moored nearby, climbed in and began to row out onto the pond. His eyes searched the water frantically as he rowed. He had only gone out about twelve yards when he noticed a dark object under the water. James took off his warm winter coat and rolling up his shirt sleeve, plunged his right arm down into the icy-cold pond water. His hand descended about eighteen inches before it touched something. He grabbed hold and pulled the object to the surface. It was the body of a woman. He summoned all his strength and managed to pull the woman out of the water, over the side and into the boat. Once inside the boat he did what any caring human being would, he attempted to give the woman artificial respiration. Sadly this was to be without success. James desperately wished he could have saved the woman and breathed some life back into her unresponsive body but he suspected she may have been there for some hours. There was nothing more anyone could do for her now. He slowly rowed the boat and its motionless passenger back to the shore where he dragged the woman's body onto dry land. He gently placed the discarded coat over her body, covering her face, and went for help. He returned a short time later with a police constable.

PC Etchell recognised immediately that the body of the woman matched the description of a local woman who had gone missing on New Year's Eve. "I suspect I know who this is," he informed the park keeper. "After the doctor has examined her I will have to inform the station and of course her poor husband. I don't enjoy my job much at times like this."

"Who do you think she is?" enquired the park keeper.

"I believe she could be the wife of a man I met on New Year's Eve. He had been concerned when his wife had gone out to visit friends and never come home. They live just across the way and have a small baby."

"Oh dear, that's dreadful. Poor chap."

"Yes, very tragic isn't it?"

"Very." James Berry was obviously moved by the situation. "I don't know what I'd do if anything happened to my wife. I can't imagine what the husband must be going through."

"No, and he seems like such a nice fellow. I shouldn't think he deserves this."

The pair waited with Hilda's body until the doctor joined them. Dr William Thomas lived fairly close by in Clapham and had not taken long to reach his destination that morning. "What a way to start the New Year," he commented as he approached. He briefly examined Hilda's body at the edge of the pond and concluded that the probable cause of death was by drowning. "I can't issue a death certificate at this stage. There will have to be an inquest into this woman's death and a post mortem which may tell us more," he explained. "Do you have any idea who she was?" He directed his question to both men. It was the constable who replied. "Yes Doctor. I believe it is the body of a Battersea woman who has been missing for the last two days."

"Have you informed her next of kin?"

"Not as yet, sir. I thought I'd wait until you had examined her first."

"I'm sure you did the right thing. I will make the necessary arrangements for the collection of the body and you can inform her family."

"Thank you Doctor." And with that the two men went about their allotted tasks, leaving James Berry alone in the park with Hilda's body, waiting for it to be collected.

It was around ten thirty when there was a knock on the flat's door. George leapt to his feet from the chair, believing there was a possibility Hilda had at last returned. After all, she had forgotten to take her keys with her. George opened the door with a nervous and almost excited feeling in the pit of his stomach. When he saw Constable Etchell standing there, that feeling immediately turned to one of horror and dread, as he realised what the constable was carrying in his arms. "Could I come in, sir?" George moved to the side and the constable stepped passed him. George closed the door and followed him through to the living room, where the baby was lying in his basket on the floor. Wyn came in to join them.

"This is my sister," explained George. "She's been helping with the baby." Wyn sat herself close to her brother, grabbing hold of his hand in preparation for what she suspected was coming next.

The constable wasted no time. There seemed no point in prolonging the inevitable. "Do you recognise these items of clothing sir?"

George did not hesitate, but nodded. "They belong to my wife," he managed to say.

"I'm afraid it's not good news, sir." Wyn squeezed his hand as George slumped down into the chair. He knew what the constable was going to say and he desperately didn't want to hear or believe it. The constable continued. "Your wife's body has been found in the water at Battersea Park. We believe that she drowned." George heard the words but couldn't take them in. Wyn started to cry. After a few moments the constable enquired if George had heard what he had just said as he had not responded.

"Yes, I heard," he replied, "but what was she doing in the park?"

"We don't know, sir."

George pushed away his sister's hand as he became more agitated. "Why would she go into the water when she knew she couldn't swim?" George wasn't thinking straight. He couldn't grasp the situation.

"We haven't got all the answers to your questions yet, sir, but we may know more after the inquest."

"Inquest?" repeated Wyn and George at the same time.

"Yes sir, and your wife's body will need to be examined by a doctor to establish the exact cause of death. It's called a post mortem."

The reality of the situation began to hit George. The most dreadful thing that could have happened was happening. His beautiful Babe was gone and never coming back. For a moment the room was silent. Not even the baby made a sound. Then, all of a sudden George sat bolt upright in his chair causing both the constable and Wyn to jump. "I want to see my wife," he demanded. "When can I see her?"

"We'll have someone contact you as soon as that's possible, sir. It shouldn't take too long."

"Can I wait at the police station?"

"It might be better if you wait here, sir. Someone will contact you when they have the body, sorry, your wife, ready for you."

The constable corrected himself quickly. There was another pause. The constable looked down at the baby who was quietly lying in his basket, not making a sound, and gently touched the child's hand. He was obviously moved by the situation. "Well, I'd best get back to the station sir, if you don't mind. I'm very sorry for your loss," he said, directing his statement at both George and Wyn.

"Thank you, constable," replied Wyn, wiping away her tears. "I'll see you out."

George managed to manoeuvre himself forward in the chair, gently lifted his son up out of the Moses basket and cradled him in his arms. Tears flowed freely down George's face. He sobbed for his and his child's loss and then baby Georgie began to cry as well. The two of them had lost someone they would never be able to replace. This spectacle met Wyn on her return to the room and moved her to tears. It was some time before they were able to console themselves.

George needed to think about what he was going to do next. He was terribly confused about the whole situation but there was one thing which was very clear in his mind. He just had to see Hilda one last time. He needed a chance to say goodbye to his dear sweet Babe. It was something he just had to do and only then would he be able to come to terms with her death.

Early that afternoon, George was contacted and allowed to see his wife's body and say his goodbyes. The event brought many feelings to the forefront of George's mind which he forced himself to ignore, as his next task was to inform Hilda's family. For George, this would be the second hardest thing he'd ever had to do.

"Doris? It's George."

"Hello George, well fancy hearing from you. Quiet boys," shouted Doris as she could hardly hear George over the noise her boys were making. "How are you both? Did you have a good Christmas?" Then she stopped herself as she realised something must be wrong. Why would George and not Hilda be telephoning her? "What is it George? What's wrong?"

George hesitated. Where should he start? "Doris, I need you to be strong. I have some bad news."

"All right," said Doris calmly, assuming the news was going to be about the baby although she didn't know why.

"It's ... it's Babe."

"Babe?" repeated Doris. "Why? What's wrong with her?"

"She was found this morning in the pond in Battersea Park." The words stuck in his throat as he spoke them. There was complete silence on the other end of the telephone. "Doris? Are you still there?" asked George.

"Yes George," was her faint reply.

"She's gone Doris. She's gone. I'm so sorry." Another silence followed and then George told Doris everything. She left him to speak as she tried unsuccessfully to take it all in. It was such a shock for her. She dropped to the floor, her head lowered as she listened and cried silent tears.

Doris eventually pulled herself together, when she heard the mention of her father's name. "I didn't think he would speak to me on the telephone, so I sent him a telegram," said George. "Could you go round there to make sure he's all right? I'm so sorry to have to ask this of you, Doris. I didn't know what else to do."

"I'll go right away," replied Doris.

"I will ring you again, later this evening, if that's all right."

"Yes, George, that's fine. Bye then."

"Goodbye Doris."

"Telegram for you mister," boomed the cheerful voice of the delivery boy, as he thrust an envelope into Edwin's hand, just as Edwin had finished serving one of his customers. "Thank you young man," responded Edwin. In his experience these things rarely brought good news, but he was ever hopeful. He went into the back room to open it in private, leaving his customers in the capable hands of his recently appointed assistant. His fingers fumbled to open the envelope and ease out the telegram. He unfolded the paper and read.

> *It is with much regret I have to inform you, your daughter, Hilda was found this morning, drowned in the pond at Battersea Park. I wish to express my deepest sorrow for your loss. Before she died, she asked for your forgiveness. I trust you may grant her this. I wish things could have been different between us. Please advise me as to where you wish her funeral to be held. George.*

Edwin read the telegram through and then he read it a second time, as he believed he had misunderstood it the first. How could this be? There must be a mistake, he thought. Is this someone's idea of a cruel joke? Folding the telegram back into its envelope and placing it in his pocket, he returned to his shop, in denial. When Doris appeared in the shop doorway, he was involved with another customer.

Edwin didn't notice his daughter at first. Having left her boys with a neighbour she had dashed round to see her father as soon as she could. She was surprised to see him in his shop and had expected to find it closed. She assumed he had not yet received the telegram. It appeared it was to be her duty to inform her father of the death of his youngest daughter. She wasted no time. "Father, we need to talk," she interjected between customers.

"Hello Doris," said Edwin, noticing his daughter for the first time. "Just let me finish serving this customer dear," he replied.

"No Father, now," she insisted. Turning to the grocer's wife she said, "I'm sorry Mrs Hone, but this can't wait."

"I understand dear," replied the woman, noticing Doris's agitation.

It was at this point Edwin realised why Doris was there. They went through to the back room where Doris broke down. "Oh Father, it's Babe."

"Yes I know," replied her father, surprising Doris. "I received a telegram earlier." Doris was shocked by her father's indifferent behaviour. He made no effort to comfort her or show any compassion for Hilda.

"Why have you not closed up the shop?" she questioned.

"What would be the point of that?" came her father's reply.

Doris did not understand how her father could be so callous. Nor had he made any attempt to discover how or when Doris had been informed. "May I see the telegram?" Doris asked. Edwin handed the telegram over to his daughter and she read it. "George wants to know where the funeral should be held," she said.

"Here of course," he said, without having to consider his answer, "where she belongs." He paused a moment, then continued. "Would you and Syd organise that for me, Doris?" Suddenly, her father appeared terribly vulnerable.

"Yes, Father. I'll go and speak to the Reverend right now. Are you all right?" she asked, uneasily.

"Can you also inform the others," he answered briskly, ignoring her concern.

"Of course I will. I'll see you later then," she said, realising he did not require her concern.

When Doris left, her father went back to his work in his shop as though nothing had happened, but his customers mostly left his shop that day with purchases they had neither asked for nor wanted. That evening the family gathered over the fish shop to remember their Babe and discuss her funeral arrangements. Edwin appeared distracted, joining in little with the discussion, but accepting what had been agreed. Over the coming days his regular customers soon heard of his loss and allowed for his mistakes as he muddled their orders, leaving his shop with no complaints, just a nod of understanding and sympathy.

After George had contacted Edwin and Doris he telephoned his mother, who immediately travelled from her home in Fulham to be with her son. His mother and sister were incredibly supportive and it was they who managed to pull George through the next few, terrible days. George's mother helped with the funeral arrangements, speaking often with Doris over the next couple of days, while Wyn took charge of the baby. George was always consulted when necessary but never troubled with trivial matters. The two women stayed with George in his flat, sleeping together in his bed while George took the armchair.

George had been further glad of their company on Sunday morning when a newspaper reporter knocked at the door. Wyn answered the door and sent him away, with a flea in his ear, stating the family had no comment to make. Hilda's death was later reported in the *South London Press*. The man to whom Wyn had spoken was obviously determined enough not to give up. After their brief conversation he had gone in search of any willing neighbour who might wish to add to his story. A couple of neighbours did and were quoted as saying, "We used to hear her singing in her flat all day." And "Her husband spent hours looking for her when she failed to return home on Thursday." Another came from Mrs Wootley who was quoted as saying, "She was always very cheerful and was passionately devoted to her son and husband." George, of course, had no interest in reading what the newspapers were writing about his wife. He was unaware they had labelled her "the singing bride".

It was now Monday and George had not left his flat since Saturday, but this afternoon his mother and sister would be returning home and he had promised he would walk them to the bus stop. "The fresh air will do you and the baby good," reassured his mother. "The poor mite could do with getting rid of that cough. As long as he's wrapped up warm, he'll be fine."

While they had stayed with George, his mother and sister had restocked his dwindling food supplies and cleaned the flat throughout. His mother had arranged for him to leave the baby with a local midwife while he attended his wife's inquest on Tuesday and funeral on Wednesday. Wyn had spoken to Joan at George's place of work and explained he would need some more time off. Joan and her father had been very supportive and understanding. Wyn and Joan had discussed the inquest at length and Joan had mentioned she'd like to attend in support of George. Wyn appreciated her kindness and hoped George would too.

It was a tearful goodbye on Monday afternoon at the bus stop. George had only ever seen his mother cry once before and that was when his father had died. He didn't know what he would have done if his mother and sister had not been there for him over the last few days. They had been his strength.

"Are you sure you don't want me to stay tonight and go to the inquest with you tomorrow?" asked Wyn, for a second time.

"No, really Wyn, you and mother have been great. I need to do this by myself. Besides, you need a break before the funeral on Wednesday."

"Well, if you're sure."

"I'm sure," confirmed George.

"I'll see you on Wednesday then and I'll make sure I'm on the same train."

"Thanks Wyn."

"Love you George," whispered Wyn, as she hugged him tightly.

When his sister finally released him, George turned to his mother. "Good bye Mother. Thank you for everything."

"Take care son," replied his mother. "I'll be praying for you on Wednesday, darling."

"I know Mum."

She hesitated as she went to kiss his cheek. "Oh I should be there," she panicked.

"No Mother, we agreed it would be too much for you. Hilda would understand."

"You're such a good man, George. You don't deserve all of this."

Relieved to see the bus arrive, George said, "Bye Mother, I'll speak to you soon. Don't worry." George watched as the two women stepped onto the bus. They waved as the bus disappeared down the street and George was alone once more with the baby.

Early on Tuesday morning George dropped his son off with the midwife in Lavender Gardens as arranged and made his way to Battersea Coroner's Court on Falcon Road. Everything George had done over the past few days had been achieved only because he had been carried along in the moment. Nothing had been voluntary and nothing had been easy. George knew that today would be his biggest challenge yet.

He entered the building, his outward appearance calm but inwardly he was in turmoil. The courtroom was rectangular and simply furnished: three short rows of chairs for the general public, a table for the witnesses, a desk for the press and a raised bench for the coroner. There was a jug of water on the coroner's bench and a box of tissues on the witness table. Tall windows let in some light but they had to be kept closed, even on warmer days, because of the noise from outside.

In the hushed minutes before the inquest began, George watched as the clerk showed people to their seats: journalists from three newspapers, the park keeper, PC Etchells, Mrs Wootley and the doctor who had pronounced Hilda dead, but George could not see Hilda's own doctor, Dr Rowland. All had been called as witnesses and sat silently, occasionally shifting in their chairs as the time moved slowly towards ten o'clock. Ruth and Joan were both there to show their support for which George was grateful, smiling briefly at them both. His nosey neighbour from upstairs had also put in an appearance, by which he was less impressed.

The clerk told everyone to stand and the West London coroner, Dr Edwin Smith, walked in, took his seat at the bench and opened the inquest. He kindly asked George if he would step up to the table and give his evidence first. George rose to his feet and the enquiry began. "Could you please explain a little about your wife's state of mind and her health since the birth of your first child?" asked the coroner.

George spoke quietly, conscious that all eyes were focused on him. "My wife had been in fair health until the birth of her first child in September. She had however experienced difficulties during the birth. My wife's doctor, Dr Rowland, was present at the birth with a midwife and a nurse. After the baby was born, her health deteriorated."

At this point a note was handed to the coroner by the clerk. The coroner read the note and said, "It appears Dr Rowland is ill at present in Bolingbroke Hospital and will not be able to attend for some time. If we want him as a witness there will have to be an adjournment." The court agreed. The coroner concluded. "This enquiry will have to be postponed, because we cannot take the medical evidence this morning. The inquest is adjourned until Tuesday 19 January," instructed Dr Edwin Smith.

At first George was relieved that he would not have to discuss his wife's private business anymore that day, until it suddenly dawned on him that he was going to have to come back in two weeks' time and endure the ordeal all over again. That thought alarmed him. He got up to leave. As he did there was a gentle tug on his arm and as he turned around he saw Joan. "Is it all right if I walk back with you George?" she asked. He smiled at her and nodded.

Ruth was waiting outside the building as they left. "Could I have a quick word, George?" she asked politely. Joan smiled at her and stepped away to give them some space to talk privately. Ruth went to hug George and he reciprocated her embrace. "I managed to get this morning off work but I have to be in at lunchtime. I'm afraid I also have to work tomorrow so I won't be able to attend Hilda's funeral."

"I understand, Ruth," replied George.

Ruth picked up his hand and held it tightly in hers. "Truth is

George, I don't think I would cope very well tomorrow anyway."

"No," replied George.

"I'm so sorry George, for the way things have turned out. I should have done more."

"No," said George abruptly. "I won't have you blaming yourself. There was nothing more any of us could have done. We tried didn't we?"

"Yes, George."

"Well then."

Ruth hugged George one more time and said, "Stay in touch George. And give the baby a kiss from me."

"I'll do that," he shouted after her, but Ruth was already halfway down the street, sobbing, as tears uncontrollably flowed down her cheeks.

Joan reappeared by George's side. "Ready to go?" she asked. George nodded.

George and Joan found themselves walking back towards George's flat. Conversation flowed freely between the two of them. George explained where he'd left the baby and that he didn't have to collect him until after the funeral and Joan tenderly asked George when he expected to be back at work. George had always found it easy to talk to Joan and it was a comfort to have her there today. He was glad of her company. Their route, of course, took them past Battersea Park. As they drew closer to the park George felt compelled to see where his beloved Hilda had spent her final moments.

"Do you mind if we go in?" he asked Joan.

"No, of course not." They entered through the tall, fancy iron gates and followed the path as it meandered through the park. It was fairly busy for Tuesday lunchtime. George felt strangely drawn to the spot where Hilda had ended her life and Joan sensed this was where he was heading.

"This is the first time I've been in here since ..." George didn't complete his sentence.

"Are you sure you want to do this?" asked Joan.

George nodded, silently. They made their way over to the boating lake. The spot was immediately obvious, as someone had placed a small posy of snowdrops, already beginning to wilt, at the exact spot where Hilda's clothes had been found. This small gesture upset George.

"Who would do this?" he demanded. His question was aimed at no one in particular. It had been the park keeper, James Berry, who had left the flowers. He had been greatly affected by the woman who had drowned in his park.

"I'm sure they meant well," commented Joan.

"Well they had no place. She was my wife. It should be me laying flowers, not a complete stranger." He turned and started to walk away, furious at what he had seen. He could only feel anger at that moment towards this stranger and the place where his wife had spent her last moments. He would never again return to the park. Joan walked with him back to his flat.

George left his quiet, empty flat very early the next morning. Smoking a cigarette and carrying his overnight bag, he made his way to Waterloo station, where he met up with Wyn and together they took the train to Farnham. Hilda's coffin had already been transferred onto the train bound for Farnham, so the two of them climbed into the closest empty carriage to the guard's van and settled themselves for the hour-long journey ahead. There was little conversation between brother and sister as both felt more comfortable saying nothing. Each knew how the other was feeling and there was no need to discuss it. They just had to get through this day as best they could and both hoped they could do it with dignity. Wyn held on to her brother's arm, her head resting on his shoulder as George stared vacantly out of the window for the majority of the journey. The funeral director and his hearse were waiting when the train arrived.

Chapter 15

1937

The sunshine was doing its best to warm up the day, trying to squeeze its way through the thick cloud cover, but on this Wednesday in early January it was a typically chilly winter's day. After exiting their vehicles on Green Lane, the ten mourners entered the cemetery through some iron gates and followed slowly in procession behind their loved one's coffin into the modest chapel. After a short service in the chapel, their reverend, a tall, gaunt, middle-aged man whose glasses kept slipping down his nose, led them to an area where a grave had been dug the day before. Situated only yards away from the chapel, this was to be Hilda's last resting place. Not one of them spoke, because all they could think about was the sad and senseless circumstances of Hilda's death. They wanted to remember Hilda for the beautiful, cheerful and loving sister, wife and friend that she was.

The cemetery was deserted apart from them, observed only by the ravens high in the trees and the souls of the dearly departed in the ground. The graveyard felt incredibly isolated. Its peacefulness was accentuated as it was winter time and this managed to instil a feeling of calm inside George which was almost tranquil.

The sky was mainly busy with grey clouds but there were breaks every so often and if you looked carefully you could see minute patches of pure blue. The sun eased its way through every now and then to make a brief appearance, casting shadows which bounced off the granite headstones and onto the grass, seemingly representing the people who were buried there. The stones and their still shadows seemed to represent not only a life but the experiences, achievements, passions and bereavements that had taken place during those people's lives.

The surrounding trees were bare and had shed the last of their leaves many weeks earlier. A caretaker had made a half-hearted effort to sweep some of the leaves into piles but had not completed his job, probably discouraged by the wintry weather. From above there came a raucous caw from the ravens that had settled high up in the trees. Those large, imposing, glossy black birds always seem to hang around cemeteries, their presence appearing quite sinister but seemingly innocent.

There was a gentle wind that day and it felt cold. If you listened carefully you could hear the breeze whistling up through the branches of the trees. The rest of the world appeared to be getting on with their day. The birds were singing, occasional traffic on Green Lane passed by, a dog barked with excitement in someone's back garden and a whisper of voices on the breeze could be heard belonging to nearby residents.

George noticed none of these things. He was encircled, protected inside a bubble which carried him along in the moment. Although composed he was quite unable to prevent himself from trembling and his body kept making little involuntary shivers of which he had no control. His whole body felt numb. He was still suffering from shock. What else could it be, when his whole life had been smashed to smithereens? He'd been thrown into such turmoil and was inwardly struggling to cope. George really had no idea how he had reached this point in his life, physically or mentally. It was a complete blur. Where had it all gone wrong? This last week had been an utter nightmare. In fact, the past few months had been a huge ordeal for him. He had never known sadness like this before. A feeling of complete and utter emptiness consumed his whole being.

All eyes focused on the mound of freshly dug soil, now only a few feet away. The mourners' footsteps crunched along the gravel path and came to rest upon the damp grass beside the gaping hole where George would soon lay his wife's body.

A number of family members were conspicuous by their absence, the most notable being that of Hilda's father. Hilda's sisters, Doris and Evelyn, like their father had felt unable to attend their baby sister's funeral. Doris had recently discovered to her surprise that she was expecting her third child and, apart from suffering greatly with morning sickness, didn't have the strength necessary to enable her to get through the ordeal. She had assisted George's mother with most of the funeral arrangements but as the funeral was taking place, she and Evelyn had thrown themselves into preparing the food for the wake afterwards. Their husbands, Syd and Jim, were at the graveside to represent their wives and give their support to George.

Violet and Nan attended, dressed in their Sunday best and full length fur coats to keep out the cold. They huddled closely, their arms linked tightly as they struggled to hold each other up. Their heads were locked together and bowed low, their tear-stained faces hidden under their black, mourning headgear. They had lost their baby sister and nothing would ever be the same again. Nothing would ever ease away the pain they felt. Syd and Jim stood next to their sisters-in-law, unable to offer any comfort to the women.

At the graveside George looked so desolate and frail. In one hand he clutched a simple wreath of white lilies which he had removed from the coffin lid as it had reached the graveside. The card attached read: With loving thoughts, Babe from George. With his other hand he held tightly onto his sister. Wyn was there to support her brother and to say goodbye to a dear friend whom she had known for only a short time. The card attached to her wreath of roses read: In memory of a sweet girl, from George's sister, Wyn. Wyn knew there was nothing she could do or say to make things any easier for her brother. She had been there for him these past weeks and she wasn't about to desert him now, when he needed her the most.

As the small crowd gathered around the grave, Reverend Roe

began his solemn committal. He pushed his glasses back onto his nose and spoke with authority but kindness. "We have but a short time to live. Like a flower we blossom then wither; Like a shadow we flee and never stay. In the midst of life we are in death; to whom can we turn for help, but to you, Lord, who is justly angered by our sins?"

George suddenly lurched forward, involuntarily, tugging at his sister's arm as he did so. A lump appeared in his throat and he had difficulty in swallowing. His mouth was dry; he felt as though he wanted to vomit and he was struggling to catch his breath. Reverend Roe glanced over at George and gestured to him with a nod, as if to ask, should he continue? In doing so, he once again caused his glasses to slip down the bridge of his nose. George responded with a nod for him to continue and after pushing his glasses back up his nose, Reverend Roe waved his hand to signal for the coffin to be lowered. As the coffin was slowly lowered Reverend Roe continued. "We have entrusted our sister to God's mercy, and we now commit her body to the ground: earth to earth, ashes to ashes, dust to dust." As he spoke, the reverend grabbed a handful of soil and tossed it down into the grave. George then led the rest of the mourners in sprinkling soil down into the grave and onto Hilda's coffin.

"In sure and certain hope of the resurrection of eternal life, through our Lord Jesus Christ, who will transform our frail bodies, that they may be conformed to his glorious body, who died, was buried, and rose again for us. To him be glory, forever and ever. Amen."

Silence fell across the graveyard once more and seconds later the small crowd of mourners laid their floral tributes and started to slowly disperse. Without any discussion they made their way back to the gravel path and out of the graveyard, through the iron gates from which they had entered less than an hour earlier.

As Wyn placed her roses next to Hilda's grave Reverend Roe approached her and George and spoke a few last words of reassurance. George hardly acknowledged the man or his words. He was staring despairingly down into the grave, still tightly clutching his floral tribute. Wyn thanked the reverend, shaking his hand with her free one, while George hung on hopelessly to her other.

George and his sister were the last to leave the grave side. Wyn stood for over ten minutes next to her brother after everyone else had left, holding onto his hand while he hung his head in silence. She gave him this time to reflect, as she shivered and felt her toes turning numb. While she waited with her brother she watched a lone male figure, whom she didn't recognise as being among the mourners, hovering over by the entrance to the cemetery. Wyn correctly surmised the man represented a local newspaper and was there to note the proceedings and floral tributes to her sister in law. At least he has the manners to wait outside the cemetery, she thought, blissfully unaware that the man had already spoken to Syd and Jim on their way out of the cemetery and gained many details which he intended to put into print.

George felt almost rooted to the spot and unable to make the connection between his brain and legs, to get them to move. All he could think about was his beautiful Babe, whom he had lost for ever. How was he going to cope without her? How was he going to bring up their son all by himself? Losing Hilda in this way had shocked him to the core. At this moment in time he had no idea how he was going to continue and knew he would never get over her death. After a few more minutes Wyn let go of her brother's hand and linked his arm, gently nudging him, hinting that it was time to leave. George took the hint and finally placed his wreath next to his sister's. The pair moved very slowing away from the graveside and back onto the gravel path. When they reached the path George turned, glancing back towards the grave, one last time.

"You did really well George," whispered Wyn, sympathetically.

George turned his body back around to face his sister. Looking her straight in the eyes he asked, "What am I going to do without her, Wyn?"

His sister gently placed her hands on both sides of her brother's face. "I don't know George. I'm so sorry, I just don't know," she said. The pair embraced each other and then the tears came, and it felt as though they would never stop.

Edwin sat alone in his front, upstairs room, unable to listen to music, read or do anything that might take his mind off the loss of his youngest daughter or the fact that her funeral was taking place today. Understandably, he closed his business for the day, although earlier he'd tried to throw himself into some work down in the shop, calculating his finances which he had recently neglected more and more. But no matter how hard he had tried he was unable to concentrate on his accounts and kept making mistakes. He had given up and retreated to the silence and emptiness of the upstairs rooms. It was later quoted in *The Farnham Herald* newspaper, that Hilda's father "was prevented by indisposition from being present" at his daughter's funeral. In reality the loss had been so great for Edwin that he was simply, physically and mentally, unable to attend. He had buried his wife only four years earlier and had never really come to terms with her death. Now he was expected to revisit all those difficult feelings, coupled with the guilt he felt for pushing his daughter away and making her think he had disowned her. The pain and regret he felt was unbearable. As he sobbed uncontrollably in his armchair, all he could think about was how he had let the whole family down, not least Hilda and of course, his dear wife, Mary. Edwin refused to receive any visitors today. His family knew better than to contact him and left him well alone. His long-time friend Lionel Smith had spoken to Edwin the previous day and attended the funeral but respected his friend's wishes to be by himself and did not call on him.

*

The congregation of mourners shared vehicles and slowly made their way back to Syd and Doris's house, a modest terraced on St George's Street in Farnham. Syd and Doris had lived there now for more than fifteen years. Their two boys, fifteen and ten years old, shared the back bedroom. Doris and Syd had the front bedroom and then there was a spare which was to be the baby's room, when it arrived. Downstairs an entrance hall led off to a front living room, a smaller room was behind that and then a kitchen was situated at the back of the house.

The front door to the terraced house was ajar as George and Wyn approached, so the pair walked straight in. Off to the right, in the front room, the mourners including Reverend Roe were tucking into the sandwiches and cakes that Doris and Evelyn had prepared. There was a quiet buzz of conversation coming from this smoke-filled room but one was unable from the hallway to pick up any actual words that were being said. Doris, Syd and Jim were fussing over the reverend, making sure he had enough to eat and drink, while Violet and Nan chatted to friends of their father, who were fellow shopkeepers.

Evelyn met George and Wyn in the hallway as they entered. "Cup of tea, you two?" she enquired. George didn't even look up.

"Yes please Evie," replied Wyn, speaking on George's behalf as well. "That would be very welcome." They followed her into the kitchen. Evelyn busied herself with making a fresh pot of tea while Wyn pulled out a chair encouraging George to sit down at the kitchen table. A selection of sandwiches and cakes were displayed on the table in front of them.

"Help yourselves to some food," said Evelyn helpfully, as she placed a fresh pot of tea on the table. Wyn picked at a few things but George touched nothing and it wasn't long before Doris and Syd entered the kitchen. Doris, who was now beginning to just show that she was expecting her third child, pulled out a chair and sat down next to George, placing her arm around his shoulder. George made little attempt to look up at her.

"We are all going to miss her terribly, George." She squeezed George's shoulder and continued. "None of us had any idea that Babe was so sick."

At this point George looked Doris straight in the eyes and said, "Neither did I, but I should have realised."

"You mustn't blame yourself, or Babe. She didn't know what she was doing." Doris was very gentle as she spoke these difficult words. It was taking a lot of courage for her to continue. "We must all try to put it behind us now George and get on with our lives. You have a son to look after now. He will help you to move on with your life."

George knew Doris was right and that she meant well but somehow her kind words were not helping him. "How was little Georgie when you left him?" enquired Doris. "Have you left him with a neighbour?"

"He's not been too good these last few days. He's had a nasty cough and cold and I think he's been missing his mother," replied George. Tears were beginning to sting the back of Doris's eyes but she managed to blink them back. "I've left him with a group of midwives who share a house not far from the flat. They seem to be doing a good job. I'll pick him up tomorrow on my way home."

"It's going to be difficult at first, George, but I know you'll both be fine as long as you have each other and you know where we all are if you need anything."

"That's very kind, Doris," said George.

George spent the next hour in the kitchen with his sister Wyn. They didn't really say much to each other, but they were both glad of the other's company. George didn't feel strong enough to be able to enter the front room and hold any kind of conversation with the other mourners, so he stayed away. As most of them had never met him before, few entered the kitchen to speak to him specifically. It was Doris and Evelyn who were backwards and forwards between the front room and the kitchen, fetching food and making fresh cups of tea for their guests. It kept them busy, allowing their thoughts to wander from Hilda occasionally.

Eventually the mourners departed, some entering the kitchen to pass on their regards to George before they left. The reverend was the first to depart, which seemed to encourage the rest in short succession. Then it was time for Wyn to leave. She had to catch her train home as she had work the following day. She and George had previously discussed her coming to stay for the weekend. George said he would really look forward to it and they agreed Wyn could travel by bus to George's flat on Friday after work and stay until Sunday. She worked in Fulham, so it wouldn't take her too long to get across to Battersea on a Friday night. She didn't want to leave George in Farnham but had little choice. She knew he was in good hands, staying with Doris and Syd overnight. She would be seeing him again in two days' time, so this made their parting a little less difficult.

Wyn and George said their goodbyes on the doorstep of Doris and Syd's house. Wyn tried unsuccessfully to hold back her tears and reassure George as she left. As George closed the front door, Doris approached him carrying a plate of food. "I think you should try and eat something," she said handing him a plate.

"Can I take it up to my room? I'd like to be alone now."

"Of course you can. I'll bring you up a cup of tea."

"Thank you Doris. Thank you for everything," said George, hanging his head low as he ascended the staircase.

George disappeared upstairs to the bedroom that Doris had previously prepared for him. He placed the plate of food onto the bedside table and slumped down onto the bed. Here he sat, head in hands until five minutes later when Doris entered with his tea. George looked up as Doris placed the teacup next to the full plate of food. "Promise me you'll try to eat something, George," pleaded Doris.

"I will. I promise," he replied, lighting up a cigarette.

As Doris reached for the bedroom door handle, George lifted himself off the bed to stand. "I'll be leaving early for my train in the morning, so I just wanted to say thank you for everything you have done today. And would you pass on my regards to your father the next time you see him."

"I'm sorry he couldn't be here," remarked Doris. "It has hit him hard."

"I understand completely. There's no need to explain." And with that the pair embraced, and Doris left the room.

George was up and dressed by seven o'clock the following morning. He had hardly slept a wink all night which now seemed to be becoming the norm for him. He made himself a cup of tea and drank it at the kitchen table as the rest of the household began to wake. It was just after nine when he left Doris and Syd's house for the station with his overnight bag. It was only a five-minute walk to the station, down to the end of St George's Road, along Tilford Road to Station Hill, but George didn't want to miss his nine thirty train and left in plenty of time. He just wanted to get home. He lit up a cigarette as he walked, drawing it in, deeply. He had no inclination to revisit the town or call in on his old employer and friend; now was not the time. Maybe he would some other day.

His train for Waterloo was on time and he left Farnham with a feeling that he was leaving something behind. The journey in total took him about one and a half hours, plenty of time for reflection and planning but George found this almost impossible. It was still too soon for him to move on.

As George arrived in Battersea, a feeling of dread washed over him as he thought about returning to his empty flat. Able to delay this for a while longer he arrived on the doorstep to the house where the midwives were caring for his son. Dressed in a dark-green woolly cardigan over her midwife's uniform the woman who opened the door invited George inside. George was informed that his son had been fine, except for his cough and cold, and that he would soon be needing his next feed. "There's a couple of bottles already made up in his bag, pet. I thought that might help."

"Thank you all very much," said George to the three midwives in the room. "You've been a great help to me."

"Any time, pet. Are you still planning to go back to work on Monday?" asked the woman in the green cardigan. George had the impression she was in charge.

"Yes, I think so."

"Well, just drop little Georgie off whenever you want. There's always someone here."

"Thank you," said George.

The baby was already in his pram and his overnight bag and bottles were packed into his bag by the other midwives before the end of the conversation. Together, George and the midwife-in-charge manoeuvred the pram through the doorway and down the single step onto the pavement outside.

"Bye pet, see you Monday," smiled the midwife. "Bye bye baby Georgie."

As George pushed his son home the baby went to sleep. He stopped, briefly, at a general store situated on a corner, and bought a loaf of bread and some milk, then continued his journey home. He struggled with the pram down the two steps outside his flat's front door but eventually managed to get himself and the pram inside. As he lifted the baby from his pram, he woke and began to cry. George turned the baby around towards himself, lifting him to head height. "It's just you and me now, lad," he said, and the baby began to cry louder. "I guess you need your bottle then," responded George and he set about the task as any caring parent would.

When the baby had been fed, changed and put into his basket, George made himself a cup of tea and a sandwich with some left-over cheese he found in the ice box. I really need to do some proper shopping, he thought. He plonked himself down at the kitchen table, forced himself to eat and began to make a list. He had only got part way through the sandwich and shopping list when he burst into uncontrollable tears. George sobbed solidly for over half an hour. He felt completely drained and bewildered. He couldn't get his head around how all this could have happened. He had no idea Hilda had been so unhappy. Then feelings of guilt overcame him. He should have noticed she was unhappy. He should have done more to help her with the baby. He should have been there more, taken some time off work, anything to help. But how could he when he didn't even know there was anything wrong? Why hadn't she said something? There were so many emotions racing around inside his head. Then George started to feel angry. Why had she done this? He couldn't understand it. She had no idea what she had done to him, and how could she leave baby Georgie without his mother? Then there was her poor father and the rest of her family. How could she do this to them? She had no idea what an impact her actions had had on everyone who knew her. How could she be so selfish? George burst into tears again. He felt so wretched.

He eventually pulled himself together and thought about what he should do next. It was quiet. Georgie was asleep. He didn't have to go back to work until Monday, so he had the next three days to get himself sorted. His sister Wyn would be there later tomorrow evening to help. She had been a huge support since he had told her about Hilda. He couldn't wait to see her again.

George wasn't sure how he did it, but he managed to get through Friday, taking the baby out in his pram and buying some groceries before Wyn arrived around six. He had only just finished giving Georgie his bottle when she knocked at the door. Wyn greeted her brother and nephew on the doorstep with a big smile. "How are my two favourite boys?" she enquired. She had been practising this greeting for the last ten minutes on the bus and she was determined to stay positive for George's sake and for her own sanity.

"Not too bad," responded George as he hugged his sister. He must have embraced his sister more times in the last week than he had done his whole life. Just for the moment though, she was his rock and one of the things that was keeping him going. Georgie was another.

"I hope you don't mind George, but I've brought some dinner for us to share. You haven't eaten have you?" she continued, not waiting for an answer.

"No, not yet," replied George. She guessed he wouldn't have. She had hardly seen him touch anything when she had been with him last. "I just stepped off the bus and a delicious waft of fish and chips greeted me, so I couldn't resist," she half lied. She just wanted him to eat something and thought that fish and chips might be the answer. As children, it had always been something of a treat on the occasional Friday night when their father had brought home fish and chips. They would have competitions to see who could eat the fastest and on one occasion Wyn had been terribly sick all over her brother and they had laughed about it for weeks. Their parents had not been so impressed with their behaviour and their father had shouted, "What a bloody waste of money." Wyn had stopped racing after that experience and enjoyed her fish and chip suppers at a more acceptable pace.

"Come in," said George as he wandered through to the kitchen. Wyn followed, closing the door behind her.

"Here, take the baby and I'll find us some plates," suggested George.

"We don't need plates George. We can eat it out of the paper, but I'll still have a cuddle with Georgie, first. Hand over my handsome nephew," smiled Wyn. As George handed his son to his sister, the baby began to cough.

"Oh dear me. You poor thing," said Wyn, as she gently patted the baby's back. The child promptly brought back half of the milk which George had just given him. The mixed vomit and mucus slowly ran off Wyn's shoulder and down her back. Quick-thinking George grabbed a towel from the kitchen side and wiped up the vomit from his sister's back.

"Sorry about that Sis, he keeps doing this," said George.

"Not to worry, no harm done," replied Wyn, sounding just like her mother. "Now where are those fish and chips?"

George, Wyn and the baby were like any other small family that weekend. Wyn helped around the house, looking after the baby, doing some washing, cleaning and cooking, while George read his paper and helped with the baby. He enjoyed his sister's company and Wyn succeeded, by and large, in taking George's mind off recent events.

On Monday morning George returned to work. Initially, he found this an uncomfortable experience. Walking into the salon and greeting his colleagues after his time away was awkward for him and just as difficult for them. They had of course been informed about his wife's death. Thankfully, later that day George found that the salon and its daily workings allowed him to take his mind off Hilda, at least for a couple of hours. It was a huge relief that his work enabled him to do this and it meant he felt less uneasy about returning again the following morning.

Joan had been wonderful. She had, somehow, known just what to say to George, encouraging him to respond in a positive way and making him feel more optimistic about his future. She left him to get on with his work, yet seemed to appear from nowhere just as he needed someone, offering resilience when his mind was swept back to his terrible situation.

And so, on the whole, George coped well during his first week back at work. Everyone said so. Each day it seemed to get a little easier for him and when he had spoken to Wyn on the Friday evening, even she had noticed a big difference in her brother. Just from talking to him on the telephone she could tell he was more relaxed about work and had settled into his new routine. He explained to his sister that his work colleague, Joan, had been a great help and that he had invited her round to the flat on Sunday afternoon to see the baby.

"You sound so much more positive George, about the future and everything."

"It must be Joan's influence," he replied. "She has this way of looking at things that makes me realise things are not quite so bad as I thought they were."

"She's doing me out of a job," joked Wyn.

"Nonsense, Sis. No one could ever replace you. You know you're always welcome here, any time."

After a long day on the Saturday and an exhausting first week back at the salon, George was glad of a lie in on the Sunday. He was pleased the baby had the same idea. He had woken George up in the night, around four, and George had given him another bottle to help him settle. It was ten before the baby woke him with his crying.

George spent the morning tidying the flat in preparation for Joan's visit that afternoon. Joan arrived at the agreed time and they spent most of the afternoon discussing work. She enjoyed playing with the baby and took a turn at feeding him his bottle. George was fully prepared this time, catching his son's phlegm-filled vomit in a towel as it left the child's mouth, before it could splatter across Joan's outfit. As George lurched forward, he frightened the baby causing him to cry and also alarmed Joan with his rapid reflex movement. "Did your daddy frighten you, sweetheart? What a silly daddy you have," laughed Joan causing the baby's tears to turn to a smile. Then the pair of them laughed together along with the baby because George had turned pink with embarrassment over his son's impropriety.

George enjoyed Joan's company that afternoon. Although she was a good ten years his junior, she had a wise head on her shoulders and was willing to share her knowledge. She had a caring way with both George and the baby, which made George feel completely relaxed in her company. She could always raise his spirits.

It was exactly one week after George had gone back to work, on the following Monday afternoon, when a telephone call came into the salon for him. Joan was waiting beside him as George replaced the receiver, looking as pale as a ghost. "What is it George?" asked Joan.

"It's the baby. He's not well. The midwives have called the doctor and want me to go too."

"What's wrong with him, George?"

"They couldn't say. I don't think they know."

"You must go, straightaway."

"Yes," said George. "I'll get my coat." He went through to the back, retrieving his scarf and gloves and struggled to get his arms into his coat. Joan followed.

"Will you call me later and let me know how he is doing, George?" she shouted after him as he left through the salon's back door.

"I will," he replied from the pavement outside.

It was around six that evening when George was passing the salon on his way home. Joan was just about to lock up and everyone else had gone home. George noticed her through the lit-up salon window. She was startled when the shop door swung open. "George! You gave me a fright."

"Sorry," he replied, quietly.

"How's the baby?" asked Joan. George broke down. "What's happened, George?" asked Joan, tenderly.

"Suspected bronchitis, the doctor said. He just wasn't strong enough to fight it. My son died in my arms." Huge tears fell from George's eyes. Joan too began to cry and naturally moved to embrace George. He made no attempt to stop her. They sat together on the comfortable salon sofa, used daily by all their clients, and George sobbed and sobbed in Joan's arms, until he had no tears left. "I'm not a bad person Joan. So why do I feel like I'm being punished again for something I haven't done?"

"Sometimes bad things happen to good people," reassured Joan. "Although, I must admit it does seem you might be getting your entire life's share, all at once."

Joan was there for George that evening, comforting, supporting, reassuring and encouraging him. They cried together, talked about baby George's short life and cried some more.

When they both felt there was little left to say and their tears had run dry, almost at the precise same moment, they remembered that the following morning George was to endure more distress at the postponed inquest into his wife's death.

"I would like to be there for you, George. If you want me there that is?"

"That's very kind of you Joan, but I can't help feeling I'm offloading too much on to you."

"I understand if you don't want me there."

"It's not that I don't want you there. It's just that I shouldn't be your problem."

"But I'd like to help, if I can, if you'll let me?"

"You're a wonderful person Joan. You don't need a friend like me, with so many problems."

"Maybe not," replied Joan, honestly. "But you need someone who can be strong for you right now. You said both your sister and your wife's friend, Ruth, will be shattered by the news of Georgie's death. I might be more use to you," she insisted.

"Very well," agreed George, realising any more resistance was futile. "I would appreciate you being there. You've more or less been there for me from the start. It makes sense you're there at the end."

"That's sorted then," smiled Joan.

It was the last thing George wanted to do after losing his son only a few hours previously, but he had no choice. The following morning, he and Joan made their way to the court house for the second inquest. They met outside. They entered together and informed the clerk about the death of George's young son. Then they went to find their seats. When the coroner entered he announced that Dr Rowland was unfortunately still too ill to give evidence. However, they would continue with the hearing.

One by one, the witnesses were called but the coroner began by asking George to recollect what he had said on 5 January. The coroner spoke gently to George.

"You said your wife had been in fair health until the birth of your first child, last September. There had been complications during the birth and that your wife's doctor, a midwife and a nurse had been present at the birth." George nodded.

"Please explain how your wife had been after the birth of your baby." George spoke quietly. "My wife made a good recovery after the birth of our child but she had worried lately about trifles and seemed very quiet."

"What sort of things did she worry about?"

"She worried about her health and whether she would be able to bring our baby up properly. She also worried about the baby's health."

"Had the baby been ill?"

"When he was six weeks old she took him to Bolingbroke Hospital and then to Tite Street Hospital."

"Did the child have to stay in hospital?"

"Yes, he was in hospital for about five days."

"And after that did the child improve?"

"Yes." George paused and took a deep breath. "Since my wife's death, my three-month-old son has also died."

"Yes, it is very tragic," replied the coroner, having previously been informed of the child's death and asked to perform a post mortem on the child's body the following day. "Everyone will sympathise very deeply with you." There was a short silence and then he continued by saying, "I must press you further. Could you now describe the events which led up to the death of your wife?"

George stood, sallow and drained while many pairs of eyes rested upon him as he recalled that fateful day. "On Thursday morning, 31 December, my wife seemed worried and asked me not to go work that day." He paused again, as he remembered how troubled she had appeared and now, how terrible he felt because he had not fulfilled her request. "I went to work and returned to our flat at 8.30pm. My wife and child were not there, but her handbag was on the chair. I looked inside her handbag and found a note."

"Was the note in her handwriting?" asked the coroner.

"Yes," replied George.

The coroner then read the note out to the court and George was forced to relive the moment all over again.

Please forgive me for doing this. You have been wonderful all through. No blame is attached to you. Mrs Wootley has the baby. God bless you both. Ask Dad and Mother to forgive me. Love, Babe.

George was close to tears. "Of course, it gave you a dreadful shock," the coroner said. George recalled his feelings. All sorts of thoughts had rushed through his head at the time, finally culminating in a feeling of anger towards Hilda. His next thought had been for his baby boy. If he was with Mrs Wootley, then maybe Hilda was there also.

"My first thought was to find out about the baby," replied George to the court.

"She had told you correctly – that Mrs Wootley had the baby?" enquired the coroner.

"Yes. I went to Mrs Wootley's address and found her mother was looking after the baby." For a moment the court fell silent as the coroner considered his next question.

"Did the police contact you on Saturday saying your wife had been found drowned?"

"Yes. A police officer came to the house on Saturday morning to say that my wife had been found in the water at Battersea Park."

"Had your wife ever threatened suicide?"

"No. Never."

"Did she have money troubles?"

"No. We had managed to save quite a sum before the baby was born." George paused for a second, and then continued. "But on occasions she had made remarks to me which might suggest she was depressed at times. My friends told me that it was usual for women after childbirth to be a little strange."

"It is not usual, but it is well recognised after the birth of a child, "agreed the coroner.

"I was told she would be all right in time."

"She did not see any mental expert?" enquired the coroner.

"No." George looked to the floor.

"Thank you. You may step down now," said the coroner.

Next to give his evidence was Dr William Thomas. The coroner asked him, "Please could you explain what you found when you arrived at Battersea Park on the morning of 2 January."

The doctor spoke clearly and precisely. "The body of a woman had been pulled from the water shortly before I arrived. I saw the deceased on the edge of the pond. She was fully clothed and I pronounced her dead at 10am. I understand the post mortem showed the cause of death was drowning."

"That is correct," agreed Coroner Smith.

James Berry, the head park keeper was the next to give his evidence. He stood nervously in the court room, having never had to do anything like this before in his life. He began, quietly. "At 9.30am on 2 January I saw a pair of gloves and a woman's coat folded up on the edge of the pond."

"Speak up lad. Could you see anything in the water?" asked Coroner Smith.

"No, but I got a boat and searched the pond opposite to where I found the clothing." Mr Berry paused to catch his breath, his throat suddenly very dry.

"Do go on," said the coroner, a little impatiently, looking up from whatever it was he had just written down.

"About twelve yards from the clothing, in mid-stream, I saw a dark object under the water."

"Yes," nodded the coroner, encouragingly.

"I took my coat off and put my arm down about eighteen inches into the water. I brought up the body of a woman." Poor Mr Berry was quite pale now as he recalled the events of that morning.

"How deep is the water there?" asked the coroner.

"It's about three feet six inches, sir."

"Carry on."

"Well, I then attempted artificial respiration sir," he paused, "without success."

"Thank you Mr Berry," and with that the man stepped down, looking genuinely distressed.

PC Etchells was the next witness to give his evidence. He stated his name and number and said that when he arrived, the woman's body had just been pulled from the water. "She was clearly dead," he confirmed with authority.

Mrs Wootley was the last witness to give evidence. After she had confirmed her name and address the coroner asked her, "How do you know the deceased, Mrs Wootley?"

"I do housework in the upper part of 89 Albert Bridge Road, sir. I knew the deceased casually because she lived in the basement."

"And how did she appear to you?"

"She seemed to be living very happily with her husband sir," answered Mrs Wootley.

"Did you ever hear the deceased threaten to take her life?"

"Oh no sir. Never sir."

"Can you describe what happened on 31 December?"

"Well sir, she asked me if I would mind her baby while she went out for the afternoon to visit some friends. I told her to take the baby to my mother until I had finished work and she did sir." At this point Mrs Wootley started to become very upset. Sobbing into her handkerchief, she was unable to control her emotions any longer. She seemed worried about something.

"The reason for this poor woman's act is difficult to understand, is it not, Mrs Wootley?"

"Yes sir, it is," snivelled Mrs Wootley.

"Unless you understand medical matters that is," continued the coroner. "Sometimes a woman's mind does go wrong after a child is born and we think that is what occurred in this case."

"I knew she worried about her baby, sir, because he didn't improve."

"That was the only thing that worried her?"

"Yes sir. I think so."

"Unfortunately, the baby has now died and this is a tragic addition to the troubles weighing on this gentleman," said the coroner as he glanced over at George.

After two hours, Coroner Smith moved to his summing up, saying, "It is obvious that this woman worried about the health of her baby. At the time of her act she would not have been responsible. The circumstances show that this woman was certainly not in a sound state of mind when she took her life by drowning." Dr Edwin Smith recorded a verdict of suicide whilst of unsound mind and offered his deepest condolences to George.

There was no inquest into his son's death but a post mortem was carried out on 22 January, again by the coroner, Edwin Smith. He concluded that the baby had died from acute bronchitis and middle ear disease. George was completely distraught and beside himself, unable to function properly for weeks after having buried his young wife and tiny son. It wasn't long before he moved out of his basement flat in Battersea. It was making him so unhappy. Too many people knew about what had happened to him and there were too many memories for him in the area.

George also made the difficult decision to change his job. He decided a complete career change was what he needed and managed to secure a position as an Insurance Assessor for a London company. He moved into rented accommodation in Lambeth, where for a short time he paid rent to an elderly widowed woman. He relinquished any contact with Hilda's family but remained in touch with Joan Sorensen, who continued to be his closest friend for the rest of his life and the only link to his previous existence.

Epilogue

Sadly, baby Georgie was not buried alongside his mother. I still have to discover exactly where George buried his son, yet I suspect it was somewhere around the Battersea area. It appears the child must have suffered with a lung infection, probably since his birth, and the repeated attacks of bronchitis weakened and irritated his bronchial airways. As the bronchial passages became inflamed they swelled and grew thicker, narrowing the tiny airways in his lungs, which will have caused his coughing spells accompanied by the thick phlegm and breathlessness. Baby Georgie's illness will have been accentuated by the many cigarette smokers around him, including his father, as the smoke will have irritated his bronchial tubes and caused them to produce excess mucus.

George went on to marry Joan Sorensen on Boxing Day in 1938. They married at St Saviour's church on Herne Hill Road in Lambeth. It wasn't until 1942 that Joan gave birth to a daughter at Morrisburne Maternity Hospital, Woking. This was originally a private house which had been converted and has since been demolished. George and Joan named their daughter Jillian Dawn. The family lived at 50 Beechdale Road, Brixton Hill, but I am unsure for how long.

Edwin never did get over the suicide of his youngest daughter in 1936. He refused to ever discuss the matter, even with his own family. Over the next decade Edwin's health deteriorated greatly. Throughout this period his shop remained open. He ran it as best he could whilst suffering greatly with an agonising and debilitating condition, caused by the tobacco he had smoked on a daily basis throughout his life. Edwin died of throat cancer during the winter of 1950. He was eighty-two years old.

*

Teddy's marriage to Eva broke down a few years after they returned to Surrey and they eventually divorced. He married again just before the Second World War to Ellen Hammond who had grown up and lived near Farnham all her life. They had no children together, although Edwin's daughter Eileen, from his first marriage, was a witness at her father's second marriage. Teddy continued to run his very successful garage business in Pirbright until the 1970s when he sold up and moved to Chiltern. Here he died aged eighty-seven in 1978.

Little is known of Mabel and her family. She and husband, Fred, lived in Blackheath in Guildford with their children. I was told by relatives she had a big family although I have only ever been able to find evidence of two children.

Lionel and his wife Gladys moved from their home in Wharncliffe Gardens, St Marylebone to Ealing and then to Hounslow. Twenty-six years into their marriage, when Gladys was fifty-one, she died at home with her husband in attendance, suffering from the same condition that baby Georgie had died from. Gladys's bronchitis was almost certainly due to her cigarette smoking and irritated by her asthma. After the loss of his wife Lionel threw himself into his work. Working as a chef, his occupation allowed him little time for socialising and he much preferred it that way. Some years later he met, quite by chance, a much younger woman, Margaret Edwards, who was thirty-seven and as yet had not married. They started to see each other regularly, enjoying each other's company and eventually decided to marry in January 1948. The following year with news of his father's decline in health, Lionel and Margaret decided to move back to Farnham. Within the year they had taken over the running of Vi's fish shop at the end of Downing street.

Doris was my grandmother. When she gave birth to my father, in July 1937, her family was complete. During the Second World War Doris juggled home life with work as an auxiliary nurse at

Trimmers Hospital, Farnham. The hours were long and often went into the night. Husband Syd worked at Farnham hospital as a clerk during the day and a fire picket by night. The couple hardly saw each other. Their youngest son, my father, would often have to be left with an elderly neighbour overnight.

All three of Doris's sons became choirboys at St Andrew's Church, along with their father who was a bass singer for the choir. After the war in 1945, Syd worked together with his eldest son, Thomas, running a fruit & vegetable, fish & poultry shop in Farnborough called Hatto's. Later, Syd and Thomas worked together again at the electricity board in Aldershot. Thomas worked in the office while Syd went house-to-house reading meters. In July 1959 Sydney died. Two years later Doris lost her eldest son, Thomas, after contracting tuberculosis. These were both terrible times in Doris's life, where she once again felt unable to attend the funerals of her loved ones.

In September 1961 my father left home to get married. By November that year Doris had sold her house in St George's Road and moved to live behind the Almshouses in Park View, Farnham. Here she lived out her days until she died in 1985 aged eighty-six.

After the war, in 1945 Evelyn and Jim purchased another residential property. This time it was a short distance from Farnham, in Frensham. This house was bigger and freed up the house in East Street for Jim's sister, Doreen. After her father's death in 1950, Evelyn and husband Jim took over the running of the fish shop. This soon proved too much for them and so it wasn't long before they decided to sell it. This was the end of an era for the whole family. In the spring of 1954 Jim died. He left his wife very well off and when she had sold The Central Garage and their house in Frensham she bought a property on Tilford Road, Farnham, to be near to her sisters. Here she lived out her days until she died aged eighty-eight in 1988.

*

Violet worked hard to make her business, the Sea Lion, a success. In 1950 she decided to retire. She sold her business to her brother Lionel and his wife and went to live in nearby Bentley with her female companion who had previously run a popular bookshop in Farnham. Violet lived here until 1967 then moved to Brighton, where she died aged eighty-two in 1983.

Muriel lived in Devon where she worked, caring for Lieutenant Colonel Arthur Pigott until he died in 1954. She married for the first time when she was fifty-four years old, to Albert Johns in Devon in 1958. Shortly after their wedding they moved back to Farnham so that Muriel could be near to her sisters. Muriel died at the end of 1987, aged eighty-three.

To this day, Hilda's final resting place remains without a headstone to mark her difficult short life. As I searched for her grave, using a map of the graveyard even proved difficult to find the exact spot. It is not known for what reason there is no headstone but I assume that at the time of burial, no one in the family could afford to have one made. As the years passed, her family pushed thoughts of Hilda far from their minds, as the circumstances of her death would always remain so painful for them. Even her husband had a new family to keep him occupied and so, Hilda was soon forgotten.

Lightning Source UK Ltd.
Milton Keynes UK
UKOW052130180612

194655UK00001B/167/P